PHASED

PHASED

VICTORIA TECKEN

Phased

Copyright © Victoria Tecken 2020

Cover art copyright © Sara Ferrari 2020

All Rights Reserved

The right of Victoria Tecken to be identified as the author of this work has been asserted.

No part of this book may be used or reproduced in any manner whatsoever without written permission from the author except in the case of brief quotations embodied in critical articles and reviews.

This book is a work of fiction. References to real people, events, establishments, organizations, or locales are intended only to provide a sense of authenticity, and are used to advance the fictional narrative. All other characters, and all incidents and dialogue, are drawn from the author's imagination and are not to be construed as real.

Identifiers: ISBN 978-1-937363-03-1 (paperback)

To Sara

This one was always for you

PART ONE

CHAPTER ONE

*D*on't fail.

Stay in control.

Don't fail.

When Val stepped into the white room, her fangs were already extending against her lips. Beads of sweat dripped down the back of her neck. Drawing in a breath, she tried to remember pine and fresh earth, but her senses were filled with the room's sterile scents. The four walls still held her prisoner, suffocating her. She glanced toward the two-way mirror at the other end of the room. They were watching, the lab techs, the scientists, the guards, all watching her like a bug under a microscope. As her body temperature rose, she repressed the fear that began to creep to the edges of her conscience.

Don't fail.

In the mirror, she saw her skin turning the ashen wolf gray beneath the simple white uniform she wore. Her blue eyes flecked with a bright violet as they began to change color. Her cheekbones jutted out, giving her face a primal edge. The speaker above her head crackled.

"Valentine, this is a control test. We need you to fully phase and then retract. If you are successful, you will qualify for the next stage of assimilation. Do you understand?"

I can't do this.

Don't fail.

Val nodded. "Yes."

The small room's stifling heat fueled her body's change. The bones in Val's face hardened, and blood pounded in her ears. The familiar rush of euphoria flooded through her. She focused on it, closing her eyes. Fangs flashed as a low growl forced its way loose from her throat, wolf overtaking human. She let go.

Instincts pushed her forward toward the door, looking for a way out. She needed to hunt, to run, to get out of this cage. She could feel the pull of the full moon outside, drawing her into its hold like a vice. A screeching sound filled the room as she raked her claws down over the surface of the metal door. She remembered the thrill of a hunt, a cabin in the woods, and blood... so much blood. Words... there were words she needed to remember... where was Lyla? She had to find her sister. Her body shuddered.

"Valentine, retract the phasing."

She didn't like the voice that spoke to her hidden behind the wall. The door should be open, and she should be hunting them. Her clawed hands curled into fists. Something inside her screamed for her to listen, to remember.

Don't fail.

Val blinked.

Fighting the barrage of instincts telling her to let go, to embrace the wolf within her, she curled into herself. She wouldn't let Lyla down. She touched the bond link hidden away in the corner of her mind, but it felt hazy. It had been months since she had felt her sister's gentle presence in her mind. She couldn't turn there for help, not yet. Not until she passed this test and they were free.

Then it will all be back to the way it was.

Shaking her head at the lie, Val dug her hands into the little grooves her claws made in the laminated tile floor. Inside, her wolf raged at being restrained. Val tried to retract her claws, her fangs… Her arms shook with the effort, muscles snapped tight.

Crackling above. "Releasing first stimulant."

Her head snapped up, eyes flashing fully violet. The scent of blood drifted into the room. Fury filled her and her senses spun out of control. The urge to hunt overwhelmed the tenuous control she had established, and she snapped at the air. Eyes blazing, she focused on the mirror across from her and the men she knew sat behind it, watching her with their white masks and white clipboards. She lunged, smashing against the wall with all the horrible force she could muster. The room shook with the impact.

DON'T FAIL.

She howled and stumbled away from the wall, head in her hands as she shook it wildly back and forth. "I can't…" The phasing held her. It felt so good, so *right*. How long had it been since they'd let her go this far? The mirror taunted her, reflecting something less human, more visceral. In this form, she was something to fear, her human features distorted. Her red hair blazed against the gray tone of her skin.

The bracelets on her wrists buzzed warningly. She growled just as the voice spoke to her overhead. "Valentine, you have thirty seconds remaining in this test."

She sank down to the floor, dragging her wild consciousness back toward its human form. She forced herself to think about her sister. Lyla could pass this test. She was calm, controlled. How did she do it? Val took deep breaths, but the smell of blood still lingered in the air. Somewhere inside, her wolf howled.

Don't fail.

…

Lyla sat alone in the conference room. The air conditioning hummed quietly, and cool air came through the vent above her head. Without it, the room would've seemed far too hot for her higher body temperature. Fighting the urge to chew her fingernails, she stared at the door. She wanted more than anything for someone to come through the door and tell her that both she and Val had passed their tests, that they were finally going to leave the Center. She tapped her foot and glanced up around the room, eyes lingering on the line of photographs neatly framed in a row on the wall.

The first was a picture of Dr. Carrington standing proudly in front of his first Carrington Labs building, the sign gleaming gold behind him. With broad shoulders, he towered over the two shorter men standing beside him.

Next was a photo taken years later in front of another sign: The Department of Domestication and Assimilation. Dr. Carrington was once again the center focus, this time wearing an expensive suit, his hair slicked back stylishly. Lyla took in the details around him, noting the tall chain-link fence and brick buildings in the background. One of those buildings was the same one she sat in now, waiting to see the very man who had founded the organization eleven years ago. Lyla's mother had once remarked that the organization would be a far greater danger to their kind than help.

Lyla fiddled with the hem of her white T-shirt, pushing the memory of her mother far away. When the door opened across from her, Dr. Carrington was the first into the room. He flashed her a broad smile. "Lyla! So good to see you."

He sat down at the table a few chairs away from her, followed by Dr. Quinn, another member of the DAO's board of directors. Dr. Quinn adjusted her wire-rimmed glasses and spread several folders and a clipboard neatly out in front of her at the table. Dr. Carrington leaned forward.

"Well, we won't waste time. I'm pleased to inform you that you have passed the final control test, and we have cleared you from the program. You've worked hard, Lyla, and I can't tell you how proud I am of the progress you've made while you've been with us."

Lyla swallowed, but couldn't find words. Her mind churned. She'd known that they would most likely pass her, but now what? She took a deep breath. "Thank you."

Dr. Carrington studied her. "You're very welcome. We have high hopes for you to have as close to a normal life as possible. We've arranged for you to be transported to one of our assimilation schools, Westbrook High. You'll be able to have a lot more freedom there, and you'll be able to interact with other students. I've assigned one of our most experienced handlers to you to help with the transition. Her name is Ms. Cormoran, and she will be your advocate throughout the next year."

Dr. Quinn glanced up over her glasses. "I have some resources for you to take. These are standard for all of our graduates." She slid one of the folders across the table to Lyla. The sticker on the front cover read *Assimilation Policies and Regulations*. Lyla flipped through the pages of small black print, but the bullet points began to blur together:

- **Involved parties will be given full access to D.A.O. resources to make them feel adequately prepared to welcome a Domesticated family or individual to their neighborhood or school.**
- **Domesticated individuals will be required to have proof of a passed control test on hand at all times. Failure to produce proof of a passed control test may result in incarceration and a retest.**
- **Domesticated individuals should refrain from using language from feral culture, especially regarding previous pack rankings...**

The lists went on and on. In the back of the folder was a single sheet of paper recounting the brief history of the DAO's program. One of Lyla's eyebrows lifted as she saw yet another photograph of Dr. Carrington and a team of scientists standing with the DAO's first program graduates. The man certainly did like to have his picture taken. Lyla looked at the two board members. They regarded her with a sort of pride. She leaned back, flipped the folder closed, and pushed it back across the table.

"I'm not going without Val."

A shocked silence settled over the room. Dr. Carrington was the first to speak. "Lyla, I understand how you might be feeling right now, but as one of our graduates, the world will truly be more open to you. With our recommendation, your potential is limitless."

Dr. Quinn glanced over her notes. "You were a stellar student here, Ms. Blackwood. This file says that you excel in arts and science. There is no reason for you not to go to school, to get a job, and to live in a Domestic neighborhood. You may still feel the influence of your primitive instincts, but they will not serve you in the future."

Lyla set her jaw. "And what about Val?"

Dr. Carrington ran his hand through his hair. "Your sister is a special case, Lyla. Her alpha behaviors are difficult to suppress, and we are not confident in her ability to control her instincts. She is much safer here for the moment."

"She didn't pass the control test, did she?" Lyla asked. The long pause following her question made her blood boil, but she managed to keep her face neutral.

"No," replied Dr. Quinn. "Perhaps with more training, she will be able to progress in the future."

Lyla closed her fists under the table. She'd just gotten her sister back. Two months. That was all the time they'd had after two years of waiting in the dark, their bond link weakened by Dr. Carrington's suppressants. Letting Val back into her mind had been a slow process, and she knew how much her sister was keeping from her. How much they'd both been forced to survive.

And she knew without a doubt that her sister would never survive this.

"I know that I can keep her calm," said Lyla. "If you separate us now, she'll never have a chance. I won't go without her."

Dr. Quinn scowled. "You're hardly in a position to be making demands, Ms. Blackwood."

Lyla looked at Dr. Carrington. "You know I'm right. You said yourself once that you've never seen anything as strong as our bond link."

"Which is still under review by the Board," Dr. Quinn interjected. "Our program strongly discourages the existence of such bonds. If we allow one exception, we lose our credibility. Your sister's test results are not encouraging."

"The bond only raises our chances of existing peacefully. Give us one chance. Let her come with me for one semester. I know she can do this."

Dr. Carrington folded his hands. "And if I refuse this request?"

Val, I made you a promise. I won't leave you. Not now, not ever.

"Then keep me here too," Lyla replied quietly. "I'm not going to live out there without my sister. If she stays, I stay."

Dr. Quinn shuffled her papers together. "I am disappointed in your attitude toward this opportunity, Ms. Blackwood. Perhaps an extended stay in our program would be for the best." She rose from the table. "I have other things to attend to, Dr. Carrington. Excuse me."

The door closed with a click behind her. Lyla squeezed her fists, eyes locked onto the wood grain of the table. She felt the brief sensation of freedom slipping farther away. "Dr. Carrington, I know that you want everyone to know how successful this center has been. If a Trueblood can be Domesticated, won't that prove how well it works?"

There was a rustle as Dr. Carrington rose from the table. Lyla looked up as he stood in front of the photographs on the wall, regarding them thoughtfully.

"You know, Lyla, students like you are the hope of the future. You've proven yourself resilient and resourceful. It would be a waste to keep someone with your talents here. Truebloods are the hardest to Domesticate, the most rooted in our feral past. But you've proven that it can be done. You've exceeded every expectation we've set for you. Perhaps you and your sister can show the world what Truebloods are capable of."

He tapped his chin. "I'll address the Board later this evening. I can't guarantee a decision in your sister's favor, but I think that further discussion is warranted."

Lyla nearly sagged with relief. "Thank you."

Dr. Carrington opened the door. "Don't thank me yet. You may have earned yourself a longer stay here as well. The Board's decision will be final." He left the room.

Lyla leaned forward on the table, resting her forehead on her arms. She reached out for the link with Val. She felt her sister's hesitant touch in response, the feeling of fingertips brushing softly over her mind. *I won't lose you again.*

...

The tall chain-link fence around the DAO campus still had the curls of barbed wire at the top. Once upon a time, the campus had been a federal prison, repurposed to house werewolves going through the Domestication program when Dr. Carrington took over the property. For the first time in five years, the two Blackwood sisters were going outside the fence.

Lyla sat on the bench, holding onto her duffel bag. The two armed guards sat in their air-conditioned station next to the gates, watching the older of the two Blackwood sisters pace back and forth next to the bench while she waited. Val was far too restless to sit down, and Lyla hadn't bothered trying to convince her.

"When did she say we were leaving?" asked Val.

Lyla glanced down at her ID bracelet, which doubled as a watch. "She should be here any minute. It's already nine o'clock."

Val spun to face the outside world, looking through the fence and down the long road leading away from the DAO center. Lyla could feel her nervous and excited tension buzzing through their bond, and it was giving her a headache. But she knew that nothing she could say would dissuade Val's restlessness, and she could hardly blame her sister for being excited. Lyla still wasn't sure how she felt about any of this. For her, leaving the DAO center felt like a crushing weight on her shoulders.

"I still can't believe I passed the test," Val said, pushing her thick red hair away from her face. Tight braids bound it back on one side of her head. Lyla was worried that the hairstyle was "too feral," but no one had said anything.

"Yeah," Lyla murmured in response. She looked down at her hands. The suppressants that she and Val were required to take would keep them from being able to voluntarily phase on normal days. But during full moons, Carrington Labs had still been unable to develop a formula strong enough to completely remove all traces of involuntary phasings. And that worried Lyla more than anything else. Was she really going to be able to keep Val under control? She shook her head. She didn't have a choice.

She looked up as a pair of hands appeared on her knees. Val was kneeling in front of her, wild hair framing a half-smile. "Hey. We're getting out of here, Lyla. It's going to be okay. We're finally going to be free."

Oh, Val. Lyla pushed her sister's hands away. "Val, we're not free. We have one chance. One shot to make this work. And if we screw it up, we're going to be back in those cells faster than you can blink."

Val's smile disappeared. "I know." She glanced up as the sound of a car approached them. "But it's closer than we were before."

But closer to what? Lyla stood up, holding her duffel bag against her chest as the blue sedan drove up beside them. A woman opened the door, stepping out onto the asphalt and smoothing her pencil skirt. Her hair was swept up into a tight bun, not a single gleaming black hair out of place. A small silver pendant hung around her throat in the small triangle of skin exposed by her collared blouse. Her heels clicked as she walked around the car.

"Valentine and Lyla! I'm so pleased to finally meet you both," she said with a bright smile. "I'm Ms. Cormoran, and I'll be taking care of everything you need from now on. I've seen both of your files. You've both made so much progress here. That's wonderful. Let's get your ID bracelets off."

Neither one of the Blackwood sisters responded as she carefully removed the thin black bands that had been around their wrists for years. Val rubbed her fingers over the skin where the bracelet had been.

Lyla felt a lump in her throat as she watched Cormoran tuck the bracelets into her purse. They'd been promoted to a new kind of guardian. Instead of lab coats and sterile masks, the handlers were licensed counselors specially trained to handle Weres who were transitioning into human culture. Lyla had heard Cormoran's name before. She was one of the best. Lyla didn't trust her.

"Well, let's not waste any more time, I'm sure you're both ready to get out of this place," said Cormoran, herding both girls toward the back seat of the car. "Feel free to ask me any questions you have. I'm here to help."

The girls shuffled into the car, settling their duffel bags in between them. Cormoran slid into the driver's seat, and one of the guards took the passenger side. Lyla glanced down at the gun strapped to the holster on his hip. She knew that inside the gun's magazine were silver bullets.

The chain-link gates opened, and the car rolled out onto the road. Lyla leaned against the door as Cormoran began to run through the list of rules that they would need to follow at the school. It was the same list that Lyla had memorized over the past few days. Lyla let herself tune out the sounds of the car and Cormoran's voice, watching as the countryside rolled by outside her window. Soon, lines of tall trees flashed by, a green blur. Her consciousness slipped away into the past.

Arka slipped through the trees like a shadow, her little feet treading soundlessly on the forest carpet of sticks, leaves, and pine needles. A few yards ahead of her, the wood grouse pecked at the ground, oblivious to the tiny hunter approaching. Looking to the side, Arka saw subtle movement in the brush to her left: Sanzi, just as silent. Both of the little wolflings were hidden well from their prey. Someday, when they were older and able to phase into their wolf form, they would be able to hunt something much bigger than a grouse hen.

Knowing that her big sister would take the first leap, Arka waited, muscles tense. A breath passed, and Sanzi burst from the brush, hair billowing fiery red in a little beam of sunshine as she leapt through it, hands outstretched. The grouse hen squealed and dashed to the side.

Arka's hands closed around its neck. A sound like a small twig snapping, and the grouse went limp. The two girls tumbled together over their prize, whooping excitedly. They rolled up to their feet, the grouse clutched tightly in Arka's small hands. Sanzi threw her head back and howled, her voice high and shrill. Then she turned to her sister with a wide grin.

"Come on," she said, pulling at Arka's sleeve. The two girls ran through the trees as fast as their short legs would carry them, exploding into a little circle of cabins in a clearing and racing for the one farthest from them. Several of the pack adults chuckled as the girls ran past them with the dead grouse dangling along behind.

"MAMA!" screamed Sanzi at the top of her lungs.

A woman appeared at the doorway of the cabin, her thick brown hair twisted up in a pile of braids and silver ornaments. A bandana held the wayward strands away from her face. The two girls scrambled to a stop in front of her.

"Mama look!" exclaimed Arka, holding up the grouse.

The woman laughed, her smile sending sparkles up into her hazel eyes. "Mighty hunters!" she said, clapping her hands. "And here I was wondering what we might have for supper."

The girls beamed as their mother reached down to retrieve the grouse. "Won't your father be proud of the two of you." She enveloped both of them in her warm embrace. Arka breathed in. Her mother smelled of earth and herbs.

"Arka..."

"Arka?"

"Lyla, are you alright?"

Lyla snapped out of the memory and realized that Ms. Cormoran was watching her in the rearview mirror. Next to her, Val was pointedly staring out the window, eyes shimmering. The memory still reverberated through the bond. Lyla hadn't realized she was sharing it. She gave Cormoran what she hoped was a convincing smile.

"Yeah, I'm fine. Just tired."

Cormoran nodded. "Go ahead and rest if you'd like. We've got a few hours to drive."

Lyla leaned against the headrest, letting her gaze get lost in the trees again. But this time she didn't let her mind wander.

CHAPTER TWO

Val followed Lyla and Cormoran toward Gibbous Hall on their first day of classes, feeling slightly constricted in the navy school uniform. The jacket was too hot, even over the short sleeve collared shirt. The other students put plenty of space between themselves and the two girls following their handler down the sidewalk. Val felt their heavy stares as she walked, gripping the straps of her new backpack. They avoided getting too close to the two Truebloods.

I guess news travels fast around here. Following Cormoran through the double doors, Val's nostrils flared, instinctually registering the scents of the students filling the hallways. All four ranks were present: alphas, betas, gammas, omegas. Human students mixed in here and there. The humans all smelled strange to Val. Their blood was less potent—quieter. The warm energy that pulsed out from the full and half-bloods was more familiar. They were more like Lyla, the most familiar scent in the building.

Val found her eyes darting everywhere, trying to identify them all. It was one of the instincts that the DAO hadn't been able to train out of her. Val took a deep breath, mentally going through the checklist to appear less like an alpha.

Don't hold eye contact too long. Slump your shoulders a little and don't angle your body toward them. Smile. Make friends. She glanced to the side and saw a pair of girls chatting with each other, standing next to the wall. One quick inhale told her that they were a beta and an omega. Neither of them returned her smile. The omega looked incredibly uncomfortable as Val walked by. Val found herself wishing she could somehow turn off the intensity that she wore like a second skin.

Cormoran led them into Principal Bleiz' office and directed them to sit down. Val did so, dropping her backpack and getting her first look at the man who ran Westbrook School. He wore a gray suit, his hair slicked back. He regarded them with a sort of pinched look. Cormoran reached across the desk and shook his hand.

"Pleasure to make your acquaintance, Mr. Bleiz. I have all the forms filled out and signed for you," she said, handing him a folder.

He glanced at them briefly and then returned his attention to the two girls. Val met his gaze and felt her instincts respond to his scrutiny. Her temperature rose slightly as she locked eyes with him, registering that he was also an alpha. A half-blood. The moment passed, and he looked away. Val smirked to herself victoriously, and then felt Lyla pinch her leg. Her sister was giving her a warning glare.

Right. Don't alpha the principal.

Principal Bleiz cleared his throat. "Valentine and Lyla Blackwood. I've been given enough information on the two of you to know that you're a risk." He tapped his fingers on the folder. "I've been assured that you both have passed your control tests and will be safe around the other students. I expect you will exhibit exemplary behavior while you are in my school."

Lyla nodded. "You won't have to worry, sir. We won't cause any trouble."

Principal Bleiz glanced at Val. "I'll hold you both to that. The safety of our students is the highest priority in this school. Am I clear?"

"Yes," Val swallowed her pride. "Sir."

Cormoran stepped in smoothly. "I will be monitoring their progress while they are here, and if you have any questions or concerns, I've included my cell number in the paperwork. We've gone over all the rules and policies with them."

"I trust you've been made aware of your schedules and the location and time to collect your suppressants?" asked the principal.

"Yes," replied Lyla.

"Good." He sighed and leaned back in his chair. "Then you'd best head to your classes. You don't want to be late."

Cormoran gave the girls a smile. "Run along now. I have a few last things to go over with Mr. Bleiz. I'll check in with both of you later."

The girls rose and picked up their backpacks, letting themselves out of the office. As soon as the door closed behind them, Lyla reached out and gripped Val's shoulder. Leaning in close, she kept her voice low.

"Val, we are not in the woods anymore. You have got to get that through your thick head. We're playing by their rules now. This is not a pack."

Val tried to look surprised. "What do you mean?" she asked.

"Don't give me that. You tried to intimidate the principal."

The smirk returned. "Tried? He backed down. You saw it."

Lyla stopped in the middle of the hallway, eyes burning into her sister's. "Val. I swear, if you can't keep your temper in check—"

"All right, all right. I'm sorry."

"This isn't easy for me either. This is the only chance we have, otherwise we are going back to those cells. Is that what you want?" Lyla asked.

Val looked down at her shoes. "No," she replied softly.

"Good. We've trained for this; it's going to be fine." Lyla said, sounding as if she were trying to convince herself as much as Val. "We've got different classes for the next couple periods, so I'll meet up with you right after, okay?"

Val made her way through the hallway to find her English classroom. The building was full of students now, and most of them stared at her. If she got too close, they would pull away as if she'd burned them. No one said hello. That may have had something to do with the concentrated scowl on Val's face. Intensity rolled off of her like waves, every step asserting her strength whether she intended it to or not.

She found the classroom and took a seat in the middle. At least that way the other students would be forced to sit around her. They all filed in, filling the spaces farthest away from her first. She heard several whispers. The word "Trueblood" was mentioned more than once. She sighed, shoving her backpack down by her feet.

Someone dropped into the seat to Val's left. She glanced up to see a tall, lanky boy with shaggy blond hair pulling a notebook from his—briefcase? Val raised her eyebrows at that. He wore thin-rimmed glasses that had slid a little way down his nose. He placed three pencils carefully at the top of his desk, each of them sharpened to a point. He glanced up, surprised to find Val watching him.

He bobbed his head awkwardly. "Hi."

"Hey," Val replied, taken aback by the fact that he had spoken to her. His scent was subdued, watered down. Human. Even more surprising.

The teacher, an older man named Mr. Harrison, stood up at the white board. He had smooth gray hair and kind eyes. "All right, class. Let's take out the syllabus and talk about what we're going to be reading this semester!"

Val pulled her schedule and syllabus out of her bag. As Mr. Harrison began to talk about the books on the list in an excited, reedy voice, the hairs on the back of Val's neck prickled. She glanced over and saw that the blond boy was staring at her. As soon as she looked at him, he dropped his gaze back down to his notebook. Val shrugged it off. It wasn't like he was the only one sneaking glances at her.

She lifted her chin, ignoring the attention. Lyla had warned her that the other students might not know how to act around them. Truebloods were rare enough, and a Trueblood alpha like Val was the strongest kind of werewolf. If she had wanted to and she wasn't restricted by a suppressant, she could have commanded any other

Were in the room to do what she wanted, and they would've listened, submissive to her will. *Maybe they're right to be afraid of me.*

Focusing on drawing in one breath and exhaling the next, Val scraped her fingernail down the side of her pencil. She glanced to the side. The boy was staring again. Once again, he immediately went back to scribbling in his notebook, pushing his glasses farther up on his nose. Val frowned.

He leaned down to pull something from his briefcase, and Val caught sight of the notebook page that had been hidden by his arm. A neat row of bullet points cascaded down the paper.

- **Trueblood Alpha**
- **Exhibiting signs of stress and anxiety**
- **Low aggression toward other students, no obvious intimidation used**
- **Central DAO Center – high risk**

Val felt nauseous as she tore her gaze away from the scribbled handwriting and back to the front of the classroom. Mr. Harrison was saying something about *Frankenstein* by Mary Shelley, but Val could not focus. How could he possibly know that she was from the Central Center? How did he know she was labeled as high risk? Why was he keeping track of her like that? Val could hardly keep herself in her seat. She watched the clock hands tick on the wall above the door that she desperately wanted to rush out of.

The moment the bell rang, Val was out of her seat and out the door, pushing past a few other students who scrambled to get out of her way. She went all the way to the end of the hall before she stopped, lifting the schedule that she'd crumpled in her hand in her rush to get out of the room.

Don't fail.

Math class. Room 107.

Steeling herself, Val pushed forward down the hallway. She wasn't about to let that boy get under her skin. She could do this.

There were already students in the class, and Val found a seat near the back of the class where she could watch the rest of the room. She breathed a sigh of relief when the door closed and the boy wasn't in her class. She opened her math textbook, grimacing at the jumble of impossible numbers and patterns that stared up at her from the page.

Lyla walked into the band room and made her way slowly back to the percussion section. She sat next to the kettle drums that were pushed into the corner, tentatively touching a finger to the smooth surface.

"Hi, you're Lyla, right?"

A male beta slipped into the seat next to her and gave her a lopsided smile. Lyla glanced at him and noticed the dirty blond hair that stuck straight up at the back of his head.

"Yeah."

"I'm Lex! I'm a full-blood."

Lyla frowned. Why would he tell her that? "Cool. Do you play percussion?"

He looked around suddenly, as if he didn't know where he was. "Uh, no, actually." He rubbed the back of his neck. "Alto sax. I'd better get down to my seat. Just wanted to say hi."

He climbed down two tiers to the woodwind section. Two other students next to him leaned in and began whispering to him, but he shrugged them off. The band teacher walked in, a brisk lady who wore a black blouse with flowing sleeves, her hair twisted up in a clip.

"Good afternoon, everyone. We have a new student with us today. Lyla Blackwood?" She glanced up to the percussion section. "I'm Mrs. Axton. I've been told you can play drums and read music. Is that correct?"

Lyla stood up and nodded, feeling uncomfortable as all the eyes in the room turned to look at her. "Yes ma'am."

Mrs. Axton's eyes crinkled pleasantly as she smiled back. "Excellent. Let's start with the "Danza Africana." Lyla, will you cover the kettle drums?"

It didn't take long for Lyla to sink back into an easy rhythm with the drums. She could feel the tension in her shoulders replaced by the muscle memory that rolled through her arms and hands. She hadn't played for years, but years of playing drums with her father had left an imprint. She let herself fade into the music, letting the heavy boom of the drums shudder through her hands. When the bell rang, Lyla took her time putting the covers back on the drums as the other students filed out of the room. Grabbing her backpack, she looked up and saw Lex waiting for her near the doorway, awkwardly shifting from one foot to the other.

"Hi," she said as she walked toward him. "Need something?"

He grinned. "No. Actually, we have study period together, and I thought maybe we could…"

ANGER.

Emotion flooded through the bond, and Lyla's head snapped toward the doorway. She pushed past Lex, frantic to find her sister. The hallways were thinning out as the students disappeared into their respective classes, but Lyla still had to weave around a few of them as she searched.

Finally, she barreled into a deserted hallway and came face-to-face with Val. Her sister's face was contorted in frustration, hands on her hips. Lyla searched her face and was relieved to see that Val's eyes were still blue. Her backpack had been dropped haphazardly on the floor with several books spilling out. Lyla took in the scene slowly, trying to figure out what she was missing.

"You okay?" she asked, still tense.

Val glanced at her and then quickly looked away, sinking down to her heels in a squat. The anger pulsing through the bond link faded slightly to something else. Lyla frowned, trying to decipher what her sister was feeling, but she could sense Val trying to mask it.

"Val."

No response.

"Val, you've got to talk to me." Still no response. Lyla looked down at her sister sternly, letting a dark edge of authority color her tone. "What happened?"

Val grumbled something under her breath, looking everywhere but at Lyla. "I hate this. You fit in because you're smart."

Lyla forced herself to be patient. She glanced down at the wrinkled schedule sheet lying on the floor next to Val's backpack. Picking it up, she found the last class period listed. *Algebra II, Room 107, Mrs. Keeling.* Suddenly Lyla realized what emotion had been coming through the link a moment ago. She couldn't help the small chuckle that escaped from her throat. Her sister was embarrassed.

She swallowed back the wide grin that was threatening to take over her face, relieved that the situation was so trivial. She couldn't resist. "So, how was math class?"

Val pressed her fingers to her temples. "I can't do it, Lyla. And it's pointless. When am I going to use this stuff?"

"You're being a bit dramatic. Even Mother and Father would've taught us math," Lyla replied. Val stared off to the side, absent-mindedly scratching her neck.

"Val? What's really bothering you?"

Val opened her mouth to respond, then her eyes narrowed suspiciously. "Someone's coming." She stood up from the floor as a lanky boy came around the corner. Lyla noticed that his glasses were perched halfway down his nose as he peered over them. He held two pieces of paper in his hands. Lyla recognized a human scent. The boy glanced between them for a moment before holding the papers out to Val.

"You forgot the homework from Lit class," he said. "Mr. Harrison asked me to give it to you."

Lyla felt the tension radiating from her sister. Val reached out and took the papers, stuffing them into her backpack and gathering up her books. The boy watched her curiously for a moment before nodding to himself and retreating toward the main hallway. Lyla poked Val's arm.

"You're not going to make any friends like that. At least say thank you."

"Not with him." Val's voice went quiet. "Lyla, I think they're watching us."

Lyla didn't like her sister's tone of voice. "What do you mean?"

"He was taking notes about me in class, Lyla. He knew we were from the Central DAO center and that I was high risk. He can't know that unless they've told him to keep an eye on us."

Looking back down the hallway, Lyla felt a cold tingle through her spine at the thought. As uncomfortable as it was, she wasn't surprised. "Well, then I guess we'll just have to keep doing what we're doing and stop giving him anything to take notes about. Come on, let's go to study hall."

CHAPTER THREE

Homework Boy was sitting in the library, a few tables away. Val watched him, her jaw set. His notebook was out again, scribbling away, just like he had been the day before in English class. Every now and then he would glance up at her before returning to his writing. Val tried to ignore the anxiety creeping into her thoughts and turned back to Lyla, who was attempting to patiently explain her math homework. Val blinked, staring harder at the page as if somehow that would help her focus. Finally, she closed her eyes.

She rushed through the trees, feeling the sweet kiss of air against her skin as she phased. The bones in her face hardened, fingertips lengthening into claws, eyes turning from blue to brilliant Trueblood violet. The feeling of being so alive, every sight and sound amplified with overwhelming clarity, was exhilarating. Power rushed through her body, almost too much to contain… a flash of light as she raced through a sunbeam.

Suddenly, walls were closing in, suffocating. Bright lights. She was surrounded by white masks. They were going to kill her. They were going to…

Val's eyes snapped open, and she didn't need a mirror to know that they were flecked with violet. She lowered her head, keeping her gaze down on her textbook. Lyla had stopped talking and was watching her. Val could sense that her sister's blood was running a fraction hotter as Val's emotions rushed through the bond. But Lyla sat calm and controlled, just like she always was.

"Keep going," Val said.

Lyla shook her head, closing the textbook and carefully placing their notes into folders. "No, I think we should call it quits while we're still ahead. We've got some time before supper." There was no argument from Val. The past two days had been a blur of classes and homework. The only other Were students that didn't completely avoid them were a group of alphas that had taken to saying "Feral" every time they passed Val or Lyla in the hallway.

Maybe we've just exchanged one prison for another, Val mused as she and Lyla trudged out of the library and out onto the lawn. They lingered for a moment in the warm sunshine. Val breathed in, taking in the faint smell of the pine trees from outside the school's high fence.

"Want to go for a walk?" asked Lyla.

There was a short trail around the outer edge of the campus that she had seen on the map when they first arrived.

"Please," replied Val eagerly.

Dropping their backpacks off in their dorm room, they hurried back outside and toward the walking path. It was smooth and paved, and soon both sisters were carrying their shoes and walking barefoot in the grass and dirt beside the path. Val relished the feel of earth between her toes. Large shade trees loomed over the trail, leaves rustling quietly in the breeze. Val reached down and picked up an acorn, flinging it over the fence and into the trees beyond. She smiled at Lyla.

"Let's do this every day."

"Okay," Lyla agreed. "Maybe soon they'll let us go outside the fence."

Cormoran had mentioned it before she'd left, telling the girls in no uncertain terms to be on their best behavior if they wanted to expand their privileges. Val knew that somewhere nearby was a National Park. If only she and Lyla were able to go out and run for a day or two. She kicked at a rock on the asphalt. Five years. Five years since they'd been totally free. Seven years since the worst day of their lives. She shoved that memory far away. She glanced at Lyla and was sure her sister's thoughts were running in a similar direction.

"I missed you."

Lyla looked up at her, surprised. "What do you mean?"

"I just mean it's nice to be back together. After so long locked up in that cell, I wasn't sure I would ever see you again." She shrugged. "It feels weird, almost. Like we're different somehow."

"We are different," said Lyla. She pulled her brown hair free of her braid and deftly reworked it, the dark strands slipping through her fingers. "I don't know if it will ever feel like it did before. You haven't really told me much of what happened those two years we were separated."

Val's face darkened. "No. I'd rather not." She felt Lyla's scrutiny, but she wasn't about to change her mind.

She lunged against the restraints, wrists burning. Everything was white.

No. Her chest tightened, and she forced herself to breathe slow and deep, carefully blocking the bond as the memories threatened to spill over the barriers that she had constructed. If she wanted to stay in control, she had to keep them out. She rubbed her fingers against her wrists, feeling the light scarring around them.

"I'm kind of surprised they let us stay bonded," she said, changing the subject. "Do you think we'll ever be allowed to blood bond with anyone else?"

Lyla shook her head. "No. It's in the guidelines for assimilation. No bonding. No new ones, anyway."

Blood bonds were relics of the past—part of a culture that could not fit in with human society. Val wasn't entirely sure why. Werewolves couldn't blood bond with a human anyway. Maybe the DAO just didn't like the idea of werewolves being able to communicate in secret. The elders of a pack were able to bond and communicate with multiple Weres. Val and Lyla's mother had been one of those gifted elders. She'd often said their blood bond, which had appeared immediately after Lyla's birth, was a rare gift even among Truebloods.

"We have to pick up our next round of suppressants on the way back to the dorm," said Lyla. "Then maybe we should play a game or something. Cormoran put some in our closet when she unpacked all the supplies for us."

Val knew that Lyla was trying to distract her, but she didn't mind the idea of a game. The two of them reluctantly left the walking trail and headed back toward the dorm buildings. They stopped in Gibbous Hall to pick up their suppressant packages from the office, and then made their way back to their room.

Val opened up the closet doors and reached up to the shelf.

"Not Monopoly," Lyla said, sitting down in one of their three chairs. "That's not fun with two people."

Val frowned, but moved her hand from the Monopoly box and grabbed another. "Chess?"

"Sure." Lyla sat across from her sister, carefully straightening the white pieces on her side of the board, and then pushed one of her pawns forward. The game was on.

A bowl of popcorn, several threats, complaints, and three chess games later, Lyla threw her hands up in defeat as Val neatly knocked over her knight for a checkmate, winning her second game. Val jumped up from the ground and whooped, throwing her fist in the air.

Lyla groaned and rolled her eyes as Val bent down and wiggled her eyebrows at her, wearing a wide grin. "You lost," Val said, elated that she finally won a game that was usually Lyla's talent.

"Yes, I'm aware. What's the loser's penalty?"

Val straightened and made a dramatic show of stroking her chin as she thought through her options. Soon a wicked smirk appeared at the corner of her mouth. "You said we should make friends, right?"

"Val… be nice."

"Oh no, you're not getting off that easily," replied Val. "Tomorrow I want you to invite one of the other students to a game night this week."

"Fine—wait what? In our dorm room?"

Val laughed. "What could possibly go wrong?"

"I'll make a list and get back to you."

"I'll be on my best behavior. Wolf's honor," Val said with a wink.

Lyla looked around the room, her eyes falling on the few personal belongings that she and Val had. "I don't know. It feels strange to bring someone else here."

"I thought I was the territorial one," teased Val. "Besides, we aren't supposed to think like wolves anymore. Humans don't have packmates. They have friends. So, let's go make some friends."

Lyla went to put on her pajamas while Val put the chess game away. She leaned against the sink in their tiny bathroom as she brushed her teeth, still grimacing at the sharp mint taste. That was one thing she'd never gotten used to. Humans brushed their teeth too much. She spit into the sink and brushed her deep brown hair off to the side, touching the short stubble on the right side of her head. She would need to re-shave that soon.

As she washed her face, she paused and looked at herself in the mirror. She looked different, even to herself. More *human*. Gone were the hair braids and beads, the dirty bare feet, and the bright eyes. She had no words for what she was now. Somewhere beneath the surface, her wolf spirit lay dormant, lulled to an uncomfortable haziness from the suppressants.

Carefully hanging the hand towel back over the ring, she left the bathroom, flicking off the light. She glanced over to Val, who was spread eagle on her bed, still in her clothes, eyes closed. Lyla paused. Her sister looked peaceful when she slept. Lyla reached down and gently shook Val's shoulder.

"Val, bathroom is open."

As her sister groaned and rolled out of bed, stumbling half-asleep to the bathroom, Lyla crawled into her own bed and buried her face in the pillow.

Somewhere, a scream. So much pain. But worse than the pain was the fear. It was eating her alive. The room was hot, far too hot. Her blood was on fire. The white masks came closer to her, reaching for her—

Lyla opened her eyes in the still dark room. She felt sweat drip down the back of her neck. Her adrenaline was racing, her breathing ragged, but these emotions weren't hers. She heard a soft whimper from Val's bed and then muffled sobs.

She pulled back her covers and climbed onto the foot of the other bed. Even in the darkness, her sharp eyes made out the red strands of hair sticking to her sister's face. Val was soaked in sweat, her fists tangled in the sheets. Her face was contorted in a mixture of rage and pain. Lyla knew better than to touch her.

"Val, wake up," she commanded. The older girl tensed, her eyes flying open as she scrambled back against the headboard. Her wild gaze fell on Lyla, and she growled. Lyla caught a flash of fangs as they began to descend beneath Val's lips. When she lunged forward, Lyla was ready for her. She caught her sister in her arms and closed her eyes, focusing on the bond and pushing her own feelings of calm and reassurance through their link.

Val's body sagged and shuddered as she came back to herself, gasping for breath. Lyla took her hands gently. "Val, you're safe. No one is going to hurt you. I need to you to tell me three things that you can see."

When her sister spoke, her voice was barely audible. She stared at Lyla's face as if she were looking through it, and then her eyes slowly flickered around the room. "Pillow. Lamp." There was a pause. "My clothes on the floor."

Lyla nodded. "Good." She waited until she saw some awareness returning to Val's eyes. "Let's try to get some sleep."

She carefully pulled the covers over Val and was about to turn back to her own bed when she saw her sister's hand reach out in the darkness. Without a word, Lyla laid down on the space Val had made for her. They turned toward each other, snuggling a pillow between them. They fell into a restless sleep.

…

Lyla was starving by the time she met up with Val to head into the cafeteria for lunch. Her sister looked relaxed, but Lyla could feel the edge in her that always followed the nightmares. They'd been happening ever since the two sisters had been reunited at the DAO center, but Lyla was sure that Val had been experiencing them for much longer. And no matter how many times Lyla asked, Val still refused to tell her what had happened the years she was in isolation. Whatever it was, it had left a mark.

They rounded the corner toward the cafeteria doors and came face to face with a small group of alphas. One of them stood toe to toe with Val as they paused in the doorway.

He stared down at her; hands shoved carelessly into the pockets of his jeans. His dark hair was tousled as if he hadn't done a thing with it after rolling out of bed.

"You're in my way, feral." One of the alphas standing behind him smirked.

Lyla sensed the shift in Val as her sister squared her shoulders and met Jackson's gaze, steady and calm. "Maybe I am."

The air between them grew tense. Jackson leaned forward. "Was that supposed to be threatening?"

Battles for dominance between alphas could escalate quickly, and Lyla didn't trust either one of them, even in the middle of the cafeteria doorway. Val stood like a statue, but the calm was deceptive. If Lyla knew anything, it was that even her years in the DAO's program might not make Val back down from a challenge. Lyla tugged at Val's elbow, but her sister pulled away from her grasp.

Lifting her chin slightly, Val gave Jackson a sweeping glance from head to toe, and then sniffed, wrinkling her nose. "Are you sure you're an alpha?"

Jackson's eyes widened, and Lyla thought he was going to attack Val then and there. But he finally scoffed. "Watch yourself, feral."

He stepped around Val and headed down the hallway, followed by the other alphas. Lyla grabbed her sister's arm and marched them into the line, grabbing two trays and shoving one into Val's hands.

"What's wrong with you?" Lyla hissed as quietly as she could manage. Val had the decency to look chastised.

"Sorry."

"Sorry?" asked Lyla. She rolled her eyes and scooped a helping of mashed potatoes onto her tray. "You want that to get back to Cormoran? I can't believe you."

Val didn't answer, following Lyla silently through the buffet line. Lyla took several deep breaths to calm her anger. Losing her control right after scolding Val for losing hers would be counterproductive.

The cafeteria was already teeming with students, and most of them had separated into little groups. Lyla took note of the scents mingling in the room. Even here, the pack mentality couldn't be bred out of the Weres. One or two alphas in each group with a following of betas, gammas, and omegas. Humans scattered throughout.

As they sat down at a table by themselves, Lyla rubbed her forehead. "Val, he's not worth your time."

The redhead speared some green beans, looking at them with distaste before shoving them into her mouth. "This is messed up, Lyla," she said around the food. "No one here has any respect for pack hierarchy. It's there for a reason."

Lyla sighed. "They haven't operated under a pack mentality for decades, Val. The D.A.O. doesn't allow us to act on those things anymore, not as Domestics. Some of these students don't even know what their rank is. They've adopted human standards now."

Curling her lip in disgust, Val glanced over at a few of the human students. "Not sure what makes them so special. They're so superficial."

"Not all of them, Val. Just like not all Weres are the same."

"I don't know what I was expecting when we came here, but it wasn't this." Val leaned closer to her. "Doesn't it strike you as odd that we are the only Truebloods in this school? Or that we weren't allowed to interact with the other Truebloods at the DAO center?"

Lyla put her fork down. "Val, I have a lot of questions too, but we won't gain anything by asking them now. We just need to get through this semester."

Val grumbled. "Some of us don't have the patience of a saint."

As her sister shoveled through the pile of greens and began to attack the chicken on her tray, Lyla treated herself to a sip of the chocolate milk. It had always been one her favorites whenever they'd been allowed to have it at the DAO center. Val drained her own carton and then glanced at Lyla's.

"Are you going to finish that?"

Lyla raised an eyebrow. "Not a chance. Hands off, beast."

Val's eyes flashed in a fake display of anger. "Please, like you're any less of a beast than I am. I've been around your phases before." She rolled her eyes at Lyla's skeptical expression. "Okay, fine. I might be slightly more of a beast than you."

Standing up from the table, Val grabbed her tray. "You're no fun."

Lyla grinned as her sister stalked off to the garbage bins. The room was filled with conversations, laughter, and good-natured teasing around the other tables. Lyla scrutinized the other students. Whenever one met her gaze, she smiled at them, attempting to soothe the distrust they obviously had of her. After a few failed efforts, one of them smiled back. The short girl said goodbye to her friends and jogged over to Lyla's table.

Her smile pushed her round glasses up a little on her cheeks. Her deep black hair was twisted into two buns on the top of her head. "Hi!" she said, dropping into a chair across from Lyla. "I'm Jules. You're Lyla, right? One of the Truebloods? I mean, obviously you are. Sorry, I knew that."

Lyla nodded. "Yeah, I'm Lyla. My sister is Val," she said, gesturing to the other Trueblood who was making her way back to the table. Out of habit, she took a deep breath, reading the other girl's scent. Omega.

"Nice to meet you! I'm one of the writers for the school paper, and I'd really love to do an article on the two of you. Would it be okay if I ask you a few questions?"

Val sat down next to Lyla. "Why do you want to put us in the paper?"

Jules stared back, and then giggled. "Are you kidding me? You're all everybody is talking about. I mean, you're *Truebloods*. You're as werewolf as it gets. And you're obviously an alpha," she said, pointing her pencil at Val. She frowned and glanced at Lyla. "Are you an alpha too?"

Quickly, Lyla shook her head. "No. Beta."

"Cool. All the students got an email that the two of you were coming this semester, but they didn't say anything about your ranks. You know how they are about that." Jules sighed dramatically and flipped open her notebook. "Okay, so we only have a few minutes before next period. What has been the hardest thing about assimilating into human culture?"

Both Val and Lyla froze. Jules' pencil hovered over the paper. She sensed the hesitation, and continued, "We haven't had non-Domestic students at our school in over eight years. I checked the records. You two were actually raised in the wild, right?"

Val made a small noise of disbelief. "I thought you were going to ask us our favorite color."

Lyla chose her words very carefully. "Yes, we were raised in the wild, but that's not really something we can talk about." Seeing the disappointment on Jules' face, Lyla felt stuck.

To her surprise, Val broke the silence. "I miss the woods. There are too many buildings and fences here."

The pencil began scribbling furiously. "Is it true that you can tell another Were's rank just by their scent? I mean, I've tried, but I can't really tell."

"You're an omega," replied Val. "You've never phased. Fully Domesticated."

Jules beamed. "Yeah, that's right. Most of us are like that. There are only a couple students here who have even partially phased." She leaned forward, eyes sparkling. "What is it like?"

The sick feeling that had crept into Lyla's stomach grew. They were already pushing the boundaries of what might be considered acceptable to the DAO. If Cormoran found out that Val was talking about phasing to another student… Lyla put a hand on Val's thigh to stop the words that were about to leave her sister's mouth and gave Jules an apologetic smile.

"Sorry, Jules. We need to get to class. We'll see you around, okay?"

Lyla pulled Val up from the table, out into the hallway, and into the milling crowd of students. She felt Val's mixed emotions through the bond, but to her surprise, anger wasn't one of them. The most noticeable was the dull ache of grief. Val pulled her arm free of Lyla's grip.

"I can find my way to class," she said. She moved away, leaving Lyla standing alone in the hallway, gripping the straps of her backpack as if they were a lifeline.

CHAPTER FOUR

Val stepped into Gibbous Hall behind her sister. The novelty of the Truebloods had faded enough that at least they weren't being openly stared at wherever they went. Val was grateful for that.

Suddenly, she heard Lyla's name being called. Val hefted her backpack up and looked for the owner of the voice. A stocky beta came jogging up to them, wearing a wide smile. Val had seen him around but didn't know his name.

"Lyla, hey!"

Val looked the newcomer up and down, and he appeared less than comfortable under her intense gaze. He offered his hand to her. Val raised an eyebrow, ignoring the human gesture. She'd never liked the idea of letting someone else grab her hand.

"Hi, I'm Lex," he said, hesitantly dropping his hand back to his side. "You must be Val."

"That's me," she replied. "I see you've already met my sister."

Lex nodded. "We had band together."

As they moved toward their last class of the day, Lex tagged along, and Val reminded herself that they were actually trying to make friends. They split up to head into their respective locker rooms before P.E.

Val sat down on a bench and pulled her gym shorts and t-shirt out of her bag. Lyla took her own clothes over to the bathroom to change. Val shed her school uniform and reached for her t-shirt.

Walking into the gym, she listened to the voices of the students echoing around the big room. She stood just outside the main group, watching. Jules saw her and waved, skipping over to the alpha's side. She grinned and elbowed Val gently in the ribs. "Hey! How's your day going?"

Even Val couldn't help the smile that crept onto her lips at the other girl's infectious cheerfulness. "It's going fine."

"Great! I submitted my article for approval. It should be out at the end of next week. Thanks so much for talking to me about it. I think it's important for everyone to learn more about you. About us."

Before Val could ask what she meant, the P.E. teacher entered with a large red ball in his hands. Val felt a surge of adrenaline when she realized what game they would be playing. It had been one of her favorites at the DAO's training center.

Val looked down at Lyla, who had appeared by her side. "Dodgeball."

Lyla chuckled and shook her head. "Don't kill anybody."

They were separated into teams, and Val wasn't surprised in the least when she saw that she and Lyla had been split up. A smirk lifted the corner of her mouth. Having two Truebloods on one team would have been more than a little bit unfair. She also saw that Lex was on the other team. As the teacher called out the last couple of names, Val found herself enveloped in a bear hug by an overly excited omega.

 "We're on the same team!" squealed Jules. "I bet you guys are great at this game."

Val forced her expression to stay carefully neutral as she disentangled herself from Jules' grasp. "We're decent. Are you always like this?"

Jules laughed. "Yep." Skipping away, she took a spot a few feet away from Val. "Don't let anybody hit me!"

Val wasn't one to turn down a challenge. She looked across the room and locked gazes with Lyla, giving her sister a wink. The teacher placed a line of red balls across the middle of the gym floor. Val eyed them and bit her lip, her body on edge. It wasn't a hunt, but it was the closest she could get to one.

As soon as the whistle blew, Val jumped forward and was the first to reach the line of red balls. She grabbed one in each hand and leapt back across the floor. Lyla's form flashed into her peripheral vision, second to the line. Val let one of the balls fly across, aiming for her sister with a throw that would've knocked a human off his or her feet. Lyla laughed and swerved gracefully to the side. The unfortunate gamma behind her took the ball to the chest with a loud "*Oof!*"

Val's blood sang with adrenaline as she dodged a throw that had been aimed directly at her head. Whipping around, she caught sight of Lex across the line, looking guilty. A low growl built in her chest, but she swallowed it, fighting her instincts.

She made sure her gaze stayed locked on him as she stalked forward, hunting her prey. Another ball whistled toward her, and she smoothly dropped her upper body forward, rocking her shoulders in a wide circle and swinging back up as the missile flew past her. She grabbed another ball as it rolled toward her on the floor. She threw the first one, expecting it to miss, and it did, but the second was right on its heels.

Lex dodged the first easily, but as soon as his head came back up, he was smacked with the second ball. He stumbled backwards, yelling out in surprise and frustration. Val suppressed the howl of victory that she wanted to let loose. Two alphas from the opposite team had decided she was their next target and were lobbing balls in her direction, calling out snide remarks as they did so. Val dodged their first volley and turned around to see Jules clinging to a ball halfway across the gym. Across the line, Lyla was drawing back, ready to lob her ball right at the omega.

Lyla zeroed in on Jules, who yelped as she lifted her leg to dodge another ball. Lyla was having no trouble staying out of the line of fire. The throws from most of the other students were predictable and slow. Val was the one player that could match her in speed and strength, but she was occupied. Lyla saw her take out Lex, moving toward him like he was a deer in the woods. He was a lost cause. Lyla turned back to Jules.

The omega was an obvious target. She wasn't in the front line, but she was close enough that a careful shot would easily hit her. Lyla threw her ball, controlling the strength so that the omega wouldn't be hurt. The ball spun toward its target. A body hurtled through the space in front of Jules, grabbing the omega and lifting her into the air, carrying her forward five feet. The ball missed them by inches. Lyla smiled devilishly. Her sister had let her guard down for a moment. A few feet away, two alphas that she recognized from Jackson's group were hurling insults at Val, throwing ball after ball at her.

"Hey Trueblood, go back to the forest!"

"Come on, show us your fangs!"

Val wasn't having trouble dodging their attacks, but Lyla could see her sister's control slipping. The bond link reverberated with their shared adrenaline and Val's growing territorial anger.

One of the alphas called out "Come on, feral! You scared?" and Lyla saw Val's hands curl into fists as she crouched slightly, her eyes tinged violet. The fangs would appear any second.

Sensing the shift in Val's demeanor, Jules ran toward her and tried grabbing hold of her hand, but Val pushed her back roughly. Lyla grabbed a ball from the floor and ran forward, grabbing a second when it rolled nearly under her feet.

Val sent two balls flying toward the alphas, and they both found their marks, but even when the other Were students stepped back and out of the game, Val didn't slow her pursuit. She crossed the line into enemy territory.

A ball smacked into her face. Hard. Val stumbled back a step, shaking her head to clear it. A second ball hit her in the side. Lyla approached warily.

"You okay?"

Val kicked a ball away and glared at her sister. "Fantastic." She stalked away to sit on the bench with the rest of her disqualified teammates. The game didn't last long after that. Val picked at her fingernails while Lyla's team finished off the last of their opponents. As soon as the coach dismissed them, Val headed for the locker rooms. She had barely reached her gym bag when she heard Jules pipe up behind her.

"Val, are you okay? Those guys are real jerks."

"Yeah," Val replied. "I'm sorry I pushed you. Are you hurt?" She glanced at the omega, who looked more concerned than hurt. Jules offered a bright smile.

"It's all right, I'm fine! I guess all the stories I've heard about Truebloods are real. You two are on a whole different level."

Val shrugged. "Adrenaline brings it closer to the surface. I have to be more careful."

"You never answered my question the other day. What is it like?"

Val reached into her bag and pulled out a clean black shirt. She had been about to answer the last time Jules asked her that question, and the words still lingered in her mind. Next to her, Lyla shot her a look and swung her own bag over her shoulder, heading for the showers. Val gritted her teeth. No matter how much she wanted to answer, she knew better. She reached back and pulled her shirt over her head, wrinkling her nose at the smell of sweat. She would need a shower before Cormoran arrived to check in on them. She reached down for the clean shirt but noticed that Jules had gone still beside her. Val paused at the girl's shocked expression.

She looked down at herself: sports bra and gym shorts. "What?"

Jules looked away. "Sorry. I just saw—you have a lot of scars. Were those from before? When you were wild?"

Val shuddered against the pain, a rasping cry breaking free from her lips. She didn't want to die. And at the same time, she did. Claws raked over her forearms, trying to shred away the bracelets, the electric current pulsing through her.

She quickly pulled the shirt over her head, covering the pale scars that littered her arms and torso. She tucked her forearms against her body to hide the deepest scars. "Some. Not all of them."

Jules didn't push it. "I'm sorry. I, um, I better get back to my dorm room." She grabbed her bag and headed for the door. Val sat down on the bench.

"Hey, I'll see you tomorrow, okay?" Jules had paused by the door, a softer expression on her face.

Val nodded. "Sure. Hey Jules?"

"Yeah?"

"Thanks."

Jules smiled and disappeared out the door. Lyla came back from the showers, her dark hair dripping onto her shoulders. All but a couple of the other students had filtered out of the room, leaving the two of them mostly alone.

"You want to talk about it?"

Val knew that Lyla was giving her a chance to get things off her chest before their meeting with Cormoran, but she wasn't sure she could string two coherent thoughts together at that moment.

"No. Let's go."

Lyla saw Lex in the hallway, waiting for them. He glanced at Val, and then back at Lyla, looking concerned. "Are you guys all right? That was—"

Lyla shook her head. "Don't worry about it. We'll see you later." Taking the hint, Lex started walking down the hallway. Lyla felt a twinge of regret, and then remembered her sister's dare. She took a deep breath and called after him. "Hey, Lex! We're going to have a game night tonight. Want to hang out?"

He looked shocked. "What?"

"Do you want to come to game night at our dorm room? We're in 213."

He grinned and flashed a thumbs up. "Yeah! That sounds great. I'll bring snacks. What time?"

"Six."

"I'll be there!" Lex flashed them the peace sign and jogged away down the hall. As soon as he was out of earshot, Val chuckled.

"I forgot about that. This should be entertaining."

"That's one word for it," replied Lyla, feeling irritable. She wasn't sure she was looking forward to this game night. Lex would probably take it as an invitation to keep hanging around them. She wasn't sure how she felt about that.

"I shouldn't have pushed Jules during the game," admitted Val during the walk back toward the dorms. "I don't know what got into me."

"I do," replied Lyla. "I've seen that look on your face plenty of times before. You're going to have to work on that. We can't turn every P.E. class into a hunting spree. But I'm glad you're getting along with Jules."

Val wiped a hand across her nose. "I wouldn't say that. She's an omega, so I feel protective of her. Pack habits die hard."

Lyla grinned, enjoying the flash of awkward tension that reached her through the bond. "Uh huh, pack habits. Or maybe you're making a friend, Val Blackwood. Would that be the end of the world?"

Val scowled. They took the stairs two at a time. Omegas were typically the weakest of the Were ranks, friendly and charismatic. They often gravitated toward alphas for protection. Lyla's lips twitched as she remembered how quickly Jules had latched onto Val. Yet another sign of how strong the inborn instincts of Weres ran. Her thoughts turned to Lex. As a Beta, he was strong, but not as commanding as an alpha. The gammas were supportive, many of them taking on peacemaker roles. Were children often exhibited signs of their rank early, sometimes as soon as age two or three.

Reaching the top of the stairs, Lyla unlocked their dorm room door. She dropped her backpack the moment she was inside, rolling her shoulders to relieve the tension. Val went straight into the bathroom to take a shower. Lyla glanced around the room to see if there was anything she needed to clean up. After moving several leftover wrappers and water bottles to the trash can, her gaze landed on the small carved wolf sitting on top of her dresser.

She ran her fingers over the smooth wood, its familiar texture bringing a rush of nostalgia. She could see it sitting in its original place on top of the fireplace mantel in their cabin, her father placing it carefully back after letting Val and Lyla play with it on the floor. It was one of the only things they'd been allowed to keep from their previous life. Seven years. It felt like a lifetime ago.

Reluctantly, Lyla removed her fingers from the carving and went to sit on one of the chairs. She dropped her head back onto the cushion and breathed deeply. The air smelled musty, even though they kept their window open a crack most of the time. Lyla heard the shower turn off in the bathroom, and a few moments later Val appeared in fresh clothes, toweling off her wet hair. Her eyes lingered on the carved wolf on top of the dresser.

"You were thinking about home."

There was no point in denying it. Lyla changed the subject. "Cormoran should be here soon. She's probably going to ask you how you've been with your control."

Val huffed and tossed her towel back into the bathroom, tying her hair up into a messy bun on top of her head. "That'll be a riot, I'm sure. She'll probably make me practice those dumb meditation exercises and recite the rules of assimilation again."

"Just go along with it. The more you cooperate, the sooner she'll leave."

"Easy for you to say. You're not the problem child," retorted Val. "It would be nice to see you bend the rules sometimes."

Lyla gave her a look. "If both of us were bending the rules, we wouldn't be here. We'd be stuck in the center for the rest of our lives. It would be nice if you made a little effort. Someday I might not be there if something bad happens, and then what?"

Val faced the window. "I guess they'll have few silver bullets ready for me, then."

Lyla gasped. "Val, don't say that!" She steadied herself. "We've come a long way. We can't give it up now."

"And where exactly are we?" asked Val. "What are we? Do you even know anymore? I sure as hell don't."

Lyla opened her mouth to answer, but she realized she had nothing to say. She'd avoided asking that same question of herself for years. She stood up. "You should grab something to eat. Cormoran will be here in twenty minutes. I'm going for a walk."

CHAPTER FIVE

When the door closed behind Lyla, the room was quiet. Val sat, fidgeting with her hands, staring straight ahead at the wall. The bond link felt strangely empty, and she knew that Lyla was masking her emotions. Twenty minutes. She had twenty minutes to collect her thoughts before Cormoran walked through the door. She glanced at the clock. Nineteen minutes.

Lyla was always the one keeping her anchored. Even in those tortured, lonely days in isolation, the thought of seeing her sister again had kept Val going. Val knew that her sister carried the weight of making sure they were able to assimilate successfully. Control and planning had never been Val's strong suit. But if they weren't able to succeed, they both knew the consequences. She shook her head in frustration as a flashback reared its ugly head somewhere in her subconscious. She couldn't let them in right now.

Instead, she took a deep breath and counted to ten. Lyla needed her right now. Her sister's anxiety had been tangible when she left the room. Val relaxed her shoulders and focused on the feelings of love and loyalty that threaded through their bond. She reached deep inside for a memory to share.

Laughing as they tore through the woods, howling and snapping at each other. Sitting on their favorite overlook on the mountain. They'd carved out a little place for themselves in the rubble of their life, just the two of them.

Val went a little deeper, allowing herself to open another door in her mind. This one was tightly closed, but she allowed it to open the tiniest crack. She allowed the memory to flood her senses.

Lyla sat in the grass, twirling a leaf around her fingers. For the first time since they'd left the DAO center, she was becoming overwhelmed with doubt as to whether or not this would even work. Val's comment about the silver bullets had her rattled, and she hadn't wanted to stay in the room and admit it. She knew that Val didn't believe that the DAO would ever truly let them be free again.

Lyla watched a group of students playing badminton on the campus lawn. In a way, she envied the Domesticated Weres. They'd grown up in a world where they'd never felt the wild rush of phasing, life out in the woods, hunting and being part of a pack. The Domestics had been used to a world that the DAO had built slowly built over decades, starting with Carrington Labs and their work creating ways to remove what they considered the violent and primitive side of Weres. For these Domestic students, denying their wolf nature was as natural as breathing. Their suppressants were so attuned to their bodies that they didn't even partially phase during a full moon. They were more human than wolf-kind.

She and Val still partially phased, even on suppressants. They'd been through the guidelines and years of training, and the school had agreed to allow them to miss classes for two or three days. But Lyla still wasn't completely sure how it was going to go around all the other students. Besides, Lyla hadn't been around her sister's phases for years. The DAO had kept them isolated during full moons.

Would Lyla still be able to stay in control? She'd sounded so confident when she had laid out the plans with Dr. Carrington. But now that the full moon was looming, only a few days away, she felt sick to her stomach. There were too many risks.

She rubbed her temples, worries and doubt swirling around in her mind like a snow globe. Faintly, she felt Val through the link. After a moment's hesitation, she allowed the mental barrier she was holding to fade. The memory that immediately flooded through the bond took her breath away.

Their father's big, booming laughter filled the cabin as he pulled Sanzi to his side, pressing a kiss to her red hair before lifting a toddling Arka up off the floor and into his arms. His red beard tickled her skin as he kissed her cheek. He held out his hand, and his daughters put their smaller ones against it, letting him cage them both in his gentle fist. Their mother leaned against the doorway, her eyes sparkling as she watched them, her dark hair wound up around her head in an intricate swirl of braids and silver beads.

From somewhere around the memory swirled a thought, gentle and clear.

"I love you, Arka. My sister."

Tears stinging the back of her eyes, Lyla stood up and walked back into the building. When she came through the door into their dorm room, Val rose from her chair, eyes shimmering with her own emotion. Lyla walked up to her sister and leaned into her, nestling her forehead against Val's shoulder. She felt Val's arms wrap around her protectively, just as they had all those years ago when they were alone in the woods.

"We're going to be okay. You don't have to carry all this by yourself," Val whispered, resting her chin on the top of Lyla's head. "We're going to be okay."

...

Lyla did most of the talking, keeping a neutral expression and laying out the details of school life as indifferently as possible. Ms. Cormoran listened to everything that had happened since she had last seen the sisters, intermittently penning notes on her tablet. She sat across from the two girls, who had pulled their chairs closer together. The small dorm room felt even smaller with Ms. Cormoran in it. The woman's hair was once again in an immaculate bun, her glasses perched studiously at the top of her nose. She wore a cream-colored suit jacket and pencil skirt with a blue silk scarf neatly tied around her neck. The two sisters knew she was a Were but had been unable to determine her rank. Val had even joked that she smelled human.

"All right, there are a few things that we should address today," Cormoran began. "Valentine, neither of you mentioned incidents of aggressive behavior that have been reported to us since you started school. One during your P.E. class and another during a lunch period?”

Val paled slightly. “Oh.”

Lyla jumped in. “She really didn’t do anything, and we were able to get the situation under control both times.”

The pause was stifling as Cormoran looked between the two of them. She tapped her pen against the side of her tablet. “Valentine, do you feel threatened by the students at the school?”

Lyla could feel the bond buzzing with Val’s anxiety, but to her credit, her sister just looked thoughtful.

“I think it’s just getting used to a new environment,” Val finally said. “Things are different here than at the center. Once I’m more familiar with it, I think things will settle down.” Val’s voice was laced with a generous amount of optimism and reassurance.

Nodding, Cormoran leaned forward. “This is a big transition for the two of you. You’re leaving a lot of old things behind and starting a brand-new life,” she said. “The two of you have made incredible progress since you started in the program. But I do need to remind you that we do not accept those kinds of behaviors in Domestic environments. The need for that aggression is in the past. You don’t have to resort to old habits to be heard.”

Lyla had to put up a mental barrier to stop the waves of disgust and barely concealed anger rolling off Val from seeping into her own emotions. But even she had to admit that she was getting tired of Cormoran’s assimilation script.

“You have your suppressants? We have a full moon coming up soon, and we need to make sure you’re extra prepared,” Cormoran reminded them. “Especially with the added stress you’ve been under transitioning into a new environment." She pulled a pair of sterile gloves from a package in her bag.

Lyla held two more white packages, still sealed. "We have them."

Cormoran took them from her and carefully inspected the seal and serial number on the label to make sure they hadn't been tampered with. "Excellent. The D.A.O. has instructed me to sign off that you've taken them, so we can go ahead and do the injections while I'm here." She ripped open the first package and pulled the syringe and vial free. After drawing the clear liquid up through the needle, she tapped her finger against the syringe.

Val was first. She rolled up her shirt sleeve, never taking her eyes off the silver needle in front of her. Lyla watched her carefully. Cormoran swiped the alcohol wipe over Val's bicep and lifted the syringe.

"Relax your arm, Valentine."

The muscles in Val's arm flexed but didn't relax. Her breathing accelerated, and Lyla could feel her effort to hold back the panic threatening the edges of her consciousness. Cormoran patted her hand kindly and smiled. "It's amazing that we have these resources available now. No more pain or fear that you could hurt someone. Slow down your breathing and count to five for me."

Val, relax. I'm right here. Lyla tried to hold her sister's gaze, but Val wouldn't look at her.

"One… two… three…" Val's rigid body relaxed ever so slightly. Cormoran administered the injection, and Lyla saw her sister flinch, eyes pressed tightly closed.

"Good," murmured Cormoran as she returned the used needle to a small box. She reached for the second package, and Lyla rolled her shirt sleeve up. Val got up from her chair and disappeared into the bathroom. Lyla visualized the barrier in her mind, directing all her focus on it as the needle pierced her skin. Val's nerves were already on edge, and an overprotective alpha was not what Lyla wanted at that moment. Cormoran returned her notes and folders to her tote bag.

"How are you doing, Lyla? Are you feeling confident about your transition in the school?"

Do I still feel confident that I can keep my sister under control? Is that what you really wanted to say? Lyla smiled. "Absolutely."

Cormoran smiled back. "Good. You know you can reach out to me any time. I will be back next week for another session. That should be after you both go through a phasing, but you know that you can reach me at any time. Remember to stay isolated. The school is aware of your situation, and you have up to three days each to miss class if necessary."

"Right. Stay away from other students, hope the suppressants work," said Val from the bathroom doorway. "Thanks for your help."

The woman nodded, pulling her tote bag up over her shoulder and heading for the door. "Of course. Remember, it is our goal to keep you here. Let's make sure we don't jeopardize that." She flashed them a smile and offered a polite wave as she left the room.

The tension in the room faded slightly and Val slumped against the doorframe, crossing her arms. "You know what the craziest thing about her is?"

Lyla leaned her head against the back of her chair. "What?"

"She actually believes she's helping us. She believes that all of this," Val gestured wildly around the small room, "is in our best interest. She's completely brainwashed."

Lyla couldn't really argue with that.

Val reached up and ripped the band-aid off of her arm. "Do you think she knows? About… everything they did to us?"

"I don't know," replied Lyla. "She wasn't assigned to us until after we finished the Domestication program. Who knows what they told her? She's never made any comments about any of that."

"Maybe she didn't know, then. They always told us that the assimilation program was a fresh start. That we were leaving our old lives behind," Val scoffed. "Like we had a choice."

Lyla didn't feel like extending that conversation, so instead she busied herself trying to find something to clean. Maybe she shouldn't have invited Lex over for a game night. If she had his number, she could have texted him and told him not to come.

"I know what you're thinking, but it'll be a good distraction," said Val. "Friends, remember?"

"Right."

Lyla began setting up the Clue board on the floor. She arranged the pieces carefully, enjoying the brief distraction. Games had been part of their training at the DAO center. The handlers had called it "Culture Therapy." Whatever that meant. She and Val had both found a measure of enjoyment on the weekly game nights that had been strictly overseen by the DAO staff. It was one of the only times they'd been allowed to interact with the other students in the program. They'd each come away with favorites. Lyla's favorite game was Clue, and Val loved Monopoly and Risk.

Lex arrived early, at 5:52 p.m. He looked almost sheepish when Val answered the door to let him in. He peered past her to where Lyla was sitting on the floor.

"Hey! I know I'm a little early. I hope that's okay."

Val stood back to let him in. "It's fine. There was nothing on the calendar for the next eight minutes. Clue sound good to you?"

Lex sat down on the floor next to Lyla, a wide grin on his face. "Oh, yeah! I love this game." When Lyla offered him the different playing pieces, he chose red.

"Miss Scarlet, every time."

Lyla glared at Val. "Val, stop pouting. You're always Miss Scarlet."

Muttering under her breath, Val grabbed the Mr. Green game piece, which was usually the one that Lyla chose. Lyla shook her head in amusement and put the Mrs. Peacock piece down on the board.

The game was one-sided from the beginning. Neither Lex nor Val was particularly adept at Clue, though they both were very enthusiastic about playing it. Lyla went along with it for a while, having fun trying to throw the other two off track. Finally, she'd had enough and made her accusation. When she pulled the cards out of the case file envelope, she smiled and placed them face up on the game board.

"What?" exclaimed Lex. "No way it's Mrs. White! I eliminated her two turns ago!" he showed them his notepad.

Val stood up. "You guys let me know when you figure out who actually won. I'm going to the bathroom."

Lex helped Lyla put the pieces back in the box. "I don't know why everybody is avoiding you two. You're pretty cool."

Shuffling the cards into a neat pile, Lyla decided to dig a little deeper. "Why is everyone avoiding us?"

Lex shrugged and sat back against the wall, studying the room as he spoke. "When we got the email from Principal Bleiz about the two of you, they made it sound like you were still half-wild. Lots of precautions and phone numbers to call if we see anything weird. You're Truebloods, and we don't see a lot of those in Domestic neighborhoods, you know? Plus, Val is an alpha, so that's another thing."

Taking in the information, Lyla nodded. She pulled her braid over her shoulder. "Something against alphas?" she asked with a smirk.

Lex laughed. "Nope. I think I'm mislabeled. I have a lot of alpha tendencies," he said, squaring his shoulders and puffing out his chest ever so slightly.

"Beta."

He looked at her with a frown. "Yeah,

I know. I still think they could be wrong."

Val opened the bathroom door and came back to sit down next to her sister. She glanced between them, noticing the miffed frown that Lex was wearing. "I missed something."

"I'm trying to tell her that I could be an alpha," said Lex. He looked imploringly at Val. She snorted.

"Beta."

With a huff, Lex gave it up. "Fine. Not like it really matters anyway."

Val grinned and shook her head, reaching for the bag of popcorn that Lex had brought. "Let's eat. I'm starving."

Beep. Beep. Beep. Beep.

When the alarm clock chirped it was pushed roughly off the nightstand. It rolled under the bed and continued its cheerful but muffled barrage. The mound of blankets that was Val growled but made no move to get out of bed. The bathroom door opened, and Lyla emerged, toweling off her damp hair. She reached under the bed and grabbed the clock while lifting the blankets. She tossed the offensive item inside with Val.

A split second later, Val was shuffling to the bathroom, grumbling under her breath. Lyla glanced out the window. It was overcast and the wind whistled. She pulled on her uniform absentmindedly, still running over the events of the last night in her mind. Overall, Lex was okay. He wasn't someone she would have naturally been friends with, but maybe having him around wouldn't be the worst thing. Val enjoyed Jules' company, so between them that was two successful friends. Maybe they were making progress.

She glanced at the calendar. Wednesday. Full moon phasing would begin the next day. It usually latched onto Val early in the cycle. Lyla sat down on the edge of her bed. Val appeared from the bathroom, freshly showered, still looking faintly grumpy. She stopped when she saw Lyla's distant expression.

"You okay?"

The two words had become something of a mantra between them. An invitation to be real, honest. Lyla rubbed the back of her neck. She must have slept on it wrong. "Phasing will probably start tomorrow. I'm just hoping it isn't a problem. The suppressant didn't make you sick this time, did it?"

"Not as bad." Val finished pulling on her uniform and then sat down next to her sister. "Who knows, maybe the dumb thing will work for real this time and nothing will happen."

As much as Lyla wanted that to be possible, she knew it was unlikely. "Maybe."

"Let's just take it as it comes, okay?" pleaded Val. She stood up, shouldering her own backpack, and lifting Lyla's with one hand. "Don't worry so much."

Lyla followed Val down the stairs and across the campus lawn. The wind was cool but felt good against their naturally warmer skin. With the full moon approaching, their blood was rising in temperature, making even moderately hot days nearly unbearable. Under the lulled haze of the suppressants, their wolf spirits were stirring restlessly.

CHAPTER SIX

When Val handed in her essay homework for English, the teacher gave her a warm smile as she took the stapled papers.

"Thank you, Valentine."

"Val is just fine, ma'am," said Val, trying to smile with the same kind of warmth as the teacher. It didn't feel right. She needed to learn to smile more. As she turned to go back to her seat, she caught sight of Homework Boy sitting off to her right, pen hovering over his notebook as always. He was watching her a little too intently. Again. She sat back down, attempting to ignore him when he glanced back at her over his shoulder.

Every time they had a class together, Homework Boy would only half-focus on the class, either writing in his notebook or reading from something that wasn't the textbook. And he glanced at her frequently. It was making Val irritated. By the end of the day she was thoroughly riled up. She ignored the voice in the back of her mind telling her that her impending phasing was making her more irritable. She disliked how her conscience sounded suspiciously like Lyla.

She wanted some answers.

After classes were over, instead of waiting for Lyla, Val stalked into the library. She caught sight of Homework Boy sitting alone at a table in the corner, a large stack of books next to him, notebook open. She walked over to the table and slid into the seat across from him. Startled, he flinched, and his gaze snapped up to her.

"Oh, um… hi."

Without responding, Val dumped her backpack next to her chair, leaning forward on her elbows and studying the boy across from her. He stared at her over his glasses, which had slipped down his nose again. For a moment, neither of them said anything. She narrowed her eyes, suddenly noticing the stack of books next to him on the table. She scanned the titles. *Phasing: Analysis of Forms. Truebloods. A Study of Pack Dynamics* was open in front of him, scribbled pencil notes all over the margins of the pages. A section on alphas was highlighted.

"Reading about alphas, hmm?" asked Val. "You know how alphas present differently than the other ranks? We're physically strongest, we're born leaders, and we can command the lesser ranks." She lifted herself up on her elbows and leaned farther forward so that her face was only a foot away from his. Her eyes pinned him to his chair, the tension thick. "And we take the protection of those we love *very* seriously. But you already know all that, don't you?"

Homework Boy swallowed. "I'm not sure what—you…"

"I want to know why you're spying on me. Are you spying on my sister too?"

He blinked. "What?"

"Do you work for the DAO? Or is this something else?" The words kept rolling, fueled by Val's paranoia. Homework Boy reached up and pushed his glasses up farther on his nose.

"I'm sorry if you thought I was spying on you," he said slowly. "I didn't mean to make you uncomfortable. I've been studying werewolves for years, and I've never had the chance to observe a Trueblood, much less one that came from a feral background."

Now it was Val's turn to blink in surprise. She sat back, crossing her arms. "So, I'm just a test subject to you? Is that it?"

He quickly put his hands up to placate her. "No, it's not like that. I'm just truly fascinated, and I want to learn all I can."

That wasn't what Val was expecting. She frowned. "Fascinated?" Humans were strange creatures. "What do you mean?"

"I'm a scientist. Or I will be someday. I want to work for the DAO until I can have my own private lab."

Disgust curled in Val's stomach. "You want to experiment on us?" she said in a low growl. It was clear that he quickly realized he'd said the wrong thing.

"No! Not at all. I want to help Weres. I know that assimilating into human culture can't be easy for you, especially with your background. I think there is a better way to still preserve some of your own culture and instincts while safely existing within human society. Honestly, my goal is to have a private lab, so I'm not bound by the DAO guidelines."

Once again, he surprised her. Val sat speechless, trying to figure out the human who was sitting across from her. "Oh."

He looked down at his notes. "My name is Christopher, by the way. Christopher Wells."

"I guess I can't call you Homework Boy anymore," replied Val. "I'm Val Blackwood, and my sister is Lyla." She figured he already knew that, but courtesy dictated that she should probably introduce herself again. Humans were constantly doing that.

"I was surprised to see you on your own," said Christopher. "Lyla is a beta, correct? I couldn't figure it out right away."

Val studied him again. He seemed genuine, and she couldn't detect any trace of deception in his blue eyes. They were turned down slightly at the corners, which gave him a sort of sad expression. She still didn't trust him. "Yeah, she is. She's up at the dorm room."

Christopher reached out his hand across the table. "I'm sorry again, I didn't mean to make you uncomfortable. Maybe we can start over."

This time, Val reluctantly decided to accept the gesture, and they shook hands lightly. She reached down for her backpack. "If I were you, I'd stay far away from the DAO if you want to help werewolves like me," she said quietly.

She stood up and turned to leave, but Christopher stopped her. "Would you be willing to meet up again sometime? I'd really like to hear more. I want to hear your side of the story."

No, you don't. And they don't want you to hear it. Val looked down at him, unsure how to respond. "I don't know."

"Whatever you're okay with. I don't want to push."

She frowned. "I guess we could hang out. But I don't want to talk about that." She reached down and scribbled her phone number and dorm room number on the top of his notebook page. "Stop by sometime."

Val gave him a brisk nod and then walked away. She wasn't sure what had gotten into her. She wasn't supposed to be making friends with this boy. He knew too much about them already. But he'd said he wanted to hear her side of the story, and whether he ever did or not, some part of Val desperately clung to that.

…

Thursday morning's sunrise was all fire. Deep orange, golden yellow, and the faintest streaks of blood red. It was spectacular, rising above the tree line beyond the campus fence. Val took a moment to appreciate it, sitting on the bench while she waited for Lyla to come back from the office. They'd decided to put in the request for their days off from school starting at the lunch period. Val had woken up with the telltale sheen of sweat over her forehead, the low burning fever starting in earnest as the full moon waited to make its appearance that night.

"Hey, Val."

She looked up at Christopher who had paused beside the bench, his briefcase held in his left hand. He was wearing a khaki trench coat.

"Hey yourself," she replied.

"Everything okay?" he asked, concern etched into his expression. Val didn't bother responding to the voice in her head that asked why he cared. She gave him a thumb's up.

"Peachy."

"Right. See you around," he said, waving as he continued on toward Gibbous Hall. There were a few other students around, and

Val suddenly noticed that she was the center of attention. Things had calmed down a bit after the initial gawking that had accompanied the Truebloods' arrival to the school. But now, the stares were back. Val frowned, trying to figure out why they were so interested in her this morning. Was her phasing so obvious, even now? She knew that her scent would be stronger.

"Hey, *feral!*"

Val snapped out of her thoughts and glanced up to see several of Jackson's "rogue alphas," as she and Lyla had started calling them, approaching her. Jackson led them, holding a paper in his hands. He held it out to her with a mocking grin.

"Didn't realize you were such a kitten at heart, Blackwood. Your training must be going well."

When she ignored him, he tossed the paper into her lap and walked away with his friends, laughing. Val scowled after them, and then looked down at the paper. It was the student newsletter. She picked it up and saw the headline.

Wild Trueblood Students Find Refuge in Assimilation Program.

She looked under the article's title to see Jules's name listed. The slow burn of anger started rumbling beneath her chest as she continued to read.

We have the privilege of hosting two new students at Westbrook Boarding School. Valentine and Lyla Blackwood are continuing their progress through the D.A.O.'s assimilation program by beginning formal education here at the school. I had the chance to sit down and speak with them over lunch during their first week of classes. Though both were raised in the wild, they expressed relief at being able to finally assimilate and enjoy a real taste of their new culture…

Val gripped the sides of the paper harder, crumpling it. The article went on and on, praising the groundbreaking work of the D.A.O. and encouraging the students to befriend the Truebloods and make them feel welcome. It dripped with forced enthusiasm. Val took a deep breath and focused on the mental image of a barrier to shut Lyla out of her emotions. She stood up and faced Gibbous Hall, balling her hands into fists. The crumpled paper fell to the ground.

Gibbous Hall was still swarming with students getting ready for their lunch. It didn't take Val long to find Jules' locker. The omega was standing there with her friend Maggie, holding a copy of the paper. Before Jules had seen her, Val reached forward and slammed the locker door shut, grabbing Jules by the shoulders, and pushing her back against the metal door. Jules looked up at her, and through her haze of rage, Val could see the flash of pure terror that crossed the omega's face.

"Val! Please, let me explain—"

"You think you've got us all figured out, huh?" Val interrupted her, forcing the words out through gritted teeth. "You're playing with things you know nothing about!"

"Val, wait!" begged Jules, squirming in Val's grasp. "I didn't know!"

"Hey!"

Val felt someone push her back away from Jules, freeing the omega. Whirling to face the newcomer, Val found herself glaring at Lex. Other students were gathering around the scene as well. Val could smell the fear in the room. Christopher appeared, pushing through the other students.

Lex held out his hands. "Val, you need to calm down. You can't attack Jules like that."

Biting back a howl of frustration, Val looked around the crowd of students. Her ears were ringing, and the fever was reaching a higher pitch. She swiped a hand across her forehead and brought it away damp with perspiration. She could feel her fangs descending. Whipping her head back to Jules, she tried to push the anger back down, but it was running wild, consuming her. Her fingernails bit into her palms until they broke the skin. She needed Lyla, but her sister was nowhere in sight.

Standing in the middle of the circle of students, Val was painfully aware of their undivided attention, watching her slow descent into partial phase with a mixture of fear, curiosity, and revulsion. If she hadn't been burning up from the inside out, it might have struck her as funny. *What a bunch of clueless... they're not even real wolves.*

She saw Lex approaching her again, his hands still out in front of him, trying to appear as non-threatening as possible. "Val, we should probably get you back to your dorm room."

"Jules, find Lyla," said Christopher. The frightened omega nodded and bolted down the hallway. Val watched her go, body rooted to the floor. Lex took hold of Val's arm and pushed her gently toward the doors leading outside. She growled and jerked away but went outside without another word.

As soon as they were outside, Lyla came running up behind them with Jules on her heels. Lyla didn't even miss a beat when she saw Val's face. She glanced over at Lex.

"Thanks. Did anything happen?"

Lex shook his head. "She got a little rough with Jules, but we got there before anything else happened," he replied. Val grimaced, and she noticed that Lex looked away when her fangs made an appearance. She put a hand to her forehead, her mind unfocused.

Jules stood a few feet away. "I'm really sorry. The article wasn't what I submitted. The staff said they were going to make some edits before they ran it in the paper. I didn't know how much they were going to change."

"Don't worry about it, Jules. We'll talk about it later, okay?" replied Lyla. She took hold of Val's wrist and guided her toward the dorms. "I've got it from here, Lex. Don't miss your class."

Lyla pushed both herself and Val through the door of the dorms and up the stairs. Every step was slow as Val fought through the war raging in her brain. Her breathing was heavy, and every few seconds, her head would tic to the side as if it were being pulled by some invisible force. The suppressants kept them from fully phasing, but it quickly became a mental war instead—one that Lyla knew all too well—as her wolf spirit fought wildly against the drugs trying to keep it at bay.

As soon as they were inside the dorm room, Lyla locked the door and led Val over to her bed. She looked down at her sister, flushed with fever; eyes glazed over, and felt a twinge of guilt. Lyla should've listened to her gut instinct when she felt Val get angry and then just as quickly return to a calm blankness.

Pulling open the door of their mini fridge, Lyla pulled out a bottle of water and poured most of it into a cup. Walking back over to the side of the bed, she pulled a chair over and sat down.

"Val, you need to drink something."

Stiffly, Val sat up and accepted the cup, taking a long drink, relishing the cool liquid. "I'm sorry that I went after Jules," she said, voice raspy. "Is she okay?"

"She's okay. What happened? She mentioned something about the article."

Val struggled to form her next words. "I'll never be what they want," she murmured. Her eyes drifted shut, and her labored breathing evened out ever so slightly as she was dragged down into a fitful sleep. Lyla set the cup down on the nightstand. This was the calm before the storm, and she could only pray that they would both come out of it unscathed.

Lyla watched as her sister curled over her knees on the chair, shoulders shaking as she held her head in her hands. She rocked back and forth, letting a low groan slip free. Lyla could see her body caught in the struggle between forms. Her eyes had turned violet, and her hands had half extended into their sharp-clawed fingers. But the suppressants were doing their work well enough.

After letting out a soft gasp of pain, Val leaned back, sweat running down her face and neck. "Wolf's blood," she whispered. "It feels like I'm being torn in half. Every time."

Lyla knew what she meant. Every full moon at the DAO center, she'd been locked inside a white cell to deal with the aftereffects of the suppressants she'd been given. The natural flow between human and wolf was ruined by the drugs. For Domesticated Weres who were half or full blood, watered down through their heritage by human ancestors, they would never know the pain a suppressant caused. It was strong enough to counteract the phasing for them. But for a Trueblood, the power in their blood raged against the suppressants with the fury of storms.

Val grabbed a cube of ice from the bowl beside her and gripped it in her fist. Within seconds, the heat from her hand had melted it into water that flowed between her fingers. It had been Lyla's idea to try the ice as a distraction, and so far, it seemed to be helping at least a little. Val looked up at her and narrowed her eyes. Lyla saw dried tear trails tracing down her sister's cheeks.

"Lyla, you're phasing too," Val said.

Reaching up to her forehead, Lyla knew what she would find there. She ignored the dampness on her fingers and grabbed the empty bowl from beside Val.

"I'll go get more ice from the freezer," she said. Val made no protest as she left the room and stalked down the hallway. In the common room, she held the bowl under the ice chute in the refrigerator and pressed the lever. The fever made it hard to think. She grabbed one of the cubes out of the bowl and held it in her palm, watching as the small bit of frozen water melted against her skin. She smiled. The little moment of distraction was calming. It took her away from the wild roaring that was building in her core.

She walked back toward their dorm room. Another student passed her on the way, but the girl stayed all the way on the other side of the hallway and picked up her pace when Lyla noticed her. Lyla rolled her eyes, irritable. Deep breaths. She needed to take deep breaths. This was all just the phasing. She looked up to see someone at the other end of the hallway, standing in front of their dorm door. It was a tall boy in a trench coat. A low cry came from inside the room, and Lyla saw him reach for the doorknob.

"Hey!" Lyla called. "Don't!"

She jogged up to him, putting herself between the boy and the door. "Can I help you?"

"Right, sorry. I'm Christopher. I know Val from class." He glanced awkwardly back toward the door. "Is she…?"

"Partially phased right now," said Lyla. Val had told her a little about meeting Christopher in the library the other day, and the pieces slowly fell into place. "Why are you here?"

Christopher fumbled in his pocket and withdrew a small bottle. "This is a mixture of blue tansy oil. I've been working on it for about a year. It's to help with some of the side effects of phasing." He handed it to Lyla, and then a slight tinge of red appeared on his cheeks. "I know it's not much, but I think it might help."

Lyla took the bottle and glanced at the dark liquid inside. Blue tansy. Her mother had kept a stock of it to help whenever young Weres went through their first phasing. It helped calm them. How could Christopher possibly have known about it?

She didn't have time to ask. Lyla reached for the door. "Thank you."

They heard a loud thud from inside the room. Christopher took a step forward. "Is there anything else I can do?"

Lyla shook her head. "Any change in that room could set her off. I really appreciate this," she said, holding up the bottle. "But you shouldn't be here."

"Right, sorry."

Lyla slipped inside. Val was standing in the center of the room, chest heaving as she stared toward the slightly open door. As Lyla closed it, she saw Christopher's eyes widen as he met the deep violet ones of the Trueblood alpha inside the room. Lyla heard a low snarl behind her. The door clicked shut.

CHAPTER SEVEN

Val flexed her hands. Her claws were bothering her, stuck somewhere in a partial phase and aching. The fever still wracked her body, but the overwhelming anger and urge to hunt were lessening. Lyla had turned away from the door and leaned against it, her head drooping forward in exhaustion.

As Val's phasing waned, she realized just how much Lyla was struggling to hold her own at bay. Feeling guilty, she stepped forward and took the small bottle out of Lyla's hand. She saw a bruise on her sister's collarbone and briefly remembered striking out in anger sometime earlier on in the evening when her phasing was still rising. It had plateaued, the pain a constant presence, but no longer flaring. Val glanced down at the vial in her hand and twisted the cap off with a little difficulty. She was hit with a deliciously calming scent. Surprised, she took another whiff, then held it under Lyla's nose.

"Smells really good, whatever it is."

Lyla's shoulders relaxed. "Yeah." She was trembling.

Val set the vial aside. "It's okay, Lyla. You need to phase."

"I shouldn't. I think I can control it, maybe even stop it completely this time," Lyla whispered, her fevered eyes focused away from Val.

Val frowned and pulled her sister into the center of the room. "Don't you dare. It's bad enough partially phasing with the suppressants. You really want to hurt yourself?" She tipped Lyla's chin up to meet her gaze. "I'm not going to let anything happen."

Stubbornly, Lyla shook her head. "No. It's my job to keep you in control," she muttered. It was dangerous for wolves to try to keep themselves from phasing. Suppressing it was one thing, but to resist it entirely when it was already underway? It could cause long-term damage. Their minds and bodies were not built to handle that kind of strain.

"Come on, Lyla. Don't make me do this."

Lyla growled in response, a warning. Val sighed, her own inner wolf alpha snapping in annoyance, wanting Lyla to obey and knowing that she wouldn't listen. She moved her hands to the front of Lyla's shoulders and shoved, hard. Lyla took one stumbling step backwards and then lunged forward, eyes flashing violet as she lost her tenuous grip on control. She came after Val with fangs bared and a vengeance uncharacteristic of her usual calm demeanor.

Val caught her, baring her own fangs. She held Lyla back as her sister swung out with her sharpening claws, and Val winced as one of them opened a small cut on her cheek. Their wolf strength consumed their muscles as much as it could, hammering angrily against the barrier of the suppressants and feeding on their rising anger. Val ducked as Lyla's teeth snapped a hair's breadth from her shoulder. Val grunted, straining to hold her own as Lyla's strength grew. Lyla whipped her head around and growled, shaking her head to keep from howling.

Pushing her sister off balance, Val stepped back as Lyla crouched on the floor cradling her head in her hands.

"Sanzi."

Val immediately dropped to her knees beside her sister and enveloped her in a hug. "I'm here." She hated seeing her sister like this, and she knew it was no better when the roles were reversed. Instead of phasing as they were naturally meant to do, the suppressants made it happen in short bursts that left them exhausted and in pain. Val felt a familiar anger rippling through her, the kind that had nothing to do with the phasing. That anger was warm and explosive. This was cold, calculating, and full of dark promise. *Someday we will be free of this.*

Lyla glared at the broken lamp on the floor. After Val had pushed her into her phase, things had gotten slightly out of control. Val had done her best, but they had toppled into the nightstand, knocking the lamp onto the wood floor. The pieces were everywhere. Val came into the room with a broom and dustpan, looking suspiciously optimistic despite the large scratch across her left cheek.

"It could definitely be worse," she said cheerfully. "One set of claw marks on the wall, some scratches and bruises and a broken lamp. I think we're getting good at this." She reached all the way underneath her bed with the broom, pulling it back with several pieces of the lamp in tow.

Lyla glared in response, still lying back on her pillow. "They could still kick us out for this, Val. I don't think Cormoran is going to feel the same way as you do."

"Maybe we can convince them to let us out in the woods for a couple of days next time."

"You know that's never going to happen. They don't want us back in an environment that encourages us to phase."

Val rolled her eyes and gestured toward the dustpan. "Good luck trying to stop it." She eyed the small glass bottle on the nightstand. The entire room smelled like blue tansy. "I do think that stuff helped. I think we would've had a lot more than a broken lamp without it."

Lyla grabbed her second pillow and hugged it to her chest. "I'm just glad it's over."

Val regarded her carefully before sitting down on the edge of Lyla's bed. "I'm really sorry I had to push you into your phase. I didn't want to."

"I know. It would've been worse if you didn't."

Val took the dustpan out to dump the broken lamp in the garbage. She returned with a water bottle, still cold from the mini fridge. She unscrewed the cap and put it in Lyla's hand. "Drink."

The water brought some life back into Lyla's exhausted body. The fever was all but gone, leaving behind the clammy nausea and dizziness that came with the aftereffects of the suppressants. She watched as Val took another sniff of the blue tansy and sighed. Lyla wrinkled her nose.

"You never told me what happened with Jules before I got there. I saw the article on the bulletin board. It was a real piece of work."

Val ran a hand through her hair. "I pushed her into the lockers, and a lot of people saw. She was trying to tell me it wasn't her fault, but I couldn't listen. I was just angry about everything." She looked down at her hands. "I'm angry at them for what they've made us. Like we're trophies for them to parade around. Like they own us."

"They won't have us forever. You know that."

Val's previously light-hearted demeanor vanished. "I don't."

Biting back the angry retort that came to mind, Lyla put the water back on the nightstand and looked out the window. Students were playing games and sitting on blankets out on the lawn. She caught sight of a familiar black-haired omega.

"You should go talk to Jules."

Val felt the stares as she walked across the lawn, hands in her pockets. Lyla had said she was resting, but Val was suspicious that her sister was watching her out the window. There were several groups of students dotted around the lawn, and Jules was sitting on a blanket with two other girls, talking animatedly and looking over a pile of pictures.

Not wanting to disturb them, Val sat down on a bench and watched the activities going on around her. She needed to re-braid her hair. After the phasing, it was a bit of a mess. She saw Jules glance over to her, and a few minutes later the girls were packing up the pictures. Jules came over after waving to her friends and plopped down on the bench next to Val.

"Hey you," she said with a bright smile. "You look pretty good, considering you transformed into an omega-eating monster a few days ago." Val grimaced, but Jules just squeezed her hand. "I knew you'd be upset when you saw the article."

"I'm sorry, Jules." Val looked down at the ground and kicked a pebble away from her foot. She wanted to say so much more, but the words had been buried for so long she didn't even know how to form them anymore. Excuses were cheap anyway.

"I don't blame you. When I turned my article in, they said they might make a few changes. I had no idea it would be that different."

Val shrugged. "They don't want us encouraging anyone, I guess."

Jules folded her hands together in her lap. "Everyone is afraid of Truebloods, Val. People talk about how you're dangerous. My family hasn't ever really thought that way, but most people do. They're afraid of what you might do."

Looking away over the fence, Val tried not to scoff at that. *They think we're the monsters.* She looked back at Jules, who was watching her curiously. "And you're not?"

Jules's voice got quiet. "I'm not going to lie, when you came up to me in the hallway, I thought… I was scared." She paused. "But at the same time, getting to know you and Lyla has made me wonder if I'm missing something."

"You're part wolf too," said Val.

Jules studied her hands. "It's so weird to hear you say that, like being a werewolf is the most natural thing in the world. It's not scary or strange to you."

It made Val sad to hear the uncertainty in Jules' voice. "No, it's not scary." Val gestured broadly to their surroundings. "This is what's strange to me. All of this. I don't know if I'll ever really belong here."

She was surprised when she felt two arms encircle and give her a warm hug. Her instincts warned her to pull away, so she sat rigid as the omega held her for a long moment. Jules let her go. "I don't know what you two have been through, but I want to be your friend. If you'll let me."

Val tried a smile. "I'm not sure how to do friends, but I'll try."

Jules laughed. "I have to get to class, but let's hang out soon, okay?"

"Sure. I'd like that." As she said the words, Val realized how much she actually meant them. Jules gave her shoulder a squeeze and then trotted off. Val sighed and looked up. The trees were beginning to turn color. She stood up to make her way back to the dorm, shuffling over the leaf-littered lawn. The air was turning cooler, a welcome change from the sauna of summer. Val's phone buzzed in her pocket.

NEW TEXT MESSAGE
From: Lyla
Meet me in the dorm entryway. Christopher wants to talk to us.

Christopher was standing with Lyla just inside the doors, hands in his pockets and looking serious. His backpack was slung over his shoulder, obviously completely stuffed with something. He nodded to Val when she came in.

"My last class got canceled, and I found something that I think might help you."

Val stared at him in surprise. After seeing her the other night, she would've expected him to keep his distance after he had seen her. "Okay, what is it?"

"Follow me."

Val raised an eyebrow at Lyla as Christopher turned and walked to the end of the long hallway. After a pause, the two sisters followed, curious. They reached the door that led to the basement stairs and Christopher turned the handle.

"Christopher, this is the basement." Val stopped and crossed her arms. Christopher flicked on the light switch and the fluorescent panels on the ceiling flickered to life. He nodded and went down to the first landing before realizing that the sisters were not following him.

"It's completely safe, I promise. There's a space down here that I think would work for your next phasing." Val and Lyla stayed where they were. Christopher pushed his glasses up on his nose with a frown. "What's wrong?"

Val stared down into the gray tunnel, and she could feel her breath growing shallower. "No offense, but I'm not in a hurry to walk down there." She met his gaze. "I'm not a fan of dark underground spaces."

To her surprise, Christopher nodded. "That's fair. I don't want to push you; I'm just trying to help. To be honest, going down into a basement with two Trueblood werewolves isn't the safest thing I've ever done."

He shrugged. "Besides, I heard you gave your neighbors a good scare last night. This might provide a better solution."

The sisters shared a look. They hadn't heard a peep from the other rooms, but they must have given the other students a lot to talk about. Lyla took two steps down into the stairwell. "Okay. Let's see this thing."

Irritated, Val stood on the top step, watching them disappear around the corner of the landing. She huffed and finally jogged down to join them, looking down at her feet to avoid thinking about the concrete that was surrounding her.

The basement of the dorm building was mostly storage. Old furniture and boxes were everywhere, creating a maze through the large open space. There were some strange artifacts, even four broken arcade games in one corner. One of them said PACMAN in bold yellow letters across the top. Val nearly tripped over a cobweb-covered chandelier and caught herself on a stack of book boxes.

"Sheesh. I don't think housekeeping has been down here for a while," she said, disentangling her foot from the long chandelier chain with a grimace.

"I'm assuming that we aren't supposed to be down here?" asked Lyla, looking around at the mess.

Christopher shook his head. "It's technically off limits, but I've been down here before to check out the extra books they took out of the library. I found an antique edition of *Les Misérables* in one of the boxes. I still can't believe someone would leave something like that packed up in a dusty old box."

At the end of the room, Christopher had moved boxes to either side of a large door. It had thick hinges and a levered handle. Lyla looked it over.

"What is it?"

"It's an old bunker," replied Christopher, pulling on the lever. The door groaned open, revealing yet another set of stairs leading farther down beneath the building. Val's breath caught in her throat. She couldn't have expressed in words just how much she didn't want to go any farther. She felt Lyla squeeze her arm as her sister followed Christopher down the second set of stairs. Val's feet felt like lead. She pushed herself forward.

The stairs took two sharp turns, leading down into yet another level below the dorm's basement. Christopher flicked on a light switch and illuminated a large room, about half the size of the gym. It was completely bare except for some shelves along the far wall and a row of metal bed frames. Val stopped at the bottom of the stairwell, looking around at the high concrete walls.

On the wall next to the door was a small shelf with a few non-perishable food items, paper plates and cups, and bottles of water. Val stepped inside the door to pick up a bag of beef jerky. "What's all this?"

"I brought a few things down here so you wouldn't have to leave. There's even a bathroom over in that corner," he pointed to a small room against the far wall. Val put the bag back on the shelf. *You can't leave.* She grimaced. That's not what Christopher had said. *We don't have to leave. We have a choice.*

Christopher grabbed the door handle and swung the heavy bunker door shut. "Look, it even locks from the inside, so while you're down here, no one will bother you." The heavy slide of the bolt echoed throughout the room. Val's eyes snapped to the door, but it was Lyla who spoke.

"Open that door."

Lyla was standing still as a stone, eyes locked on the room's only exit, and suddenly Val was seeing the door through her sister's eyes as the bond between them opened. She saw another door, saw it closing slowly, the lock being pulled shut. *Alone. I'm so alone. Let me out.* Lyla's fear echoed through her head.

Christopher attempted to open the door, but the bolt stuck. He pulled on it again, but it held. The tension in the bond snapped like a whip, and Lyla jumped forward to the door, wrapping both hands around the bolt handle and throwing her weight against it. The long metal bar slid back with a loud creak. Lyla leaned her head against the door. The bond went completely silent, and the emotion that had been flowing through moments before stopped.

Val stepped forward and wrapped her arms around her sister, holding her. Lyla's hands trembled, still grasping the bolt. Val placed her hands over Lyla's.

"Let's open the door."

Together they pulled back the handle and the door swung free. One of the lights in the stairwell flickered. Val squeezed Lyla's shoulders.

"Look. What do you see right now?"

"The door. The door is open," Lyla whispered.

Val nodded against her shoulder, burying her face in the back of Lyla's shirt. "Yeah, it is. And it's going to stay that way as long as you want it to." She needed to calm her own racing heart. "Breathe with me."

The shallow breaths that Lyla was taking evened out as they stood silent, facing the open door. Christopher stood a few feet away, watching closely but not daring to interrupt the moment between them.

Val turned Lyla to face her. "Hey."

Eyes still somewhat unfocused, Lyla was slowly coming back from the place in her mind that Val could not follow. "I'm okay," she said. "Sorry, I don't know what happened there."

Before Val could respond, Christopher took a few shuffling steps toward them. "I'm so sorry," he said. "I should've asked if you were okay with it."

"It's not your fault," Val replied quickly. "Just let one of us shut the door next time."

"Yeah," Christopher said. He was wringing his hands together, but it wasn't pity Val saw in his eyes. Whatever was going on in his mind was, she couldn't read it.

"If you don't want to use the room, that's really no big deal," Christopher said. "We could find some other way—"

"No, it's fine." Lyla brushed imaginary dirt off her pants. "I'm fine. It was really thoughtful of you to show it to us. I'm just going upstairs for a bit." She headed into the stairwell and disappeared around the first landing.

Val wrapped her arms around herself. "I bet that wasn't in your textbooks," she chuckled, not feeling the amusement she forced into her tone. She looked up at Christopher as she turned to go up the stairs.

Christopher met her gaze. "No. But maybe it should be."

CHAPTER EIGHT

When Lyla got the text message from Cormoran, she wasn't surprised. She'd been hoping that the incident between Val and Jules might have been swept under a rug somewhere, but they were scheduled for a meeting with Principal Bleiz after their last class of the day. Cormoran wasn't supposed to visit them until the end of the week.

Val was already sitting outside the conference room beside the office, pulling at a string on the hem of her uniform sleeve. Lyla opened her mouth to say something, but the door behind Val opened and Jackson appeared. He shot a smirk toward Val.

"Finally got yourself in some real trouble, huh? That didn't take long." He walked away down the hall.

Before Val could respond, Principal Bleiz stepped out, wearing his usual scowl. "Come in."

Inside the office, Cormoran was wearing a navy suit, hair still pulled back into the sleek bun. She gave the girls a tight smile when they sat down in the chairs across from the two adults at the conference table.

"I've been informed of a particular incident between Miss Blackwood and another one of our students," the principal gestured to Val. "And I've heard all the details of it from several other student witnesses."

Lyla grimaced. That explained Jackson's involvement. Principal Bleiz clenched his fist on top of the desk. "When the DAO informed me that they were placing the two of you in this school, I had my reservations. Student safety is my priority, and while we do not recognize rankings here, I will address the fact that this *alpha* behavior is contaminating the atmosphere of our school. It appears that in spite of the good work of Dr. Carrington's program, you are unable to control yourself." He turned to Cormoran. "We were assured by your senior management that having Truebloods in this school would not be a danger. It appears that the concern over this was not misplaced after all. Perhaps the suppressants are not sufficient to prevent these types of incidents."

Cormoran tried to reassure him. "They are. I would discourage you from the belief that this was the product of any kind of ranking system. I have reason to believe that Valentine's behavior in this incident had more to do with human emotion. The phasing may have exacerbated it, but I don't believe that it is the core issue here."

The principal looked less than pleased with that answer. "And I suppose we should be grateful that she didn't take these human emotions farther and attempt to control our vulnerable students?"

There it was. Lyla bit back her own thoughts on the matter, but she couldn't help the feeling that the odds were against them.

Cormoran was right, Val hadn't been using any kind of alpha behavior with Jules, other than perhaps the extra dose of aggression that fueled her anger. But in Lyla's experience, people like Principal Bleiz were not willing to believe something other than what they already assumed. And he believed that Val was dangerous. Lyla ignored the tiny question that whispered into the back of her thoughts. *Is she?*

Val spoke up softly. "I don't want to hurt anyone. I'm sorry. It won't happen again."

Principal Bleiz turned to her. "No, it won't. The only reason you are still enrolled in this school is because Miss Ollren spoke on your behalf this morning when I questioned her about the incident. She was well within her rights to report you or press charges."

Jules. Lyla should have known that Jules would've been called to the office as well. She breathed a quiet word of thanks to the little omega for sticking up for Val. Principal Bleiz gestured at Ms. Cormoran.

"I have a staff meeting to get to. See that you take care of this. I will be turning in my full statement of complaint to Dr. Carrington first thing tomorrow morning." He picked up his briefcase and left the room. Val hadn't looked up from her hands since they sat down. Cormoran placed her bag on the table and pulled two file folders from it.

"Principal Bleiz and I have agreed that upping the dosage of your suppressant will be the best course of action, considering all the circumstances."

Val's head snapped up. "But I'm already on the strongest dose. You can't—"

"The DAO labs have recently passed a new formula into the field-testing phase. You're a perfect candidate. Just think, it could take all of this away for good." Cormoran offered what was meant to be a kind smile. "It might restrict your phasing all together."

Val's breathing quickened. "Please. I'll do anything."

"Valentine, I understand how hard this is for you, and I'm doing the best I can to help you. If you want to stay here at the school, this is the way that we accomplish that. Otherwise, you will have to return to the center and continue training there."

The terror pulsing through the bond made Lyla nauseous. "Ms. Cormoran, I really don't think it's necessary. Like you said, the incident with Jules was an emotional response. It had nothing to do with her wolf—"

"Her phasing, Lyla. It was just a phasing. Remember, we talked about how using certain words make it harder for the assimilation process to work well."

Gritting her teeth, Lyla continued. "Her phasing, then. Who knows what a stronger suppressant will do to her?"

"Don't, Lyla," Val interrupted. "I can speak for myself."

Ms. Cormoran smiled encouragingly. "Val, why don't we go into the next room and have a minute to ourselves. I want you to have a chance to speak your mind."

Lyla began to shake her head but stopped when she saw the smile leave Cormoran's face. She squeezed Val's hand as her sister stood up. The shaking in her hands was subtle, but Lyla saw it. She could feel it like a bubble around her sister. When the two of them left the room, Lyla groaned and leaned forward, letting her head drop to the table. When she lifted it, she glared at the chair where Cormoran had been sitting. And then her eyes fell on the manila folder tucked neatly under the tote bag. Val's name was typed on the tab.

Val watched warily as Cormoran slid her chair closer, withdrawing a white package from a small bag on her lap. It looked the same as the others, except it had a large red stamp across the seal that read: TEST PHASE. Val clenched her fists.

"I don't want that."

Cormoran's gloved hands never stopped moving. "Changes like this are always hard. It's important for you to stay positive while you work through this program. And you know I'm always here to support you."

Val bit her lip and swallowed back the angry tears that were threatening to spill out past the edges of her tightly held control. She watched as Cormoran drew the liquid out of the vial with the syringe. The silver needle caught the light and flashed. Val's face grew pale.

The needle pierced her arm, and the liquid was fired like a bullet into her bloodstream. At first, she could feel nothing. Then, white hot fire spread through her veins. The screaming she could hear in her head sounded so much like her own voice. Her wrists rubbed raw as she struggled against the restraints.

"No."

"Valentine," Cormoran's voice was soft but hardly comforting. "This is what needs to happen for you to stay with your sister. And I know that's what we both want."

Val's shattered gaze lifted to Cormoran, and then fell back to the syringe that the handler held in her hand, waiting. An eternity passed in Val's mind, until she stiffly removed her uniform jacket and rolled up the short sleeve beneath. She flinched at the cool moisture of the alcohol wipe, and then the sharp sting of the needle. The cords in her neck stood out as she fought to keep the terror from consuming her mind. She focused on her arms, staring at the deep scars running up above her wrists.

Don't fail.

Lyla pulled the folder toward her, heart pounding in her chest as she opened it. Val's photos stared back at her. One of them was a recent capture of Val in her school uniform. But the other was older, much older. It had been taken when they had first arrived at the center. Val's eyes were red-rimmed and scared, her face gaunt and dirty. The memory of that day still haunted Lyla. She still remembered waking up in the cave next to Val on their last morning of freedom.

Flipping past the photos, Lyla began scanning through the documents. After the first few pages that recorded their previous history and medical information, there was an in-depth psychoanalysis written by the therapist they'd seen at the very beginning of the program. Lyla scanned through the conclusion comments.

Volatile behavior. Subject responds with hostility to emotional triggers and appears to react strongly to negative stimulants. Strong phasing response. May require stronger Domestication methods. Early analysis suggests that Subject may not be suited to assimilation.

Lyla resisted the urge to roll her eyes. She could've written that, and she was no psychotherapist. As she moved further into the file, she paused when she reached an envelope labeled *Intensive Therapy Results*. Frowning, she pulled out the papers inside, and when she began reading the typed print, she felt her stomach drop to the bottom of her feet.

Silver Injection Therapy Observation

Day 12: Lethal Injection Capacity – Subject #523 V. Blackwood. Second attempt.

0700: Subject exhibits strong resistance to current suppressant formula. At 0800 we will attempt a lethal injection of silver compound to determine Subject's tolerance level.

0802: Injection given.

0806: Subject begins cardiac arrest.

08:08: Flatline heart rate. Resuscitation protocol activated.

0811: Subject was successfully resuscitated.

0840: Injection successful. Accurate levels of lethal injection were determined.

Lyla sank back into the chair. She couldn't breathe. She flipped through the rest of the results pages, and each one added to the unbearable pain growing in her chest. *Shock Therapy. Solitary Confinement and Isolation. Neuro-stimulants. Forced Phasing. Starvation Response. Triggers and Limitations.* Lyla couldn't stomach another page, but she didn't want to stop. She had to know.

The door opened, and Cormoran stepped in. She stared at
Lyla, who stared back, the folder in between them like a detonator.

CHAPTER NINE

Cormoran smoothed her skirt and carefully extracted the folder from Lyla's tight grip. She organized the papers and put them back in her bag. Then she sat down, taking her glasses off and placing them off to the side on the table. Lyla waited for the woman to speak. Her own voice was currently held captive by the hard lump in her throat. Cormoran watched her, searching her face for something. The room was far too silent, each waiting for the other's first move.

"Where is Val?" Lyla forced out.

Cormoran smiled. "She was feeling a bit tense, so she went for a walk. I'm proud of how she handled today. Let's talk about the anger you're feeling right now."

Lyla gaped at her. "The anger I'm…" She pointed at Cormoran's bag. "Did they do all of those things to her?" One desperate piece of Lyla's heart wanted more than anything for Cormoran to say no, that it was all just a misunderstanding.

"For some patients, more extensive therapy is required to fully understand their capabilities. It's for their safety as well as everyone else's."

Lyla slumped back in her chair. Whether or not Cormoran knew what had happened to them was no longer a question. Lyla set her mental barrier firmly in place to keep Val out of the intensity of the emotions she was feeling. The last thing she wanted was for Val to find out that she knew like this.

Every memory for the past several years suddenly made more sense. Val's growing anger and resistance to the first years of the program, and then the separation. The first few months of isolation, the pain and fear that had bombarded their bond link until Dr. Carrington had developed a way to smother it with his drugs. Then, the soul-crushing silence. Two years of it, only seeing each other in brief glimpses if they were allowed to come outside.

The first time she'd seen Val again a few months ago, they'd sat in a white room across from each other, each desperately searching for the sister she'd lost in the eyes of the stranger across from her. They were the same, but they were not the same at all.

Val's despondent behavior hadn't lifted after they'd been reunited. She refused to say anything about what had happened when they were apart. The nightmares and strange things she called out during the night had been only glimpses. Lyla had seen the scars on her sister's body, but Val wouldn't tell her anything about them. Lyla had never imagined anything like this.

Cormoran broke the silence. "Lyla, it's important that you understand the confidentiality of this information. It would be unfortunate for someone to have access to any personal history. If you and Val are going to have a better life, we can't jeopardize that in any way. Your sister's safety depends on your cooperation. Do you understand?"

Lyla met Cormoran's gaze, stone cold. "Perfectly. If you have nothing else to say, I'm going to go find my sister." She picked up her bag and walked to the door, her whole body on edge.

"Lyla."

She paused, waiting.

"Take good care of her. She needs you."

Lyla didn't slam the door behind her, no matter how hard she wanted to.

The leaves fluttered down to the trail, surrounding Val in a little autumn flurry. She was already feeling nauseous, and it didn't help that her stomach was tied in knots. Walking slowly down the trail, she studied the gravel under her feet. She made no move to sweep the hair away from her eyes, allowing it to shield her face. Her arm burned.

She should have waited for Lyla, but she needed a moment to herself. Lyla was under enough stress, and Val certainly didn't want to add to it. She was too tired to block Lyla from their bond, but she wasn't worried. She was so numb she doubted if her sister would be able to feel her presence at all.

Val felt a wave of nausea sweep through her body. Turning to the side, she dropped to her knees, barely pulling her hair away from her face before she vomited into the grass on the side of the trail.

"Val!"

A hand rubbed her shoulders gently as she leaned over, and a tissue appeared beside her. She took it and wiped her mouth, still shivering slightly. Perspiration lined her eyelids.

"Sorry," she croaked. She turned to face Lyla and was surprised when her sister pulled her into a hug. Even though her brain was moving sluggishly, she still realized that Lyla's grip was abnormally tight. They held onto the hug for a few minutes, leaning on each other's shoulders.

Val was concerned. "What's wrong?"

"I'm just glad you're here."

Val didn't know how to respond to that, so she leaned into the hug, letting Lyla hold her for a few more seconds. Finally, Lyla sat back. "Let's go back to the dorms."

The lawn was vacant, most of the students were eating dinner in the cafeteria. One couple sat on a blanket watching the sunset together. Lyla pulled her phone out of her pocket and noticed several texts that she had missed from about twenty minutes ago.

NEW TEXT MESSAGE
From: Jules
Want to hang out? Lex was looking for you a while ago.
Christopher ate supper with us and he's here too.

NEW TEXT MESSAGE
From: Jules
Where are you guys?

NEW TEXT MESSAGE
From: Jules
Ok srsly. I'm sending out a search party if I don't hear
from you soon.

Val was reading over her shoulder. "We should go. They're the only people who still want us around."

"You're obviously sick, Val. We can hang out with them tomorrow."

Val shook her head. "No, I want to. I don't want to sit in a quiet dorm room right now. It'll be nice to have a distraction."

Lyla looked at her for a minute, and Val wasn't sure what she saw shimmering in her sister's eyes. She realized that their bond was still closed on Lyla's side, but guessed that her sister was just trying to give her some space.

The school's weight room was quiet during the dinner hour. But Jules' bright laughter floated into the hallway as the two sisters approached. Inside, Lex was lifting weights and Christopher was sitting on a chair with a book. The instant she caught sight of the Truebloods, Jules bounced up from where she'd been sitting on a stationary bike.

"There you are!" she exclaimed. "Val, you look awful. Principal Bleiz didn't give you a hard time, did he?"

"I'm okay. Just tired."

Jules didn't look like she believed that excuse, but she put her hands on her hips. "I told him not to send another email out to the student body, but he did anyway. I'm so sorry."

"It's not your fault, Jules," said Val. "I shouldn't have acted the way I did." She gave the omega a tired smile. "Thanks for sticking up for me. That means a lot."

"Of course I did. That's what friends do. Besides, that lady from the DAO gives me weird vibes."

Val laughed. "Cormoran? Yeah, that's fair."

Lex curled the weights one more time before setting them back on the stand, stretching his arms. He glanced at Lyla and grabbed a towel from his gym bag, hanging it around his neck. "Are you guys going on the field trip to the zoo? It's in two weeks."

"You need a parent or guardian to sign the permission slip, right?" asked Lyla. Lex nodded, and Lyla gave a hopeless shrug. "Yeah, we probably can't go."

The email with all the details had come through a few days back, and Val remembered the vibrant photos of the zoo's exotic animals. It was over two hours away in the closest large city. Away from the school and the tall fence. It would have been the first time she and Lyla had been allowed outside of a fence or a car between fences since they'd started the program at the DAO.

"Sorry," Val said. "That's my fault. Maybe you can go, Lyla. I'm sure that Cormoran would sign for you."

Jules scoffed. "That's ridiculous. You should at least ask, the worst they can do is say no." She pulled her phone out of her jeans pocket. "I'll be right back, okay? Maggie wants to talk to me about something outside."

The omega jogged out of the room, wrapping her pink scarf around her neck to add a little warmth to her thin sweater. Lex walked over to another machine and reached up to the bars, doing a couple of pull ups. Lyla sat down on a bench near him, and he dropped down to the ground, grinning at her.

"Truebloods are supposed to be super strong, right?"

He reached out and grabbed large weights from the bottom of the rack. Val nearly laughed out loud when she saw the irritated look on her sister's face. Lyla was definitely not in the mood for Lex's antics. Lex curled one of the weights up to his shoulder and then held it out toward Lyla. While it was true that all Weres except the omegas were stronger than humans, alphas were much stronger than the other ranks.

Without looking at him, Lyla shook her head. "No, I'm good, thanks." She picked up a pair of twenty-pound weights.

"You sure? You could probably handle the forties."

"Maybe. But I don't have anyone to impress," she replied, nonchalantly curling the weights up to her shoulders. Val saw a red blush bloom in Lex's face, and she shook her head with a smile, reaching up to the bars that Lex had just vacated. She pulled herself up effortlessly, letting out a long breath at the feeling of strength that surged through her. But with it came a fresh wave of nausea and she quickly dropped back down, face pale.

"Val? You okay?"

Lyla was watching her closely, and Val saw Christopher look up from his book. She nodded and rubbed her hands together. "Yeah, I'm good. I might grab a breath of fresh air. I'll be right back."

She headed down the hallway and out the front doors of Gibbous Hall. She breathed in, enjoying the rush of cool air through her system. Around the corner of the building, she heard voices. She paid them no attention until she recognized that one of them was Jules. Three other voices reached her sensitive ears, and she searched her mind for their names. They were all friends of Jules. Maggie and Lauren were two of them, but she didn't recognize the third.

"This isn't a game, Jules. You're in danger."

"My brother says that Trueblood alphas can control your mind. And she's already tried to hurt you once."

Val immediately started paying a lot more attention. She leaned against the brick next to the doors. Jules spoke up again.

"They're not like that, Elise. They're my friends, just like you guys are."

"Friends? They're feral, and they're not safe. You have to stay away from them."

Maggie was next. "You have to choose, Jules. I don't want anything to do with them, so if you want to hang out with us, you need to stop."

"I know you guys are scared, but what about them?" Jules asked. Her voice was quiet, placating. "They hardly have any friends. You don't know anything about them."

"Neither do you! They haven't been here that long! Aren't you scared of what they could do to you?"

There was a pause. "Sometimes. But I trust them. I don't know why, but I do. Maybe if you guys tried talking to them—"

Lauren laughed, but it was angry. "I can't believe I'm hearing this. Come on, I have homework to do."

Val pressed herself flat against the side of the building, hidden by the dark shadows of the corner. She saw the three girls stalk past her, walking briskly and talking amongst themselves. Val waited until they were far enough away not to notice her and then stepped around the corner of the building.

Under a dim light over one of the exit doors, Jules was sitting on the ground, knees pulled up to her chest. For a moment, Val wondered if she should turn around and go back inside, but she made up her mind. Jules had said they were friends. This was what friends did.

Jules heard her as she approached, and the omega glanced up in surprise, quickly wiping her hands over her cheeks. She smiled, but it didn't reach her eyes.

"Hi." She looked away. "Did you hear any of that?"

Val eased herself down next to Jules. "I didn't mean to, but I heard something about Truebloods and how I'm going to control everyone's mind."

A giggle escaped Jules' lips. "It all sounds so ridiculous, doesn't it?"

Even though Jules couldn't know it, Val knew that there was a kernel of truth in all of the misconceptions that her fellow students had about them. She didn't know much about her abilities to control other Weres. It was something that the DAO had strongly opposed. But as a Trueblood alpha, theoretically she did have the potential to be able to command the others. Val sighed, leaning her head back against the wall.

"They might be right."

Jules looked at her in surprise. "What do you mean? Val, you're not like that."

Val felt a sudden desire to be honest. "I did come close to hurting you, Jules. I'm really sorry for that, and I don't ever want to repeat it. But when they say that I might not be able to control myself, they're not wrong."

"It did scare me," said Jules, looking out into the darkness. "Your eyes were, well, I've never seen anyone like that. I don't really know what I'm doing."

"That makes two of us," replied Val softly. "I'm sorry."

"It's not right, what they're doing." When Val frowned, Jules continued. "I don't know what you and Lyla have been through, and you don't have to tell me anything. I just think it's not fair that everyone is treating you like this." She turned to look at the Trueblood next to her. "I don't know why, but I trust you."

Val blinked and swallowed, looking away. "Thanks, Jules." She wasn't sure what else to say. The feeling of being trusted was familiar, but it was an old echo from days long past. It frightened her. "I don't want you to lose your friends over us. I want you to do what *you* want to do, not because anyone is pressuring you. You know I won't think any less of you."

Jules sniffed. "I don't think they should tell me who I can be friends with." She lifted her chin. "And I want to be your friend. As long as you still want to be mine?"

"I don't know."

Jules looked shocked. "What?"

A tiny smile played around the corners of Val's mouth. "You're kind of scary."

Jules crossed her arms. "Me?"

The grin broke through as Val looked at her, eyes twinkling mischievously. "Everybody thinks the alphas are the ones to be worried about. Omegas are the real danger to society."

Laughing, Jules shook her head. Val stood up and reached her hand down, helping the omega to her feet. "Should we go back in?"

Wiping the last of the tear trails from her face, Jules nodded. "Let's go be dangerous."

When Lyla woke the next morning, she saw Val passed out across from her, spread out on her bed still wearing the same clothes she'd had on last night. Lyla shook her head and got up to take her shower. As usual, Val was still sleeping when Lyla left the bathroom, toweling off her hair.

By the time they were leaving the dorms, they only had five minutes to make it from their room to class. Val followed Lyla grumpily, dark circles under her eyes. She hadn't said a word since Lyla had dragged her out of bed. Her face was paler than normal.

As they ran into Gibbous Hall, Lyla stopped when she heard her name being called. Turning around, she caught sight of Principal Bleiz standing in the open door of his office. When Lyla turned to walk back toward him, he held out two pieces of green paper.

"What's this?" Lyla asked.

Principal Bleiz pushed the papers into her hand. "Cormoran put in the request and signed the permission slips for your field trip." He glowered at them. "This goes against my better judgment, and if it were my choice, you would not be going. I expect you to be on better than your best behavior."

As he disappeared back into the office, Lyla looked down at the permission slips in shock. Val hovered over her shoulder and stared at the fancy signature at the bottom of the paper.

"Wow. I can't believe Cormoran actually signed these."

"I'm not going to ask questions," replied Lyla, uncomfortable at the reminder of their handler. So far, she'd managed to keep her knowledge of what Val had suffered in the center to herself, but she didn't know how much longer she could manage it. She frowned. Was Cormoran testing them to see what would happen if they were given a little more freedom? Did she actually want them to succeed?

Lyla rubbed her neck, trying to relieve the tension in her muscles. As they walked to class, she chewed on the end of a pencil. Whatever Cormoran's reasoning was, she was sure of one thing. She and Val could use the change in scenery.

CHAPTER TEN

Val pressed her cheek against the glass as she watched the trees rush past the bus. She had cracked the window slightly, and the sight and smell of forest and fresh air were glorious. It was almost too much, but she couldn't pull away. Even though she'd experienced the same smells on the school campus, the rushing breeze and sweet sense of freedom, however small, made it more irresistible. She knew Lyla was watching her, feeling that same pull toward the forest that had begun the moment they had drawn breath, the wild singing through their blood.

Ever since the meeting with Cormoran and Principal Bleiz, Lyla had been quieter, more distanced. Whenever she looked at Val, there was something different in her eyes. Whatever it was, Val didn't like it. She'd asked Lyla about it several times, but Lyla always evaded the answer.

Val hated that Lyla was shutting her out. But at the same time, she knew she couldn't blame her sister. Val had her own secrets. Lyla would never look at her the same again if she knew the truth.

And Val couldn't bear the thought of her sister knowing everything. Not yet.

A smiling face popped up over the back of the seat in front of them. Jules had her hair arranged in the two messy black buns on top of her head, her huge round glasses adding to the look of childlike excitement on her face.

"Hi!"

Val smiled back. "Hey Jules."

"I hope our next field trip is a shopping mall," Jules said with a sigh. "I'd really love to shop for you guys. I can't keep my inner fashion designer hostage forever!"

"Sure, Jules," replied Val, amused. "But no pink."

The omega looked confused. "Obviously. It's not your color, honey." She beamed and flipped back around to sit down in her seat. Val leaned over to Lyla.

"I have a color?"

Lyla smirked. "Jewel tones. Some earth tones. Blues and greens, but not bright." She laughed at Val's shocked expression.

"How do you know that?"

"I pay attention. I'm assimilating."

Eavesdropping from the other side of the aisle where he was sitting next to Christopher, Lex leaned over. "I bet I know what Jules' colors are." When the two sisters looked at him, he grinned from ear to ear. "Jewel tones."

Christopher chuckled next to him, and Jules huffed from her seat. "Really, Lex? That's horrible."

Val watched the two boys for a minute. As far as she could tell, they hadn't really become friends until they'd all started spending time together. They were an odd pair, but they seemed to get along well. She turned back to the window.

The outskirts of the city began rolling past the bus windows. Val recognized some of it from the last time they'd driven by, going the opposite direction away from the D.A.O. center and into a new life. More freedom than they'd had in years. Finally, larger buildings came into view, and she saw a brown sign directing them to the zoo at the next exit.

By the time the bus rolled up to the entrance and stopped, Jules was already bouncing out of her seat, fidgeting impatiently as she waited for the students in front of her to leave. The others followed her out of the bus, somewhat less enthusiastically. Jules swung her drawstring bag up onto her back and skipped toward the ticket window.

"Let's go see the penguins first, they're so cute!" exclaimed Jules. The large group of students began to split off in different directions. The rogue alpha group, as she had begun calling Jackson and his friends, pushed past them, and headed down the left path toward the big cat enclosures. Jackson tossed a wink at Val as he followed the others.

"Welcome home, feral," he called over his shoulder. Val felt heat rise in her chest as she glared after him. Even though it was a Domestic insult, she still burned with the insinuation, no matter how many times Lyla told her to let it go.

She let Jules drag her away toward the penguins.

Lyla followed the others, listening to their playful banter and Christopher's random commentary of facts about each of the animals they encountered. They wandered from exhibit to exhibit, until they reached the doors leading into the building that faced the wolf enclosure. A bronze wolf statue stood guard at the entrance. They all walked inside to see the large posters all over the walls describing the different types of wolves and their life in the wild.

Lex pointed at one of the infographics. "Look, the average pack size is five to eight wolves." He looked around at the others. "We're average, guys!"

Shocked, Lyla turned to say something, but stopped short when she saw Christopher and Jules laughing. Val had a big smile on her face. Lyla's fingernails dug into her palms. *We are not a pack.* They'd been told to make friends, and they had. This was a mockery. Val looked over at her, feeling the anger through the bond.

Lyla walked stiffly over to the observation window and leaned against the railing, seething. *They meet a couple of Truebloods and suddenly they think they know everything.* She swallowed, angry at the tears that suddenly stung her eyes.

"They're beautiful, aren't they?" Val leaned against the railing beside her. "You okay?"

Lyla looked into the grassy exhibit and saw a white wolf standing solemnly under the trees, watching them. A dark gray wolf came up beside it, and the two rubbed against each other in a friendly greeting.

"Yeah."

Val's gaze moved from the wolves to her sister. Lyla focused intently on the glass and gripped the railing with white knuckles. She was tired of using so much of her mental energy to keep Val out of most of her thoughts. She couldn't risk letting a memory of what she'd seen slip through. She knew she was keeping Val in the dark, but the alternative was worse.

"You going to let me in?" asked Val, softly enough so that the others couldn't hear.

"I don't want to talk about it right now."

Val sighed, but didn't push her. Lyla knew that sooner or later her sister wouldn't take no for an answer.

"Come on, Blackwoods!" Lex called from the doorway. "Jules wants to see the snow leopards."

Val put a hand on Lyla's arm. "Let's go see some cats."

"Go ahead. I want to watch them for a little bit," Lyla said, gesturing toward the wolves. "I'll catch up to you." Val looked undecided for a moment, but finally left to follow the others.

On the other side of the glass, the wolves were now gamboling in the grass, snapping playfully at each other. The beta gray wolf nipped at the heels of the white, only to turn tail and run for the trees when the alpha turned on him, fangs flashing. There was something relaxing about how easily the wolves acted on their instincts, simply being what they were. Deeply buried, the wolf in Lyla longed for the days when she and Val had run free, lost in the exhilaration that only runs through the blood of things that are wild. The two wolves appeared again, flopping down in the grass, the feud forgotten.

The doors of the viewing area opened, and Lyla caught sight of the rogue alphas as they came into the building. Lyla moved down the railing until she was in the corner, still watching the wolves but staying out of the way. Jackson soon caught sight of her and came over to stand a couple feet away, looking out at the now sleeping wolves.

"You know, it's too bad that you had to come to Westbrook with your sister," he said. "You're not half bad, Blackwood."

Lyla didn't respond. She had no intention of allowing Jackson's comments to get to her. He would have to leave eventually. Instead, she looked out and watched as the white alpha in the enclosure rolled over, stretching his neck out under the nose of the beta as they slept in the sun. Jackson moved away from the railing.

"That's where your sister belongs," he said. "Behind a glass wall. You know it's only a matter of time before she really hurts somebody. Are you sure you can live with that?" He took a step away, grinning to himself. But he was stopped by a firm hand on his arm. Turning around, he faced Lyla.

"You know nothing about my sister, and you know nothing about me. Leave us alone, and don't push me," she said. Jackson frowned, and she could see something in him responding to her commanding tone. He leaned toward her, his eyes dark.

"When are you going to stop this charade? No one wants you here. We all know that you're dangerous. You can't keep pretending forever."

Lyla was vaguely aware that Jackson's friends had made a loose half-circle around her, watching them. She kept her gaze on Jackson, knowing that if she could keep him subdued, the others wouldn't attack her. Val might be too far away to help her in time even if she called through the bond. Suddenly, Jackson glanced at something over Lyla's shoulder and his eyes narrowed, expression curling into something resembling disgust.

"Freak. Come on," he jerked his head to the side, signaling his friends to move back. "Watch yourself, Blackwood. Your time is coming."

They left Lyla standing alone in the observation room. She took a deep breath and closed her eyes. Suddenly, the hair on the back of her neck prickled and she remembered Jackson's look over her shoulder. She turned around.

The white and dark gray wolves had been joined by two more, and all four of them were standing rigid behind the glass, facing her in a line. The white alpha's lips were lifted in a low snarl. Then Lyla realized that they weren't looking at her. They were facing the doors beyond her where Jackson had just disappeared. A shiver ran down Lyla's spine. She turned to face them, and the white alpha met her gaze. His tongue lolled out of his mouth, and he dropped back down to the ground.

Lyla caught up to the others in the gift shop. She could feel the beginning of a headache behind her eyes, and she rubbed her temples to alleviate the pressure. Wandering into the rows of stuffed animals, she tried to look interested. It wasn't long before Jules found her. She grabbed a stuffed sloth off the shelf and wrapped it around her neck.

"So cute! What's your favorite animal, Lyla?"

Lyla glanced over the shelves, forcing herself to stay in the present. She couldn't think about Jackson right now. Or Val's file. Or all the other things that were constantly on her mind. "I've always thought horses were pretty cool."

"I love the penguins. But I'm getting the sloth because he gives great hugs," Jules said. She grabbed Lyla's hand. "Come on, Val wanted to show you something." Lyla gently pulled her hand free but followed the omega toward the familiar red-haired girl standing in front of the shelf of snow globes. Jules skipped away to look at masks with Lex. Val reached up to the shelf and pulled one of the globes down, holding it gently in her hand.

"This one reminds me of home."

Lyla caught her breath as she looked into the little glass globe. Inside, a tiny forest glistened with glitter snow. A hill rose from it and two wolves howled; their feet buried in white. Barely visible in the trees was a small cabin with a thin trail of smoke rising from the chimney. Lyla took the globe out of Val's hand and gave it a small shake. Tiny snowflakes sparkled around the wolves.

"I'm going to get it," Val said softly.

Lyla swallowed and put it back up on the shelf. "No, we shouldn't. Cormoran only sent us enough money for lunch."

"I'll get it if you want." Lyla looked up and saw that Christopher had come over to them and was standing next to Val. He started pulling out his wallet, but Lyla shook her head.

"Thanks for the offer, but I don't think Cormoran would approve. There are rules we have to follow about things from the past," she said. Christopher hesitated, but put his wallet back into his pocket. An awkward silence fell over them for a moment before it was broken by Jules. Before Lyla could react, Jules was holding something up to her face.

"Oh my gosh, Lyla put this on, and here's one for Val," the omega said. "We can all take a picture with these on!"

Lyla frowned. In her hands was a flimsy mask, two eye holes cut into the white underside. She flipped it over and her blood ran hot. It was a wolf mask. She looked up and saw that the others were good-naturedly complying with Jules' request. Even Val gave her a shrug.

Lyla's hands trembled, and she set the mask down on the shelf next to her. Jules noticed right away and picked it up. "Come on, Lyla, it's just for fun!"

"Not today, Jules."

"Lyla, loosen up. Let's do it," Val said.

The other four huddled together and Jules handed her phone to Lex. "Here, you take the picture, your arms are longer." Her eyes crinkled behind the mask she wore. "Our first pack photo!"

All the emotions Lyla had been holding in for days finally boiled over. "We are *not* a pack!" she snapped. "This is a sick joke!"

Jules slowly crumpled in front of her, and Val stepped forward immediately. She pulled the omega behind her and faced her sister, putting a hand on Lyla's shoulder. "Lyla," she said calmly, fighting the rush of anger Lyla was sending her way. "Back down."

The two girls locked gazes, the tension rising. Christopher opened his mouth to say something, but Lyla interrupted.

"I can't believe this."

She turned on her heel and left the gift shop, forcing her feet to move until she had walked all the way out of the zoo's entrance and back toward the bus. The driver opened the door for her as she pulled herself up the steps.

"You all right, there?" the older man asked.

Lyla wiped her sleeve across her eyes. "Yeah. I'm fine." She found a spot in the back of the bus and slumped into the seat, huddled against the wall.

The bus ride home was quiet. Lyla ignored her sister, who had come back to sit next to her. Jules had avoided her gaze when she got on the bus and was sitting a few rows ahead. *I still can't believe I almost lost it in the gift shop.* Lyla had seen the fear in Jules's face.

Thankfully, she had been able to pull herself back before it escalated. Val wouldn't have hesitated to protect the omega, and something about that made Lyla feel uncomfortable. Her sister's instincts to protect were natural, but this was the first time they'd been put at odds with each other over someone else. The closer their new "friends" came, the harder it would be to protect Val.

She pinched the inside of her arm to pull her attention back to the window. She didn't want to think about that. She was dreading the imminent conversation with Val more than she wanted to admit. She could tell that Val was holding it back, just waiting until they were back at the school and she could talk to Lyla alone.

When the bus finally slowed to a stop and the doors opened, Lyla pushed past Val and headed straight for the dorms. She made it up the stairs, dropped her bag next to her bed, and locked herself in the bathroom. She heard the dorm door open and close outside. After a while, she finally admitted that she couldn't hide forever.

Opening the bathroom door, she was surprised to see Val sitting silently on a chair, reading through one of their textbooks. Lyla sat down across from her, not sure what to say.

"You're actually wearing your glasses."

Val nodded. "You actually came out of the bathroom. I thought you died in there." She set the textbook down next to her. "Are you going to tell me why you snapped at Jules?"

"I'm sorry, I just have a lot on my mind," said Lyla. "There's no way I was going to put a wolf mask on my face." Now that she said it out loud, it did sound a little ridiculous. "I really don't want to talk about it. I just need to sleep it off."

Val removed her glasses and set them aside, a muscle in her jaw tightening. "You were pretty hard on her. She wasn't trying to irritate you."

Anger sparked somewhere in Lyla's tired mind. "I'm sorry I upset your omega."

Val glowered. "What? She's not *my* omega. I don't own her. She's my friend. And she's trying to be yours too."

"Oh, that's right. I forgot we're a *pack*."

Val calmed herself with a deep breath. "Is that what you're so worried about? Honestly, Lyla, I'm not that stupid. The only person in my pack is you."

It was too much. Lyla felt her control slipping further from her grasp. "We don't have a pack anymore, Val! They're all dead, remember? They're dead and we're still here and nothing is going to fix that." Lyla couldn't stop the words. Her head was giving way to her heart.

Shock registered on Val's face. "Lyla, where is all this coming from? What happened?"

Lyla paced around the room, grabbing at the roots of her hair. "What happened? Oh, I don't know, maybe seven years of our lives being a complete nightmare. Maybe years of torture and being locked up in a cell underground wasn't enough, maybe seeing our parents killed outside our cabin didn't wreck you, but it wrecked me."

Val rose from her chair. "You don't think it wrecked me? I kept you alive in the woods for two years after they died." Val's calm demeanor was gone.

"Oh, I'm sorry. I'm not the *alpha*, right? I'm just the good sister, the one who does everything the way I'm supposed to while you do everything you can to keep us here forever!"

Val growled, and then she grabbed Lyla's shoulders, searching her sister's face. "Stop pushing me away. Why are you shutting me out?"

Trying to jerk away from her sister's hands, Lyla retorted, "Are you even listening to what I'm saying? You're not the only one who has been damaged by this, Val. And now I have to deal with the fact that they tried to kill you! They filled you with silver and tried to kill you too!"

As soon as the words left Lyla's lips, she wished she could take them back. When they sank in, Val's face paled, and she dropped her hands from Lyla's shoulders as if they were dead weight. Her breathing grew shallower.

"How much do you know?"

Lyla looked away. "I saw your folder when Cormoran took you out of the room the other day. I saw everything. All the things they did to you. It's all true, isn't it?"

Val gritted her teeth, and her eyes fixed on a point beyond Lyla, unfocused. "You can have the room to yourself tonight," she said.

Lyla didn't even have words to answer as the door opened and then closed. She just let her body fall until she was lying against the wall, knees pulled to her chest as she hugged herself desperately.

"No! Please! I can't do it again!"

Val blinked and dug her fingernails into her arms, trying to ground herself. *The screaming. Was that her voice? Everything was white, and the faces watched her.* Val dragged in a breath. She had to control her breathing.

The straps around her wrists were so tight. Silver needles coming closer... closer... she couldn't breathe through the pain.

Jules opened her dorm door when she heard the soft knock. "Hey Val! I wasn't expecting…" she trailed off. "Val?"

Val didn't look up. "Can I sleep on your futon tonight?" she whispered.

"Oh honey, of course you can," said Jules softly, reaching out and pulling Val into her room. "What happened?"

Val tried to swallow. "Everything is falling apart, Jules."

Without another word, Jules reached out her arms. Val walked into them, leaning her head down on her friend's shoulder. When Jules started rubbing her back reassuringly, Val finally choked out a broken sob.

CHAPTER ELEVEN

Lyla skipped class the next morning. She woke up with a raging headache that was only partially affected by the ibuprofen she took. She silently cursed her wolf blood for reducing the potency of modern medicine. Finding any herbal remedies in the school was unlikely. By the time it was almost lunch period, she felt like she didn't have enough of an excuse to stay in bed, she was getting restless anyway. She pulled on her school uniform and trudged over to Gibbous Hall. The cafeteria was full of loud students, and the smell of a chicken dish was wafting through the air.

Walking through the lunch line like a zombie, Lyla carried her tray back to the table with her friends. She had debated eating by herself, but she wasn't that desperate. She set her tray down beside Lex, fully aware that Val was ignoring her across the table. She dug into her chicken and rice, suddenly aware of how hungry she was. She hadn't eaten anything since lunch the day before.

The normal chatter was a bit subdued. Everyone tried to ignore the strange tension between Val and Lyla, but only Jules seemed to be undeterred. "Right. What are you guys doing after class? Let's hang out. Maybe we can all do a game night tonight."

No one said anything. Val stood up and took her tray away, and then stalked out of the cafeteria. Christopher rose slowly and followed her.

Jules gave Lyla an apologetic smile. "You guys really need to talk this out."

"Did she say anything?" asked Lyla dully.

Jules shook her head. "She hasn't told me what happened between you two if that's what you're asking. But I've been around you guys long enough to know she wouldn't just quit talking to you over peanuts."

Lyla awkwardly pushed her fork around in the last bit of her food. "I've got to get to class." She ignored Jules's look and grabbed her backpack. She didn't like the awkward concern that the others were projecting, it made her feel uncomfortable. If Val wanted to talk to Lyla, she would've done it.

Barely able to focus on any of the classes, Lyla mostly watched the clock as the hours ticked by. After her last period, she saw Val walk out of Gibbous Hall with Christopher. They were heading toward the walking trail.

"Lyla!"

Recognizing Lex's voice, Lyla knew she should respond, but she wasn't sure if she wanted to. She reluctantly turned around to see the beta jogging up to her.

"Hey. Um, I was just wondering if you wanted to hang out for a little while."

"Not really, I should go do some homework..." Lyla realized it was a lame excuse, but she wasn't sure that she wanted to be around anyone for the rest of the day. Lex reached out and squeezed her hand. Lyla froze, surprised by the gesture.

"Okay. But tomorrow I'm not taking no for an answer," he said with a smile. "Being alone isn't going to make things better." He let go of her hand and walked out of the building. Lyla frowned. Readjusting her jacket, she took a deep breath and started walking back to her dorm room.

Val watched Christopher out of the corner of her eye. He walked slowly, clearly enjoying the smells of autumn and the warm breeze. He was never urgent about anything. He walked as if he were going to live for a thousand years. The trail around the campus was quiet, and none of the other students were anywhere within earshot. She pulled at the sleeve of her jacket, wondering why she had agreed to go when Christopher had asked her to take a walk. The anxiety she'd been feeling for the past few days was coiling in her stomach.

Since she'd confronted him in the library, he had respected her wishes not to talk about her past. He'd never asked any questions about it. He'd simply been content to spend time with the group, reading, writing in his notebook, and occasionally making comments on the conversation. Val studied him. He always acted as if nothing in the world ever bothered him. What would it take to ruffle his feathers? She saw him glance her way out of the corner of her eye and felt her stomach clench tighter. Why was she so torn between not wanting him to ask his questions and at the same time wishing he would? She was almost ready to turn around and make her way back to the dorms when he finally spoke.

"I haven't been completely honest with you."

Val stopped in her tracks. Had he been lying about spying on her? "That's not encouraging."

He nodded. "I realize that. But it didn't feel right to tell you before. Will you let me explain why?"

"Okay." She supposed she owed him at least that much.

"Four years ago, my dad and I went on a fishing trip. On the way, we stopped at the DAO Central Headquarters, and we took a tour for my dad's work." He pushed up his glasses. "It was clean. White and gray everywhere, even the furniture. The man who gave us a tour said he was a handler, and it was his job to be a mentor to new Weres who had completed the Domestication process and were ready to start the assimilation program."

Christopher stopped in the middle of the trail. "He took us through the little museum at the visitor's center, showed us the classrooms and the occupational therapy rooms where they taught their residents how to live like humans. It was all very professional."

Val had to bite her lip at that. *Professional,* she repeated to herself. That was the image they wanted. She waited for Christopher to continue. The idea of him being in the DAO center made her uneasy.

"My father asked a lot of questions, especially about the wild Weres that he'd heard were in the program. We got special clearance, and our guide took us to a lower level of the laboratory building. We didn't go far, just into the main control room right next to the elevator. We couldn't see very much because he had the operator turn several screens off. He said it was for the privacy of the residents." Christopher finally looked at Val, and his gaze made her uncomfortable. "One of the cells was empty except for a white bed, and a girl was lying on it."

Bile rose in Val's throat. She wanted to stop Christopher from saying anything more. She'd already been forced to relive too many memories this week, and whatever was coming next, she didn't want to hear it. But she couldn't bring herself to stop him.

"I thought she was asleep, but my dad noticed the restraints on her arms and legs. The guide said that she was a high-risk resident, a Trueblood alpha, and that the restraints were only in place to keep her from harming herself. He said they had great hopes that she would pass the program with flying colors."

Val sank down, crouching close to the ground. She put her hand down on the asphalt, and focused on the cool, gritty feeling against her skin. She squeezed her other fist against her knee.

Christopher continued. "I recognized you as soon as you came to school, Val. Ever since I saw you on that screen, I've had a lot of questions. About the DAO, about Weres, and about Truebloods. I wanted to help people like you. I thought the DAO was the place to do that. Now I'm not so sure."

The leather was too tight against her wrists. That was the first thing she felt as she slowly woke from her drug-hazed sleep. Her head pounded, and the bruises on her ribcage throbbed with each breath she dragged into her lungs. Why was it so hard to breathe? Where was Lyla? Her eyes were unfocused, but all she could see was blurred white. Four walls. The ceiling. All of it, white. White. White. The same color as the blinding pain crowding the edges of her memory. A tiny red blinking light in the camera in the corner of the ceiling was the only contrast.

"Val?"

Somewhere, far away, someone was screaming. The electricity coursed through her like fire. White figures in white masks in a white room. The phasing hurt so much. She couldn't do it anymore. She crumpled to the floor, aching and exhausted. But they wouldn't let her sleep. Phasing over and over. Flashes of violet in the mirrors. Broken shards cutting across her hands as she smashed against the glass. Her own claws raking over her skin, trying to break free from the bracelets and their maddening electric currents.

"*Again.*"

The flashbacks were slamming against her mind like sharp fragments. She couldn't do this right now. Her fingers shook with the effort it took to keep herself grounded. She knew she had dropped the barrier holding Lyla back from their bond link, but she didn't have the mental strength to keep it up. She shook her head and placed both hands flat on the asphalt, digging her fingers into the gritty rocks. Squeezing her eyes closed, she desperately clung to the last threads holding her to reality.

"Val."

She felt a hand gently close around her own and was surprised by the warmth in it. His voice was close and gentle. "Can you open your eyes and tell me what you see?"

Tell me what you see right now. Val had said the same thing to Lyla in the bunker. She forced her eyes open. They'd never been this close before, and the first thing she saw was the blue of his eyes. He had kind eyes. Her gaze flickered to the faint stubbled lines of a beard along his jaw. He squeezed her hand.

"We're safe here. It's going to be all right. Can you walk over to the bench?"

She nodded shakily, letting him lead her a few feet away to the bench at the corner of the trail. There were no other students in sight, and they were hidden from the main campus lawn. Val sat down, running her fingers absent-mindedly over the scars above her wrists, caught somewhere between the world in her mind and the one outside of it.

Christopher spoke again. He sounded sad. "What did they do to you?"

Squeezing her fists and holding for five seconds, Val let out a breath as she relaxed her hands, and then did it again. She could feel the familiar numbness wrapping around her mind, pulling her into a blissful detachment. She leaned forward with her elbows on her knees.

"I'm not supposed to talk about it," she said, avoiding his gaze.

"But you want to." It wasn't a question, and he wasn't wrong. Val's jaw tightened, undecided. Would it really make a difference, in the end?

"You didn't come to the program of your own free will. I've guessed that much," said Christopher softly. "And if you don't want to tell me any more than that, I won't ask you to."

"I was twelve. Lyla was eleven. We'd survived on our own for two years after… after our parents were killed." She looked at him. "If you're such a historian, you already know about the Culling."

He nodded. "People got scared after a string of Were-related murders. It turned into a witch hunt. The DAO was created as an alternative, a way to incorporate Weres into our culture instead of exterminating them."

"Our entire pack was wiped out. My father was able to hide us under the floorboards. When Lyla and I finally came out…" she shook her head. "We evaded the DAO in the woods for a couple years, but they caught up with us. Lyla and I were separated shortly after we were tested to confirm our ranks."

"That's when you started the Domestication program?"

"Yeah. That's the nice name they have for it." Rubbing her temples, Val decided she'd come far enough already. "Forced phasing was one of the first things they did. They wanted to see what triggered it, how strong I was, how much control I had over it. Lyla went through that too. Weeks of it. So much that I thought my body would fall apart. They didn't even acknowledge me— talked about me like I was an animal. After the first couple of years they said I was high risk and moved into what they called intensive therapy. I spent months locked away alone in a white cell."

Her breath grew shallow again, but she surged ahead. "I have a documented lethal silver injection limit. Do you know what that means?" When Christopher shook his head, she continued, crossing her arms protectively. "They injected a dose of silver into my bloodstream to see how much I could take before I died. Sometimes I wish they hadn't brought me back. Afterwards they purged the toxins out of my body so I wouldn't have seizures."

Val felt a tear slide down her cheek. "I'm not sure what you were expecting to hear, but if you want me to cheer for you when you say you want to help us, I can't. I don't want any more help from anyone."

Christopher shook his head. "I don't even know what to say, Val. There are no words for this." He looked at her, brow furrowed with emotion. "I'm sorry. Can you tell someone? If you don't expose what they're doing, they'll never stop."

Those words snapped Val back to the present. She stood up from the bench. "You can't tell anyone what I just told you. If you do, we'll be taken back to the center, and they might not let us out again."

Christopher calmly looked up at her. "I promise. But will you promise me something in return?"

"What?"

He rose from his seat, looking down at her intently. "If you ever need someone on your side, you'll tell me."

Val didn't know what to say. She nodded, avoiding his gaze. "Thank you."

"You said earlier that you weren't supposed to talk about any of this. So why did you?" he asked quietly.

Val studied him for a few seconds. "I don't know. Maybe because I'm tired of always shutting people out."

Christopher reached down and unzipped his backpack. He pulled out a little brown box and awkwardly held it out to her. "Here, I want you to have this. I need to get back. Are you going to be okay?" When she nodded, he pulled his backpack onto his shoulders. "Maybe you can't tell anyone today, but someday you will. And I hope I'm there to see it."

He walked away down the path, leaving Val standing alone with the box in her hands. She pulled it open carefully, and then felt her eyes burn as she saw what was inside. Cradled in the white tissue paper was the little snow globe from the zoo, the wolves proudly howling on top of their tiny hill.

CHAPTER TWELVE

Lyla had hoped that Lex would forget his promise to hang out with her. But as she walked out of her last class the next day, the undeterred beta hurried to catch up with her, his signature goofy grin plastered across his face. She groaned silently but was surprised when she noticed a basket in his hands. She wasn't sure she wanted to ask, so she didn't. Lyla followed him out onto the campus lawn. They found a secluded spot in the sunshine, and Lex plopped the basket down. Opening it, he took out a blanket and spread it out on the grass. Lyla watched, speechless, as he took out a box of crackers and some cheese.

"Sorry it's not fancier, but I brought food!" he exclaimed proudly. He sat down and patted the open spot next to him. Lyla stared. It took a minute, and then Lex slapped his forehead.

"You don't like crackers. Oh wow, I should have asked you."

Lyla didn't move. Lex glanced down at the food, confused. "Cheese? It's the cheese. Are you lactose intolerant? If you are, it's fine, we can just sit on the blanket and talk, we don't have to eat.

I'm sorry for not checking with you first. I didn't even think about that."

"This is not a date," said Lyla.

Lex blinked a few times, and then his cheeks turned a deep red. "Date? Oh gosh, this is definitely *not* a date. Yeah. No."

Dropping her backpack, Lyla sat cross-legged on the blanket, ignoring the intensely awkward atmosphere. She could tell that Lex was embarrassed, but if it wasn't a date, she wasn't sure why. She reached for the box of crackers and pulled it open. Lex slowly moved to slice the block of cheese. He handed a piece to Lyla. She glanced down at it, wishing that it included meat as well. The herbs smelled like something her mother would have grown. Lifting it to her lips, she remembered to eat small bites. Humans ate food in the most infuriating ways.

"That's good," she said.

He smiled. "I'm glad you like it."

"So why did you want to do this?" asked Lyla curiously, grabbing another cracker. Lex shrugged and sliced more cheese. Lyla noticed that he was being very meticulous about cutting perfect squares. The perfectionism of food preparation was something else she'd never understand. As far as she was concerned, it was far simpler to pick it up and eat it however you pleased.

"Just thought maybe you could use a change of pace. You know, with you and Val being kind of… not talking."

Lyla nodded. "Yeah."

"You guys seem pretty down in the dumps. Jules didn't tell me anything, but I know that Val's been sleeping in her dorm room. Christopher said he talked to her yesterday."

The cracker shattered between Lyla's teeth, and she looked away. That wasn't a particularly pleasant memory. She had felt Val's grip on the barrier loosen, and for a moment, the bond link had been flooded with flashbacks. From what she'd seen and felt, Lyla guessed that Val had shared enough of her past with Christopher to make him dangerous. But more than that, Lyla was angry. And she sure wasn't ready to have that conversation yet.

"Are you okay?"

She swallowed and reached for more cheese. "Peachy."

Lex waited for a minute before saying what was on his mind. "Lyla, whatever this is about, you really should talk to her." He leaned back on his elbows. "Even I can see how much it's wearing on you."

Lyla wasn't sure how to respond. Was he expecting her to open up to him more than this? She couldn't let herself relax here. Lex was being kind, but she couldn't jeopardize their situation any more than Val might already have done. As she brooded over it, Lyla caught sight of Val and Jules at the other end of the lawn. Jules was reading something from one of their textbooks in a dramatic tone. Val was watching with a smile, but Lyla could tell that it didn't reach her eyes.

"Sometimes I wonder if I'm doing enough," she admitted softly. "No matter what I do, it seems like we're always falling a little bit short."

Lex sat up, following her gaze to see Val and Jules. "For what it's worth, I think you're doing amazing. Everybody has arguments. Plus, your friends are here to help."

He tentatively reached out and brushed his fingers against Lyla's hand where it rested against the blanket. A breath passed before she pulled her hand away. No matter what, she couldn't let him in.

Lex turned toward the food and began putting everything back into the basket. Lyla was still focused on the two girls across the lawn. When she looked away, she saw Lex watching her.

"Are you phasing soon?" he asked, gesturing to her forehead.

She reached up and touched her damp skin. "Yeah, I guess so." Curse the full moon. No matter how controlled they were the rest of the month, it always chased them, driving them back into their own personal wilderness. She looked out at Val, who was still talking with Jules. None of her usual phasing signs were there. *Just how well did that new suppressant work?* Lyla wondered. Whatever the answer was, the amount of time before they would be locked in the bunker together was dwindling quickly. And when that day came, Lyla had no idea what would happen.

…

Lyla could feel her temperature rising until even the air-conditioned dorm room was too warm. She had to admit that the cool underground air of the bunker sounded heavenly just then, regardless of what might be waiting in it. She called in to the school office and let them know that she would be out of classes for a day or two. She hoped that Val had done the same. As she prepared to leave the dorm room, her phone buzzed on the desk.

NEW TEXT MESSAGE
From: Jules
She just went downstairs. If you guys need anything, just let me know.

Lyla shoved her phone in her bag and headed down the stairs to the basement, passing through the first door. Heat rippled through her body as she walked through the maze of boxes to the back of the huge room. The bunker door was open. Knowing that Val was already inside, Lyla stepped through and pulled the lock, shutting them both in. Part of her wanted to stay on the top step and ignore the basement's other occupant, but she knew better. This was only going to work if they faced each other. She was done trying to keep her distance.

Val was sitting on the floor. She was sweating, but Lyla was surprised that her phasing hadn't progressed further yet. When Val looked up at her, there were only a few flecks of the Trueblood violet in her eyes. Val hadn't bothered to put the barrier back up, but their link was stretched and fragile. Lyla could feel it trembling between them, strained.

When Lyla entered the bunker, Val already felt on edge, as she always did before a phasing. Stewing over it all day hadn't helped, and she still didn't know what to say to her sister. Lyla dropped her bag against the wall and folded her arms. Neither of them spoke. Lyla was already well into the beginning of her phase, and Val felt a sudden worry that she wasn't feeling more of the telltale physical signs. Just the unending nausea. She wasn't ready to face the fact that she might not phase at all this time.

"What did you tell Christopher?"

Val glared at her sister. "Really, that's the first thing you're going to say to me?" her voice was husky.

Lyla shrugged. "What am I supposed to say?"

Shaking with a sudden tremor, Val grimaced. She could feel the wolf within her attempting to force its way past the dark barrier of the suppressant. "I don't know, maybe something like 'I'm sorry.' Start there."

Her sister scoffed. "You're one to talk. I suppose you want me to apologize for trying to keep you out of a laboratory cell."

Val felt another tremor, but she stood up to face her sister, rage consuming her. She pointed a finger toward Lyla's face. "You think I need some kind of babysitter? Admit it, you don't trust me."

"Oh, we're talking about trust now?" Lyla spat back. Her fangs were fully descended, and the veins in her neck and face stood out against the ashen gray of her skin as her body pushed as far into the phase as it could. "I felt those memories while you were talking to Christopher! You've kept me in the dark this whole time, but the minute someone butters you up, you cry on his shoulder and tell him all the sad things that happened to you!"

It didn't matter to Val that her sister was losing herself in the phasing. She was saying things she would probably regret later, but they stung Val to the core, and she growled, fangless but fierce. Reaching out, she shoved her sister as hard as she could.

The younger stumbled, but quickly caught herself and charged back toward Val. They locked arms and struggled, each trying to throw the other off balance. Val leaned into her sister, trying to keep herself braced against Lyla's much greater strength. Lyla tightened her grip around Val's forearms and threw her to the side.

Crashing into a metal bedframe, Val's body was now desperately fighting the suppressant, and the impact sent a flash of white-hot pain through her, magnified by the war waging inside her. Val let out a breathless gasp and struggled to her knees, gritting her teeth as she pushed herself. She was no match for Lyla as she was. But the pain brought with it the darkness that always haunted the edges of her consciousness.

She could no longer remember her name or where she was. All she knew was the blinding pain racing through her body. It owned her, twisting her into some broken thing. She was dying. Trapped in the suffocating haze of agony, she realized with insane clarity that she wanted to die.

Let me go.

Then her sister was on top of her, dragging her to her feet. Val gripped Lyla's shirt, trying in vain to pull away and get underneath her sister's arm to regain the upper hand. There was no sisterly bond here, just anger and pain and words unspoken. Val pushed further and was rewarded by claws forming on her right hand. She swiped them across Lyla's side.

With a deep growl, Lyla tossed her like a sack of flour. This time, Val's back hit the wall, and she dropped to the floor with a cry as she curled into herself. Lyla stalked toward her, the wolf completely clouding her self-control.

Shaking, Val pushed harder, rage building in her as the suppressant forced her phasing back again and again. She let the pain fuel her anger, focusing on it, embracing it. When Lyla grabbed her by the collar of her jacket, she ducked her head and pushed all her weight forward, throwing her sister off balance. Inside, her wolf was overpowering the haze.

The two squared off, both breathing hard as they phased as far as they could. Val could feel the suppressant giving way slightly, but she didn't have time to see how much farther she could push. Lyla came after her, a raw snarl ripping out of her throat as they crashed into each other. Val felt the familiar strength rushing into her muscles. Human gave way to wolf, and the two of them snarled viciously at each other. Then they charged.

The sharp ends of Val's claws scraped across Lyla's forearm as she ducked beneath her sister's outstretched hands. Lyla retaliated without a sound, twisting hard and kicking Val's feet out from under her as she rolled gracefully to the side. Val went down hard, catching herself on her shoulder. Even partially phased, she still winced at the jarring impact.

Val glowered at Lyla as she backed into a corner. Her lip was split and there was a slight gash on her forehead. The wolf ebbed and flowed through her veins, still angry, still hungry for justice. But as she was now, unable to fully phase, her human energy was close to giving out.

Breathing heavily in the middle of the room, Lyla watched her. They were both predators and prey in that moment, each moving in sync with the other. Val knew that if she attacked again, Lyla would meet her without hesitation. The anger she felt was still burning brightly and showed no intention of fading. Closing her eyes, she growled, frustrated at herself. She could feel the suppressant working again in her bloodstream, making her hazy.

Val made her decision. She pulled herself up straighter and walked stiffly over to the mattress lying on the floor, sitting down with a soft grunt as her body began to register the aches and pains. She lay down and rolled onto her side, facing away from her sister. After a few minutes, she heard Lyla shuffle over to another part of the room, and the bunker fell into an uncomfortable silence.

Neither one of the sisters said another word for the next sixteen hours. They sat in opposite corners of the bunker, silent and fevered, each trapped in her own thoughts. When the wolves began to fade, they were left with bruises, scrapes, and an embarrassed tension between them.

Val gathered her things and stuffed them back into her bag. Her shoulder ached from taking the brunt of her fall to the floor. The gash on her forehead had already begun to seal over, which let her know that the suppressant hadn't completely removed her ability to heal. But she knew she couldn't show her face in the classrooms like she was now. Principal Bleiz would likely expel her on the spot. Val could tell that Lyla was favoring the side that had claw wounds. Regret was beginning to settle in now, but Val had never been good at apologetic advances. She pulled at her hair in frustration, wishing for the hundred-thousandth time that they could have just stayed in that little cabin in the woods.

As she moved around, her body protested. She propped herself against the shelf of food to catch her breath.

"Are you okay?"

Lyla's voice was flat, but Val felt a trickle of concern through the bond. "I'll be fine."

She trudged up the bunker stairs a few feet behind Lyla. Nothing had been resolved, and the next week would likely be the same as the last. They emerged from their self-imposed prison, and Val nearly ran into Lyla as her sister stopped short at the top of the stairs. She peered around Lyla's shoulder to see Jules standing a few feet away, pinning them with a stern gaze.

"Well?" she asked expectantly. "Do I get my futon back?"

Val blinked. "How did you know we were coming upstairs?" she asked, ignoring Jules's original question. Jules narrowed her eyes.

"I told Lyla to text me when you were done. You look horrible." The omega glowered at them. "Don't tell me that temper tantrum downstairs didn't even end with you two talking about this."

When Val refused to meet her gaze, Jules threw up her hands in exasperation. "Goodness *sakes*! I even baked cookies for you to celebrate." She pointed a finger at the sisters. "I will not be eating them all myself. You two are going back down into that bunker to open your mouths and talk like civilized beings, and I will not let you out until you've forgiven each other."

The two sisters hesitated, and Jules squared her shoulders. "I'll call Christopher and Lex, and we will carry you down the stairs if you won't go yourselves."

Val couldn't help but smile a little, wincing at the pull against her split lip. "Small but fierce, you are."

Jules' eyes twinkled. "I'm a werewolf too. Now get to it."

And then, they were right back where they started, and Val found herself sitting across from her sister on the floor, lowering herself down with a soft grunt. The dull ache was still present throughout her body, and a slight edge of nausea was lingering. In truth, she felt half-alive, as if something had been stolen from her the previous night. Cormoran liked to say, "just a phasing," but it was so much more than that. Val fidgeted with her hands.

Lyla shifted. "Why didn't you tell me what happened?"

Let's get right to it then. "I was afraid of how you would look at me. Of how we," Val gestured between them. "Would be different."

Lyla frowned. "How I would look at you?"

"Like I'm broken. The only thing keeping me going is that everyone believes I'm strong, sure of myself. I'm a Trueblood alpha, and that's what they see. I don't want anyone to know the truth."

"What's the truth, Val?"

Hesitating, Val sifted through words in her mind, trying to understand herself enough to express how she felt. "I don't know how to say any of this." Lyla waited patiently. Finally, Val sighed and rubbed a hand over her eyes.

"You said you want to keep me out of that laboratory cell," Val said quietly. "I *died* in that cell, Lyla. There's a part of me that won't ever leave it. Every day I relive those moments in my mind, and I can't—" she stopped, shaking her head. Val had never allowed herself to say the words out loud. "Some days I wish they hadn't brought me back."

Lyla reached out, grabbing hold of her wrist. "When I was locked in isolation, every day I spent imagining the day we would get to see each other again. That's what got me through."

"It's what got me through too," replied Val. "Lyla, I'm sorry. For all of this. I just couldn't bear the thought of you knowing. Part of me still can't."

"I'm sorry too, Val. We'll get through this. Can we promise not to shut each other out anymore?" Lyla asked.

"Promise." Val hesitated. "Did what Lex say about us being a pack really bother you?"

Lyla looked down. "I just can't have that kind of a mentality about them. Our pack is gone, Val. Mama, Papa, all of them. And they're never coming back."

Val squeezed her arm. "Maybe not, but what I do know is that our friends are the first people to really care about us since we were captured on that ridge all those years ago. I'm not going to let go of that."

"I'm not going to ask you to. I'm just not ready for that yet."

"That's fair." Val smiled. "Are we good?"

"We're good."

Val nodded and rose to her feet, ignoring the aches. "Awesome. I want those cookies. Do you think Jules has some of that concealer makeup?"

"Why?"

Val offered a sheepish grin. "I think we're going to need it before we go back to class."

CHAPTER THIRTEEN

"**V**alentine Blackwood and Megan Finnigan."

Val blinked, looking up from doodling on her notebook as her English teacher called out the pairings for their next project. Val hadn't been paying any attention, and she had missed all of the guidelines for the presentation. Hopefully, her partner had written them down.

The bell rang. Val shoved her books into her backpack. She noticed the girl that she'd been partnered with talking animatedly with the teacher before leaving the room. Val hurried toward the door to catch up. The other students moved out of her way as they usually did. She paid them no mind as she followed the girl who had left in front of her. Finally coming up behind her, Val reached out and tapped her on the shoulder.

"Hey! It's Megan, right?"

The girl tucked her blonde hair behind one ear, eyes darting around the hallway. Her gaze landed on Val briefly before flitting away.

"What do you want?" she asked.

Val tried smiling. "We're partners. For the project. For class. I was wondering when you wanted to get together to work on it. You can come to my dorm room if you want, or I could come to yours. Or maybe the library."

Megan took a step back away from her. "I don't want you to come to my dorm room. I'm switching partners."

"But—"

"Please don't talk to me again." Megan turned and walked away. Val stood in shock for a minute, watching her leave. Several of the other students nearby were pretending not to eavesdrop, but she knew they'd heard the conversation. Val put her head down and headed for the cafeteria, jaw clenched.

She rounded the corner and made a beeline towards the table where her friends were sitting. Lex and Christopher were sitting across from Lyla, who had already picked up an extra tray of food for her sister. Val felt a nudge of concern through the bond. Of course, Lyla would've picked up on her mood already.

"Hey. You okay?"

Val couldn't even remember how many times her sister had asked her that question in the past few weeks. After the bunker talk, things had been a little easier between them, but they still didn't talk about the past. Lyla didn't push Val to share more than she was willing.

Val took a sip of her water. "Fine."

"Okay." Lyla gave her a look. "You sure?"

Stabbing her pasta salad with a fork, Val tried to organize her thoughts. She really didn't want to talk about the way the other students still looked at them, acted around them. Time had seemed to put more strain, not less, between the Truebloods and their peers.

"Hey, Jules!" said Lex suddenly.

The omega came walking up to the table, her normally cheerful face pulled into a scowl. She sat down in between the Blackwoods and the two boys. "Have you guys heard what's going around the school today?"

Val shook her head. "We're not usually in the social gossip circles, Jules."

Lex focused on his food. "Yeah, I've heard a few things." Both sisters looked up at him, and he shrugged. "I didn't want to bother you guys with it."

With a huff, Jules dropped a newspaper onto the table. Surprised by the omega's anger, Val pulled the paper closer to her, eyeing the bold headline across the front page. **TRUEBLOOD ALPHA SUSPECTED IN ATTEMPTED MURDER CASE.** Pushing the paper across to Lyla, Val put her fork down. The little appetite she'd had was gone.

"Everyone in the school knows about it by now. I found the paper in the computer lab. I can't believe that the staff is allowing this in the school," fumed Jules.

"It's the news," said Val dully. "I guess they have a right to know."

Lyla set the paper down, tapping the table with her forefinger. "He was being held in a high-level penitentiary. It says that he escaped by using an alpha command on the guards and attacked a human family in the next town."

Christopher looked up from his notebook with a frown. "That's strange. Don't they usually have security measures specifically for werewolves for things like that?"

"Yeah. They're called suppressants," replied Val.

"Which he should have been on," said Christopher. "A suppressant will lower the probability of an alpha command's potency. Although in the case of a Trueblood, it might still be strong enough, I suppose."

"Christopher. Not helping," Jules broke in. "The point is, this guy isn't Val and Lyla, and everyone in the school is talking about it like they're all the same! It's not right."

Val smiled a little. "It'll probably blow over eventually. It's just a news article."

"Hey feral," said an all too familiar voice. Val glanced to the side and saw Jackson sauntering toward her. She frowned. What was in his hand?

Jackson stopped at the table and held up a raw steak. "Thought you might be having a hard time eating all this civilized food, so I got you something a little more to your taste." He held the steak out under her nose, and then dropped it on her tray. Everyone around the table stared at him, but Val looked down at the large piece of meat, the scent drawing her attention. And suddenly, Val just felt tired of it all.

She smiled at Jackson. "How did you know? I've been starving for some real werewolf food." Without another word, she picked the steak up off the tray and bit down on the end, tearing off a large chunk. Across the table, she saw Christopher watching her, and she could have sworn she saw a twinkle in his eyes. Val leaned her head back, savoring the meat.

"You going to hog all that meat to yourself?" Lyla asked, reaching for the steak.

Val chuckled. "Just like when we would hunt and kill our own food," Val said, catching the ripple of mischief coming through their bond. Her sister bit off a piece as well and grinned, handing it back to Val.

"Jackson, you must be dying to have some, you being a werewolf alpha and all," said Val sweetly, offering the meat to him. "Don't be shy." She could see the students around them staring, their normally loud conversation hushed. *Might as well give them a real show. They want it, they got it.*

Meeting Jackson's furious eyes, she smiled again, then put the meat back on the tray. "I guess not."

He seethed, and leaned down, on hand resting on the back of her chair and the other on the table. His face was inches away from hers. "You think you're the top of the food chain, don't you? Well guess what, this morning three students were pulled out of the school because of you two. How long do you think it's going to be before Principal Bleiz figures out that getting rid of you two would be easier than losing the rest of us? Everyone knows it's only a matter of time before you turn back into wild animal."

Val kept her hands firmly planted where they were. Jackson was leaning over her in a position of dominance, and she knew there was an unspoken challenge behind his words. Then she felt a gentle reassurance through the bond from Lyla, and she lifted her chin.

"Don't worry. I'll try not to hurt you."

Jackson scoffed. "You're not as scary as you think you are."

"You could've fooled me. You seem desperate to prove that you're more of an alpha than I am, but you know what the truth is?" She leaned forward, closing the gap between them to a narrow sliver of space. "You won't ever make me back down. You're not strong enough, and you never will be."

She saw a muscle in the side of Jackson's jaw twitch, and he pulled back. "Enjoy your freedom while you can, feral." He turned and stalked away out of the cafeteria.

Val took a deep breath and released it slowly. Her muscles relaxed, and she rolled her neck to the side. When she turned back to the table, she saw her three friends watching her. Christopher's pencil was frozen over the notebook page. Val shook her head and picked up her backpack, slinging it over her shoulder.

"Okay, well I'm heading back to class. You guys are going to catch flies if you leave your mouths open like that," she said with a wink. "Jules, you can finish the steak if you want."

"No, I'm good," said Jules. "But that was really cool."

Val shrugged. "I just figured Christopher could use the notes. See you guys for game night later." She turned and headed out of the cafeteria. Now that the adrenaline was fading, the room was starting to feel stuffy. She heard Lyla's familiar step behind her.

"We need to talk tonight," her sister said quietly.

Talking was the last thing Val wanted to do, especially since she figured it would probably turn into a scolding about her behavior with Jackson. But she nodded anyway.

...

Later that evening in their dorm room, Lyla pushed the newspaper she'd grabbed from the cafeteria table into Val's hands.

She was bothered by something, and she needed her sister to tell her she was being paranoid.

"Look at this again."

She watched as Val sank down into the nearest chair and picked the paper up, her forehead wrinkling as she frowned, studying the article. Her sister read through the page and then glanced up at Lyla with a shrug.

"Is this what you wanted to talk about?"

"Yeah."

Val chuckled. "Here I thought you were going to yell at me for what I said to Jackson in the cafeteria. I wanted to put him on the floor in front of the whole room."

"No, I thought you controlled yourself pretty well, considering," replied Lyla. "Now, will you please look at the newspaper."

Val returned her attention to the article. "Guy sounds like a real winner."

Lyla leaned down and pointed at the photo of the suspect. "No, look at him. Does he look familiar to you at all?"

Val squinted, and then Lyla saw her features relax. "Yeah, he does, a bit. You've obviously seen him before, so do you want to help me out here?"

"I kept looking at the picture through my last class, trying to place him. But I think I finally figured it out. I'm going to try and share this with you if I can." Lyla closed her eyes and focused on the memory she'd pulled to the forefront of her mind.

He gripped her left arm, walking her briskly down the long hallway to one of the lab rooms. She looked up and saw the security badge on his collared shirt, a thick neck, and a light scar beneath his right cheekbone. He stared straight ahead, pulling her along—

Lyla stopped and looked at Val, who was also opening her eyes. They were wide with surprise, and she leaned back in her chair, shoulders slumped. "He was a security officer at the center. A beta. He took me to the labs a couple of times too."

Grabbing the newspaper, Lyla pointed at the photo. "So why is he listed as a suspect in a Trueblood alpha attempted murder case?"

"They probably used the wrong photo."

Lyla gave her a look. "Really, Val?"

"No, I'm serious. They probably ran the story before they had all the details, right?" asked Val. "And even if there was some kind of mix up, what does that have to do with us?"

Tossing the newspaper aside, Lyla sat down, raking her fingers through her hair. She played subconsciously with the stubble along the shaved side. "I don't know. I'm just worried about all of this. Everyone thinks there is a Trueblood alpha out there who is trying to murder people."

"No wonder Megan didn't want to be my project partner," mused Val.

"What?"

"Never mind. Look, Lyla, I get that everything is crazy right now. But right now, we can't do anything about it. Let's wait for this to blow over and enjoy Monopoly with our friends tonight. Okay?" Val tilted her head down to get in Lyla's line of vision. "You should be more worried about how I'm going to bankrupt you."

Lyla's attempt at a smile disappeared as soon as Val left to go to the bathroom. Did she worry too much? She rubbed a hand over her face. Maybe Val was right. She felt like she was seeing shadows in every corner. Jackson had said that three students had already been pulled from the school, probably because their parents had decided it wasn't worth the risk.

There was a knock on the door. Lyla frowned. They were twenty minutes early. When she opened it, Christopher was standing outside, holding a plastic bag of grapes. Lyla raised an eyebrow. He glanced down.

"Oh, I just had some extra. Grapes are good, right?"

Lyla shrugged and opened the door wider to let him in. "Sure. Grapes are fine."

"I know Val likes them, so that's why I thought they'd be okay," said Christopher. He put the bag down on top of the mini fridge. Val came back into the room.

"Hey Christopher. Ready to lose Monopoly again?"

He smiled. "Last time was close."

Lyla pulled the game box off of the closet shelf and set it down on the floor to start setting up. Val sat cross-legged next to her. Lyla noticed that Christopher was still standing, and he hadn't taken off his coat yet.

"You are staying for game night, right?" she asked.

He nodded. "Yeah, yeah. Sorry, I came early because I wanted to ask you something. I felt bad how things are at the school right now, and I thought it might be nice for you both to have a break."

Val sat up straighter. "What do you mean?"

"Well, it's almost Thanksgiving break, and so I called my dad this afternoon. He and my mom are inviting you guys to stay with us over break. Jules can't come, but Lex said he might be able to."

Before Lyla could politely decline, she caught sight of Val's face. Her sister looked excited. "Lyla? Do you think Cormoran would sign off on it?"

Not a chance. Lyla wasn't sure if she was speaking for Cormoran or herself. The two of them staying with a human family for several days seemed like a horrible idea. Lyla glanced at the newspaper lying haphazardly where she'd tossed it. "I don't know."

Christopher took off his coat, draping it carefully over the back of the chair. "No pressure, of course. My dad suggested that we could maybe even go camping one of the nights. Our house is at the edge of a big forest."

Lyla inwardly groaned, and she didn't miss the way Val's eyes lit up. There was no way that her sister would be willing to listen to reason now. "Can we give you an answer in the next few days? Cormoran is coming to visit us tomorrow, we can talk about it then."

Christopher nodded. "Of course. Whatever you want to do."

Lyla silently began setting up the game while Val started asking Christopher questions about the forest and his parents. Lyla tried to imagine what it would be like, staying with a strange family—a human family. Did they know what kind of friends Christopher had made? Besides, Thanksgiving break was over a full moon. If that wasn't the perfect set up for disaster, Lyla wasn't sure what was. They'd have to stay out in the woods, since she was willing to bet that Christopher's parents didn't have a bunker in their basement. Lyla stopped, irritated at herself as she counted out the starting cash for each player. She shouldn't even be thinking about this. Cormoran would never let them go.

CHAPTER FOURTEEN

Cormoran was five minutes late and knocked on the dorm room door just after Val had decided to go searching for her. Lyla had given up trying to talk some sense into her sister, wanting her to realize how unlikely it was that they would even get permission. But Val was undeterred. The moment they had all sat down, Val leaned forward, hands clasped in her lap to keep from fidgeting.

"I have a request."

Cormoran arched a perfectly plucked eyebrow. "Oh?"

"One of our friends asked us to come to their house for Thanksgiving. His parents offered. It's not far away. I'd like to go. Will you sign the permission slip?" Val's words tumbled together in her haste to get them all out.

"And do you think that is a good idea?" asked Cormoran.

Up to that moment, Lyla had struggled with how she wanted to handle this. She couldn't shake the anxiety in the pit of her stomach, but she knew how much this meant to Val. "If you really want us to assimilate, how better to do that than to try a weekend away with someone who already knows us?”

Cormoran smiled. “And how would you manage your phasing in a strange environment with a human family?”

Lyla was sure that Val hadn’t even considered it, and the flash of worry through the bond confirmed her suspicions. The next full moon was right over the Thanksgiving weekend. Even though Christopher lived in a wooded area, Lyla didn’t know how his family would feel about having two phasing werewolves on their property. The more she thought about it, the more Lyla realized that they were on a sinking ship. There was no logical reason why Christopher’s family would accept that kind of risk. Neither sister answered the question. Then Cormoran surprised them.

“I received an email yesterday evening from Mr. Wells,” she said, withdrawing a piece of paper from her bag. “He expressed his familiarity with our program and his desire to be of assistance. The DAO relies on the support of human families who are willing and able to participate in the assimilation of our students, and the Wells’ are well aware of your needs. The board is confident that you will be in good hands.”

“They’re letting us go?” Val looked thunderstruck. Cormoran held out a signed permission slip, and Val took it between her fingers as if it might disappear at any moment.

Cormoran reached into her bag. “Yes. With several conditions. I’ve already pre-packaged your suppressants. You will take them with you, and they will be administered in the presence of Mr. and Mrs. Wells. We have also sent a second set to Mr. Wells to use in the event that these are misplaced.”

Lyla nodded. The implication was clear enough. There would be no avoiding the suppressants, even far away. Cormoran set the packages on the little coffee table. "You will take them the day you arrive. Mr. Wells has graciously agreed to provide a private space for you during your phase." She paused, making sure she had both of their full attention.

"The last condition is that any sharing of sensitive information regarding your experiences in our program or your past history is strictly prohibited. I don't think I need to remind you of the consequences should that condition be ignored. Your safety is extremely important to us."

Lyla chose not to respond with her thoughts on that. "I don't understand," she said instead. "Why would a human family take a risk like this? I'm assuming they know what we are."

"And what is that, dear?" asked Cormoran.

Irritated, Lyla retorted, "Truebloods. You know that those suppressants don't completely erase the symptoms of our phasing. We're still werewolves, Ms. Cormoran."

"You are Were students," corrected Cormoran. "And they are aware of the risks. We have already approved the space that Mr. Wells provided. He is familiar with our safety protocols."

Is he really? Does he have a laboratory full of cells too? Lyla didn't want to give Cormoran the pleasure of seeing her irritation. She sensed Val's confusion through the bond and returned a strong intention to keep the questions to herself, making sure that Val did the same. She saw her sister's teeth click together, biting back whatever she was about to say.

"I want to commend you both on the excellent progress you've made this past month. I'm proud of you," said Cormoran as she put her clipboard away. Lyla noticed ruefully that the case files were no longer in the bag. It was a little too late for that precaution.

The moment the door closed behind Cormoran, Val let out a long breath and ran her hand through her hair, dropping her head back. "I'm definitely not the only one who thinks she let us have that way too easy, right?"

"Nope."

Val groaned. "Any guesses?"

"Not yet. I don't trust her. Maybe this is a test of some sort, to see if we will take advantage of the family or try to escape. Jules said that there have been other news articles circulating about Truebloods, so I can't understand why they would let us out in society so easily."

Val stood up and shrugged. "I don't care what Cormoran has up her sleeve anymore." She flashed Lyla a grin. "This trip is totally worth it. We're going to be in the woods again."

Lyla stared across the room into the chair that their handler had just vacated. *I'm not going to let this ruin the first taste of freedom we've had in years.* Whatever this Thanksgiving had in store, Lyla was beginning to feel as if they could handle it. She glanced down at the suppressant packages. Seeing Val's response to them during the last phasing, she couldn't help the dread she felt. Little by little, Cormoran kept chipping off little pieces of them, and Lyla had no idea what would be left when she was done. She could only hope that they were long gone before they had time to find out.

Jules demanded a girls' sleepover night in her dorm room before they all left for break. Val claimed the futon and Lyla dragged her mattress down a flight of stairs just to have a more comfortable bed for the night. After consuming bowls of Rocky Road ice cream and watching one of Jules' favorite chick flicks—which Val and Lyla suffered through, attempting to keep their sarcastic remarks to themselves—Lyla took their bowls to wash them out in the sink and get ready for bed.

Val lounged against the futon's thick cushions. "I'm really sorry you can't come with us this weekend, Jules."

"I know, I'm super bummed. Missing camping with my two favorite Truebloods is a blow to my heart," Jules said, dramatically pressing a hand against her chest. "But I haven't seen my family since I left for school, and I know my grandparents would be heartbroken if I didn't come."

Val smiled. She knew that Jules' family was close knit, and it was nice to hear her talk about them. It soothed the ache that Val felt whenever she thought of her own family. Jules's parents were supportive of other Weres as well, which is why they'd sent their daughter to an assimilation school, and why Jules herself had warmed up to the Trueblood sisters so much faster than many of the other students. Jules had said several times that her parents would love to meet Val and Lyla. Perhaps someday, but Val knew that a trip that far away would be much harder to get the DAO board to agree to. It made Val wonder why other families chose to send their children to Westbrook.

"Do you think that Christopher actually wants us to visit for Thanksgiving, or do you think he just feels sorry for us?" asked Val.

Jules shrugged, and Val saw lips twitch as if she were hiding a smile. "Not sure. You'll have to ask him. Want some more ice cream?" she asked, standing up. Val glanced at her skeptically.

"Jules."

"What?"

"Jules."

"…what?"

Val pinned her with a stern gaze. "You know something. What's going on?"

"I don't know why I would know anything. He's probably fine."

Val stood up and lowered her voice. "What are you hiding? And don't tell me that you don't want to talk about it either."

Jules scowled in indignation at Val's authoritative tone. "Don't use that on me."

"Why not?" Val grinned wickedly and made a grab for the omega. Jules squealed and made a mad dash around the room. Val chased her.

"Stop it!" Jules' attempt at sounding stern was lost amidst the giggles that erupted. Lyla opened the bathroom door and took in the sight of her sister chasing Jules around the dorm.

"Val, what…?"

"She's acting weird and won't tell me what's going on," Val replied, still eyeing Jules who'd been cornered next to the mini fridge.

"Oh. Okay."

Val regarded the omega for a moment before her eyes lit up and she grinned, snapping her fingers. "I know what this is about."

Taken off guard, Jules frowned. "You do?"

"Mhmm." Val crossed her arms. "I think you have a crush on Christopher."

Jules' jaw went slack as she stared at her friend, and Val felt a rush of pride at having figured it out. She glanced at Lyla, who looked amused. Jules straightened her shoulders and stepped forward, standing toe to toe with the alpha, a grin stretching across her face.

"No, you clueless dork. He's got a crush on *you.*"

...

Val sat rigid in the backseat of Lex's tiny two-door car, trying to avoid staring at the curly blond hair of the boy sitting in front of her in the passenger seat. Thankfully, Lyla had not said a word to her about the uncomfortable incident last night. Val wasn't about to bring it up. After the initial shock of Jules' comment, she'd laughed it off and they'd gone to bed. But she couldn't sleep, her thoughts pulled to the little snow globe she kept on her nightstand. She figured that Jules was seeing things, but some small part of her worried. *What if she isn't?*

The whole trip had been awkwardly quiet. Val was normally the one who initiated conversation, but she was not in the mood. Lex ended up playing music over the radio, and Lyla leaned against the window and dozed off. It was only a two-hour drive to Christopher's house, which Val was thankful for. Lex drove into a secluded neighborhood with large houses nestled into the trees. Val pressed her nose to the glass and watched as the forest rolled by. The thought of living in the middle of it for four whole days made her feel almost giddy.

Christopher directed Lex to pull into the last driveway on the road, which wound through a grove of carefully maintained trees and landscaping to a large two-story colonial house. Giant white columns dominated the front façade, and a stone path led up to a large wooden door with a wrought iron handle. Several sculpted topiaries guarded the flowerbeds in front of the house. Val stared and felt her jaw go slack. Lyla glanced at her with a raised eyebrow.

Val stepped out into the fresh air as soon as Christopher slid the seat forward for her. She didn't know where to look first. Turning away from the grand sight of the house and garden, Val looked over her shoulder at the wilderness surrounding them. She took a deep breath, filling her lungs with the scent of the wilderness. It was so close she could taste it. She glanced over at Lyla, who was looking around at everything silently.

The front door of the house opened, and a middle-aged woman appeared, her hair swooping lightly to the side over her pearl earrings. Her eyes sparkled above a warm smile. Christopher walked into her embrace, and she lifted herself up on her tiptoes to hug him tightly. Then she turned to the other three. "Welcome! We've been so excited to meet you all. I'm Christopher's mom, please call me Lucy," she said. When Lyla reached out a hand, Lucy waved her off.

"We're family now, sweetie. I'm a hugger," she chuckled, wrapping her arms around Lyla. Val grinned as she saw her sister return the hug hesitantly. When Lucy approached her, Val accepted the hug and was surprised at the kindness and warmth that seemed to radiate from the woman. Christopher had told them that his mother was from the South, and Val was still trying to understand what that meant. The idea that humans were different depending on where they lived in the country was a strange one.

"Thank you for letting us stay with you, that was really nice," Val said, hefting her bag as she followed the others into the house.

"It's our pleasure, sweetie. Mr. Wells should be home any time, and our Thanksgiving dinner is just about ready. We've got a big turkey this year—I hope you like to eat."

Better if I could hunt it myself, Val thought in amusement. "Thank you, Mrs. Wells. That sounds really good."

Lucy beamed. "Oh, bless you, call me Lucy. Christopher, darling, why don't you show our guests to their rooms?"

The inside of the house was even grander than the outside. The four friends carried their bags up the curved staircase. A huge chandelier hung from the ceiling, dominating the entryway. Val almost felt guilty for walking on the pristine mosaic tiles. Christopher led them to a wing of rooms and opened the third door on the right for Val and Lyla, then continued down the hallway with Lex.

Val closed the door behind them and dropped her bag on the plush carpet. A queen-sized four-poster bed sat against the wall between two carved wall sconces. The furniture all looked as if it had come out of a Victorian-era movie set. A bookshelf full of classic novels sat next to a comfortable chair in the corner of the room. There was even a little writing desk in front of the window with a quill pen lying across the polished wood.

"Wow," said Val, glancing around the room. "This is crazy."

"I know. I don't really want to touch anything," Lyla replied. "I don't know what I was expecting, but this house is huge."

Val fell back onto the bed, throwing her arms out to the side with a long sigh. "If you try to steal the sheets, I'm kicking you out."

"You are definitely worse. I better not wake up with your foot in my face," retorted Lyla. She walked to the window and pulled the curtains slightly to the side, looking out at the grounds and the woods beyond. "We're going to go out there tomorrow."

"You ready?"

"I don't know."

"I am. I don't even know if I want to wait around for the turkey," admitted Val. She slid off the bed, noticing that Lyla was still looking out the window.

"Are you okay?"

Lyla turned and nodded, straightening her shirt. "Yeah. I can't believe I'm saying this, but I miss Jules right now. She would've made this a lot less awkward."

"Don't worry. If we keep everything surface level, we won't have a problem. Christopher and his dad know enough about the DAO that they probably won't ask us that many questions. Besides, Christopher knows that we're not supposed to talk about it."

Val frowned as she saw Lyla bite her lip. "What?"

"I got another text message from Cormoran earlier today, reminding us to keep everything confidential." Lyla looked at Val. "Now that Christopher knows, there's no guarantee he wouldn't have told his parents something he shouldn't have."

Even though Lyla wasn't trying to make her feel guilty, Val still felt a twinge of regret, knowing that she had shared too much. If Cormoran ever found out, there was no telling what the consequences might be. But then her thoughts drifted back to what

Jules had said the previous night, and a strange warmth filled her. With all the uncertainty, she was certain of something at least: she could trust Christopher.

CHAPTER FIFTEEN

Mrs. Wells had set the table with crystal glasses, beautiful painted china plates, and silver utensils. A huge stuffed turkey sat on a platter in the middle of the table, surrounded by heaping bowls of mashed potatoes, buttery biscuits, black eyed peas, cranberry sauce, and corn bread. At the head of the table stood a man who looked exactly like an older version of Christopher.

He smiled at the girls when they entered the room and shook hands with them. "Christopher has told us so much about you both. It's a pleasure to meet you in person."

How much has he told you? Lyla wondered. They all sat down at the table, and Mr. Wells said grace, thanking God for bringing Christopher's friends to their table. Lyla felt a twinge of discomfort. *I don't know if you'll be thanking Him later.* Even so, she was surprised by how genuinely kind Christopher's parents were. As Lucy began to dish up everyone's plates, Val was pulled easily into a conversation about school, everyone's food preferences, and dream vacations. Mr. and Mrs. Wells were thoughtful in their questions. Lyla didn't say much, but she felt herself relaxing as she began to eat. The biscuits were heavenly, melting in her mouth with buttery warmth.

Lyla had just turned to her turkey and black-eyed peas when Lucy asked her a question. "Did your family have any special Thanksgiving traditions, dear?"

Everyone at the table glanced her way, and Lyla wasn't sure what to say. Of course, they would know that she and Val didn't have living parents. She tried to sift through her memories for an answer that wouldn't give anything away. They all felt so distant.

"Not Thanksgiving, no. But my mother loved to raise and dry her own herbs," Lyla said. "She always cooked everything fresh, and my father would help her. Our whole… family… would come and eat with us outside the cabin together." The memory of their faces began filling Lyla's mind, and she quietly pushed them away just as she always did. There was a pause.

"I remember everyone laughing a lot," added Val, squeezing Lyla's hand under the table for support. "And a woman from the nearest town taught our mother to make apple pies. I can still remember the smell of the dough and cinnamon."

"That's beautiful, honey. They sound like wonderful people."

Lyla spoke around a lump that rose in her throat. "They were. The best people I've ever known."

No one knew what to say after that. The clink of silverware against the plates filled the silence. Lex looked around the table and then piped up. "My mom used to make little turkeys out of Oreos and candy corn!"

Lyla caught his gaze and gave him a small smile in thanks. After everyone finished eating, they all cleared the table and helped

Lucy clean up and wash the dishes, despite her protests that they didn't need to. After she finally put the last plate away in the antique hutch, Lyla was ready for bed, eager to have some peace and quiet for the rest of the evening. As she said goodnight and headed toward the staircase, Mr. Wells stopped her.

"Lyla, I'm sorry to bother you. I know you must be tired. Will you and Val please bring your suppressants to my office? I was told that you would be bringing your own, but I was sent extras in case those were misplaced."

And just like that, reality came back, pulling Lyla out of the comfortable haze she'd been enjoying through the meal. She nodded. "We brought the ones Cormoran gave us. I'll go get them."

When she returned to the main floor, Val met her at the bottom of the stairs. "I was enjoying the feeling of not being a lab rat for one day."

"Come on, let's go." Lyla didn't feel like joining Val's rant about their situation at the moment. They both walked into Mr. Wells' office, which smelled like cedar and old books. Mr. Wells sat on the edge of the desk, and Lucy gave them a supportive smile from the armchair in the corner.

"Do you need help?" asked Mr. Wells. The girls shook their heads. Early on, they'd been taught how to administer their own suppressants. They just usually chose not to. Lyla took her worn hoodie off, leaving her in a simple black t-shirt, the same style as the one Val wore. Suddenly self-conscious, Lyla averted her eyes from the well-dressed couple sitting on the other side of the room. The holes in the knees of her jeans felt like giant beacons drawing attention to just how different of a world she and Val came from than the one they were sitting in now. Between phases and the general higher physical nature of their lifestyle, the clothing supply they received from the DAO didn't always keep up with them.

Val took one of the packages from Lyla and ripped the paper open with her gloved hands. Lyla saw spots of color in her sister's cheeks as she withdrew the syringe and pierced the skin on the inside of her elbow with a grimace. She depressed the plunger and slid the needle free, jamming it back inside the package.

"Need anything else?" asked Val quietly. Lyla pulled on a pair of gloves, feeling the effort Val was putting forward to keep her true state of mind from showing. It felt wrong, this vulnerable part of them exposed to people they hardly knew, and Lyla's fingers trembled slightly as she withdrew her own syringe from the package.

"No, thank you, Val," replied Mr. Wells calmly. "Let us know if we can do anything else for you. Our room is at the end of your hallway upstairs. Our home is your home while you're here with us."

Lyla ignored the cool sensation of the suppressant as it entered her bloodstream. She carefully put the used syringe back into the package and put it into the box Mr. Wells offered.

"Thank you for letting us stay," she said. "We're really grateful."

"It's our pleasure, sweetheart," replied Mrs. Wells, her kind smile bringing out the light wrinkles around her eyes. Lyla pulled her hoodie back on and followed Val out of the room.

An hour later, Lyla slid into the cool bedsheets and relaxed against the mattress. The bed felt too comfortable, and she was still getting used to the idea of being able to use all the expensive things in their room. It had taken Val nearly ten minutes to decipher the uses of the five different knobs and spray nozzles in the tiled shower stall. Lyla had lost herself in one of the books from the shelf beside the bed, attempting to escape the way her body was beginning to feel sick from the suppressant.

The satin pillowcases were slippery. Lyla rolled to the side and tried to get comfortable. She felt the bed creak as Val climbed in and wiggled down into the sheets.

"Lyla?"

"Yeah."

"It was really nice, wasn't it? Being around a family like that again," said Val. "It almost felt normal for a little while."

"They're very nice people."

Val paused. "You don't trust them?"

"I just said they're nice people. How does that translate to 'I don't trust them'?" asked Lyla, rolling her eyes. The irritation she felt wasn't because Val questioned her; it was because she knew Val was right. If she was honest with herself, she didn't trust anyone except Val.

Val snorted. "I know you better than that. I don't know, maybe I'll be wrong about them too, but nothing is going to keep me from enjoying this camping trip tomorrow. I don't care what happens."

Lyla didn't respond, and soon she heard Val's breathing deepen and slow as she slipped away into sleep. The dim light of the moon shone through the light curtains and painted a splash of light on the colorful rug. Lyla stared at the light. When they were young, she remembered seeing the moonlight through their windows in the cabin, watching her mother and father slip outside, already beginning to phase. Back then, she couldn't wait until she was old enough to go with them—to hunt in the forest and feel the power racing through her blood. She'd never gotten the chance, and part of her would always grieve that.

Next to her, Val's breathing had steadied. Lyla glanced over at her sister, watching the peaceful expression on her face and the way her chest rose and fell lightly as she slept. For a moment, she looked the same as she had so many years ago: young, and unburdened. Lyla took a deep breath and slipped out of the blankets, treading silently across the floor.

She descended the stairs and went into the kitchen, Mr. Wells' words circling through her mind. *Our home is your home.* Lyla couldn't imagine treating this giant palace of a house as if she belonged in it, but she figured that getting a drink of water couldn't hurt. She reached up to the cupboard of glasses and took one down, filling it halfway from the tap on the sink. She heard a footstep behind her and turned, fingers gripping the glass tightly to keep from dropping it.

Mr. Wells stepped into the kitchen and set a book on the counter. "Hello, Lyla. Need anything?"

She lifted the glass. "Just getting a drink of water. Is that all right?" she asked, suddenly wondering if she'd overstepped.

He smiled and pushed his glasses up on his nose in a perfect imitation of his son. "Of course. You're welcome to anything you need. Is your room comfortable?"

Lyla took a sip of her water. "Yes, thank you. It's a really nice house."

"Good. I'm glad that you were all able to visit us this weekend, I know it means a lot to Christopher. He seems very fond of the three of you."

Lyla ran her finger over the rim of her glass, not sure how to respond. "He's a good friend," she found herself admitting. She noticed that the blue plaid bathrobe that Mr. Wells was wearing over his pajamas was threadbare. One of the pockets had come loose a little and folded over on itself. Mr. Wells caught her gaze and looked down.

"Pardon the fashion statement," he said. "I've never been able to let Mrs. Wells throw it away. We put sentimental value on strange things sometimes."

"You're reading one of Christopher's books," said Lyla, her attention turning toward the book on the counter. *Truebloods.* She'd seen Christopher carrying it around many times. Mr. Wells nodded.

"It's from my library, actually. Christopher has been doing quite a bit of his own research into the subject. My shelf of books on werewolves is missing quite a few of its volumes lately," he said, amused.

Lyla was surprised that he would refer to them as werewolves. It was a word that was almost completely removed from any Domestic conversation. She watched the man across from her, feeling bold. "What made you so interested in studying us?"

If he was taken aback by her honesty, Mr. Wells didn't show it. He tapped his finger against the book. "The Culling," he replied. "I'd never seen destruction like that before, such wanton disregard for life. I set myself the task of learning as much as I could with the intention of making the world a better place. A lofty notion, perhaps, but I believe that we can all change the world in our own small way."

It was easy now to see where Christopher's philosophies on the subject had originated. Lyla decided to keep going, curious. "Christopher told us that you'd worked with the DAO in the past?"

"I have, yes, although it has been in a limited capacity. They are a very private organization and they take the safety and confidentiality of their clients quite seriously, from my experience. I have had the opportunity to tour several of their main campuses over the past few years."

Lyla studied her fingernails. *How much do you really know?* She knew she was pushing her luck even pursuing this topic. But she had to know. She had to protect Val, and she needed to know if Christopher had honored his promise to keep their secrets. "I'm sorry if our being here has been an inconvenience. You probably had to follow a lot of protocols to have us here. I know that we present a considerable risk to your family."

Mr. Wells regarded her thoughtfully. "Lyla, I'm aware that you are unable to speak freely about your position here. Ms. Cormoran was thorough in her explanation of the policies this program follows. I may not know the specifics of your history, but please be reassured that my son's concern for you and your sister is reason enough for us to welcome you both into our home."

Her eyes burned, and Lyla turned to rinse out her glass. "Thank you." She stepped around the kitchen island and headed for the doorway, speaking around the lump in her throat. "Goodnight."

She didn't wait to hear his response, but she heard a quiet "goodnight" behind her as she walked back up the stairs.

CHAPTER SIXTEEN

"Okay, the camping spot is right through here," said Christopher, walking into the carpet of dead leaves and branches. Val helped Lex pull the wagon along the footpath. While the three Weres were not as affected by the cooler weather, Christopher was bundled up to the top of his head in a heavy coat, thick cargo pants, gloves, and a thick beanie hat was pulled over his ears. Val had thus far resisted the urge to tease him about it. After all, it wasn't his fault he was a human.

They finally reached a little clearing beneath the canopy of tall trees. The smells attacking Val's nose from the fresh forest air were nearly driving her crazy. Even through the suppressed haze, she wanted nothing more than to lunge into the trees and hunt. She wondered how good the game was.

"Do you ever go hunting out here, Christopher?" she asked. He pulled one of the tent bags out of the wagon and gave her a questioning glance.

"No, I never have. But my uncle does sometimes."

Christopher and Lex began to set up their tent, and Lyla dragged the second bag over to a spot about ten feet from them.

"Val, come help me," Lyla said. Val quickly jogged over and helped her sister pull all the tent poles out of the bag while Christopher dug a large hole for a campfire. Lex meandered over by the wagon and began digging around in the other supplies.

Val threw both her sleeping bag and Lyla's into their tent and pushed one of the stakes farther into the ground with the toe of her boot. Val straightened up after double checking all the tent stakes and noticed that Lex was still crouched next to the side of the wagon. He hadn't moved for a couple of minutes.

"Hey Lex, you okay?"

The beta flinched as if he'd been pulled from a trance, but then stood up. "Yeah. Yeah, I'm good!" he replied, turning around and giving Val a thumbs up. Val shrugged it off and grinned at Christopher meticulously straightening out their tent and tapping the stakes into the ground with a small hammer. She stretched out her arms and heard the soft bubble of water somewhere nearby.

"Lyla, want to go check out the stream?"

"Sure." Lyla crawled back out of the tent.

Val waved at Christopher. "I saw a stream on your map. It's nearby, right?"

He nodded and came over to hand the map to her. "Yep, right here," he pointed to a spot close to their campsite.

"Cool. We'll be back soon."

Lyla walked more slowly than usual, and Val moved just ahead so she could find the best way through the brush. After Val's experience the previous month, Cormoran had issued the same dosage for Lyla, in hopes that it might continue to remove all symptoms of phasing, and Lyla was feeling the side effects already. Val hadn't said anything to her sister, but she was feeling more and more detached from her own wolf—as if it had been locked away in a soundproof room somewhere she couldn't reach. The suppressant was working, just as she'd feared. She found herself wondering if she would ever be able to phase fully again. Even now, the day before a full moon, she felt nothing.

"I'm sorry you're not feeling well," Val said, pushing a branch out of her way.

"I'm fine."

Val knew it wasn't worth a response. Her sister was always more irritable when she was sick, but she knew that Lyla wouldn't have missed this camping trip for anything. Val could hear the stream up ahead, and a few more steps brought them to the edge of it. The sound of the water was soothing, a little bubbling brook through the trees. Val knelt and put her hands in the cold water. Lyla crouched next to her and put her own hands in the stream next to Val's. She smiled.

"This feels good. Remember the stream that we used to play in behind the cabin?" Lyla asked. "We used to let the little minnows nibble our fingers."

"I remember," replied Val. "I'm glad we came. Hey, Lyla?"

"Mhmm?"

"I know things aren't completely back to normal between us after before, but I'm really glad we're together. We might not be free yet, but this feels pretty darn good."

Lyla nodded. "I'm glad too. I talked to Mr. Wells last night for a few minutes. I don't think Christopher has told him anything."

Frowning, Val ran the words through her mind several times before she decided how to respond. At first, she felt a strange annoyance that Lyla hadn't trusted Christopher's word. But she knew that Lyla was just trying to be careful. "I'm glad. I think everything is going to work out. This is just the beginning."

They sat for several minutes with their hands in the stream, listening to the softly rustling leaves and the distant sounds of the woods. Val withdrew her hands when they began to tingle and feel slightly numb from the cold. Somewhere back the way they'd come a strange cry sounded. Val frowned and stood up, eyes snapping back toward the trees.

"Did you—"

Lyla turned to face the sound too. It came again, louder. There was no doubt that it had come from one of the boys. And then they heard a sound that turned Val and Lyla's blood cold: the unmistakable howl of a werewolf.

Val took off running through the trees, crashing through the brush. The howl had spurred her own wolf out of its sleepy haze, and she could feel her fangs pressing through her upper and lower gums. She heard the brush crackling behind her and knew that Lyla was only a step behind. They charged back into the campsite clearing, bodies on edge.

Christopher was standing behind the wagon, eyes wide with fright and a large stick in his hands. Across from him, his back facing the two girls, was Lex. His jacket had been thrown to the side and muscles rippled through his arms. The veins in his neck stood out, and a dark grayish hue colored his skin. His mouth was open, revealing his long fangs. The bones in his face had thickened, pressing out against the skin, his ears lengthening to tips.

Christopher caught sight of Val and Lyla, but he stood frozen in his spot behind the wagon, desperately trying to keep it between himself and Lex.

Val stood frozen with shock as she took in the scene. *He's fully phasing.* Lyla took several steps toward Lex, and the beta's head whipped around. His eyes were blood red, and his long claws were already past the tips of his fingers.

"Lex!" said Lyla. "I need you to step away from Christopher." Val saw her scowl in frustration.

Lex growled, eyes narrowing, and turned back toward the human. His wild first phase rendered him nearly immune to Lyla's command. Val knew that if Lex charged, there was no way she could reach him before he got to Christopher. Lyla took another step toward the phasing Were, but the crack of the branch she stepped on was all it took for Lex to leap forward. He hurtled into Christopher, and the two boys crashed to the ground. Christopher yelled in pain as Lex's claws raked down his arm, leaving bloody gashes behind.

Christopher managed to roll out from under the enraged werewolf as Lex drew back for a second swing, and he took off running. Val's voice was still trapped in her throat as she watched her sister surge forward and leap onto Lex's back, fighting to pull him to the ground. The beta shoved her off and went after Christopher. Val knew that Christopher had no chance of outrunning Lex, and if he was caught, he'd be as good as dead.

Val felt as if she were watching everything unfold through a thick layer of glass. She put one foot forward, and then another, following the others in slow motion. Lex reached Christopher and shoved him forward. The human boy lost his balance, tumbling onto the forest floor and rolling a few feet away. He pulled himself up against a tree, holding his torn arm, blood trickling through his fingers and soaking his sleeve. Lex stalked forward.

Lyla threw herself onto Lex's back again, eyes flashing Trueblood violet. She howled, and Val felt the shock of her sister's pain flash through the bond. Lyla was trying to push her body into a forced phase. Lex reached around to grab hold of her, but Lyla yanked him backwards. They both toppled to the ground.

"Val! You need to phase, now!" Lyla screamed at her.

I can't. It's gone. Val could feel the suppressant dulling her, pulling her wolf back down into the fog. She kept moving forward, her body numb as her mind desperately tried to detach from the reality around her. Her sister was struggling to keep Lex on the ground, and there was no way she could overpower him by herself.

This isn't real. This isn't real. This isn't real.

"Val! Phase!"

Lyla's voice cut through the fog in Val's brain, but the fear held her paralyzed in place. Every second ticked by as if it were a minute. She knew the only chance they had was if she and Lyla were both able to push through the suppressant and phase. But even if they could, their energy wouldn't last nearly as long as Lex's unbridled and newly phased strength. Val felt helpless, the wolf deep inside unresponsive. Was it even there?

Her sister's fevered gaze and violet eyes found her. "VAL!"

They're coming for me. It hurts so much. I can't do it again. Please don't make me do this again. Not again. It's gone. I don't know if I can do this.

Val tore her gaze away from her sister, who had locked her arms around Lex's neck, his flailing claws raking against her sides.

Christopher stood, bleeding and fearful against the tree trunk, staring at them, his face pale with loss of blood and shock.

One thought pierced through the rest. *I have to protect him.*

Val closed her eyes, reaching deep inside to her wolf, cowering beneath the suppressant. She ripped it free, forcing it to the surface, tearing it through the fog. She felt the first sharp wave of pain lace through her body. Forcing past a suppressant felt as if her body were being torn and shredded, attacking itself. She snarled at the pain, letting the anger take her. Her eyes snapped open. She saw Lex break her sister's hold and throw Lyla to the side like a rag doll. He resumed his hunt, leaping to his feet and focusing his gaze on the human cowering by the tree.

No.

Val lunged forward, fangs beginning to descend as she threw herself between Christopher and Lex. The beta snapped furiously at her, swinging at her head with his sharp claws. One of them glanced off Val's cheek, leaving a cut behind. Waves of pain crashed through Val's phasing body one after the other, a torturous onslaught. Lex hesitated, and then Lyla was on him again. Val had given her the breath she needed to push her own phasing farther. Her face was twisted with the pain as she snarled and snapped at Lex.

"Val, you have to do something! We can't hold him back!" Lyla shouted, crying out as Lex sank his teeth into her shoulder. Val barreled into Lex, her momentum carrying them both backward into a tree trunk. Lex's head flew back against the bark with a loud crack, and he fell to his knees.

Lyla gripped her bleeding shoulder. "He's too strong. I tried to command him to stop, but he's fighting it."

I can't phase any farther. Val crouched and readied herself for another blow as Lex picked himself up off the ground, looking angrier than ever. Val caught her breath and forced as much authority into her voice as she could muster.

"Lex! Stop."

The beta paused, shaking his head from side to side and snapping at the air, fighting her alpha command. Val held her ground until another wave of pain nearly brought her to her knees. Lex howled. Val clenched her fists. Her authority wasn't strong enough. She knew she wouldn't be able to keep her body in this state much longer. And Lex was heading straight for Christopher. Val looked at Lyla, both of them bleeding and ragged, and Val realized that there was only one other thing that could save Christopher, but at what cost?

"I only need a minute."

Lyla immediately turned on her heel to face Lex. "Go." She straightened her shoulders and met the beta head on. Val ran for Christopher, lifting her arm to her mouth as she approached him. She sank her teeth into her skin, letting the deep red blood rise to the surface. Val ignored the shock and fear on Christopher's face as she slid to a stop inches from him. He turned to run, but she grabbed his wrist.

"I claim you," she breathed, drawing her arm across his face, shoulder, and chest in a wide sweep, leaving a swathe of red behind on his skin and clothes. She bit down on her arm again and repeated the same action, leaving Christopher covered in her blood.

Her head swam with the scent, and she threw her head back, howling. Her mind grew clearer, awash with pain and power and a new sensation, drawing her to Christopher like a magnet.

"Lex!" she shouted, voice deep and visceral. "He is mine. I claim him."

The beta stopped a few feet away and sniffed the air, lips rising above his fangs. Rage filled his face, but Val saw the wolf beneath the surface recoiling from the blood he smelled on his prey. It was one of the oldest Were rituals, binding protector and protected together for life. Now, instead of the smell of fear and the thrill of a hunt, Lex's senses were overwhelmed by the blood of a Trueblood alpha.

"Lex, enough." Lyla spoke from the ground, her voice tired, but commanding. "Go into the forest."

Lex growled, still watching Christopher, and smelling the air. Val stood between them, eyes locked on the beta, ready to defend with her life if he took one more step forward. The new threads connecting her to Christopher sang with a wild energy. Lex snarled and turned, loping away into the trees. Lyla rose to her feet stiffly.

"He needs to hunt. I'll follow him farther into the woods. He's going to need someone with him when he starts coming back."

Val nodded curtly, still rigid. Lyla jogged into the trees, following Lex's retreating form. The moment they were out of sight, Val dropped to her knees, breath coming in huge gasps. She heard crunching leaves and was vaguely aware of Christopher kneeling beside her.

"Val?" his voice was hushed.

"We should go back to the campsite. I need to eat, drink something. In case he comes back," she said, shivering as her adrenaline rush faded. "And we need to look at your arm." She stood up and made her way back through the trees. Christopher didn't say a word behind her.

When they found the campsite, Val rummaged around in the sealed bins of food until she found some jerky and trail mix. She tossed a couple packets to Christopher, and then pulled out a bottle of water. She glanced over at the blood coating his face, arms, and clothes. He looked as if he'd been pulled out of a crime scene. Awkwardly, she looked away as soon as he met her gaze. She could feel the thin hold she'd had on her wolf slipping as it descended back into the dull haze of the suppressant. Her body felt as if it had been through a meat grinder.

"What if Lex comes back?" asked Christopher, carefully putting the empty trail mix wrapper into his cargo pants pocket. His hands were shaking so much that it took several tries.

"His wolf will respect my… my…" *Claim. It was a blood claim, Val.* She bit her lip. "My scent." *That sounds way less creepy. Good job.*

"Let's look at your arm," she said, pulling the first aid kit out of a backpack.

Christopher's face turned a dark shade of pink. "I think it's okay, actually." He turned to the side, showing Val the ripped sleeve and the arm underneath. The skin was tinged red with drying blood, but the deep claw wounds had shrunk to dark scratches. Val stared at it.

"What on earth?"

"Werewolf blood is a potent healing agent for human wounds. Your healing abilities work even more quickly on us," he explained. "It was something I read about a long time ago, and I thought it wouldn't hurt to try. Most medical practices ban the use on the off chance that it could cause a human to change, but that's not likely."

Val frowned. "We're not supposed to mix our blood."

"It takes a lot more than that to change a human into a werewolf. I'd have to be nearly dying. The werewolf blood takes over the body while the human side dies. It's far too complicated for something like this to be a concern. Did you never learn anything about it?"

Val shook her head. "No. Our parents wouldn't talk about it. They only told us that turning a human would get us a death sentence. And the D.A.O. never let us study anything from our own culture. All the books were banned."

Running his fingers over the scars on his arm, Christopher looked down at his shoes. "Val, what you did back there… it was a blood claim, wasn't it?"

How on the green earth does he know about that? Val guessed she shouldn't be surprised. "Yeah."

"It's permanent."

It wasn't a question, and Val sucked in her breath. "I'm really sorry, Christopher. I didn't know what else to do."

"Don't worry about it," Christopher said quietly. He stood up and started heading toward the stream. Suddenly unable to stand the thought of him being alone, the blood claim pulled her to her feet, and she followed him. Her steps were silent behind Christopher's crunching footfalls. Val knew she'd had no other choice, but her decision to name herself Christopher's protector was not a simple fix. The blood claim was irrevocable. She'd seen her father use it once when a scared omega had come looking for shelter, running from her pack. And Lex had responded the way Val had hoped he would.

Thinking of Lex brought more questions to mind. How had he been able to fully phase? The only logical explanation Val could think of was that he had forgotten to take his suppressant. She scowled, planning exactly what she would say to him when he returned. The thought of him being around Christopher filled her with rage. She closed her eyes as they reached the stream. *This is the blood claim talking.* Val hadn't realized how strong the protective urge would be.

"It must be hard not being able to fully phase. I've never seen anything like that," said Christopher, sitting down on a rock beside the water. "I could tell that it was hurting you."

Val eyed him. "It's not something I would do for fun," she quipped, trying to lighten the mood. She scratched at her arms, watching the last of the gray hue fading from her skin. Christopher looked up at her seriously.

"Do you think you'll ever be able to fully phase again? The way Lex did?"

Val didn't want to think about that question, much less answer it. She kicked some leaves around with her boot. "I don't know what's going to happen." Much to her chagrin, Christopher didn't look away. He reached out and gently brushed his fingers over her hand. Heat flooded her face.

"You're a lot stronger than you give yourself credit for, Val Blackwood." He smiled and pulled his hand away, reaching down into the stream. "And thank you. For what you did."

Val swallowed hard and turned away from him, leaning against a tree. The surge of feelings in that moment was confusing to her.

Beneath the strong protective instinct she now felt for Christopher, there was something else. Something she didn't want to let go of. Something she'd been convinced she'd never feel for anyone.

PART TWO

CHAPTER SEVENTEEN

Everything was so clear in moonlight. Every faint scent was magnified, overwhelming. Far away, a woodpecker tapped its beak against a tree. In Lex' ears, it sounded as if it were right next to him. Energy thrummed through him, every muscle still on fire from the adrenaline of the chase. He glanced over at the carcass of the deer a few feet away. Now that the insatiable urge to hunt and eat had been appeased, he was faced with a myriad of conflicting emotions. Phasing was nothing like he'd imagined. It was no fairytale; it was raw and unbridled strength, every sensation pushed to the extreme. He'd felt purely animalistic, instincts driving his every step. He didn't think he could ever face Christopher again.

"Hey."

He looked over his shoulder to see Lyla rejoining him. She had participated in the hunt a little, but then left him alone to eat. Even Lyla's presence set him on edge, and as soon as he had brought down the deer, his territorial instincts had flared. Lyla hadn't said a word, but she seemed to know that he needed space. She'd simply walked a safe distance away and sat to watch him eat. As if this kind of thing happened every day in her life.

She had partially phased, but he hadn't seen her lose her composure once. Not even during the hunt. Her eyes had flickered back to violet on the hunt. But when he had finally brought their quarry down, she had pulled back instantly while the smell of the deer's blood had nearly set his own on fire. Now that he had felt the absence of the suppressant he'd known since he was young, he felt like a stranger in his own skin. For the first time in his life, he could feel the wolf running through his veins, charged, and freed from the suppressant.

Lyla watched him with that same calm expression she always had. Lex reached up to run a shaky hand through his hair and stopped at his jaw, feeling the protruding bones. His skin felt rougher, and his lips were pulled taut over fully descended and sharp fangs. He dropped his hand and felt thankful there was no mirror nearby. He wasn't ready for that. The full moon shone up above them, and he glared at it. He sat down on the carpet of leaves and pine needles, leaning forward to rest his chin on his palms. Lyla didn't say anything, and he was surprised by that. He'd expected a scolding at the very least. She had every reason to be angry with him. So did Val and Christopher. Lex pushed the unpleasant memories from earlier away. His brain was chaotic enough without those. Instead, he studied Lyla. She'd always seemed to have a calming effect on those around her. The last traces of her phasing had dimmed, and he could see the tired dark circles beneath her eyes.

"I'm sorry." It was the only thing he could think to say. His voice was low, gravelly, and sounded like it belonged to someone else. To his surprise, Lyla smiled.

"You should've seen Val the first time she ever phased," she said, clasping her hands over one knee. "I'm surprised the world survived it."

He frowned. "And you?"

"I don't remember much of it, honestly. Val took me up in the mountains and helped me hunt."

"Your parents didn't take you?"

She looked away. "No. They were already gone by then. I was twelve when I phased for the first time. Val started early, she was only eleven, but I think the stress of losing our parents and living on our own had something to do with that."

Lex looked down at his hands. "Did you hurt anybody?"

She shook her head. "No. We were far away from anyone else." When he didn't respond, she leaned forward. "Lex, I'm going to assume that you didn't do this on purpose. You couldn't have known what was going to happen, especially since you've never phased before. The first time is more intense than any other phasing you have. It's almost impossible to control it."

"How do you and Val do it?"

She chuckled. "There's a reason we hide in the bunker. The control we have has come with years of practice."

"That's all it was, practice?" he asked, giving her a pointed look.

"No," she admitted. "That's the word that people want to hear."

Lex knew she wouldn't say more than that. He was suddenly very tired, and his body was beginning to ache. He wanted answers, both from himself and from the girl sitting across from him. But he didn't even know what to ask. What would his parents say?

"Your eyes are starting to come back," said Lyla. "We should head back to the campsite first thing in the morning."

Lex shook his head, ignoring the pervasive memories of what had happened only hours earlier. "I don't want to hurt anyone."

Lyla brushed a dead leaf off her pants. "You won't. Your phasing is past the dangerous point now. Besides, Val's blood claim would keep you from doing anything to Christopher."

"That thing she did, the blood claim, what was that?"

Obviously uncomfortable with the subject, Lyla shifted her weight. "It's an old tradition, usually done with a ceremony. Val was placing Christopher under her protection, and from now on, other Weres will recognize the scent of her blood on him. It's not something she can reverse now."

Lex paused. "Is that illegal?"

Lyla looked up at him, her eyes dark. "Yes."

His shoulders slumped forward. "I'm sorry, Lyla. I've really made a mess of things. I'll tell them it wasn't her fault."

Lyla moved forward until she was kneeling in front of him. She put her hand on his shoulder and waited until he met her gaze. "Lex, it's going to be okay. Tomorrow we will go back and talk it all out together."

He swallowed, his muddled brain registering how close she was. Her eyes were sincere, the left side of her face framed by the rich brown strands of her hair. He felt fresh guilt for the trouble he'd caused. She pulled away and moved to a spot a few feet away from him.

"Let's get some sleep," she said, curling up on the forest floor.

Exhaustion was starting to settle in, and Lex looked forlornly into the forest, watching the dark shapes of leaves rustle in the dark. His eyes drooped and he stretched out. The comforting scent of the forest enveloped Lex as he drifted away.

…

When Val woke the next morning, she stretched out, sliding her arms over the slippery coolness of her sleeping bag. As she blinked, groggily clearing the sleep from her eyes, she realized she was still alone in the tent. Lyla and Lex hadn't returned. Val leaned forward, rubbing her temples. She'd used a blood claim yesterday, and the memory sent a chill down her spine. She felt the tether binding her wolf to Christopher somewhere outside. She paused. *Binding just my wolf... or me?*

Val unzipped the tent door and stepped out into the morning air. A light fog was spreading through the trees. She looked around the campsite. The remains of the fire that she and Christopher had built the night before was long dead, a charred and crumbled pile of ash in the ring of rocks. She trudged over to the boys' tent and leaned close to the door. All the windows were zipped shut.

"Christopher?"

No response there either. She called his name again, a little louder. A branch cracked behind her, and she whirled, settling into a defensive crouch. Christopher stood at the edge of the campsite, holding his hands up in mock surrender.

"Just me." He was carrying his notebook. "I went down to the stream to write for a little while. I had a lot of things to record from yesterday."

Val straightened. "Are you serious?"

He frowned. "Yes."

"You could've died yesterday. You do realize that?" asked Val, incredulous.

Christopher nodded. "I do," he replied. "Writing things down helps me process my thoughts. Makes things feel less overwhelming." He pushed up his glasses, and suddenly the eye contact made Val incredibly uncomfortable.

Val turned on her heel and walked over to the wagon to pull out some food for breakfast. She felt a soft touch on the bond link. Val glanced out to the trees and grabbed two oranges. She tossed one to Christopher.

"You should eat something. They're almost here."

Christopher just held the orange in his hand and shook his head. "Even after all the research I've done and all the things I've read, your bond with Lyla still amazes me. Almost nothing has been written on how it works, what the limitations are. It seems unique to each pair. I'm trying to list the differences between a bond link and a blood claim." He looked up at her and then quickly looked away. "I just want to know what I'm in for, I guess."

Val's fingernail shot through the orange, and juice splattered against her face. She gritted her teeth. "

"I guess so." Val peeled her mangled orange, removing every little string from the juicy slices. "It's always been there. I don't even really think about it. There were other bonds in our pack too. I never asked."

"Can she hear your thoughts?"

Val snorted. "She'd like to think so, but no. Between Lyla and I it's mostly just feelings. But the memories we share are clear." She suddenly realized what Christopher might be getting at. "Oh. I can't hear your thoughts if that's what you're asking."

Christopher nodded, ducking his head back over his notebook. "Okay cool."

Val popped another piece of orange in her mouth, searching for something else to talk about. "Some of the elders in our pack could send clear messages and specific words through a bond link, but it takes decades of practice to be able to do that. My… my mother could do it."

As soon as she brought up her mother, Val wished she hadn't. She didn't want to remember the beautiful, smiling woman who had taught her how to protect others and not to be afraid of the dark.

"There's nothing to be afraid of. The dark holds all of our wishes, all our secrets, and keeps them safe for us."

Gunshots and the sound of screams. Val huddled in the cold cellar beneath the fake floorboards, her arms wrapped protectively around Lyla, who was shivering with fright. And in the midst of the chaos happening above them, the last words of her mother touched her mind with a calm, soft voice.

"I love you, my darlings. Protect each other."

Val picked at her orange, her appetite waning. She never allowed herself to return to the sight that awaited the two terrified children when they finally left their hiding place. All the names and faces held so dear—lifeless, bloodied. And now, it was as if the world had forgotten them and left only Val and Lyla to keep their memory. She could feel Christopher watching her, silent. The constant tug toward him hadn't let up since the blood claim. She focused on the orange.

Val.

The soft suggestion of her name rippled through the bond. She turned around and saw Lyla and Lex approaching from the tree line, figures still veiled slightly by the dissipating fog. She gave a slight shake of her head at her sister's concerned expression. She knew that Lyla had seen the memory as well.

Lex stayed at the edge of the trees, looking anywhere but at Christopher and Val. Lyla leaned in and said something softly enough that only he could hear. Lex nodded and awkwardly stepped closer to Christopher, waiting for the other boy to stand up before he spoke.

"Christopher, I'm so sorry. Are you okay?"

The older boy held out his hand immediately. "I accept your apology. I know it wasn't your fault, Lex." They shook hands. "I'm okay. Just give me a head's up next time, yeah?"

Val passed out fruit and granola packets as they all sat down on the logs. Christopher tapped his chin thoughtfully with his pencil and then pushed his glasses up farther on his nose. "I don't understand why you phased in the first place. Did you forget to take your suppressant?"

"That's the strange thing," replied Lex. "I did take it. Before we left, I went to the nurse's office and she said they'd run out. She went to the back room and was able to find one in an older crate. I took it right there."

Lyla picked at the granola in her hand. "It should have worked. You've never phased through them before, right?"

Lex shook his head. "Never. The first few times when I was younger, I could feel something strange, like that part of me wanted to come out, but it never did. My parents haven't phased for years. They've lived as Domestics since before I was born."

Surprised, Val stopped chewing and frowned. "How long has the DAO been manufacturing this stuff?"

"Carrington Labs opened officially in 1987, but the government didn't give them much attention until 1998 when all the murders happened, and then the Culling. By that point, Carrington Labs already had developed a prototype of the suppressants and presented it as an alternative," Christopher replied. "That was right before the DAO was founded."

Val crumpled the granola packet in her fist. "Yeah, that sounds just like the posters in the museum. Like they saved the world from monsters."

"The suppressant should have worked," continued Christopher. "Maybe there's something to the idea that Truebloods can influence other Weres—make their phasing more prominent."

Anger tingled through Val's body, and she gritted her teeth. "So, you do believe all the garbage they're spreading? I suppose you'll suggest that I tried to alpha him into phasing next."

The other three watched her with concern. Val felt Lyla's tentative touch through their bond, but she pushed back forcefully. "Don't, Lyla. I don't want you in my head right now."

"Val, it's going to be okay. None of this is our fault."

The redhead glared at her. "No, it's not, but I'm not an idiot either. We're always the scapegoat, Lyla. They're going to find some way to twist this so that Lex gets off scot-free and we get the blame."

Lyla's tone lowered warningly. "Val. That's not fair."

"No, you're right. It isn't fair. Lex phased during a full moon. It's the most natural thing in the world. And I put a blood claim on Christopher because it's the only thing I could do to save his life. But somehow, they're going to blame us. Who knows if they'll ever let us out after this."

Christopher looked remorseful. "I'm sorry, Val, I didn't mean it like that. I was just trying to think of what could've happened. Both Lex and I can tell our side of the story if it comes to that."

Suddenly, Val shook her finger at them, eyes brightening. "We don't have to tell them anything. No one would know if none of us tell. It'll be like it never happened!"

They were all silent for a minute. Val noticed that Christopher shifted uncomfortably in his seat, avoiding her gaze. She frowned.

Christopher sighed. "I called my dad this morning. He knows."

The three Weres stared at him. Val stepped forward. "You did *what?*"

"Look, Val, yesterday was… I was a little shaken up," admitted Christopher. "My dad just wants to know what happened. I told him that everyone is okay, and the danger is past. He's coming to get us soon."

Val seethed. "It's so easy for you, isn't it? Do you realize what they could do if they find out that I used a blood claim? I've told you what happens in that laboratory."

"Everyone, calm down," said Lyla sternly. "Lex, this concerns you as well. When the report is filed, you'll most likely be taken in for some basic testing."

The beta's face paled. "I didn't even think of that."

Val chuckled humorlessly. "What's the matter, Lex? Scared of some DAO tests?"

Lyla shot her a dark look. "Val, stop it. We're all in this together, and if we are calm and honest about what happened, they're not going to do anything drastic."

"And if you're wrong? What are you willing to gamble?" challenged Val. The atmosphere shifted, and the uncomfortable intensity between Val and Lyla grew. Their gazes stayed locked, silent. Val's rigid posture and aggressive expression radiated her alpha rank. Lyla was calm, relaxed. Except for her eyes.

Val suddenly relaxed and dropped her gaze, looking away from her sister. She saw the shock on Christopher's face, and pursed her lips. *Better that you don't know some things yet.* As soon as the tension eased, Lyla turned back to the boys. "Look, the suppressant was probably expired. If we keep our heads about this, it'll be fine. Val, why don't you go for a walk and cool off."

Val nodded, looking tired. "Yeah."

Christopher stood up and walked over to his tent. "I think I'm going to take a nap for a little while. My dad should be here in about an hour."

As soon as she and Lex were alone, Lyla leaned forward and rested her head in her hands. She was still tired, and her body ached from the exertion of the fight with Lex the day before. She focused on breathing deeply, taking in as much of the forest as she could. Who knew how long it would be until she and Val could return to a place like this?

Her mind was already formulating a plan for the coming days. First, a conversation with Christopher's parents, and then with Cormoran, both posing their own difficulties.

"You know, you really should open up more," Lex remarked. He hadn't moved from his log seat. "You spend a lot of time fixing other people's problems, and I owe you one after you kept me from turning Christopher into a gravestone yesterday."

"What do you want to know?"

He chuckled. "Not exactly what I had in mind." He stretched his arms and turned, cracking his back. "I don't know, tell me something that no one else knows about you." He paused. "Or something only Val knows."

He's so strange. Even with that thought, Lyla realized that Lex deserved at least something, since he'd been suddenly dropped into a world he wasn't supposed to be in. Lyla pondered, sifting through her options. "My real name isn't Lyla. When we were born, both Val and I were given wolf names by our parents. The DAO chose new names for us when we came into the program," she said. "Wolf names don't exactly fit their Domestic image."

Lex looked like he wanted to say something else, but he finally asked, "What is your real name?"

It had been so long since it had passed her lips. Even Val rarely called her by that name now. It was hard for both of them, too close of a reminder of their family and their beloved home.

"Arka."

Lex looked out into the trees. "Arka. That's a beautiful name." He swallowed. "It's really nice, I mean. My parents just named me Alexander."

Crunching leaves from the tree line heralded Val's return. As her sister's figure approached, Lyla glanced at Lex. "Just don't go calling me that in front of anyone."

"Scout's honor."

She eyed him with a smile. "Wolf's honor means more."

Lex laughed. "Fair enough. Wolf's honor, then."

Val gave them both a skeptical look as she began pulling out the tent stakes. Lyla got up to help her, unzipping the door and pulling their sleeping bags out. Lex stood up and sauntered over to the wagon to pack up the rest of their supplies.

"So, Val," he ventured.

"Yeah?"

"What's your wolf name?"

She straightened up in surprise, and Lyla gave a slight nod. Val went back to the tent stakes, pulling them out with a sharp yank. "Sanzi. But if you call me that, I'll serve you on a plate."

CHAPTER EIGHTEEN

Mr. Wells hadn't asked them any questions the whole car ride back, and now he simply arranged them all in chairs in his office so they could talk. Lyla felt as if she carried the world on her shoulders as she took her seat. They'd all agreed that she would be the spokesperson for the group, with Christopher supplying extra information.

As she looked across at Mr. Wells, and then at the face of his wife— obviously worried, —next to him, Lyla swallowed. She explained the events of the previous day thoroughly, leaving out no details except the conversation she'd had with Lex out on their hunt. Mr. Wells listened to the entire story without interrupting, his hands folded in his lap. When Lyla was finished, he nodded solemnly and gestured to Val and Lex.

"Do you both attest to the truth of this?"

They nodded. Lex was rubbing the palms of his hands together and making a careful study of the carpet. "Yes sir. I'm really, really sorry. I had no idea it was going to happen."

"I believe you," replied Mr. Wells. He tapped his finger against a stack of papers on the desk. Lyla saw the phrase 'Host Family Policies' on one of them. "My immediate concern is the injuries that were sustained during this event. I think a trip to the hospital might be in order."

"Mr. Wells, we are all right. We heal faster than humans, and most hospitals aren't trained to handle our kind," Lyla said. Her fingers subconsciously found her shoulder, feeling the puncture wounds left behind by Lex's fangs. They had already begun to knit together, and the pain was much less than it had been the day before. They would be fully healed in the next day or two.

Mr. Wells didn't look particularly pleased by the idea, but he turned to his son. "Christopher, we will need to take you in to have you looked over. You said your arm was healed by Val's blood?"

Christopher flushed subtly beneath his glasses. "Um, yes. The healing properties of werewolf blood work very quickly on human subjects, even faster than on themselves. It's really fascinating."

Lyla didn't miss the way that Mrs. Wells shifted in her chair, looking uncomfortable. Lyla couldn't blame her. At the DAO center, they'd been told over and over again that things that might be normal to Weres were horribly barbaric to humans.

"And Val, please tell me more about this… *blood claim* you placed on my son."

Now it was Val's turn to blush, and her face went completely red. "I saw my father do it once. It, uh, it tells other Weres that he's under my protection."

"Permanently?"

Val looked down. "Yes. I didn't know how else to keep him alive. My alpha command didn't work on Lex because of the suppressant. I'm really sorry. I promise that it won't cause any problems."

Mr. Wells sat back in his chair, shuffling through the papers in front of him. "I put in a call to Ms. Cormoran this morning," he said. Lyla's face fell, and he noticed. "I have reassured her that we have things under control. You'll be going back to the school tomorrow morning, and Ms. Cormoran will meet you there. There are people investigating the crate of suppressants in question. From what I've been told, the situation may not negatively reflect on you since the circumstances were out of your control. Lex, your parents have been notified and you will have to go through a basic set of tests now that you have phased."

Val eyed him suspiciously. "Mr. Wells, do you mind me asking what exactly it is that you do?"

He smiled. "I am a private investigator and consultant for the government."

Lyla wondered just how much Mr. Wells knew about their situation and how much he was keeping to himself. He looked at each of them in turn.

"I do think we will be invoking house order to rest for the remainder of the day. Lex, I'm sure your parents would appreciate a phone call." Lex nodded, leaving the room while pulling his phone from his pocket. Mr. Wells turned to his son. "Christopher, would you give us a moment, please?"

The door clicked shut behind the two boys. Mrs. Wells excused herself after them. Lyla braced herself. *Here comes the real reaction,* she thought.

"I want to express my deepest gratitude to you for saving my son's life," said Mr. Wells seriously. "You both acted selflessly and bravely, and I think that shows a greatness of character."

Neither of the sisters knew what to say. Lyla felt Val's surprise mirroring her own through the bond. Lyla found her voice. "Thank you, sir. When we were in our pack," her voice faltered on the word. "We protected each other."

"Then you've done them proud," said Mr. Wells with a kind smile. He reached out across the desk, holding out a small piece of paper. "This is my card. If the two of you ever need someone in your corner, give me a call. I expect that Ms. Cormoran will have much more to say."

Lyla took the card and slid it into her pocket. Val leaned forward onto her knees. "Mr. Wells, I didn't expect you to understand."

He smiled. "I can assure you that I will be taking measures to make sure that a repeat of yesterday never happens on my property. I was made aware of the risks when we applied to be an Assimilation Host Family. Christopher was under strict instructions to call me every few hours to let me know how things were going. Though I must admit that I was not expecting the danger to come from Lex."

"We were told that we wouldn't qualify to stay with a human host family," said Lyla, suddenly curious.

Mr. Wells nodded. "Christopher convinced me to press Ms. Cormoran for the opportunity. She wasn't terribly keen on the idea at first, but we were able to persuade her. Here, you can look at the guidelines if you like."

Val took the folder from Mr. Wells and held it between them so Lyla could see. Lyla saw her sister's fingers pause over the header labeled *Compensation and Benefits*. After a moment, Val handed the papers back.

"Well, thank you for giving us a chance, Mr. Wells."

"Of course. Please get some rest; I'm sure you're both tired."

They left the office and trudged up to their bedroom. Lyla pulled off her socks and hoodie and climbed into the bed. The last two days had finally caught up with her, and she wasn't sure she'd ever felt so heavy. Val glanced at Lyla's shoulder.

"You sure that's okay?"

Lyla tenderly probed the healing flesh with her finger. "Give me a day or two and ask me again. I forgot how sharp our fangs are."

Val grinned. "Sorry. Good battle scars, though." The bed dipped as she climbed in next to Lyla. "What do you think they're going to do about this?"

Closing her eyes, Lyla burrowed her face into the pillow. "I wish I knew."

. . .

Christopher rolled over beneath the cocoon of blankets he was wrapped in, restless as he wavered between sleep and half-awareness. He stopped precariously close to the edge of his bed, and a sound from outside his room pulled at his consciousness. He struggled to open his heavy eyelids. He heard the sound again, and his sleep-muddled brain registered that it was a cry of pain. It was enough to jog him awake, and he reached for his glasses.

Stumbling out into the hallway, he ran into his parents, who had haphazardly thrown robes on over their pajamas. The cry came from Val and Lyla's room. Christopher frowned, immediately nervous as he tried to figure out if one of them might be phasing again. Unlikely. Then he remembered Val's panic attack on the trail. Overwrought with worry, he was about to reach for the doorknob when his father caught his wrist. Shaking his head slightly, Mr. Wells lifted his hand to knock. Christopher swallowed. He should've thought that through.

Before his father's hand could knock against the door, they heard Val's voice. It was still heavy with sleep, but frantic.

"Please let me go! Please let me go! I can't do it anymore…" a soft, despairing moan accompanied the words. Lyla's response was harder to hear.

"…not there… safe… five things you can see."

Christopher's mother placed a hand over her mouth. "Oh, honey," she whispered through her fingers.

Christopher's heart twisted at the broken sound of Val's voice as she tried to ground herself from whatever terrors were chasing her. The voices inside the room grew even quieter, and Christopher could no longer make out the words. Then silence.

His father pulled at his elbow. "I think they'll be all right."

Christopher didn't want to leave the door, but he felt his father put a hand on his shoulder and squeeze. "They know where to find us, son."

Christopher nodded. He whispered goodnight before returning to his room. He let himself fall back onto the bed and stared up at the ceiling. He'd never spoken a word of the story he'd been told that day on the trail bench. He'd even managed to keep the worst of the secrets from his father, which was no small feat, especially when Mr. Wells had questions of his own about the DAO's operations. After what they'd just heard, he was sure that those questions would be even more present. He sighed and rolled over onto his side, watching the blinking red numbers on his alarm clock.

As soon as they all came down for breakfast the next morning, Christopher could tell that something wasn't right. Val wouldn't meet his gaze throughout the entire meal. He jumped up to ask them if they needed help bringing down their bags, but Lyla just shrugged and said they were fine. Whatever had happened the previous night seemed to have put Val in a somber mood, and Christopher decided to take the route of chivalry and give the lady her space. But this resolution only lasted until they began to pack up the car, and his imagined chivalry gave way to concern.

He dragged his backpack and overnight bag down the stairs, jogging a little faster when he noticed that Val was just ahead of him. Out onto the driveway, his feet crunched over the gravel as he hurried to catch up with her.

"Val are you… is everything okay?" he asked her, pushing past his nerves. She dropped her bag next to the trunk of the car. She didn't meet his eyes.

"I'm fine. I'm just ready to go back."

Christopher didn't buy that for a minute. "Did you, um, have a good time? I know the camping trip didn't quite follow the agenda I had, but—"

"Why are you doing this?" Her eyes rose to his.

He stared at her, backpack still in his hand. There was a strange edge to her voice, and he found himself desperately wishing that all his observation and notes had prepared him to decipher the way she was looking at him. He'd seen her anger, her skepticism, and her pain. But this was different.

"Doing what?"

She rubbed her palm over her neck. "Whatever it is you're doing."

… that's helpful. Christopher tried to sift through his memories of the past couple of days to figure out if there was something he missed. "I'm not sure what you mean. Did I say something wrong?"

Val kicked a few rocks down the driveway. "I know that your family is getting paid a lot of money to host us." She looked visibly tense, searching for words. "Do you really want to be my friend, or is this still an experiment?"

Christopher thought over his next words very carefully. At first, he considered saying, "Every friendship is an experiment of sorts," because it sounded philosophical. But something told him that wasn't what Val was looking for just then. Her red hair cascaded down across one side of her face, offset by new, tight braids running down the other. He noticed that she had put two silver beads in each braid. She hadn't done that for a while. Christopher pushed his glasses up, palms sweating.

"I want to be your friend." As soon as the words left him, he felt their weight, realizing how much he truly did want to be there, standing outside his house in front of her. He was still trying to convince himself that the fragile girl he'd seen strapped to a gurney was the same as the strong, vibrant redhead in front of him now. She'd haunted him since the moment he saw her.

"Why?"

Her blunt question shouldn't have surprised him. And the multitude of answers that he could've said were things that he could not bring himself to say out loud. Her hand was resting on the top of the car trunk within easy reach of his own. He kept his arms at his sides.

"I just figured you needed one."

Faint spots of color rose in her cheeks. She opened the trunk and pushed her bag inside. "Okay," she said, shoulders straight. "I'll get the rest of the bags."

She walked back to the house, leaving Christopher to slump against the side of the car. He pulled at his hair. If he were braver, he would run after her and tell her the rest. He would tell her that he had needed a friend too. He would tell her how long he had wanted to be her friend, to learn everything about her. But he wasn't that kind of person, and suddenly, he despised himself for it.

...

Val sent a text message to Jules as soon as they arrived back on the school grounds. She and Christopher hadn't said much on the way home, leaving Lex to strike up a mostly one-sided conversation with Lyla about old action movies. Val had to give him kudos for trying. Part of her was still skeptical, still trying to convince her that Christopher was only her friend because the DAO was paying his family. But the rest of her knew better, and that made her feelings all the more confusing. Val's phone buzzed.

Pushing the door to their room open, Val only had a brief moment to frown in confusion over the text message before a smaller body wrapped around her in a bear hug. She grunted from the impact as Jules's beaming smile flashed up at her. The omega disentangled herself and then continued her attack with a hug for Lyla. Val dropped her bag.

"How did you get in?"

Jules's smile seemed permanently fixed in place. "I might have bribed the dorm manager with cookies," she said with a wink. "Or I might still have Val's spare key from when you guys came for your sleepover. Pick one."

"Slightly creepy, Jules."

The omega rolled her eyes and fixed her scarf. "I haven't seen you guys forever, and now you're calling me creepy? Thanks, Val."

Lyla carefully maneuvered herself into the dorm room, slipping past the other two who were creating a roadblock. "Good to see you too, Jules."

"See? Someone in this dorm room has manners," approved Jules. "Now, you have to tell me everything that happened over break! My grandparents bought me the cutest sweater, and my aunts argued over skin care products. I got to bake gingersnap cookies with my Gran. Her recipe is the best ever." Jules dropped down into one of the chairs.

"Tell me everything. Are the romances blossoming?"

Lyla joined them. "Jules, seriously stop with that."

"Fine," Jules relented. "But did you have a good time? I was so jealous; you got to enjoy the delights of camping in a forest while I was stuck in Florida. I didn't get a single text!"

The two sisters shared a glance, and neither of them had anything to say. Val had intentionally avoided texting Jules after letting her know that they'd arrived at their destination. When everything had happened with Lex, she'd ignored her phone until they'd begun the drive back to school.

"Okay, I can tell something is up. Spill the beans, sisters." Jules looked between them, waiting for the explanation.

Val leaned her head back against the arm of the chair. "Lex phased. There was something wrong with the suppressant he took."

Silence fell over the room as Jules stared at them. "He what?" she managed after a minute. "How… what happened?"

Val didn't really want to recount the story, but she managed to give Jules the stripped-down version, including some of the discussion with Mr. Wells afterwards. Jules leaned back against the chair, back slouched.

"Wow. I don't even know what to say. Is Christopher okay?"

Lyla nodded. "Yeah, he was a little shaken up, but he's fine."

"I didn't even know that you could do something like a blood claim," said Jules. "Things just keep getting crazier with you two. At least the semester is almost over. Only three weeks until winter break."

Val didn't want to think about winter break. "Christmas at the DAO center is always a riot."

Jules chuckled. "Really?"

"Our therapist gave us self-help books last year. Wrapped them in some snowflake paper and everything," Lyla replied. "But one of the other Truebloods got ahold of some fancy chocolate bars and put them in everyone's stockings."

Jules frowned. "You know the other Truebloods?"

"We weren't allowed to be together without strict supervision," Lyla replied. "But we met for activities sometimes. Why?"

Brows furrowed, Jules licked her lips. "When I was at home, Mom and Dad told me that things are getting a little tense about the Truebloods. Some of the assimilation schools have requested extra security as a precaution. People are actually afraid of some kind of takeover. They showed me some of the newspaper articles that have been going around, talking about the Trueblood students that were sent to each school and wondering what the DAO is going to do to keep things under control." Jules shook her head. "At least we got you two!"

Val rubbed her temples. "Not sure that's a bragging right, short stack."

"Whatever. Look, I didn't want to tell you to make you worried, but I just thought you should know what's going on. You two rest, okay? I'll see you tomorrow for class." Jules headed for the door, swinging her chunky pink scarf around her neck. "Try to stay out of trouble at least that long." Throwing them both a kiss, she closed the door.

CHAPTER NINETEEN

Lex jogged down the steps from Gibbous Hall head down and fists clenched at his sides. Several students moved quickly out of his way. He went to the edge of the campus lawn and sat down on the ground, jerking his backpack off, and letting it slowly fall over next to him. He ran his fingers through his hair and pulled at it, leaning his elbows on his thighs.

Lex had always been well-liked. He was easy to get along with. He'd always had a group of friends. He enjoyed being the life of the party, making people smile and laugh. One wrong syringe had brought it all crumbling down around him, and for the three days since he'd been back at school, it had been a nightmare.

When he looked up, he saw Val coming across the lawn. She sat down a few feet to his left on the grass and folded her legs underneath her. "Hey."

"Hi."

"Jules sent me to tell you not to pay the losers any mind. Her exact quote," said Val. Lex chuckled, and pulled up a blade of grass, twisting it around his fingers. Val copied him.

"You look like you need to get something off your chest," she said. "You've been off the last few days. Even Lyla is worried."

Lex looked up. "Really?"

"Yeah, but don't tell her I said that." Val grinned. "So, what's eating you?"

It was the same question Lex had been asking himself all morning. "I don't know. I guess I just keep going over and over everything in my head and none of it makes sense. I know it happened, but it's like I'm in the wrong place now. You know what I mean?"

Val didn't respond. Lex turned back to the blade of grass. It snapped in half. He looked up, trying to gather his thoughts. Val leaned back, supporting herself on her elbows and crossing her ankles. She squinted up at the bright fall sky.

"It's the way they look at you. The way that you're trying to convince yourself that somehow the fact that you phased, and it wasn't your fault, makes sense with the way they're treating you. And now it feels like the world is a place that doesn't want you to be in it." She glanced at him. "Am I close?"

"Something like that."

"What happened? You left class in a hurry."

Lex grunted, pulling up more grass. "Everyone got an email this morning updating my status as a non-Domestic. If they didn't know before, they all do now."

"And what do they know?" asked Val.

"That I phased. That I'm now taking a higher suppressant dose to keep everyone safe." Lex tossed the blades of grass at the ground. "Didn't you get the email?"

Val shrugged. "Yeah, I saw it. Some of them are even saying it was because you were with us. It's kind of funny, the way they act like we're something they aren't. Most of them are werewolves. They just don't want to admit it. But we can't change what we are. We just have to make the best of it."

"It doesn't bother you?"

She smiled a little. "Of course it does. There are a lot of things I wish I could change. But at the end of the day, I'm a Trueblood alpha. I have to own that."

Lex nodded. "Do you ever wish you weren't?"

"No. Never." Her serious tone changed. "If I weren't what I am, what would Jackson do with himself? He wouldn't have anyone to yell 'feral' at in the hallway."

Lex knew she was trying to lighten the mood, but there were a lot of things in his mind, and Jackson was one of them. He'd been at the receiving end of the slur earlier that morning. Hearing the word 'feral' directed at him had been a blow he hadn't realized would hit him so hard.

"He used to be my friend."

Val's eyebrows went up. "You and Jackson? What happened?"

"We've been in the same school for years. I don't know, he just started to change. Started pushing people around, acting like he was better than them. He wouldn't talk to anyone who wasn't at least a beta."

"Well, his loss," said Val, punching him lightly on the shoulder. "He's just full of hot air."

Lex shook his head. "He's smarter than you think, Val. I don't know why he's got it out for you and Lyla, but he's not someone you want to mess around with."

"I can handle Jackson," reassured Val. She stood up, brushing off the back of her pants. "Come on, let's go play a game or something. I'll text Jules. She's got chocolate drizzle popcorn." She hoisted her backpack up to her shoulder and walked off. Lex watched her move confidently through the students on the lawn toward the dorm building. They all moved away from her, avoiding her gaze, but she didn't seem to notice them. She held her chin high.

Lex rose from the ground. This would get easier. He nodded to himself. This would get easier.

…

Christopher loved autumn. The smells, the colors, the slight chill in the air that could be held back by a good trench coat and scarf—all of it. He stopped in the middle of the trail to pick up a perfect golden leaf and twirled it in his fingers. The late evening sky was still flooding warm hues across the campus as the sun retreated. Christopher sighed, content, his mind slowly working through the details of the social studies paper he was turning in the next day.

The trail was quiet, and Christopher enjoyed the peace. It wasn't hard to find it if you knew where to look, even on their relatively small school grounds. But even on the empty trail at the edge of the campus, Christopher found his thoughts trailing after him. Most of them centered on a certain red-haired Trueblood alpha.

Christopher frowned. She'd kept her promise and hadn't said a word about the blood claim since they'd come back to school. But while Lex's new status had been broadcast to the other students by way of a politely worded note from the principal, Christopher's was literally written in his skin. He and Val were now inextricably linked, whether they wanted to be or not. If his previous association with the Truebloods wasn't enough to condemn him, the blood claim had assured his exile from the good graces of his peers. Christopher had considered talking to Lex about it, but he wasn't sure how. He knew that Lex was dealing with his own concerns, and he wasn't sure if the beta considered them good enough friends to discuss their emotions.

Christopher heard footsteps behind him, and moved to one side of the trail courteously, waiting for the other person to pass him. But to his surprise, a strong arm descended over his shoulders, and he found himself walking stride for stride with Jackson.

"Christopher Wells. Let's go for a walk," the alpha said. He sounded cheerful, but the hair on Christopher's arms prickled. He tried to move away, but Jackson kept a firm grip on his shoulders, walking them further down the trail.

"I have to admit, I knew you were in trouble when you decided to take their side, but I can't believe you actually let her mark you. How does it feel to be a Trueblood's pet?"

Christopher bristled despite himself. "It's not like that."

Jackson leaned in and inhaled right by Christopher's ear. "You can't lie to me, Wells. I can smell her all over you. Are you helping her? What is she planning?"

Suppressing the shudder that went down his spine, Christopher pushed away again, and this time was able to remove himself from beneath Jackson's arm. He glanced down the trail but saw no one. The trees were thickest here, and he could barely see the buildings. He held up his hand.

"I need to get back."

"Is she calling you? I bet she can feel me threatening you right now," Jackson sneered. "I know they're up to something. They're dangerous, you know that, right?"

Christopher met his gaze. "Right now, I'm not concerned about Val and Lyla."

Jackson grabbed the front of Christopher's trench coat, pulling him in close. Christopher saw a flash of red through the alpha's eyes. He looked away.

"Yeah? Well you should be," replied Jackson. "But let me guess, she told you that she's protecting you now with this blood claim, right? That she'll come running if you're in danger? Don't be stupid. Every single werewolf in this school knows who you belong to now, Wells. But you picked the wrong side."

"Jackson, let me go," said Christopher, still looking down at the asphalt. "This isn't about sides."

"Yeah? When your Trueblood girlfriend murders half the school, are you still going to be singing that tune?"

"She's not like that—"

Jackson shoved him, hard, and Christopher felt his hip bruise as it connected with the trail. He rolled to the side and was about to sit up when he felt a heavy boot press down on his chest. Jackson pointed at him.

"You're going to tell me what they talk about. What are they planning?"

Christopher struggled to breathe around the weight Jackson was putting on his chest, shaking his head. "You won't believe me. Why are you doing this?"

"Because I need to find a reason to get them locked up, and you're going to help me," Jackson said, voice low.

A twig snapped, and a dark shape barreled into Jackson from behind, knocking him off of Christopher and down to the ground. Christopher sucked in a deep breath and sat up. Jackson was rolling to his feet, and Val stood between them, body rigid, every inch of her radiating authority. Christopher pulled himself up quickly.

"Val, it's okay."

Jackson laughed. "I wondered when you were going to show up. What are you going to do? You going to attack me?"

Val growled. "Get away from him." The words sounded strangled, as if she were forcing her voice to cooperate. "I'm sure Principal Bleiz would love to hear about this."

Jackson shook his head. "He's not on your side, feral. You've got no proof of anything. Just my word against yours. Wouldn't the principal love to hear how you attacked me because you were jealous over a human you claimed?"

"You're a liar."

He took a step forward. "You can't be with him all the time, feral. If I have to use him to get to you, I will."

Christopher felt his stomach drop, and he saw the change in Val's eyes. He knew without a doubt that if Jackson threatened him again, Val would retaliate. But this time, they weren't hidden away in a forest, and this wasn't an accident. And Jackson knew it.

"It would be so easy to make it look like you did it," Jackson said.

A snarl, and Val moved forward faster than a snake. Her fists stayed at her sides, but she pushed into Jackson, their foreheads touching as he gave way, stepping backwards. Val kept pace with him, staying right on him as he tried to back away. Christopher found himself walking forward, reaching out.

"Val!"

His hand touched her shoulder, and she flinched. But she didn't move from her quarry. Jackson held his ground as much as he could, eyes dark with anger. Val kept her face inches from his.

"If you hurt him, I don't care who is in my way."

She turned and took hold of Christopher's wrist, walking away down the trail. Christopher kept up with her long strides and didn't say anything. He could feel the fury in her, the barely contained power threatening to burst free. He'd seen it before. He remembered the sight of her in the forest as she'd stood between him and Lex. He was beginning to wonder if the strongest suppressant in the world would be enough to stop her if Jackson followed through on his threat. The blood claim increased Val's protectiveness exponentially. He found himself wondering if she would have reacted the same way without it.

There were too many thoughts circling through Christopher's mind for him to understand what he was feeling. As he let Val lead him toward the buildings, he replayed the scene over and over and over again. Why was Jackson so fixated on the idea that Val and Lyla were planning something? Had the fear of the Truebloods taking control of the Were population truly spread so deeply? Or was it personal?

His thoughts were slowly drained away by the sensation that was quickly overpowering the rest: the feel of Val's grip on his wrist. He saw the tension that had never left her shoulders, the tight new braids lacing across the left side of her head, disappearing beneath the waterfall of red hair that dropped below the collar of her jacket. He wanted to say something. Anything.

The blood claim wasn't the only thing linking them together anymore. The feeling that had been growing in his chest for the past few months had a name, and he suddenly knew without a doubt that he would do anything for her. He turned his hand and entwined their fingers. He wasn't sure if she noticed or not, but she didn't pull away.

. . .

"Val's not here," Lyla said. She dropped her book on the bed, glancing over at Jules and Lex, who were sitting on opposite ends of the futon, textbooks open. Jules frowned.

"She came down but then she left again. She told me she'd be right back, but I'm starting to wonder if something is wrong," the omega said, rubbing her hands together. "She seemed kind of upset when she left."

Concerned, Lyla turned to reach for the door, and it nearly hit her in the face as it was pushed open from the other side. Her sister came rushing into the room with Christopher in tow. Val's face was drawn and angry. Lyla immediately chided herself. When she'd felt the bond go quiet a little earlier, she should've known that something was up. Nothing good ever happened when Val went silent. Lyla quickly scanned them both, but they looked unharmed. Christopher's face was flushed.

"What happened?" Lyla asked, grabbing hold of her sister's shoulder to slow her down. Val turned to her, eyes still flecked with violet. Her whole body was trembling.

"Jackson threatened Christopher. He's trying to get to me, I need to go find him. You stay with Christopher and keep him safe, I'll –"

Lyla shook her head. "Not a chance. You're not going anywhere like this. Take a breath and tell me what happened."

As Val caught her breath, Lyla's attention dropped to where her sister's hand was still interlaced with Christopher's. Avoiding Lyla's raised eyebrows, Christopher gently disengaged his hand from Val's, unlacing their fingers, and then answered for her.

"Jackson found me on the trail. He thinks you and Val are planning some kind of violence against the other students. But it doesn't make any sense. Lyla, I don't think he would go this far without something driving him. He knows about the blood claim, and he's trying to use me to provoke Val." He pushed his glasses up on his nose. "She didn't hurt him."

Lyla raked her fingers through her hair. Every time she didn't think that Jackson could push his luck any farther, he managed to find a way. She was honestly amazed that Val had been able to control herself considering her protective instincts were heightened to a frenzy when it came to Christopher, thanks to the blood claim. Jules went to Val and wrapped her arms around the tense alpha. Lex stood up behind her.

"You okay, man?" he asked Christopher. The taller boy nodded but didn't take his eyes off of Val. Lyla noted the deep concern written on his face, his brow furrowed as he stayed within arm's reach of her sister.

"Lyla, he said he could make it look like I... if Christopher got attacked..." Val swallowed the rest of her words and looked at the wall. Jules squeezed her tighter.

Lyla nodded. It was time for answers. "I'm going to go talk to him." She held up her hand when Val moved to come with her. "No. You're going to stay here. Lex, don't let her leave."

With a wide grin, Lex patted Val's shoulder. She glowered at him. Satisfied that her sister and Christopher were in good hands, Lyla turned to leave, but Lex stepped out of the room behind her, gently closing the door behind them. "Lyla."

"Yeah?"

"You sure you don't want me to come with you? You might need a wingman."

She sighed. "No, I need you to stay here with Val. I need to know she won't come after me. I'll be fine."

He searched her face, his cheerful grin gone. "Be careful."

Lyla found Jackson leaning against the side of Gibbous Hall, hands shoved into his pockets. His eyes glittered as she approached, and he flashed her a smile. Lyla glanced at their surroundings. She didn't put it past him to have some of his alpha friends with him. He had to have known that Val wouldn't let him off so easily.

"Two Blackwood sisters coming after me in one day. What an honor," he drawled.

Lyla calmly stepped up to the side of the building and leaned against it a couple feet away from him. "I'm not in the mood for that, Jackson. We need to talk."

He chuckled. "So, the feral one sends you out to fight her battles for her? Not surprising, with that cool head of yours. Your sister is a ticking time bomb."

Now Lyla was really starting to hand it to Val for keeping her temper in check as long as she had. She sorted through how she wanted the conversation to go. *Find out what he's up to. Get in, get the information, get out. Don't let him under your skin.*

"I'm not here for her sake. I'm here for yours."

"Oh, I'm sure. Half the student body is waiting for her to turn on them in the hallway. Your little pack is really gaining a reputation. Never thought you'd turn Lex, though. Didn't think he had it in him. Guess there really is something to that Trueblood control."

"Why do you care so much about Val and I being here?" she asked calmly. "There's obviously something going on."

"You're not good for the school," replied Jackson easily, as if he'd rehearsed it. His tone betrayed him, and it was clear that he didn't believe in the words any more than Lyla did.

"I don't buy that," she said. "If you really cared about the school and the students in it, then you wouldn't have cornered Christopher."

"He's not one of us anymore, he's with her. I don't owe him anything." Jackson settled farther back against the brick. "He's no better than that omega that hangs around with you."

Lyla bit back her initial response to that comment, and instead studied Jackson. She didn't know that much about him except for the tough exterior that he wore like armor. It suddenly surprised her how many similarities he had to Val. What was beneath the armor? Lyla reached into the vault of memories of their meetings with Cormoran and how she always tried to draw out Val's fears.

"Is it because you're not the highest-ranking alpha? Are you afraid of being seen as weak?"

Jackson's attention snapped back to her, angry. "You think this is just about me? This school has security measures to handle Weres like your sister. Did you know that? One call from Principal Bleiz, and your sister is back in her lab rat cell."

Lyla blinked, shocked. *Cell... how could he know that?* Noticing her reaction, a slow smile spread over Jackson's face again as the conversation's upper hand passed back to him.

"I hear she's pretty allergic to silver." He leaned toward her. "I also hear they fixed the results of her safety test to bring her here. Is that true?"

"Your sister is a special case, Lyla. Her alpha behaviors are difficult to suppress, and we are not confident in her ability to control her instincts. She is much safer here for the moment."

"She didn't pass the control test, did she?"

"No."

If Jackson was asking her if it was true, then he didn't know. Her sister's test results were still only hearsay. Lyla locked eyes with him, anger overtaking her initial fear. "What do you know?"

"I know quite a bit about you," he taunted easily. "And wouldn't you love to hear it all?"

Lyla eased herself away from the side of the building. "I would. And you're going to tell me."

He eyed her. "Oh really?" He moved to stand closer to her, tense and waiting. "Not likely, sweetheart. You may be a

Trueblood, but you're a beta. Why don't you go get your sister? Let her off that short leash."

Lyla swallowed the growl that rose in her throat. She closed the bond. A deep thread of authority rumbled through her voice. "Tell me what you know. All of it. What do you know about me and my sister?"

Jackson blinked as his brain sluggishly registered the command. He shook his head, grunting in surprise as her tone pushed him to reply. Lyla snarled softly.

"Tell me. Now."

His words tumbled out. "Principal Bleiz is trying to find a reason to get you sent back to the center." His jaw tightened. "He wants me to find a way to prove you're dangerous."

"Why?"

"Truebloods aren't safe. He knows you're planning something. And whoever he's working for knows it too," Jackson gritted out, eyes snapping angrily as he glared at the girl in front of him. Lyla held the control in an iron grip, ignoring the flashes of pain as her wolf bound Jackson to her will through the suppressant's hold.

"Why are you helping him? What do you get out of it?"

Agony laced through Jackson's features as he fought the command, and she saw in his eyes that she'd found something behind the armor. He braced himself against the wall. "If I help him, I don't have to go home. I don't have to live with…" the words disappeared into a gasp. "No! Stop."

Lyla frowned, easing back. Whatever she'd found, it was personal, and she saw how desperately he didn't want to let her in to that part of him. She left it alone.

"What do you know about Val?"

His shoulders went rigid. "Stop… I don't know… just that they did experiments, something with silver. Principal Bleiz thinks they changed her test results."

The suppressant dragged Lyla's control back into the fog, and she felt her breath leave her in a rush. The strain of holding control over Jackson left her body feeling weak.

He was laughing. It was a hoarse, broken sound. He was leaning on one shoulder, looking as exhausted as she felt. But his eyes locked with hers.

"I can't believe it. All this time."

Lyla's heart began to race as the calm, logical side of her brain began to process what she'd just done, and then she felt bile rise in the back of her throat. She saw satisfaction in Jackson's eyes, and he pointed above her head. Without looking, she knew what was there. The security camera that hung on the corner of the building. She turned to run, but Jackson's voice followed her.

"You're an alpha."

CHAPTER TWENTY

Val. She had to find Val. Lyla stumbled back into the dorm, and the moment she was through Jules' door, she saw Val rising from the futon, arms open as she felt the fear and desperation Lyla was flooding through the bond. Lyla grabbed hold of those arms and felt herself pulled tightly into Val's embrace. She began to shake, and Val sank down to sit on the floor, bringing Lyla with her.

"Lyla, what happened?" asked Jules.

It was too late. Lyla knew that Jackson was already on his way to Principal Bleiz. After months of worrying about Val, Lyla had given them what they needed. She couldn't bring herself to look at Val, whose fingers were gently combing through her hair.

"He knows I'm an alpha."

The fingers froze, and the whole room went silent. Out of the corner of her eye, Lyla saw Lex, and for once, he looked speechless. Val drew back to look at Lyla's face.

"Are you sure?"

"Hold on, you're a what?" interrupted Jules. Her hands paused halfway through unscrewing a cap from her water bottle. Lyla didn't feel like explaining, and Val stepped in.

"She's an alpha. I suppose if he knows it's only a matter of time before everyone else does too." She sighed, her arms still locked around Lyla. "They tested us both when we first arrived at the DAO center. Lyla's results were inconclusive, so they marked her as a beta. We knew that being a beta would be safer, so we never told them the truth."

Jules sank back on her heels, water bottle forgotten. "That explains a lot."

Lyla finally allowed herself to meet Val's gaze. Her sister's blue eyes were soft, her calm demeanor almost unsettling. "Lyla, what does he know?"

"He knew that you've been," Lyla hesitated. "That we've been experimented on. He knows some things about us that he could only have found out from someone who's read our files. Principal Bleiz is trying to find a reason to have us sent back to the center. It sounds like he's working for someone else. I gave Jackson an alpha command to find out what he knew, and I think it's on the security camera footage."

Val's shoulders slumped, and Lyla felt her careful concealment of her emotions. They'd managed to keep Lyla's true rank a secret for so many years. Lyla's control had served her well, and they'd gotten their chance at freedom because of it. The DAO would never have allowed two Trueblood alphas to stay together, especially outside of the center. Betas were subject to less testing and scrutiny than their hot-blooded, commanding superiors. It had saved her from the level of treatment that Val had endured.

Lyla's mind flooded with the blurred memories she'd seen from Val's perspective, the pain, and the fear. Guilt overwhelmed her. Lyla tried to put up a barrier in the bond.

"Lyla, don't. It's okay," Val said, placing her hands on either side of her sister's face. "You didn't know what they were going to do. It's not your fault. You got us out of there." She smiled, but Lyla could see a shimmer in her eyes. "It's about time you got in trouble for once."

Lex spoke up. "Lyla, what do you mean that you were experimented on?"

The knowledge of the DAO's true nature was a closely guarded secret, and Lyla knew that they'd already put themselves in a dangerous position by letting their friends in as much as they had. She saw Christopher staring at the floor, his hands tightly clasped together. Lyla realized how much she dreaded Lex's eyes being opened to their history. She didn't want him to pity them. To pity her.

"The DAO separated us for a long time after we went through the first round of tests. They did… horrible things to me, and worse to Val. They're not what everyone thinks they are. I don't think I want to say more than that right now." She swallowed. "We're a danger to society, you know."

She saw Jules's eyes fill with tears. The omega sniffed and wiped her eyes impatiently. "I'm so sorry, Lyla. I suspected it was something like that, but I wanted so desperately to be wrong. I can't believe they would do anything like that to you."

Christopher suddenly rose from the futon and went to the window, laying his closed fist against the sill. Val's eyes flickered over to him. Lyla knew that whatever was between them, it was growing into something more than friendship. But whatever it was, it wouldn't be allowed. They couldn't live normal lives. That had ended the moment they'd seen the floorboards cover them in the cabin, heard the sound of werewolves fighting, dying. The moment they'd walked out into a different world. Lyla swallowed, regaining her control.

"It's really important that what we've told you doesn't leave this room," she said quietly. "We're not allowed to talk about our time in the program, and if they found out that we told anyone, we could be locked in a DAO cell for the rest of our lives."

Lex shook his head. "I think I can speak for all of us when I say that we would never do that to you. Is there anything we can do to help?"

"You're the first real friends we've had since our pack," said Val. "I can't tell you how much that has meant to me."

Jules reached out and put her arms around the two sisters, hugging them fiercely. To Lyla's surprise, Lex followed suit, moving down to the floor, and wrapping his arms around them from the other side.

"We're here for you, no matter what," said Jules.

Lyla felt her phone buzz in her pocket, and the two friends sat back, releasing her from the warmth. When Lyla pulled her phone free, her heart dropped. "It's Cormoran." Foolishly, she'd thought they might have more time. *I just want to go home.* The phone rang in her hands. Once. Twice. Three times. She felt Val's fingers brush against her own as the phone was gently removed from her grasp.

…

The first thing that Lyla noticed was how tired Cormoran looked. Her pencil skirt and suit jacket were immaculately ironed, her hair smoothed into its normal bun without a single flyaway hair. But it was in her eyes: a deep weariness as if she'd been up all night. She sat in her chair across from the two girls, clipboard in hand. She adjusted her thin spectacles, daintily balancing her silver pen in her fingers.

"Principal Bleiz called me late last night, but you're both aware of that. There's been an accusation leveled against you, Lyla, that you kept your true rank hidden from the DAO. I'd like to hear your thoughts on that."

Do you actually want to know my thoughts? Lyla sensed Val's confidence through the bond and was grateful that her sister was attempting to give her a boost. She knew that Val would stand by her no matter what.

"I am an alpha. I've known since we started the program." There was no point in denying it, not after she'd given Jackson an alpha command and there was a security camera over the doors to Gibbous Hall.

"And why did you feel the need to keep that information secret from the organization?" asked Cormoran, steady as always.

Val broke in. "If you want honesty, my experience with the DAO as a Trueblood alpha doesn't give you a glowing review," she said, bluntly meeting Cormoran's gaze. "She was safer as a beta."

Already protective, it wouldn't take much for Val to lose her temper. Lyla silently placed a hand on her sister's arm.

"I understand how it might seem that way," Cormoran started. "But remember that our organization has specific policies in place for safety. Betas are not tested as thoroughly as alphas who come through the program, because they do not pose as high of a risk during assimilation. It is important that we are aware of the extent of Lyla's abilities and phasing."

Val tensed beneath Lyla's hand. "If you think I'm going to apologize for the fact that my sister was not subjected to your *safety testing* as thoroughly as I was, you're kidding yourself. Don't act like you don't know what they did to us." Her eyes darkened. "For all I know, you watched it happen."

"Valentine, that's unkind," Cormoran chided. "I answer to the Board, and I have nothing to do with the testing itself. My job is to act as a mentor as you work through the process of assimilation. Lyla, we have to give the situation here some serious thought. The Board is meeting to discuss options. Two Trueblood alpha students in one school is a difficult thing to ask of the principal."

"Yeah, we wouldn't want to make him uncomfortable," retorted Val.

"Valentine."

Val ground her teeth together and looked away. Cormoran tapped her pen against the top of the clipboard. "We have to consider what the best course of action is for everyone involved. Those options include the possibility of separating the two of you and placing you in different schools for the next semester."

Lyla knew that if they reacted too strongly to anything Cormoran said, their chances of actually staying together would drop significantly. She reached through the bond and tried to push Val's rising fury back. Her sister glanced over at her, knowing what she was doing and why, but still struggling to keep her emotions in check.

"Cormoran, I know this may not make a difference in the Board's decision, but during my conversation with Jackson, he also revealed to me that he is aware of our past history to some extent, and that the information was given to him by Principal Bleiz. Principal Bleiz has not made it a secret that he does not want us here. Jackson has told me that he is actively trying to find a reason for us to be removed."

Fully expecting Cormoran to dismiss her concerns, Lyla was surprised when the woman jotted a few notes down on her clipboard with a short nod. "I believe that the Board should be informed of all the available details. Thank you for bringing that to my attention. The only decision that has been reached thus far is that the two of you will stay here through the next two weeks until school ends for the semester. Outside of class, you will be confined to your room. We have supplied Principal Bleiz with extra security for that time, and they will be armed."

Val scoffed. "Just in case we try to save another student?"

Cormoran gave her a look of disapproval. "It was a compromise. Principal Bleiz asked for your removal immediately. I appealed to the board to let you complete the last two weeks."

"Thank you," replied Lyla. Cormoran gave her a genuine smile. As much as she didn't like the woman, Lyla knew that Cormoran was trying to act in their best interests. It was such a tangled mess. Lyla didn't know what had made Cormoran such a dedicated follower of the DAO's mission, but Lyla hadn't seen so much as a flicker of doubt in her devotion.

"When the semester is over, you will both return to the DAO center with the rest of the Trueblood students from the other schools. Lyla, you will need to complete several tests that were left out of your previous records that are specific to alphas."

Val looked at the floor. "Will they test her for the…" she couldn't finish the sentence.

"Lethal silver limit?" replied Cormoran. She saw Val flinch slightly, but her voice was kind. "The Board is confident that Lyla's risk is low enough to forego that procedure."

Val nodded curtly, and Lyla felt her own relief at the reassurance. Val hadn't said anything about it, but Lyla knew that they'd both been afraid of the possibility.

"Do you have any other questions for me? I'll be checking in with you twice a week until you come back to the center."

The girls shook their heads. Cormoran put her clipboard away. When she stood to leave, she paused and looked down at the two of them. "I'm going to be here every step of the way. If you need anything at all, please call. I'm available at any time of the day."

When the door closed, Lyla leaned over and rested her head on Val's shoulder. Val reached her arm across her sister and tugged her closer. Lyla wasn't sure which of them needed the comfort more.

"You okay?" Val whispered.

Lyla closed her eyes. "Not right now, but I will be."

…

The two final weeks of the semester passed by all too quickly, and Val soon stopped counting the days that were left before they returned to the DAO. Allowed a select number of visitors, they had game nights nearly every night, surrounded by their friends. To the best of their ability, they played, they laughed, they teased each other with the warm familiarity that had grown between the five of them the past few months. Jules tried her best to keep up the energetic positivity that was her specialty, and she ended up sleeping in Val and Lyla's room several times, talking long into the night.

The extra security that Cormoran mentioned came in the form of two large adult betas who kept an eye on everything that happened around the school. Val wasn't sure because she couldn't see anything, but she suspected that they carried some kind of tranquilizer guns.

On their last day of school, Jules pressed a small box into each of their hands when her parents came from the airport to pick her up. Her eyes glimmered with tears, and she made them promise to call her if they could, to tell her that they were all right. She hugged both sisters so tightly that they nearly had the breath squeezed out of them. Inside the boxes were a pair of gold necklaces matching the one that Jules was wearing.

When Lex left a few hours later, he made sure to visit the girls at their dorm room. At first, he kept his hands tucked awkwardly into his pockets. Lyla told him that he should take care of himself and text them once in a while. He had turned around to go, but at the last minute he reached out and gave Lyla a hug, leaving before they got a good look at his red face.

Christopher was the last. He shook hands with Lyla and told her that he and his father were there to help if they could. Then he turned to Val, gripping the brim of his fedora hat.

"Val, I'm—"

"Thank you," Val broke in. "For everything." She silently cursed herself for the way he closed his mouth, looking down at his hat, putting away whatever words he'd been about to say. But Val knew that it was better this way. She wasn't ready to let him go. Anything he said would only make it harder. The blood claim drew her to him like a magnet, but she had promised herself she wouldn't let it change their friendship.

But when he reached out to hug her, she let him.

She felt his arms wrap around her, felt the way that he kept enough distance between them to be respectful. For the briefest second, she rested her head against his shoulder, and closed her eyes. Then it was gone. He nodded to her, handing her something and walking away down the dorm stairs. Val looked down to see his copy of *Truebloods*. She opened the first page and saw a soft pencil inscription beneath the title.

I hope this helps you remember why the world needs people like you.

Your friend,
Christopher

CHAPTER TWENTY-ONE

All too soon, the tall fence appeared with its coils of barbed wire at the top. Val chewed her fingernails nervously, tapping her other hand against her thigh to the music in her headphones. The rhythm calmed her. She felt Lyla's fingers brush against hers and glanced over to see the reassuring smile on her sister's face. Val cursed silently. She wasn't the only one testing as an alpha now.

The gate buzzed obnoxiously and let them through, then closed with a squeal and groan behind them, locking them in. Val was determined not to weigh Lyla down with her own panic, so she forced herself to go numb. Her fingernails dug into her palms.

They stepped out of the car and rolled their suitcases into the reception area, where they loaded the bags onto the conveyor belt to go through the security check. A guard swept and patted them both down to check for weapons. Cormoran signed them both in at the front desk and returned with their wristbands. The little black metal circles clicked around their wrists, then blinked several times as they came to life. Val twisted hers, fiddling with the hinge as she had done for hours on end in her cell. They'd never come apart.

The heavy, bulletproof glass doors were the next gateway, leading them farther into the main building. Their suitcases were returned to them, and Cormoran led them out onto the green space between the three buildings on the center campus. Once inside the smallest structure, B Wing, they were led through the main living area, which was a giant gym-sized space full of couches, TVs, game tables with puzzles, ping pong and pool tables, and a reading library in the far corner.

Bringing them up a flight of stairs to their small room, Cormoran left them to get settled, promising to return in the morning. Before she left, she confiscated their cell phones. The two girls had been careful not to include any incriminating conversations in their text messages with their friends. Their phones would be heavily scrutinized by a tech team.

Val dropped back on one of the two twin beds and grimaced. She had to admit that the mattress was more comfortable than the one she'd been sleeping on at the school, but she would've traded any number of springs in her back to be on the other bed. Lyla crossed to their window.

"The other Truebloods are coming back too," she said, noting several other Were students led across the green by their handlers. Val craned her neck to see. Two boys presented a comical pair, one tall and muscular, the other short and scrawny and trying to keep up with his partner's long strides. The smaller boy looked familiar, but Val couldn't remember his name. She thought he might be a gamma. The taller of the two was an alpha named Mark.

Val leaned back on her pillow. It was only a matter of time before she and Lyla were separated again. This time, there would be no hiding, and Lyla would have to face the alpha testing. They would push her to her farthest limit. Val had tried to give her some idea what to expect, but the DAO was unpredictable.

"Jules texted me on the way here. She said that her parents hung a welcome home banner over the front door, and that if we ever come to visit her, she'll make us a bigger one," Lyla said with a chuckle.

The memory of the omega's last hug was bittersweet. "I wonder which one of us will be going back," Val admitted softly.

"We don't know what the Board will decide. Come on, let's go downstairs for a while and play a game. Cormoran said we had free time tonight as long as we stay in the common areas."

Mark and the scrawny gamma student were already playing pool, so Val and Lyla headed for the ping pong table. It ended up in a heated match, both Val and Lyla flushed and laughing as they tried to outmaneuver the other. Val drew her arm back and smacked the white ball onto Lyla's side, and it bounced once on the far corner before flying off onto the floor. She threw her arms up in victory.

"Woohoo! That's how you do it!" she gloated. Catching the rolled eyes that Lyla sent her way, she laughed. "Good game, kiddo."

Lyla came back to the table, the white ball captive in her hand. "You haven't called me that in a long time," she said, brushing her flyaway brown hair out of her eyes. Val set her paddle down on the table.

"I always thought you hated it."

"I don't mind."

Val grinned. "Okay then, kiddo."

"Don't push it."

They realized they had an audience. Mark and the gamma had put their pool cues away and were leaning against the table, watching them. The tall alpha tipped his head with a roguish grin, eyes crinkling at the corners good naturedly.

"Blackwood sisters, right? How was your semester?" he asked.

Val hadn't had a lot of interaction with Mark before, but the few times they'd spoken in passing he had seemed nice enough. Even though he was an alpha, his strength and authority were translated through his confident presence more than aggression. He was edgier than Lyla, but that wasn't a hard standard to reach.

"Made some friends, saved a human, passed math class. The usual," said Val, leaning against the ping pong table.

The gamma leaned forward, messy carrot red hair sticking out in all directions and framing his face full of freckles. "We heard that a Domestic student fully phased at your school. Our school had extra security during the week make sure no one else had bad suppressants. Was everyone okay?"

Lyla wasn't sure how much she should share, and she didn't want to expose Lex. "Yeah, we managed okay. We were in the right place at the right time."

"I need details," said Mark. "You'll have to tell us all about it sometime over break. From what I heard, we're going to have more free time to get to know each other this break. Not sure what encouraged the generosity, but I'll take it!"

Val glanced at the gamma again. "Sorry, if we're going to be spending a bunch of quality time together, I'll have to admit that I don't remember your name."

The boy's smile revealed some uneven teeth. "My name's William, but all my friends call me Dodger."

Lyla's eyebrows went up. "Dodger?"

"He's too fast for his own good," explained Mark. "You should see him during Phy Ed. He's impossible. Did you like getting out of the good old DAO for a few months? This is your first semester out, right?"

Val felt the weight of her wristband heavier than before, grazing it with the fingers of her opposite hand. She knew that their conversations weren't private; she and Lyla had discovered that early on in their time at the Domestication program. They'd discussed possible plans for escape, only to find out that their handlers had been alerted by the security team. Several other times they had been scolded for voicing unpleasant opinions of the program in general. Val twisted the band.

"Um… it was great."

"No worries," Mark gave her a knowing look. "Let's go grab some dinner, and we can swap school stories. There aren't a lot of alphas at ours, only a few besides me. I've basically got the run of the place," he said. There was no sense of exaggerated bravado like there was with Jackson, he just said things the way they were.

They sat at a table together for the meal, which was light and bland but nutritious. Lyla never thought she would ever prefer food from the school cafeteria, but she'd forgotten how tasteless the DAO food was.

They found out that Mark had been able to try out for the basketball team, which was something he had enjoyed in his early school days. Unlike Val and Lyla, his family had attempted self-assimilating, but when Mark was old enough to be ranked as an alpha, they were convinced by a DAO representative to send their son to the program to help him "understand his responsibilities" and learn to control his natural Trueblood alpha tendencies.

Mark didn't seem to want to talk about the testing he had undergone, but he did mention that things could've been worse. He'd become a bit of a poster child for the DAO's alpha program, especially since his parents financially supported the organization.

"I mean, they did a photoshoot with me for all the new posters and flyers," Mark said, chuckling and shaking his head. "The photographer kept telling me to look determined and confident, like I was heading into a bright future."

Val made a dramatic show of awe. "Can I have an autograph? You're famous!"

Dodger laughed. "Yeah, famous for eating a dozen donuts when you think your coach isn't looking," he teased. "I share a room with you. I've got so much blackmail."

There were one or two other alphas besides Mark in the dining room, but most of them were betas or gammas. There were three omegas, but they weren't like Jules. They had a harder edge to them, still jovial and friendly, but more guarded. Val didn't even want to think about what would happen to Jules in a place like this. She glanced at the heavily armed security betas stationed at each corner of the room. No, the light-hearted atmosphere brought on by the conversation with Mark and Dodger was only an illusion. They weren't at Westbrook anymore.

Back in their room, they spent the last hour before Quiet Time resting on their beds. Val listened to music and Lyla read a mystery novel that Lex had passed on to her a few weeks back. Every move was visible to the security team, and Val tried to ignore the little black dome in the corner of the ceiling. The bathroom was the only place where privacy was allowed.

The whistle blew for lights out, and Val pulled the chain on her nightstand lamp, wiggling down into her sheets. She swallowed, wide awake and staring at the dimly visible white walls around her. Four walls. Four corners. One door, locked. She tried to relax. *Five things I can see…* she closed her eyes. That wasn't going to work. *I don't want to be here. I want to go home. Don't fail.* The gears in her brain sluggishly began the age-old mantras that had plagued her for years.

Five things I can remember. She took a deep breath, trying to steady her ragged breathing. *Jules's ridiculous fluffy pink sweater. The leaves on the trail. Christopher pushing his glasses up on his nose… Christopher's fingers interlacing with hers.*

The uncomfortable edge in the back of her mind that told her that he was too far away, that she couldn't protect him, was relentless. The blood claim held her, even here. It was just the blood claim. She felt a hot tear slide down her cheek, soaking into the pillow next to her ear. *It's not just a blood claim.*

"You okay?"

The soft whisper from Lyla's side of the room broke through Val's hazy tears. She sniffed and wiped her hand across her eyes.

"Fine," replied Val. She knew she sounded anything but. She felt Lyla's soft touch through the bond, a gentle reassurance that her sister was there with her. Flickering memories trickled between them, the bond wide open. Together, they struggled through the night.

...

The murders before the Culling rocked the tender balance of peace between wolfkind and their human neighbors, tipping the scales. For decades they had stayed separate from each other, bound to their own laws.

Dangerous werewolves were taken care of by their own, meeting the swift retribution of pack justice. Werewolf honor and loyalty was strong, and the elders of each pack were strict on the involvement with humans. Elders were most often Truebloods.

Some werewolves chose to assimilate themselves into human culture, going through safety tests and proper documentation. As the 1900s ended, the two cultures merged together more and more. It was quickly apparent that neither one was prepared for the consequences.

It was proposed that a new system should be put in place to document the werewolves and track them, storing their every secret in a public database. The idea spread like wildfire and was widely approved of by most of the human population and a select group of the packs. But when the government began to organize the new system, the murders began.

Groups of werewolves went rogue, leaving the jurisdiction of their packs and disappearing, only to reappear later in horrible crime scenes. Fifty-six human lives were lost over the span of six months. It appeared random at first, until a pattern began to emerge. Every one of the victims had been an outspoken advocate for the most severe treatment of wolfkind.

The elders of the packs were desperate to catch the responsible rogues and whoever was leading them, knowing that the actions of a few would spell disaster for the rest. They aided the government search as much as they could, but the damage had already been done. The desired effect was completely lost in the nationwide panic that followed.

After six long months of searching, the leaders of the ghastly crimes were finally discovered and caught, and every one of the eighty-six members of the werewolf rogue pack that called themselves The Phased were incarcerated, given the death penalty by both the government of the United States and the order of their own elders.

But it wasn't enough. The rift between humans and werewolves had been driven too deep. The murders were horrific, but what followed them was a massacre. The Culling quickly became the most devastating event in the history of wolfkind. For four years, masked figures hunted them by the dozens, and whole packs were wiped out. The perpetrators seemed organized, but their origin was a closely guarded secret.

The same Were leaders who had apprehended the original murderers proposed a new plan to keep peace, an organization that would regulate the assimilation of werewolves into human culture and provide a program to Domesticate them.

One of the leaders, Dr. Carrington, was a medical scientist, and he brought forward information and statistics from a new product that he had been testing: a suppressant that could reduce the aggression of a werewolf during phasing. He claimed that his formula would eventually be able to keep any Were from phasing, even a Trueblood.

Val closed the book, wincing as her body protested her hunched position on the bathroom floor. She ran her fingers over the worn spine, tracing the letters. *Truebloods.* She wasn't surprised that the book was banned in the DAO center. The author took a non-biased point of view of the history of everything that had gone on between werewolves and humans. She sighed and glanced at the clock on her watch. Cormoran would be coming to get them soon.

Leaving the bathroom with the book safely tucked under her shirt, Val knelt down next to her bed, pressing her shoulder against the mattress. To the camera behind her, she would appear to be opening her backpack to put something away, but she carefully slipped the book between the mattress and the box spring. There was a knock at the door. Val glanced up at Lyla, watching her from the other bed.

"Are you ready?"

Lyla tucked her hair behind her left ear. "No. Let's go."

CHAPTER TWENTY-TWO

The board members were already sitting in their chairs. Several had black notepads in front of them. One of them, a middle-aged woman named Dr. Quinn, was flipping through some stapled papers showing a variety of graphs. Her hawk nose and stern gray eyes were framed by salt-and-pepper black hair.

Val knew every one of them by name. She had taken great care memorizing the faces she'd seen twice in the months after they'd graduated from the Domestication phase of their rehabilitation. She glanced around the table at each one. Dr. Beatrice Quinn. Mr. John Willows. Mrs. Jennifer Thenard. Dr. Alan de Rainault. Mr. Jack August. And the one at the very head of the table: Dr. Robert Carrington, medical scientist and mastermind behind the DAO's structure and mission. Three of them bore the blood of werewolves, but they'd become such perfect masters of their chosen lifestyle that not a trace of rank was detectable. Mr. Jack August, Mrs. Jennifer Thenard and Mr. John Willows represented human interests in the organization.

Val suppressed a shudder of disgust when Dr. de Rainault's gaze flickered over her. He leaned back in his chair and rested his chin on a hand glittering with gold rings. He was world renowned for his work in the psychology field, according to the biography in the glossy brochure.

Cormoran delicately placed her clipboard and both Val and Lyla's files on the table in front of her, setting her pen at a perfect parallel to the paper. "Lyla and Valentine, thank you for coming, the Board is interested in hearing more about several of the incidents that occurred during this past semester."

Dr. Quinn spoke, looking at them over her thick black-rimmed glasses. Her deep red lipstick was a stark contrast to her teeth. "We've been informed of the logistics. But we'd like to ask you a few questions and hear your point of view."

"Why now?" Val blurted out.

Cormoran gave her a slight shake of her head. "Valentine."

"It's all right, Ms. Cormoran." When Dr. Carrington spoke, he exuded a thinly veiled power over the room. Val would've sworn that he was an alpha. "Ms. Blackwood is free to speak her mind."

Val's mind reeled from the contradictions that statement implied. She felt Lyla tap her thigh slightly under the table. "I just mean this is the first time you've asked for our point of view on any of this."

Dr. de Rainault tapped his fingers against the table, his rings clicking. "Ms. Blackwood, the two of you may be the most important Truebloods we've ever had in this program," he said. "You're very special, and we'd like to explore the possibilities that the two of you represent."

Val wasn't ready to tell them just how much those words made her want to vomit. Whatever they were planning, she wanted no part of it. Dr. Carrington spoke again.

"We received the report filed by Mr. Peter Wells. You were staying with his family during your Thanksgiving school break, correct?"

"Yes."

"We were told that you saved the life of a human friend of yours during that stay. I commend you for your heroics. There was some consideration as to whether or not your full-blood friend's phasing was a result of the Trueblood influence he had been exposed to." When he saw Val's expression darken, he waved his hand dismissively. "We were able to confirm that the fault was with an expired crate of suppressants that was not meant for student use. They have been disposed of properly, so we can avoid a similar mishap in the future."

Expired. Mishap. Heroics. Influence. Disposed of. Every word was so clinical, premeditated with great care, and each one fell like a deliberate weight against the walls of the room.

"What do you want to know?" Val asked.

"Mr. Wells' report mentioned that you were able to subdue the beta student without excessive violence. I'd like to know the details of that exchange," replied Dr. Carrington.

Sensing Val's immediate panic, Lyla stepped in. "We tried to restrain him at first, but he was stronger than we were. We were… we were able to force our phasing enough to hold him back. I drew him away into the forest, and…" she paused, and Val could feel her uncertainty.

"Be honest," said Mrs. Thenard sharply. "We're giving you a chance to tell your side of the story. We won't ask twice."

"Mrs. Thenard, there's no need to be unkind," replied Dr. Carrington quietly. "Lyla?"

"I took him out in the forest to hunt. It was enough to keep him calm until his phasing could pass," said Lyla.

Mrs. Thenard's face twist in disgust. "This is exactly the sort of thing we need to eliminate. The thought of two of our students gallivanting about in the trees, hunting like animals… it's an offense against nature."

"Your nature, perhaps, my dear Mrs. Thenard," replied Dr. de Rainault smoothly. "But remember that these young ladies were raised in such a forest. It is as natural to them as breathing. Their instincts are fascinating."

Val tried to keep her emotions off of her face. Dr. de Rainault described them as if those same natural tendencies didn't exist in his own heavily suppressed bloodstream. She noticed that Dr. Quinn was making notes on her notepad, the silver pen moving easily across the paper, leaving perfectly neat letters behind.

"Valentine, did you use any influence over the beta student during this event?" asked Dr. Quinn, her pen pausing.

"I …" The memories of that day were hazy, but Val knew exactly which one they wanted, which one they would pick apart like vultures. It had been drilled into her over and over in the program that her use of alpha commands was a punishable offense. "Yes. I tried to use a command to keep him from attacking our friend."

"And?" Dr. de Rainault leaned forward, eyes glittering. "What else?"

They know everything. Of course, they know. Everyone in the school knows. They're playing with me. Val felt more like prey in the presence of a pack of wolves than she ever had before in her life.

Suddenly Val felt very tired.

"I put a blood claim on Christopher to protect him," she admitted. Mrs. Thenard gasped in revulsion, but she saw Dr. de Rainault and Dr. Carrington nod in approval. "I didn't know what else to do," she whispered.

"A blood claim is quite a feat for one so young," broke in Mr. Willows, his silk shirt and velvet jacket lapels far too lavish for the plain room. "They are only potent with strong loyalty."

Val clenched her fist beneath the table. She would go to her grave before she would talk about her feelings with this group of prowling predators. "He's my friend," she responded. "We protect each other."

"A noble sentiment," replied Mr. Willows, watching her intently. "And to the other Ms. Blackwood, I am curious to know more about this blood bond that you two seem to be so proficient with. It is something you were born with, correct?"

"Yes. My parents told us that it wasn't uncommon among siblings," Lyla said.

Dr. de Rainault seemed far too pleased with that bit of knowledge as he addressed the room. "She's correct, but what is unique to these two particular siblings is that their blood bond is particularly strong. Ms. Cormoran has told us that they even seem to be able to sense each other's location or communicate specific emotions. As I've said before, this deserves a much more thorough set of tests to determine its full effect."

Dr. Carrington interjected, "I believe we have much more to discuss regarding the blood bond, but that is a topic for another day. For now, we will need to decide on the best way to move forward. Principal Bleiz has filed a formal complaint with us regarding the placement of two Trueblood alphas in his school. Had we known the truth about Ms. Blackwood's rank prior to their enrollment, we would've placed them separately."

"If I may interject, Dr. Carrington, I'd also like the Board to consider the information we've collected regarding the principal's less than ethical actions. There are allegations to consider there as well," said Cormoran.

"You're quite right, Ms. Cormoran," said Dr. Carrington. He smiled at the two sisters. "You've created quite the stir since the day you arrived with us, my dears. We will act in your best interests and place you where you both will have the best chance of a smooth assimilation. Ms. Cormoran, will you escort our guests back to their rooms?"

Val studied her hands. It was over. There was no way that the allegations against Principal Bleiz would be enough to keep them together. She was going to lose her sister again.

"Wait." Lyla pushed her chair back and stood up. "I know that you think separating us will give us the best chance of assimilating, but I know that's not true. Val and I have always looked out for each other, and it's because of our bond that we've been able to … to survive all of this. The best chance we have is to stay together, and I think if you want to make the right decision, you should listen to the people who are going to be affected the most."

The one person in the room who had been silent during the entire meeting leaned forward, hands still subtly fidgeting with a silver ring. It was shaped like a lion head, gaping maw stretched around his finger, teeth pressing lightly into the skin. Jack August, the billionaire owner of several large media companies, was a quiet man.

"You're brave, Ms. Blackwood. I'll give you that." He settled back into his chair with a small smile. "Next time don't let your hands tremble."

...

Group talk sessions happened twice a week, overseen by one of the handlers. The Trueblood students were split into groups, then brought in, made to sit in a circle and talk about how their days were going and what struggles they might be having with assimilating. The conversation was always gently guided away from any specific words or topics that were deemed too feral.

Val dropped into a seat, saving a space for Lyla next to her. Since leaving the conference room a few hours earlier, Lyla had been quiet and reflective. Val knew better than to push her to talk about it. Meeting with the Board hadn't given either of them much confidence. She needed to find a way to lift her sister's spirits.

Mark and Dodger's handler, Mr. Gibbs, was sitting in the circle of chairs with his two charges. Mark winked at the sisters when they sat down. Val smirked. *Alphas.* Dodger was spinning a fidget ring on his finger, but he flipped his shock of carrot red hair to the side and gave them a nod. There were four other students in their group, and Val only knew the name of one of them.

"All right everyone, we've tried to make the groups a little larger so you can all get to know each other and build some positive relationships," said Mr. Gibbs. "Let's keep it easy for our first day back. Let's talk about your semesters at school. What was the most challenging thing you faced and what was something that went really well? Sophie?"

The only omega in the group was a slender girl with kind brown eyes. She reminded Val of Jules, but with less enthusiasm. "I made a lot of friends, which was nice. I think the hard part was trying to adjust to being more independent."

"That's an important part of the assimilation process, because all of you will eventually be responsible for yourselves," replied Mr. Gibbs. "Thank you for sharing that with us. Valentine?"

"Well," Val began, taking a deep breath and furrowing her brows in thought. "I don't know how comfortable I am talking about this, but…"

"It's important to work through these things," Mr. Gibbs encouraged.

"There was something that I really had a hard time adjusting to during the semester. Even the tutoring here at the center didn't prepare me for just how hard it would be." She paused, looking around at the faces watching her. "It made me feel like a failure, and I honestly don't know if I can go back."

Mr. Gibbs nodded. "What happened?"

Val looked up at the ceiling. "Math."

Dodger let out a barking laugh. The other students snickered briefly before Mr. Gibbs quietly restored order. Even he was attempting to hide his smile. "All right, everyone. Thank you for the share, Valentine. Lyla?"

Val glanced to the side, leaning her arm over Lyla's chair dramatically. "What challenges did you have this semester?"

"Well, the biggest one I can think of is sitting right next to me. It was a real pain."

Val's heart soared as Lyla's familiar mischievous twinkle lit her eyes and the rest of the group started laughing again. Even if it was just for a moment, her mission had succeeded. She smiled in satisfaction and gave a mock bow when she saw Mark give her a thumb's up.

When they got up to leave, Val felt a soft touch on her elbow and turned to see Dodger standing behind her. He smiled.

"Just wanted to say thanks."

"For what?"

"Making us all laugh in there. It's not easy to do, especially with whatever you two have been through. But you're still holding your heads up."

A newfound respect for Dodger bloomed in Val's heart. She shrugged awkwardly. "I'm glad if it helps. I'm surprised Mr. Gibbs was okay with it."

"Eh, he's not as stuffy as some. You've got people rooting for you, Blackwood." He grinned over his shoulder at her as he left.

…

In the first two days, there was one group therapy session, one meeting with Cormoran, and several hours a day when the girls were allowed to exercise and spend time in the recreation hall. The meals were always nutritious but unimaginative—a perfect balance of protein, greens, and fruit. Val and Lyla spent a lot of time reading. Cormoran did let them see a text message they'd received from Jules. According to her, Christmas break was ruined because she'd burnt her first batch of sugar cookies.

They didn't see Mark and Dodger again over the next two days. Now that they were all settling in, the individual students were being scheduled for tests. It was snowing on the day that Cormoran came for them. She walked into the room and scanned both of their wristbands into her data pad. Val had always sarcastically joked that she had to check them out like books from a library. But today Cormoran seemed to have a stoic heaviness to her movements as she instructed them to follow her down to the labs.

The labs.

Val couldn't suppress the chills that she felt as Cormoran led them on a familiar path away from the main buildings to the smallest on the campus. There were double the number of security guards inside, and the blank white walls seemed to lean in, matching the cold blanket over the ground outside. The labs held no other similarity to the soft, pure flakes falling from the sky outside.

"Valentine, please follow Mr. Gibbs. Lyla and I will rejoin you shortly," said Cormoran, motioning to the second handler waiting for them off to the side. The man was grim and quiet, a far cry from the jovial demeanor he'd portrayed at the first group session. Val started to follow him, forcing herself to focus on the texture of his brown suit coat. She fought against the urge to close the bond. She'd promised Lyla that she wouldn't. Not that it would matter soon. The DAO had psychotic drugs that would close it for her. And she'd be in the dark again.

Mr. Gibbs led her into a small room with a table. The only thing on the table was a strip of wide black cloth. He picked it up and stepped toward Val. "I'm going to use this as a blindfold. You will be safe. The test is quite easy. They will explain everything when we arrive," he said calmly.

Val didn't say a word. She couldn't. The panic was rising again, crawling its way up into her hands, arms, and squeezing around her chest. She'd given up trying to understand the madness that was the DAO. She stood silently while Mr. Gibbs gently tied the black cloth over her eyes and made sure that she could not see anything. She felt him settle his hand against her elbow and begin leading her forward. She hadn't been afraid of the dark in years, and she was determined not to begin again now.

She walked for a short distance, following the handler's lead, brushing her shoulder against the edge of a doorframe. Her feet shuffled against the floor helplessly. Suddenly, Mr. Gibbs' hand was gone from her arm. She waited for an explanation, but there was none. Then she heard the sound of other shuffling footsteps somewhere nearby. They stopped, and then the silence returned.

"… Lyla?" she asked softly.

"Mark," replied a voice threaded with exhaustion. A crackle of speakers sounded overhead, and then Val heard the unpleasantly smooth voice of Dr. de Rainault.

"This is a simple test to determine the strength of two blood bonds. There is a short maze in front of you both. Both Lyla and William are here in the control room with me. They will attempt to lead you both through the maze to find an object, and then back out. This is not meant to be a competition; we are evaluating you each separately."

Val felt bile rise in her throat as she realized the most likely explanation for Dodger and Mark's disappearance the past few days. They hadn't been blood bonded before. As far as she knew, she and Lyla had been the only ones in the center to have one. According to what she knew, new blood bonds could be delicate and disorienting. And if it had been unnaturally forced… Val didn't want to think about that. She heard Mark's strained breathing beside her.

"Begin," crackled the voice over the speakers.

CHAPTER TWENTY-THREE

Lyla took a deep breath, watching her sister through the glass window in the control room. Val stood, tense and waiting, the black blindfold keeping her in total darkness. Lyla waited for her instructions, listening to the technicians rustling around the room in their lab coats, the tapping of fingers against keyboards, and the hushed voices they were all using to communicate. A few feet away from her sat Dodger, and Lyla could hardly bring herself to look at him.

His usually pale face was close to bedsheet white. Dark circles hung beneath his eyes, and his hands were trembling in his lap. He stared out toward the maze with an unfocused gaze, sometimes wincing and lifting his left hand up to his forehead. Lyla noted the heavy bandage wrapped around his right arm.

Anger filled her. The DAO took everything beautiful about their heritage and twisted it, using it for their own gain. Blood bonds had never been meant for this.

"Dodger…"

"Begin!" Dr. de Rainault boomed into the microphone on the other side of Dodger. The boy flinched. Lyla turned back to the window. Her sister waited, and Lyla felt the confusion of her emotions through their bond. Val started walking forward into the maze. One step. Two steps. She was getting close to the first turn to the left. Lyla sent a flash of concern through the bond, and Val stopped short. Val lifted her hand and pointed to the right.

Not that way.

Val turned to the left and took a step forward again. Lyla focused on the bond, trying to be as clear as possible. She knew Val couldn't hear her words, but the intent would come through enough to tell Val which way was right or wrong.

In the other side of the maze, Mark stepped too far forward and hit the first wall, letting out a grunt of surprise. Dodger hadn't moved an inch, still staring out at the alpha he was connected to, pain etched into his expression as he tried to focus.

Lyla returned her attention to Val. There were ten more changes in direction, each one a smooth transition as Lyla communicated silently with her sister. After the final left turn, there was a pause, and Val cocked her head to the side, waiting.

Val, reach up.

She didn't move. Lyla frowned, and tried something else. She focused on the image of her sister standing beneath the little blue flag hanging from the ceiling, and let it flow through the bond.

Val reached high above her head, waving her hand until it brushed against the fabric. She gripped the corner and yanked it down, and then turned to follow Lyla's instruction back out of the maze. The return trip took even less time. Mark was still bumping and cursing his way through the maze. Dodger now had sweat running down the sides of his face.

Stop, Val.

Lyla leaned back as her sister ripped off the blindfold. Val took two steps toward the glass window, and Lyla could see her anger, feel it boiling between them. Her sister had seen her mental projection of Dodger. Val fixed a look of disgust and hatred on the one-way mirror window, eyes flickering back and forth, searching for any sign of the people she knew were behind it. She crumpled the blue flag in her hand and tossed it aside.

On the other side of the window, Dr. de Rainault watched it all with a wide smile. He tapped his fingers against the desk and stood up, holding his hands out to Lyla.

"Brilliant, both of you. I've been waiting so long to explore your bond link. It's uncanny how sensitive it is compared to a newly formed bond. Come with me."

Hesitant, Lyla looked at Dodger. But Dr. de Rainault urged her along. "Don't worry about your friends," he said. "They will be well looked after."

Lyla lifted her chin and rose from the chair, gently brushing the tips of her fingers against Dodger's shoulder as she passed him, escorted by Dr. de Rainault and two security betas. Out in the hallway, Val joined her, still looking like a thundercloud.

"You okay?" Lyla whispered.

"Peachy."

Dr. de Rainault pushed them to the brink of their mental capacity for the rest of the day. He tested their ability to transfer emotions, how strong they were, and how accurately the other could guess what her counterpart was feeling. He asked them endless questions, pressing deep into what they knew about their bond. Lyla felt as though they were being opened up on a table and picked apart. Her brain was exhausted, and she knew that Val was losing the last reserves of composure that she had left. They were both able to answer the questions without revealing much in the way of memories.

Lyla was also surprised to notice that as they went on, the clarity between them was growing stronger. It was being stretched and built up like a muscle, torn down and then rebuilt again. By the end of the day, she was even able to communicate more clearly with specific words and images. They were still hazy, and sometimes Val took a few minutes to understand, but the bond thrummed and felt alive. They'd never relied on it so heavily.

Finally, Dr. de Rainault flipped over all the pages of his copious notes and clicked the *off* button on his recorder. "I believe I have what I need to organize the next steps." He smiled at them. "The two of you are going to change the history of this organization. Pure gold!"

When Val and Lyla stumbled back into their room and heard the door lock behind them, Val sank down against it, arms wrapped around her knees. It was already dark outside their window. A basket with a small sandwich had been left on each of their beds for a late supper. Val's stomach growled and Lyla gestured toward the food.

"You need to eat something."

Val took a bite of the sandwich and grimaced. "I think they're trying to starve us. Wouldn't be the first time," she muttered. Lyla sat down on the edge of her bed.

"Did they tell you why?"

Surprised, Val looked up around the next mouthful of food. "Why what?"

"What they were trying to find out before? Why they starved you?" asked Lyla. She knew she was treading on dangerous ground.

Val set her basket down on the floor. "When I phased, they wanted to see if it increased my aggression."

"Did it?"

Val took another bite. "You know how I am when I don't eat."

"Glad I missed that party."

Val grinned, finishing the last of her sandwich and setting the basket aside. Lyla watched her for a minute. "You seem better, you know. More like yourself lately. You handled today like it was the first time we'd ever seen the inside of the labs."

Val didn't answer right away. Lyla didn't bother reaching through the blood bond, it felt raw and worn. She was just about to say that they should get some sleep when Val responded.

"I think it was our friends," she smiled wistfully. "I never thought we would find any hope when we left this place. It feels good to belong somewhere again. I feel like there are people outside these walls that want us to be free."

...

To avoid the height of the phasing period, the cafeteria prepared a special early Christmas dinner for the students with pineapple hams, mashed potatoes and fruit breads added to the assortment of side dishes. For dessert there was a triple-tier chocolate cake. Val wasted no time digging in. As she started in on her second helping of ham, she noticed that Lyla was eating very slowly, barely picking at the food on her plate. Val frowned, fork pausing in the air. Then she saw the sheen of sweat on her sister's forehead.

Val stared. Lyla was almost never the first one to phase. Neither one of them had been given suppressants when they returned. Lyla's wristband beeped, flashing a temperature reading. Val reached over and tapped her on the shoulder.

"Do you want to go to our room?" she asked. Lyla nodded sluggishly, her eyes taking on the familiar hazy stare. Val slid her chair back and was just about to reach down to grab her tray when several security guards came through the cafeteria doors, followed by Cormoran. Val's shoulders tensed as she moved to stand between them and her sister.

"Valentine, we need to take your sister to the lab now," said Cormoran, her gentle tone strained as she tried to pass the young alpha. "She will be perfectly safe."

Val met her gaze. "Just like I was?"

"Valentine," warned Cormoran. "This is not the time. Will you step aside, or do I need to have you taken to solitary?"

Angry, Val gritted her teeth. "You're going to hurt her."

Softening for a brief second, Cormoran reached out and put her hand on Val's shoulder. "The Board wants to test her ability to self-suppress. That is all."

"You can't take her," Val said, lifting her chin, her tone beginning to take on the edge of authority. Something like regret passed through Cormoran's eyes, and then Val felt an icy shock shoot through her system from the black bracelet around her wrist. She doubled over.

"Take her to a holding cell, she's not stable. Valentine, I'll come by to check on you shortly."

Two strong betas marched Val out of the cafeteria. The electrical current left Val weak and shaking. She was deposited in a small white cell on the first level of B-Wing, and the locks clicked into place behind her. She scrambled to the door and slammed her fists against the cold metal, cursing the DAO, Cormoran, and every one of the six Board members. She leaned her forehead against the door.

She reached out to the bond, but the thick haze that surrounded Lyla invaded her own brain. She knew she was dangerously close to provoking her own phasing. Self-suppression. If Lyla could do it, so could she. She wouldn't phase. Lyla needed her. She took a deep breath and closed her eyes, willing her mind to close out the emotions that were threatening to overwhelm her. *Focus on Lyla. Calm. Strong. Don't fail.*

. . .

Lyla watched as the lab technician filled a syringe from a small vial. Behind the mirrored glass in front of her, she knew that Dr. de Rainault and Dr. Carrington were watching her. As the lab tech injected her with the serum, she expected to feel the deep pull of the suppressant, bringing her back down into a state of lulled complacency. But as Lyla was left alone in the four white walls sitting on her chair, she realized that something was stirring inside her that she hadn't felt for years.

Her wolf was rushing to the surface, and nothing was holding it back. Clarity rushed into her senses, amplifying every noise, every sight. Her nostrils filled with the pungent scents of disinfectant, sweat, and Dr. de Rainault's cologne. She wrinkled her nose, head tipping back as she felt the claws extending from her fingers. Her lips lifted to reveal her fangs, fully elongated and sharp as knives. Her eyes flashed into their Trueblood violet.

Something was wrong. It was too much, too strong. Somewhere in the confusion she felt a sense of calm flowing through the bond, and a twinge of surprise came as her mind slowly realized Val must be trying to send it to her. She reached into the bond, grasping hold of that reassurance, and flooded the bond link with the intensity of her phasing. She felt Val pull back, but she surged forward, not letting go.

She rose from her chair, unable to hold her body or her mind back as the enhanced phasing took over. It felt foreign, and her wolf was torn between the pull of fully phasing and trying to understand what was happening. Through the bond link, she surged after Val, trying to draw her sister back to her.

. . .

Val lurched backward as if she'd been shoved, holding her head in her hands. She tried to pull away from the bond, tried to regain control over it, but Lyla was too powerful. Val felt her mind shudder with the impact as her sister pulled, her wolf howling through the space between them. She wanted Val, and in her phasing, her emotional capacity had become subdued. She couldn't feel Val's fear emanating back to her.

Val dropped to the ground, pressing her hands to her ears, using all of her strength to close the bond. The barrier inched up moment by agonizing moment, and she suddenly felt the rush of anger and frustration as Lyla redoubled her efforts. Something wasn't right. Val clenched her fists and pushed as hard as she could, slamming the barrier into place. Lyla's fury echoed through her as the whirling emotions faded. Val sank to the floor, chest heaving and mind numb as she lay alone in the small cell. Her body temperature was rising. She shook her head.

If Lyla can do this. So can I. Don't phase. They're coming for me. Don't phase.

…

At first, Lyla didn't hear the voice coming through the overhead speakers. Everything was a red blur, her eyes darting around the room. Val had closed her out of the bond, and Lyla felt nothing but a stinging fury at being rejected. She didn't understand. Val shouldn't push her away. She smashed her emotions against the bond link again, but the barrier held. She howled, feeling nothing but the pure hunting instinct flowing through her. Her sister was acting like prey, running, and hiding. She stalked to the door of the room and wrapped her clawed hand around the doorknob. The door groaned but held. Lyla was tired of the cage. She turned to the glass window. She couldn't see them, but she could smell them. She could smell excitement, apprehension… and disgust.

The fury mounted. How dare they be disgusted by her? She lunged forward, slamming against the glass. BOOM. The sound echoed through the room.

"Lyla!"

The voice spoke ominously from above, and she snapped her head up, searching for the source. When her eyes found the speakers built into the ceiling, she growled. Crouched on the floor, fangs bared, she waited.

"Lyla, you've been given a stimulant to enhance your phasing. I need you to try to self-suppress. Try to control it."

She snapped angrily at the window, eyes flashing pure violet, her Trueblood heritage on display in all its glory. Control it. Why would she want to control this? Her muscles were tense, ready to spring into action. If even one person came through that door…

She closed her eyes, grounding herself with what she could feel. Her fingers softly brushed against the slight layer of grit over the floor tiles, rolling the tiny pieces of rock between them. Her shoulders shook with the effort to suppress the wild rage of the hunter inside. She forced her mind to accept the fact that this wasn't normal. She was acting under the influence of a stimulant.

Val.

The force she'd used to attack the bond was far too intense for her sister to withstand. And yet somehow, she'd done it. That was the only moment of calm Lyla had as she floated between the aggressive phasing and control. She tentatively touched the bond, and felt the resistance melt away. Val was shaken, but still holding it together. Guilty, Lyla tried to reassure her as best she could.

And then the first wave of pain hit. Lyla collapsed to the ground, body curling in on itself as it resisted her suppression. She gasped, desperately clinging to the thread of control she'd established. She stayed on the floor, unable to move as wave after wave of nauseating agony crashed through her body. But still she held firm. She would not allow herself to become a monster.

As the struggle inside continued, Lyla was watched silently by the faces behind the window. She knew they were there, but she couldn't bring herself to care. Faintly, she felt panic that wasn't her own, and then anger. She slipped into the blissful dark.

CHAPTER TWENTY-FOUR

Something cool and damp touched Lyla's forehead, stirring her back to consciousness. Her eyes fluttered open slowly. The room was too hot. Her skin felt clammy beneath the weight of a thin blanket. She was lying on a cot, still in the same room that she'd been in before. She felt strange and realized that her fangs and claws were still there, her senses still heightened. She struggled to filter everything she was taking in. A presence loomed next to her, and she recognized Cormoran's face, carefully neutral.

"How are you feeling?"

"I've been better," croaked Lyla, wincing at the dryness of her throat. "Can I go now?"

Cormoran's smile was tight, forced onto her lips. "Not yet. You did very well. Dr. Carrington said he's never seen control like yours. It's amazing, Lyla."

Lyla wished that she could feel as optimistic about her abilities. But it just gave her a feeling of dread. She was beginning to wonder if she and Val were going to end up being lab rats for the rest of their lives. Her suppression ability must have worked well because she felt totally numb, even though she was still partially phased. It was as if she was suspended between two states of being, and neither one of them had truly claimed her.

"Where's Val?" she whispered, trying not to irritate her voice.

"She'll be joining us shortly," replied Cormoran. Lyla sensed the hesitation, and she turned to look at her handler. She also realized that the bond link was so faint she could barely feel it.

"Cormoran, what's wrong? Why can't I feel her?"

"They gave you a sedative. Valentine has begun her phasing, and we wanted you to be able to sleep. It will wear off soon."

Lyla hated the way that Cormoran was always neatly dodging her real question, trying to reassure her with that forced gentleness. "Did they give her the stimulant too?" There was no answer. "Cormoran?"

Cormoran met her gaze. "You don't need to worry, Lyla. Every step of these trials has been carefully planned to ensure safety for everyone involved. Today is important, and both of you are valuable to us."

The same script, every time. Lyla gave up, relaxing her body into the cot. She closed her eyes to rest, knowing there was nothing else to do but wait. *She slipped away from control, her wolf raging beneath the surface of her skin. The pain was so strong, it was tearing her apart.* Lyla's eyes snapped back open, her breathing shallow through the tight pressure building in her chest. She'd had flashbacks like these before, but it had been so long.

Cormoran sat with her in silence for almost an hour. Slowly, Lyla's phase receded, taking the violet in her eyes back down to brown, her hands and face returning to their normal shape. After a while, the data pad that Cormoran held beeped loudly, and she tapped it to read a message.

"They're ready for us. Lyla, how are you feeling?"

Lyla didn't answer. Cormoran sighed and stood up, reaching out a hand to help Lyla up off the cot. The young Were ignored the gesture and carefully rolled up to a sitting position. She needed to see Val.

Cormoran took her down two hallways and into a control room. The only people she saw were the operators, lab techs, and Dr. Carrington. Dr. de Rainault was nowhere to be seen. Dr. Carrington smiled when he saw her.

"Hello, Lyla. I'm glad you had a chance to rest a bit. You performed marvelously, exactly as we had hoped. Now, I have a special assignment for you. You've proved that you can suppress your own phasing, and we'd like to see if that ability extends to others."

Confused, Lyla glanced at the window facing into a wide white room just like the one she had just left. It was completely bare, except for a single chair in one corner. On the chair sat Dodger, and the look of fear on his face made Lyla's stomach twist.

"What is this?" she asked softly, not wanting to hear the answer.

"Come sit," said Dr. Carrington. "Dr. de Rainault will join us shortly; he is with Valentine at the moment."

Lyla hesitantly sank into the chair he pulled out for her right in front of the window. She watched Dodger fidget, leg bouncing up and down. "I don't have a blood bond with him. I can't communicate with him that way."

Dr. Carrington nodded, typing something into his data pad. "Of course, I can see why this would be confusing for you. We're not going to ask you to communicate with William, but with your sister. She's going to be released into this room in a few minutes, and I want you to attempt to suppress her phasing."

Mouth open in shock, Lyla stared at him. "Suppress… how?"

"You have the ability to reach into her mind. You need to control what she is feeling and bring her back to a level of calm that can be managed."

Horrified, Lyla stood up. "I can't do that!" she spat. "Do you have any idea what that would do to her?"

"Lyla, I can understand your concern. You have a chance to make a better life for your sister. She's been through so much pain and confusion. You can take that away for her. If it's possible, it could change the course of your future and the future of the DAO program. Perhaps even guarantee more freedom."

He was tempting her with a promise she knew would never be worth the cost. No matter what freedom might hang in the balance, Lyla would never be able to do that to her sister. It was such a violation of trust that she didn't know if they would ever heal from it.

"No, I won't do it."

"Ah, my dear," said Carrington gently. "We do require your help. In a moment, your sister will be released into the room, and it will be up to you to keep her from harming William."

"You wouldn't let her…" suddenly Lyla wasn't sure if she believed that. They were all means to an end, and if some of them were sacrificed to achieve the goals for a greater good, Lyla was sure that it was a price the Board was readily willing to pay.

"Of course not," replied Carrington. "But I don't believe you will enjoy the alternative."

Dr. de Rainault opened the door, walking in, his white lab coat flaring as he whipped it behind him to sit in his leather chair next to the window. "Lyla, good to see you looking more like yourself again." He leaned forward and spoke into a small desk microphone. "Whenever you're ready."

The side of the wall opened in the white room, revealing a short doorway into a tunnel. There was a flash of violet, and Lyla felt her heart drop to her stomach. When she reached out to touch the bond tentatively, she flinched and drew back as if she'd been burned.

Watching Val burst into the room, eyes wild and pure violet, claws and fangs bared… Lyla hadn't seen her sister fully phased since she was eleven years old. Her sister's first phases at the DAO were spent in solitary confinement while Lyla was hidden away in another room. She looked so horrifically wild in the pristine white room, red hair flowing over her gray tinged skin. The harsh lines in her face pulled her expression into an intense scowl.

There was nothing left in her eyes that made her Val. Her warmth and bravado were gone; the stimulant had pushed her so far out of her humanity that Lyla barely recognized her. She stared hard at the window, looking at a space to the right of Lyla, knowing that the people she wanted to hunt were behind the glass. Her lips curled over her fangs in a threatening growl.

Don't… please don't…

Lyla didn't want to go back to the bond. The merciless aggression she'd felt had broken her heart. She could see Dr. Carrington watching her from his seat, paying no attention to the feral werewolf in the white room. Internally, Lyla begged her sister to find some semblance of control. She saw Val raise her chin, smelling the air. Then her violet eyes narrowed. She turned, settling into the tense rigidity of a hunter stalking its prey.

Dodger cowered in his chair, the enhanced intensity of the alpha making him incredibly uncomfortable. He shook with fear, gripping the seat of his chair with white knuckles. There was nowhere for him to go, and he knew enough about alphas to know that running was the worst possible thing he could do.

Lyla gripped her own chair. She couldn't do it, she wouldn't betray Val. But she couldn't leave Dodger defenseless either. She was gambling with another's life. Just as she tentatively reached out to touch the bond again, to try to reason with her sister, Val lunged for Dodger.

Dodger let out a shriek and threw himself off of the chair, using the piece of furniture as a shield in a desperate attempt to protect himself. Less than two feet from the terrified gamma, Val froze as if she'd been suspended in place, every muscle pulled tight. Her eyes were wide, mouth open in a silent scream. She fell backwards, convulsing several times on the floor. The shaking stopped after a few seconds, and she pushed herself up, shaking her head angrily and slinking over to the wall, lips pulled back from her fangs as she scratched at the black bands on her wrists and around her neck.

"Lyla, every thirty seconds from now on, Dr. de Rainault will raise the intensity of the electric pulses emitted through the bands. They will be activated whether she attacks or not. Now, I do not like this any more than you do, but you understand that we need to ensure your participation."

Val was closing in on Dodger again. Dr. de Rainault's finger hovered over the button on the data pad. Tears stung the back of Lyla's eyes, and she couldn't tear her gaze away from her sister.

She reached through the roaring wild of the bond with a gentle touch, flinching from the painful force bleeding into her mind from Val's. *Forgive me, Sanzi.*

At the sound of her name, Val stopped in her tracks, turning back toward the glass window in surprise, realizing for the first time how close Lyla was. Then Lyla pushed past her side of the bond and into Val's fevered mind for the first time.

Val howled, fury mounting to an unbearable pitch as she swung her head from side to side, crashing against the wall as she fought against the intrusion. She reached up and clawed at her head. Lyla pushed farther, focusing on setting up a system of control, sending tendrils of calm in all directions. She felt Val's pain at her betrayal. She felt her sister's wild fear and the flashbacks that were invading her vulnerable mind.

White fire. White masks. White walls. It hurts too much. I just want to go home. Val's thoughts merged with her own as Lyla kept up her steady breathing. *It's okay. Breathe deep, focus on my voice.* Lyla's voice reverberated through Val's mind, as did a cacophony of others.

"Hey feral!"

"Subject has been resuscitated. Heart rate stabilizing."

"Sanzi, don't be afraid of the dark."

"Lyla has a better chance without me. I wish they'd never brought me back. I've never been able to protect her the way she protects me."

Tears rolled down Lyla's cheeks as Val's innermost thoughts were laid bare in front of her. An image of Christopher's face flashed by. *I think I love him. I don't want to. He's not safe with me.* As her wolf retreated beneath Lyla's strong influence, Val let out an agonized cry and fell to her knees, still cradling her head in her hands. As the phasing was suppressed farther, crippling pain rippled through them both. Lyla gasped, grabbing the arms of her chair to keep herself steady. Val's voice came, faint and trembling. On the same side of the bond, the words were clear.

Lyla.

I'm here.

Let me go.

I'm so sorry, Val. I'm-

Get out.

Lyla drew back, leaving her sister alone with her thoughts once again. She was left with a quiet mind and a heart that felt as if it had been split in two. Tears rolled down her cheeks. Val still curled in on herself, fighting the pain and nausea flooding her body. Dodger was still sitting on the floor, watching Val with more concern than fear. He slowly inched toward her and said something only she could hear. Val murmured a response, and he reached out to touch her shoulder. Lyla swallowed, grateful for at least a small measure of comfort toward her sister.

Dr. Carrington sat comfortably in his chair, handing his notes to Dr. de Rainault, who was reviewing scans on a screen. Lyla saw her sister's name on the top of the bright neon colors that shifted and changed in the silhouette of the brain.

"This is incredible," said Dr. de Rainault, staring at the scans. "Simply incredible."

"You've done very well today, Lyla," said Dr. Carrington. "Now, Ms. Cormoran, if you would be so kind as to take Lyla back to her room. I think some solitude might be appreciated."

CHAPTER TWENTY-FIVE

Val woke up in the quiet of her own room on a bed with crisp white sheets. The sun streamed through the window, and the warmth felt gentle against her bare skin. She sat up slowly, the pounding headache she'd had for the past two days finally beginning to fade. Her mind was still numb, and she'd kept it that way. Outside, the snow glistened in the early morning glow. One staff member walked from the main building toward the dorms, engulfed in a puffy coat. *It must be very cold outside.*

Val found herself wanting to feel that cold. She wanted the shock to her system, the fingers of frozen winter to startle her out of the haze. She hadn't seen the outside of her temporary room for nearly forty-eight hours. Cormoran had visited once, but she hadn't pressed Val with any questions or stayed longer than was necessary to hand her some pills for her headache. A staff member from the cafeteria brought up simple meals three times a day, but she never said a word. Val didn't mind. The silence had been welcome.

She knew that she couldn't stay in the room forever. It was only a matter of time before she'd be dragged back into the labs again… She stopped herself. No thoughts. Just the bliss of nothingness. Her emotions were dull and sluggish anyway, thanks to the sedative and drugs that she'd been given when she left the labs. The bond link was nothing but a distant hum, barely noticeable. She couldn't have felt Lyla even if she tried.

She wasn't sure how long she sat there watching the sun climb slowly up to the center of the sky, shining in a golden smear through the winter sky. There was a soft knock at the door, but she didn't turn, thinking it must be the cafeteria lady with her lunch.

"Valentine?"

Cormoran. Val blinked and reluctantly tore her gaze away from the blurry sunshine. She lifted her eyebrows when she saw Cormoran standing in khaki pants and a simple white, collared dress shirt. A light gold chain with a diamond pendant glittered over her collarbones. Instead of the tight bun, her hair was pulled back into a clip, a few strands tucked behind her ears.

"I've cleared some time for you to exercise. You need some fresh air. Get dressed and meet me out in the hallway," Cormoran said. The door shut behind her.

Managing to pull on her hoodie and sweatpants, Val shuffled out into the hallway and followed Cormoran down the stairs. Val glanced around as she walked, hoping to avoid a certain brunette alpha. She wasn't ready to face her sister yet.

Cormoran held the door open for her. "Take a walk around the lawn. They just shoveled the walkways this morning. The recreation hall is open too if you'd rather spend your time there. I'll be close by, so if you need me, just push the button on the side of your wristband."

Val stepped out onto the sidewalk, and the chill seeped into the fabric of the hoodie within seconds. Her naturally higher temperature was enough to take the edge off, but the cold still gave a slight shock to her system. She shoved her hands into the sweatpants pockets. The air smelled fresh, but not nearly as satisfying as the forest outside Christopher's family home.

While they hadn't expected Lex's aggressive phasing, Val missed how alive she felt in those moments. Her parents had often helped younger werewolves in the pack with their first phases, taking them out to the woods, teaching them how to control the powerful urges to hunt anything that moved. Lyla and Val had always looked forward to when they would be the ones running out into the trees with their parents, being taught the secrets of their kind. But life had dealt them different cards.

Val's first phasing had started by shivering through a fever, hidden away in a cave. Lyla had been terrified, and eventually Val realized that she would have to leave her sister alone just to keep her safe. Lyla hadn't moved from that spot in the cave for a whole day, hiding behind a boulder and waiting for her sister to come back and tell her that everything was going to be all right.

Val followed the path around, but her steps slowed as she approached the looming lab building. Almost of their own free will, her feet turned until she was heading down a different path that wound back toward the main hall and the dormitories. She sniffled, her nose running slightly in the cold air, and she brushed her long red hair out of her face, scratching the side of her head that sported the tight braids.

She didn't look up until she had nearly made a full circle. About thirty feet away, Lyla sat on a bench next to the main hall. She was dressed in the same sweatpants and hoodie as Val, eyes fixed on the ground in front of her. Val's shuffling footsteps slowed. She didn't want to keep moving toward Lyla, but she did. She kept walking until she reached the bench, and then she sat down on the opposite end from her sister.

Lyla cleared her throat. "You okay?"

Val didn't have anything to say to that, so she didn't. Neither of them had ever been particularly good at communicating, even with each other. They'd always kept their struggles under a tight lid. Val had covered it up with her sarcasm and bravado. Lyla had chosen to mask it with a tight grip of control, both over herself and over the environment around her. Finally, Val spoke, using her voice for the first time since she'd been in the testing room.

"We're a pair. The two of us trying to keep up this façade and pretending like we're not holding together by threads."

"Say what you want to. Just don't go silent on me again," said Lyla.

Val looked out over the sparkling snow. "Cormoran let you out so you could come talk to me, didn't she?"

"Yeah."

"Okay." The air between them was so awkward it made Val want to pull her hair out. Lyla still wasn't looking at her.

"Have you been having nightmares?"

Val shook her head. "No. The sedatives and pain meds for my headaches keep me pretty knocked out. I guess there's a silver lining in everything."

"Are the headaches from—" Lyla's voice trailed off as Val's jaw tensed. "I'm really sorry. They were hurting you, and I didn't know what to do."

"If you think those electric currents hurt half as much as you forcing your way into my head, you're kidding yourself," retorted Val. "All those years in the program, there were two things that kept me going. Getting back to you, and the fact that no matter what they did to me, they couldn't get inside my head. It was the one thing I had that was always mine."

Val bit her lip. She'd already said more than she wanted to. She didn't need the bond to know Lyla was desperately trying to hide the guilt that was eating her alive.

"I know it wasn't your fault," Val said softly.

Lyla lowered her head, and it took only a few seconds before Val realized that her shoulders were shaking, tears rolling down her cheeks. Val mentally berated herself. Circling both arms around her little sister and pulling her close, Val let Lyla's tears soak into her shoulder.

"It wasn't your fault." Val repeated. The words felt clumsy on her tongue, but she wasn't about to deprive Lyla of hearing them. "I love you." She bit back her own tears. "I love you."

"I love you too." Lyla rubbed at her eyes. "We don't ever have to talk about any of it if you don't want."

"What's to talk about? It's not like I have any secrets anymore," replied Val with a snort. "You saw it all. Heck, I don't know, maybe it was for the better."

"You can try and do the same to me," offered Lyla. "I won't stop you."

"No," said Val forcefully. "I would never do that, Lyla. And I'm not saying that to make you feel guiltier than you already do. It wasn't your fault, and I mean that."

"I thought we might get split up and sent to different schools, and you wouldn't talk to me again," said Lyla. "I couldn't stand the thought of you leaving and being angry with me."

"They might let us go back to Westbrook together. I bet Jules goes hysterical when we see her again," Val said, amused at the thought. "It'll be okay. We'll survive this, I promise."

"Isn't it supposed to be my job to say that?" asked Lyla, smiling beneath the drying tear trails on her cheeks. Val smirked at her.

"You've got to let me be the big sister sometimes."

"Deal."

...

Dr. Carrington held the brain scan lightly between his fingers, lips pursed as he studied it and the page of notes he held in his other hand. Dr. Quinn sat next to him, and Mr. Jack August finalized the sum total of the room's occupants.

"The data is revolutionary. If we could achieve this level of control with other bonded pairs, we could present a convincing argument to implement this nationwide," said Dr. Quinn, her silver pen still for once. "It might even be a safer option to pursue at this point than the first. The manual creation of blood bonds was never considered before the Blackwood sisters came to us. I believe it could very well be the future of this program." She flipped through her notes. "The blood bond between Mark King and William McLane has stabilized. We have high hopes for their continued success."

Setting the pages back down on the table, Dr. Carrington tapped a finger against his lips. "I am glad to hear it. But as to our plan for the Truebloods, we will stay on course. The manual blood bonds have enough data and legitimacy behind it now that we can present it to our partners in the government. It will keep them satisfied for the time being."

Dr. Quinn frowned, and Dr. Carrington swiveled his chair toward her. "Can I still count on you to support us in this venture, Dr. Quinn?"

She paused, and clicked her pen shut. "Have I given any reason to doubt?"

He smiled disarmingly. "Never, my dear Beatrice. You're as steady as they come. Have you finalized the shipment of crates to the schools?"

"Yes. Everything is stocked as you specified. With all the precautions observed."

"Excellent." Dr. Carrington turned his attention to the quiet man who was sitting halfway across the table, shrewd eyes watching the exchange between the two doctors. "Mr. August. I've been impressed with how quickly your media outlets work. It seems the whole country is on edge when it comes to the Truebloods. The story about the escaped alpha was a particularly poignant touch."

The man nodded, teeth flashing as he leaned back in his chair and smiled. "A little flair for the dramatic is always a good trait in my line of work. People feed on fear like parasites. Always looking for something to worry about. All I do is give them a nudge in the direction that we want them to go. We are primed and ready, we just need the players and the stage."

Dr. Quinn eyed him. It was no secret among the board members that the two of them shared a deep dislike of each other. She cleared her throat. "I would feel better if we were able to pinpoint a lethal silver limit with the younger Ms. Blackwood. We still don't know enough about her limits."

Dr. Carrington nodded. "A valid concern, but the recovery period for such a procedure is far too lengthy for the timeline we are working with. We need Lyla Blackwood to be capable of playing her part."

"Do you think it is a mistake to keep the handlers in the dark? They might prove useful to us in this."

"I think not," replied Dr. Carrington. "They're invaluable assets to us, undoubtedly. But some of them have grown too sentimental where their charges are concerned. And we must always keep our eyes on the objective prize."

There was a knock on the conference room door. Dr. Carrington turned his chair to greet the newcomer. "Ah, Ms. Cormoran. Time to discuss the future of our favorite Blackwood sisters."

CHAPTER TWENTY-SIX

Jules' legs bounced up and down as she fidgeted, her red mittens clasped up around her mouth. Her huge circular glasses perched on her reddened nose. Her matching fluffy earmuffs were bright against her loose black hair. She shivered even in the warmth of her winter parka. Lex stood beside her in a light jacket. He watched her for a minute, amused.

"You could wait inside, you know."

"Can't. Want to be the first to give hugs," Jules chattered.

"Jules, I'm pretty sure you'll be the only one giving them hugs," laughed Lex.

She blew on her hands, and then glared at him. "Well, whose fault is that? I swear between the four of you, I'm getting some gray hairs. You should tell her how you feel."

Lex shrugged. "Jules, she doesn't like me that way."

"Whatever," she replied flippantly. "I can't believe Christopher hasn't actually talked to Val either. Neither of you sent them a single text message?"

Lex had the decency to look ashamed of himself. "I figured she'd have enough on her plate without talking to me. Besides, they said they might not be able to use their cell phones."

Jules threw up her hands and let out a frustrated groan. "Ugh! Honestly, you two. Do I have to do all the work myself? Tell Christopher to come out here."

"Jules, he'll be even colder than you."

A black van appeared at the gate, slowly rolling over the gravel and snow. It pulled to a stop in front of the dorm building. Jules let out a loud squeal and went running. The moment that the tall redhead stepped out of the middle seat onto the driveway, Jules tackled her from the side. Val lost her balance and wrapped her arms around Jules' midsection just as they tumbled off to the side in the snow. Jules gasped, her excited exclamation of welcome turning into a string of apologies.

"Oh my gosh, I'm so sorry!" she gasped, rolling to her feet. "Val, are you okay?"

The alpha rose to her feet, brushing the snow off the back of her pants before turning back to her friend. "I'm okay, you crazy kid. And they call *me* a feral," she teased.

"I'm just so glad you're back," said Jules breathlessly. She stepped back to look Val over, and frowned when she saw her dark, sunken eyes. There was a slight gauntness to Val's face as well, as if she hadn't been eating well. Lyla stepped around the back of the van and gave Jules a small smile.

"Hi, Jules."

Jules gave Lyla a calmer hug than the one she'd given Val, and then stepped back to look at them both. "Are you guys… are you really okay?"

Val circled her arm around the omega's shoulders. "We're glad to be back. I wasn't sure if we were both coming until a couple days ago." Jules had questions, but she was interrupted by the sight of a familiar woman stepping around the side of the car, her faux fur coat collar ruffled from the wind. Cormoran gave Jules a smile before addressing the Blackwood sisters.

"ID bracelets stay on this time, I'm afraid," she said. "And remember the requirements. I'll be checking in with you every evening over the phone. If the bracelets register a temperature higher than the limit, I'll be notified. Do you have any last questions for me?"

Jules watched the way that both sisters avoided her gaze, shaking their heads in tandem. Cormoran folded her hands.

"All right. I'll see you both soon."

She stepped back into the car with the armed security beta. Jules glanced toward Gibbous Hall where the two on campus security guards were watching over the new arrivals. The black van pulled away.

"Let's go inside, I'm cold," Jules said, tugging on the sleeve of Val's hoodie and breaking the strange spell of silence Cormoran had left. "The boys are waiting to see you."

She caught the glance that passed between the two sisters, but paid it no mind, grabbing both of their hands, and pulling them toward Gibbous Hall. Lex still stood outside the doors, hands shoved into his pockets, breath leaving his mouth in little smoky puffs. When they came closer, he grinned and nodded at them.

"Long time no see," he said. "I'm glad you guys are back."

Jules pointed at the doors. "Go get Christopher. We can help them take their bags up to their room."

Before Lex had even turned around, the door opened to reveal the tall blond boy with a dark red scarf wrapped around his neck, covering most of his mouth. "Hi."

"Hi," said Val quietly. Jules didn't miss the way Christopher's eyes twinkled when he saw her, or the way Val's cheeks heated with a barely perceptible blush. Jules managed to keep the smile that threatened to take over her face to a minimum. She picked up one of the bags.

"Come on, friends. Let's get these ladies moved in."

Several hours later, the three girls were all dressed in pajamas, sitting on Val and Lyla's floor with mugs of microwaveable hot chocolate. When Jules had discovered that her two best friends had never experienced mini marshmallows, she threw a fit and retrieved a bag from her room. She watched them take their first sips.

"Good, right?" she asked, intently watching their expressions.

Val stared down at the little floating puffs of white. "I don't know. They're kind of weird and stick to my lip. And they're so sugary."

"That's the point." Jules giggled. "The more sugar the better."

"You really don't need any extra sugar, Jules," said Lyla. "If anyone in the world was made out of sugar, it's you."

Jules flipped her black braid over her shoulder and fluttered her eyelashes. "Why thank you. It's a lot of work to be this sweet."

"I think I'm getting a cavity," groaned Val. She laughed when Jules smacked her lightly on the shoulder.

"Valentine Blackwood, don't be so mean. I texted you every day over winter break even though I knew you wouldn't respond. I missed you guys."

Val smiled. "We missed you too, Jules."

They talked late into the night about everything and anything except for Val and Lyla's time at the DAO center. When Jules curled into her sleeping bag on the little foam pad on the floor, she gave a contented sigh.

She didn't know how long she'd slept when a sound stirred her awake. She blinked, eyes adjusting to the darkness. A soft cry came from Val's bed. Jules sat up. She knew that Val had nightmares. They'd come nearly every night when Val had stayed in her room months ago. Once, she'd tried to wake Val by saying her name, but there'd been no response.

Jules crept toward the bed. Val was twisted in the sheets, hands clenched into fists. Jules could just make out the slight sheen of sweat on her face. She reached out, fingers slowly inching toward the alpha's shoulder. Val's ID bracelet flashed red.

"Jules! Don't!"

The warning from Lyla came too late as Jules leaned over the older girl, putting her hands-on Val's shoulders. Immediately Val's hands let go of the sheets and swung wildly, fighting off the hidden terrors plaguing her mind. Jules yelped as one of Val's hands connected with her sternum. She fell backwards and felt Lyla catch her from behind. Val's eyes shot open, laced with violet.

Just as quickly, she groaned and put her hands to her head, glaring at Lyla. "Get out of my head."

Lyla held Jules steady. "You hit Jules."

The other alpha's eyes widened as she took in the sight. Jules rubbed the bruising skin beneath her collarbone, and Val scooted off her bed. "Jules, I'm sorry. Do you need some ice?"

Jules sniffed, irritated as her eyes filled with tears. "No." She reached out and wrapped her arms around her friend. "I hate that they did this to you. I'm sorry. I'm so sorry."

Val patted her back. "It's not your fault. I feel like I'm saying that to everyone lately." On the nightstand, Val's phone buzzed, and the redhead flinched.

Lyla picked up the phone. "Yeah, it's fine. Val had a nightmare, that's all. Nothing else happened." Jules heard a smooth voice on the other end of the line, and she assumed it was Cormoran. *Wow, they're not joking around.*

Hanging up, Lyla put the phone back down. "Let's get some sleep."

Peering at Val in concern, Jules went back to her sleeping bag. She watched as the two alphas climbed back into their beds. They were so on edge that Jules could practically feel it radiating off of them. She sat watching them until their breathing grew steady in sleep, remembering the first day she'd seen them walk through the school. Something in her had awakened that day, something she'd never even known she had. Somewhere far within, she knew that her wolf had stirred for the first time. The papers were right. Truebloods could influence other Weres.

But they were also so, so wrong about what happened when they did. Jules snuggled back into her pillow and wished she could do something to help.

. . .

On the first day of classes, Principal Bleiz called the two Blackwoods into his office during their free period. Sitting down across from the oak desk, Val slouched in her chair, waiting for yet another scolding. Principal Bleiz looked irritable, and Val was guessing that the tall mug of coffee sitting in front of him wasn't the first he'd had that morning.

"The DAO has made it clear that the two of you will be staying here through the rest of your school year. My hands are tied on this, but I will have you know that the security betas will be staying as long as you both do. I expect you to be on your best behavior."

Val pasted an offended expression on her face. "Aren't we always?"

"Go. You both have class to get to," scowled Principal Bleiz, ignoring her. "I don't want to see you in my office again unless it's absolutely necessary."

"Yes, sir!"

Val dashed for the door. She turned to go down the hallway and ran headfirst into Christopher. She put her hands out to stop herself and planted them directly on his chest. He caught her arms to steady her. Immediately, both of them flushed red.

"Uh…" Val sputtered, shoving away from him. "What… uh, what are you doing by the office?"

Christopher shifted his bookbag over his shoulder uncomfortably. "My next class is that way," he said, pointing down the opposite hallway. "And Jules said you guys had a meeting with the principal. I was just coming to see how it went."

Val shrugged, wanting to escape as quickly as possible. "It's fine. Everything's fine. I gotta get to class." She maneuvered herself around Christopher, trying to get control of her flaming face.

"Um, Val?"

"Yeah?" she paused, groaning silently. She really didn't want this conversation to go any further. She glanced back at Christopher, who shifted his glasses up farther on his nose.

"Your shoelace is untied."

"Oh, thanks."

Still blushing furiously, Val continued down the hallway. She wanted to be out of sight of the boy next to the office. She knew Lyla was behind her, and the fact that her sister had seen the whole thing just made it worse. The bond link hummed lightly with Lyla's attempt to contain her amusement.

"Can you please keep your thoughts to yourself?" grumbled Val as they turned into their classroom. Lyla just chuckled. Irritated at her sister, Val made sure to choose a seat as far away from Lyla as she could. She dropped her bag and reached down to tie her shoe.

At the end of her last class nearly a week later, Val received a text from Christopher asking her if she'd be willing to talk later that day. She wanted nothing more than to hide in her dorm room and ignore the message. She left Lyla in the library and headed across the campus to the chosen meeting spot. She passed Jackson on the lawn, but he didn't even look her way. Val noticed that he looked drawn, almost as if he were sick. She wasn't about to complain about his lack of interest.

She shoved her hands into the pockets of her cargo pants and headed for the bench at the corner of the trail. Ahead of her, she saw the familiar figure wrapped in his trench coat, a furry bomber hat perched on his head. A small smile played at the corner of her mouth, despite her resolution to be completely objective in the forthcoming conversation.

When he caught sight of her, he jumped to his feet. "Hey."

"Hi."

They stood awkwardly for a minute before Val moved to sit down on the bench. Christopher hesitantly sat down on the other end. "How was your winter break?"

Val folded her arms over her chest. "It was fabulous. Five stars. But I don't think you wanted me to come out here to ask me how my break went."

He winced. "No, I didn't." It took him a moment, and he seemed to be unsure what he wanted to say. Val sat quietly. She wasn't about to start the conversation.

He scratched his nose. "I'm not good at this kind of thing."

"That makes two of us," replied Val with a shrug. "But you wanted to talk about something, so let's at least give it a shot."

He sighed. "I've had a lot of time to reflect on everything. At Thanksgiving, you asked me if I was being your friend as an experiment. I realized that if you really saw me that way, that I didn't want to be that person. And I didn't know how to show you that I wasn't. Do you really think so little of me as that?"

Val opened her mouth to respond, but the words died on her lips. She dropped her gaze, unable to look at him anymore. "No, I don't think that little of you," she admitted. "I actually think a lot of you."

She noticed the way his lips curved upward at that. When he looked up at her again, she felt as if he could see her. Not the façade she wore to protect herself, but the vulnerable side of her hidden far away.

"I'm your friend because I want to be," he said. "I know that you've trusted me with a lot, and I don't always know what to say, but I'm truly honored."

"I wasn't supposed to tell you," whispered Val.

"But you did. And I'm glad." He shifted closer to her. Val felt her heart pound as he touched hesitant fingers to her cheek. She was surprised by how warm his hand was. She swallowed, torn between all the emotions that were vying for her attention. She knew she had to stop him. The blood claim's faint rhythm was constantly challenging her, telling her that her feelings could not be trusted. Tears flooded her eyes, and she stood up from the bench, taking several steps to put distance between her and the boy on the bench. The boy who had given her a snow globe and listened to her story.

"I can't do this."

He looked confused. "I'm sorry, I shouldn't have—"

"No, it's not that. It's this, all of this," Val gestured wildly around herself, breath forming tiny clouds of fog as it met the air. "Whatever this is. I put a blood claim on you, Christopher. I'm supposed to feel protective of you, care about you. But I don't think it's meant to be anything other than that. I'm sorry, I promised this wouldn't change anything."

He gently took her hands. "Val, this doesn't have anything to do with the blood claim. I don't care about that. I think I'm falling in love with you."

His candid confession left her speechless. She'd heard the word sometimes in her quietest thoughts, but hearing it so plainly spoken into the winter air chased every chill from her. He was looking down at her, eyes earnest, baring his heart.

And what can I offer him in return? It was the question she had asked herself over and over. She knew the answer. *Nothing. A broken girl who will break his heart.*

She blinked away her tears. "Christopher, you've been a better friend than I could ever have asked for, and this is all…" she paused, looking down where he held her hands between them. "Please just be my friend."

Hurt washed over his face, and Val wanted to take it all back. But she stood, staring at him while he stared back, silently begging him to understand. He lowered their hands and released her. He swallowed and gave her a smile that didn't do anything to hide the pain in his eyes.

"Always."

CHAPTER TWENTY-SEVEN

When Val came back to the library, Lyla could see that she'd been crying. She sat down at the table with Lyla and pulled off her thin gloves. Closing her textbook, Lyla resisted the urge to use the bond link. Val was still sensitive to that, and Lyla was letting her set the boundaries. Whatever Christopher had said must have had an impact, and Lyla was fairly sure she already knew how the conversation had gone.

"Want to talk about it?"

Val's gaze snapped up. "Everything's fine. We're still friends."

"I think that's exactly what you're having a problem with." Lyla fully expected the glare she was given. "Val, I think we can all see that it's more than the blood claim at this point."

"Yeah, well I'm glad you can see it so clearly."

Lyla knew that she'd seen too much that day in the test room. They hadn't talked about it since, not really, because that's what they did best. Lyla sighed. "Val, you love him."

There was no answer, which was answer enough. Val scraped at the edge of the table with her fingernail, staring at it as if it held the secrets of the universe. Lyla waited. Finally, Val grimaced and shook her head.

"I guess it just doesn't matter. Whatever my feelings are, you know how the DAO would react to a relationship between a Trueblood alpha and a human. Plus, I'm a mess. It's bad enough that you have to deal with it. I won't put that burden on his shoulders too."

Lyla shrugged. "All true. But you can still admit your feelings for him."

"Yeah? And what about you and Lex?" asked Val with a scowl. "You feel something for him, but you hold back too. So why is this any different?"

Lyla shifted in her seat. "I guess I just don't have time to think about Lex that way. Besides, I think we both know it's not exactly the same thing." Val went quiet, and Lyla leaned forward on the table. "Val, I'm sorry."

Val blinked and looked away. "It's fine. It's going to be fine."

...

Lyla and Val stood in line with a small crowd of other students in front of the nurse's office. It had come as no small surprise that Cormoran had instructed them to receive their suppressants like everyone else that month without her supervision. There was a wide bubble of space between the Truebloods and the rest of the students, but they were used to it. The unrest surrounding the presence of Truebloods in society had stayed consistently high.

Christopher had even told them that his father had been called in to several special meetings on the very topic.

In Lyla's opinion, things would be much better for everyone if the Truebloods were all allowed to go back to the forests and be left to themselves. The night before during their heated game of Monopoly, Jules had even remarked, "I mean, they're the ones that wanted you guys here in the first place, and now they don't. Can they make up their minds?"

The nurse finally called them in. "Next."

Val and Lyla walked in together and sat down in the cushioned chairs. The nurse gave them both a warm smile. "How are you two doing today? You haven't been in my office before."

"They're letting us out on a longer leash," quipped Val with a grin. The nurse chuckled and set the two packages on the small table next to her. Both girls rolled up their sleeves, baring their arms. The nurse swiped the alcohol over their skin. Lyla glanced at the nurse's name tag. *Marge.* The smells of the medical supplies almost completely masked her scent, but Lyla guessed she was a gamma.

"Okay, quick sting," Marge said, sliding the needle into Val's arm first. The alpha hissed, turning her face to the side. "Sorry. Nobody's a fan of these things, I know."

"Something like that," muttered Val.

Lyla sat stoically as she was injected, ignoring the sharp bite of the syringe. Marge gently smoothed band aids on each of them. "All right, you're set. If you notice something out of the ordinary, feel free to come back. I'll be in the office late for the next three evenings in case anyone needs anything."

"Thanks."

Lyla stepped out of the office and around the trailing glares that followed them down the hallway. Val threw an arm around her shoulders. "Ready to get schooled, Lyla Blackwood?"

Side-eyeing her, Lyla smiled. "You're in a good mood, all things considered."

Val threw her head back and took a dramatic inhale. "It's just that I can't wait to be locked up in a bunker with you for two days again. Jules even added a bag of mini marshmallows to our food shelf."

It felt good to laugh. Lyla followed her sister into the locker room.

Val dodged around Lex, passing the ball over to Lyla, who was being guarded by Christopher and Jules. Weaving around the much slower omega and human, Lyla sent the basketball up over the rim of the hoop and swishing easily through the basket. Val whooped and reached out for a high five from her sister. Lex threw his hands up in the air as Jules retrieved the rolling ball.

"This is ridiculous. Why are you two on the same team again?"

"What's the matter, Lex? Can't handle a couple of Truebloods?" teased Lyla. She wiped the sweat off of her brow, breathing only slightly heavier than normal. Jules fell dramatically to the gym floor, feigning exhaustion and holding onto the basketball.

"You guys are crazy. Why did I get talked into this?" she complained. Val walked over to take the basketball from her, but Jules tightened her grip and scooted away, throwing in a growl for good measure. Val raised an eyebrow and turned to look back at her sister.

"We've got a wild one."

"Can't have that," shrugged Lyla, taking a swig of her water bottle. Val grinned and headed for Jules again, picking the omega up and slinging her carefully over her shoulder. Jules squeaked and protested, tossing the ball to Lex, who took the opportunity to race up to the hoop and make a basket. Jules shook her fist in the air, still upended over Val's shoulder.

"YES!"

Val set her down, protesting, "That's cheating!"

"Says you." Jules flashed her a wide smile.

Lyla laughed. "I'm pretty sure the score was in our favor."

The five friends sat down on the gym bleachers, sipping from their water bottles. Christopher went back to his notebook. Val noticed that he'd moved on to a new one this week, having filled yet another for the shelf above his desk. She'd seen it once when they had stopped by his dorm room the previous semester. His room was exactly the way she would've expected it to be: two extra bookshelves, a desk with an antique lamp, and notebooks piled and stacked on nearly every surface. He'd even hung up several paintings on the walls. It was more like a professor's office than a student dorm room. Since he didn't have a roommate, he was free to decorate how he liked. He looked up from the notebook, and their eyes met. Val looked down and studied her water bottle cap.

Jules poked Val in the side. Val grunted and glared at the omega, who paid it no attention. "You feeling okay? You looked like you were daydreaming."

"Yeah." Val frowned. "Actually, yeah." She realized that the side effects that usually accompanied her suppressant weren't bothering her this time. She glanced at Lyla, who also looked like she felt fine. Then she noticed that Jules looked slightly pale.

"What about you?" she asked the omega.

Jules put her water bottle back in her bag. "I'm feeling a little gross, honestly. I think I might turn in early, guys."

The others said their goodnights and headed back to their own rooms. The moment they had closed the door, Lyla cleared her throat.

"I'm not feeling nauseous this time."

"Me neither," said Val. "But I'm not complaining. Maybe the suppressants will stop our phasing for real this time." As nice as it sounded, Val hated the thought. She couldn't let them take it away like that. "Do you think it will come back when we leave the program?"

Lyla set her bag down on the floor of their bedroom. "I guess we'll find out."

...

Nearly half the student body was out sick the next day of classes. Val and Lyla sat in Advanced English, glancing around at all the empty seats. Mr. Harrison made an announcement at the beginning of class that if anyone felt sick and needed to leave, they would receive a pass from the school nurse.

"It can be completely normal for students to feel negative side effects when we receive new suppressant formulas from the D.A.O.," he reassured. "Everyone will be back to their healthy selves by tomorrow."

Jules was absent all day. Lex showed up for their shop class, but Lyla noticed that even he looked a little more tired than usual.

Since none of the human students were affected, the ratio of Weres and non-Weres was much more balanced that day. In the nurse's office, Marge was kept busy giving out anti-nausea medication and taking temperatures. Lyla finally concluded that the new suppressant formula must have been the one that Cormoran had tested on them a few months ago. She and Val still felt healthy, which was a nice change.

After classes and supper, they decided to visit Jules to bring her some food and company. She hadn't even texted them. When the two Truebloods arrived in her dorm, they were immediately confronted with the sight of the omega rolled in her comforter, lying on the futon next to a box of Kleenex and a half-eaten chocolate bar. Val set down the steaming bowl of chicken noodle soup and knelt next to the futon, lifting the edges of the comforter to peer at the sickly omega inside.

"Hey short stack," she said softly. "We brought you something to eat."

The lump in the comforter moaned. "I'll probably just throw up again." Her voice sounded raw and painful. "Thanks for coming to see me." She sat up stiffly, her black hair sticking out in all directions around a face that was a strange shade between pale and green. She rubbed her eyes, looking down at the bowl of soup. "The chicken smells really good."

"Awesome. I slaved over it. Poured it out of the can myself," replied Val with a sassy wink. The omega looked up at her friend, and Val felt her heart drop. In the depths of Jules' dark eyes were flecks of red. Lyla saw it too, and Val felt her sister's immediate concern.

"Jules? Your eyes… they're turning color," said Lyla.

The omega took the bowl out of Val's hands. "Yeah, they do that sometimes," she sniffed. "Sometimes they look more hazel than brown."

The two sisters shared a look. Lyla tried again. "They're turning red."

The perspiration lining Jules' forehead and the way her hands were trembling slightly was far too familiar. Val noticed that the omega's fingernails had sharpened to points. "Lyla, she's phasing." She quickly grabbed the bowl of soup, saving it from pouring all over the omega's lap as Jules let it fall from her hands.

"I'm… no, there's no way I could… Val?" her eyes grew wide and scared. "This is a joke, right?" The telltale outlines of her fangs were just visible through her lips.

Val's voice was quiet and soothing, more than Lyla had thought her capable of. "Jules, there's a chance you could've gotten a bad suppressant, like Lex did. But you're going to be okay."

The red flecks in Jules' eyes slowly flooded through her irises, and when she glanced down at her hands, she gasped at the sight of the claws, revealing her fully descended fangs. Lyla felt herself freeze as her brain worked through the possibilities. As an omega, Jules' phasing would hardly be a danger to any of the other students. She was more likely to hyperventilate. Lyla put a hand on Val's shoulder.

"I think you need to go get Marge."

Val nodded and squeezed Jules' hand. "Don't worry; I'll be right back with the nurse. You've got this." She rose and hurried out the door. Jules' breathing continued to increase, and soon she was panting, squeezing her eyes shut and trying to cope with the foreign strength rushing through her body.

"Jules," said Lyla. "Can you try to take some deeper breaths?"

"I'm not supposed to phase. I took my suppressant, this isn't supposed to happen," Jules mumbled, shoulders shaking. Lyla took her hands.

"There's nothing wrong with you. I'm here, I won't let anything bad happen," Lyla reassured, silently urging Val to hurry. Jules struggled through a few deeper breaths, and calm began to settle over her features. When her blood red eyes met Lyla's, she blinked, and then gasped.

"Lyla, your eyes—"

Somewhere outside the room, there was a terrified scream.

…

Val jogged easily up the sidewalk toward Gibbous Hall. She frowned up at the full moon, silently giving it the full measure of her opinion. She swiped a hand over her brow and surprised herself when it came away covered in sweat. When she looked down, she saw the ashen gray color of her skin. She skipped a beat, her jog slowing down to a walk. She felt her upper fangs pressing against her lower ones, pulling her lips back into the feral snarl of a wolf. Shock filled her as she realized that the normal haze of the suppressant was completely absent. On her wrist, the red light on her ID bracelet began blinking.

The dark sky rumbled overhead, a crack of thunder splitting the clouds after a bright flash illuminated the buildings. Val trembled as her body rushed through the phasing, and the clarity flooded into her senses. When it came, the scents of other werewolves flooded her nostrils. Back in the direction of the girls' dorm, she heard a faint scream, and then a strange crashing sound from inside Gibbous Hall. Her wolf pulled her forward, and she realized with a strange dread that it was being drawn by other wolves. She fought back to keep her control intact.

Val… calm down…

The echoes of Lyla's voice reverberated through her mind. She took a deep breath, pulled the doors open and slipped inside. She could hear a loud commotion echoing from somewhere else in the building, and it sounded close. The lighting had been dimmed for the night, but her eyes were sharper than normal. Every edge stood out; every smell magnified. She took more steps forward toward what sounded like growling, claws on sheetrock and metal and angry snapping of fangs. The smell of them was all sweat and primal fury. Alphas and betas. Several gammas.

One of them smelled closer than the others… her head whipped to the side as the slightest shift of movement reached her ears. Fangs flashed in her face as a fully phased beta flew out of a classroom doorway to her right and hit her full force. They crashed against the opposite wall, denting the sheetrock, and sending a shower of dust all around them. Her wolf raged at the attack, but she reined in her instincts hard, twisting under the other Were. She lifted him up and shoved him into the wall again. He crashed to the floor, but rose a split second later, shaking his head. Shoulder down, he charged, catching her in the stomach. The breath rushed out of her in a loud grunt. The two of them crashed backward through the doors of Gibbous Hall.

CHAPTER TWENTY-EIGHT

Carrington sat in front of his marble fireplace, sipping bourbon in a small glass. He watched the flames dance over the fake logs, appreciating the way that the heavy glass restrained most of the heat. There was a pleasant warmth in the room, but it was not too hot. Perfectly controlled. He tapped his fingers against the arm of his leather chair, and waited in his quiet house, listening to the crackle of the fire. Years of preparation had all led to the moments ticking down on the ornate clock in the corner.

"The players… and the stage…" he muttered to himself, taking another sip. "Time to play, girls."

The Blackwood sisters had been the nugget of gold he'd been sifting for since he'd founded the program. Truly remarkable. A bonded pair of feral Trueblood alphas. And such a pair! Valentine's unbridled power and Lyla's impossible control. And he'd managed to get his hands on them. He sipped the bourbon.

His phone rang.

"Dr. Quinn," he said smoothly. "What do you have for me?"

Her voice was calm and unruffled, as it always was. "Project Trueblood is officially underway. We're receiving initial security footage from the cameras now. Principal Bleiz is on site. I've informed him to hold fire unless he has a clear shot."

Dr. Carrington clinked the ice cubes against the side of the glass. "Excellent. Are your extraction teams on standby?"

"Yes."

"I want them, Beatrice. Whatever shape they're in, they go to the location I specified. Understood?"

"Everything is in place. The teams have access codes, and I've covered their tracks. Congratulations, Robert. It seems you will prove to be right after all."

He smiled. "I appreciate it, but this is only the first step of many we still need to take. After the news of this spreads, it will be up to the public to take up our banner and return society to the way it was intended."

"Of course."

"I look forward to our glass of champagne, Dr. Quinn." He ended the call and set his phone on the table next to him. He returned his gaze to the dancing flames.

…

There was a crash outside the door. Jules whimpered, cowering against the wall. Lyla stood up, her violet eyes narrowing as she sucked in a deep breath. The scent of phased wolves was flooding through the door.

Suddenly, the bond became flooded with broken fragments of the scene outside. Lyla saw the charging alpha from Val's perspective, and felt her sister's realization at the same time it came to her. For all they knew, every werewolf student on the campus was phasing, and except for a select few, none of them had ever felt the effects and strength of a phase before.

Lyla headed for the door, realizing just how much danger the human and less aggressive Were students were in. The sounds from outside were growing louder. Something pulled on her sleeve, stopping her, and she turned to see Jules, wide eyed and shaking.

"We can't go out there, Lyla!"

The alpha gripped her friend's shoulders. "Jules, I need you with me right now. There are other Weres phasing, and if I don't stop them, they could injure or kill anyone they feel like hunting. Do you understand?"

Jules shot a panicked glance toward the door, but she nodded. "Okay."

"Stay behind me."

Lyla opened the door and stepped out into the hallway. Immediately, they were thrust into a scene of chaos. At least three Were students were fully phased and facing off, eyes blood red and wild. A door opened a few feet away and an alpha appeared, dragging a human student by her arms.

Lyla dropped her shoulders and locked gazes with the other alpha, letting out a low warning growl. The girl was taller than her, but Lyla felt no fear. She'd squared off against her sister far too many times to be intimidated by height. The other alpha pulled her human captive behind her and turned, ignoring Lyla. That was her mistake.

Lyla moved forward with inhuman speed, twisting the alpha's arm behind her back, and catching her with a hard fist to the jaw. The human girl dropped to the floor, and Jules rushed in to pull her to safety. The fighting betas farther down the hallway took notice of the commotion and dove into the fray, white fangs glittering. Lyla ducked as one grabbed for her and flinched as her shoulder was grazed by claws. The alpha was lying in a daze on the ground, and Lyla found a split second to be grateful that she'd been knocked out relatively easily.

Jules screamed. "Lyla look out!"

Lyla instinctively felt the rush of air behind her head and dropped down to her knees just as the two betas collided above her. She drove every ounce of authority into her voice that she possessed and spat at them.

"Enough."

Their bodies froze, trembling with unsatisfied anger and the fierce urge to hunt. Power flowed through Lyla, unhindered by suppressant or fear. She felt the strands of her control tightening around them. Out of the corner of her eye, Lyla caught sight of another Were student peering out from a doorway. It was a gamma, fully phased but somewhat in control. When she saw Lyla holding off the two betas, the gamma rushed forward to stand at Lyla's side, squaring her shoulders to look as intimidating as possible.

"Go," Lyla spoke slowly. "Stay on the lawn."

Her hold over them was growing. It was easier to subdue them than the alphas, but Lyla hadn't ever established dominance over more than one Were at once. She had a plan; she just didn't know if it would work. The betas stalked toward the doors, still rigid but obedient. Lyla winced as a strong sensation of pain came through the bond. Val was in trouble somewhere.

She waved Jules and the others forward. "Basement, now. You need to get to the bunker."

The metal door to the basement squeaked open. Jules hurried the other students down into the stairwell. There was a loud crack over the building that seemed to shake the walls. The lights flickered, and then went out.

...

Val skidded backward into the gravel, crying out as the icy rocks scraped at her shoulders. She scrabbled against the ground, trying to get some kind of a grip on her momentum. Swinging her leg sideways, she managed to pull away as the roaring beta tackled the space she had just left. Two alphas charged toward them, drawn by the fighting. The parking lot was lit by a huge flash of lightning, and the following thunderclap sent a shiver through the ground. The parking lot lights dimmed into nothing.

Darkness was interrupted only by the flashes of lightning. The freezing sleet was heavy now, and Val frantically swiped her hair away from her face as the strands stuck to her skin. All she could see in the dim light was the glowing red eyes around her and the outline of the other two alphas stalking toward her. The beta behind her rose, a rumbling growl deep in his throat. Val took a deep breath, eyeing him over her shoulder, feeling the hair on the back of her neck lift as the three Weres around her settled into a formation to hunt. A chill ran through her, her clothes soaked through and clinging to her gray skin. The wolf inside her hummed with anger, wanting to be released. But Val knew that if she wanted to keep control, she couldn't it let go. If she did, she could very well turn from protector to predator.

As the three Weres charged, fangs flashing, Val braced herself. She locked arms with the first alpha, spinning to the side to get him in between herself and the other two. But it wasn't fast enough to avoid the beta's claws. They skimmed down the length of her back, and she gritted her teeth against the sharp sting. She ducked her elbow down and then back up hard, connecting with the jaw of the alpha in front of her. He flew backward and landed hard in the gravel.

Val turned just in time to see the beta charging in and the alpha right behind him. Out of nowhere, a dark shape blurred through the rain, smashing into the alpha with a roar. The beta coming toward Val slowed his movements in surprise, and she took the opportunity to smash her clawed fist into his chest. He grunted and fell backwards, gasping for air as the wind rushed out of his lungs.

Still tense, she turned on the newcomer, only to be met with a familiar face. Lex grabbed hold of her arm, eyes red and full of panic. "The security betas opened fire on the Weres in Gibbous Hall, they're shooting silver!" he shouted at her.

Shooting silver… Val glanced toward the girls' dormitory. Her sister was safe, she could feel Lyla's calm determination and understood her mission to safehouse the other students in the basement bunker. And then it hit her. The thin protective strand that linked her to Christopher snapped like an angry electric wire. Danger.

No! Turning on her heel, Val headed for the boys' dormitory.

Lex shouted after her. "Val, what are you doing?" he ran to catch up, pulling at her sleeve. She shook him off.

"The boy's dormitory!" Val yelled back at him. "They're going to be slaughtered in there!" She didn't wait to see if Lex had followed her when she continued her mad rush toward the doors. She had to save Christopher.

…

Lyla felt herself slammed into the wall by a heavy body as the dorm plunged into complete blackness. A split second later, the generators kicked in, flooding the building with an eerie red glow from the emergency lights.

She kicked out as hard as she could and then swung with her claws. The gamma howled and stumbled back, instantly falling to her knees in submission as the irate Trueblood whirled on her. Lyla commanded her to go outside, and she slunk down the hallway.

"Jules! Keep everybody down in the bunker. You stay here by the door and don't let anyone in unless they give you my name." Jules nodded and pulled the door shut. Lyla waited until she heard the heavy lock click into place before heading down the next hallway.

She took a glancing blow to the thigh from another alpha but managed to order out the weaker gammas and betas while she dealt with the others. A group of Weres were battering against a locked dorm room door, smashing against the wood with their claws and shoulders. There was no logical urge here, only a chaotic and violent need to destroy, hunt, and kill as the Were students were consumed by their wolves for the first time. Knowing there were students trapped inside the room, Lyla whirled into the pack.

They had nearly broken the door down, it was rattling on its hinges, large chunks of the wood ripped free around the handle. Inside, Lyla could hear the terrified voices of the trapped students.

The alpha of the group faced her, lips drawn and snarling. Her eyes flashed an eerie color in the red lights. In any other situation, Lyla would've found it amusing that this half-blood alpha was challenging her. She gave them the same alpha command, her voice strong and dark. While the others backed down, the half-blood jumped forward angrily, unwilling to accept her dominance. Lyla caught clawed fists with her own and lifted the alpha off her feet, shoving her hard against the wall and repeating the command. The challenger faltered, finally averting her eyes.

Without another word, Lyla let her go and headed for the trapped students, knowing that the other Weres would follow her command, no matter how unwilling they might be. She knocked on the door.

"I'm here to get you guys out," she said quietly. "I can take you somewhere safe."

Hesitantly, a human student opened the door, and Lyla was immediately struck by the smell of the wounded omega lying on the floor. One of the other girls had been smart enough to wrap a shirt tightly around her leg to staunch the bleeding. Lyla's wolf flared at the smell, but she calmly addressed the group.

"Let's get her to the basement door. There's a bunker down there with other students, you'll be safe until we get help." She led the motley group out into the hallway, the wounded omega supported by two of her friends. Lyla reached out for Val, but she could barely feel her sister's emotions. The sounds of fighting erupted upstairs. *God, help us.*

CHAPTER TWENTY-NINE

The boys' dormitory was bathed in red light. The eerie glow added to the horrific scene that Lex and Val found themselves in. They'd pushed past a few frantic students who were rushing out into the freezing rain, safer outside than they were in the death trap that was the dormitory. The moment that Val stepped inside, her stomach turned. The dark stain of blood smeared the walls and floor like a morbid painting.

The smell of death was everywhere, filling her senses and clogging them, choking her with the fear that still gripped her chest. She couldn't breathe. She stumbled out of the cabin. They were all so still, so quiet. Just hours before they had been so full of life.

Val knelt beside the first student she saw, a gamma with a head wound. He was still breathing, and she guessed that he had been knocked out. Lex passed her and started opening dorm doors. The third one he opened revealed a shivering pair of human students hidden away in the closet.

I have to get to Christopher. Val rose from the ground and grabbed Lex by the collar as he came out of the room with his two charges. "Get them out of here. Find Lyla."

She turned and ran for the stairs, heart pounding. Two bodies came hurtling down the staircase at her, snapping and snarling as they clawed and bit at each other. Val braced herself, but their combined weight toppled her backward, rolling over and over until they hit the ground. The moment one of them turned to snap at her, Val backhanded him away and roared menacingly. She leapt to her feet and grabbed him by his shirt collar, holding him up to her face as she locked gazes with his red eyes, all wolf. He whimpered, backing down, and she released him with a shove.

"Go out and wait on the lawn," she growled. "Don't hurt anyone."

The second Were, a beta, slowly rose to his feet and cowered to the command. Val felt the strain that the command put on her energy, but she ignored it as soon as her way up the stairs was clear. *Please be okay.* Her blood pounded in her ears, adrenaline raging through her like a wildfire. Her feet couldn't carry her forward fast enough. Two more students lay immobile on the stairs, their heartbeats faint. Val could smell them only distantly as they clung to life. Nearly driven to panic, she tore up the landing and toward the second door on the farthest hallway. She caught sight of a group of Weres as she flew past the first hall of rooms, heard them snapping and fighting over something.

The door to Christopher's room was broken clean off its hinges, lying against the wall opposite the frame. Val felt her breath catch in her throat as she stepped inside. Books lay everywhere. Val's boot crunched against the pieces of a broken lamp just inside the doorway. She scanned the room, hoping beyond hope that he had been able to get out in time. The window was still intact, but a giant ragged hole had been torn in the wall between his room and the neighboring one. She could smell scents she recognized, all of them belonging to Jackson's alpha friends. And then she saw him.

Half hidden behind his armchair, his glasses had been knocked from his face and shattered. His eyes were closed, a dark gash standing out against his forehead and cheek. He was deathly pale and completely still. Edges of a horrific wound were just visible through his torn shirt.

Val let out a guttural cry and crossed the room in two strides, falling to her knees and pulling his body up into her lap, her clawed hands wrapped gently around him. Her mouth opened, but there was no sound as she struggled for breath against the tightness of her chest. She cradled Christopher against her body, shoulders shaking with sobs that she could not force out of her lips. Every second slowed to an agonizing crawl as her senses were overwhelmed with grief. *No, no, no.*

She threw her head back and howled, a broken sound in the eerie red room. She rocked him back and forth on her knees. The control she had sustained was breaking, releasing the fury of the wolf inside her.

Her father lifted her chin with his fingers, his eyes serious. "No matter what, we always protect our pack. We protect each other. Alone we are weak, but together we are strong."

Val glanced over to where her sister slept peacefully on their double bed. "I'll always protect them, Papa."

Always...

"Please be my friend."

Always...

Red eyes glared at her from the doorway. Low grumbling growls and the strong heady tension of hot-blooded Weres ready to kill permeated Val's burdened senses. Jackson's rogue alphas. With great care, she lowered Christopher's broken body to the floor, and then rose up like a sentinel behind him. Her violet eyes fixed on her quarry, and the last threads of humanity were dormant behind the cool gaze of a hunter.

Cold rage fueled every breath as Val faced the pack at the door, and she lunged into them with the fury of an avenging angel. Her claws flashed, leaving deep furrows through the thigh of the front alpha, who was unfortunate enough to take the brunt of her first attack. She was dimly aware of the wound opened in her side, but she was numb to the pain. Teeth flashed and she whirled, sending the alpha flying against the wall. She dropped to one knee and swung her claws in a wide circle, connecting with whatever she could reach. A second later she was flying between the alphas again, her movements graceful and impossibly fast. Her Trueblood heritage gave her an advantage in speed.

The familiar red haze swept over Val as she reached her full phasing. She had lost all sense of the bond link. The only thing that filled her mind now was the image of the boy lying on the floor in the room behind her. Fangs buried themselves into her arm, and she roared, grabbing the alpha by the shoulders, and dragging him into the room, throwing him against the window. The glass shattered. She dragged in deep breaths, turning back to the remaining alphas.

To her surprise, another Were was already amongst them, snapping and growling. She vaguely heard a sharp alpha command. They disappeared from the view of the doorframe. The dominant alpha was left alone to face the raging Trueblood inside the dorm room. He turned to look at her, and Val frowned. The face was familiar, even through the fog that held her mind captive.

Jackson.

Fully phased, his face was a more intense version of his normal sinister smugness, framed by the white fangs behind his lips. But he wasn't smiling now. Val dropped her shoulders, crouching down as she prepared to attack. But to her shock, Jackson held his hands out, palms open.

"I'm not here to fight, Val."

She realized that his scent was the one that had been missing when she had entered the room, and his simple words took the fight out of her with a rush. She turned to look at the still form of the boy on the floor. As if in a dream, she reached out for him again, but stopped when she felt a hand on her shoulder. She snapped at Jackson, forcing him to take a step back.

"Val, he's still alive, but we need to get him out of here fast, or he won't make it," said Jackson quietly. Val searched his eyes desperately for any sign of a threat, but it wasn't there. She watched as he lifted Christopher carefully up in his arms as if the human boy weighed nothing.

"Let's go."

"Where?" the voice that came out of Val's mouth didn't even sound like her own.

"There's a trauma unit in the back of the nurse's office," said Jackson as he carried Christopher out toward the stairs. "It's the only chance he's got."

Val wanted more than anything to stop him, torn by her mistrust of Jackson's intentions. But her overwhelming desire to save Christopher's life at any cost won out. "If you hurt him…"

"Cool it, Blackwood. This time I'm on your side." Jackson took the first few steps down. Val followed right on his heels, eyes never leaving the human boy's pale face.

…

The last students hurried down the stairwell, carefully supporting the wounded. Jules called after them, directing them down to the bunker. Lyla slumped against the doorframe for a brief moment, catching her breath while Lex kept an eye on the hallways. Jules reached out and touched Lyla's arm.

"Lyla… are there any that didn't make it?"

The Trueblood pushed her stringy hair away from her sweat-slicked forehead, meeting Jules' gaze evenly. "Yes." She saw the omega fight back tears. "Jules, help the ones you can. They need you."

Jules nodded and shut the basement door without another word. Lyla turned around, refusing to let herself feel the exhaustion. She knew that her authority over the Weres gathered outside could snap at any moment, flooding the halls with their wild rage. She closed her eyes.

"Lyla, hey." Lex turned her to face him, his palms resting gently on the sides of her face. "Stay with me. What do you need me to do?"

Lyla reached out to the bond and was immediately flooded with broken fragments of images and emotions. Val was having a hard time holding her control. *Christopher…* Lyla saw a brief flash of the boy lying on the floor, blood staining his clothes. Shaking herself back into reality, Lyla pointed toward the back door. "We need to get to Val."

The two of them left the building, sprinting across the brief space between the two dorms. Lyla felt the rain hitting her face, and the freezing water snapped her awake again, sending a rush of energy through her body. It was so cold, the wind and sleet hit her body like shards of glass. They barreled into the boys' dormitory, nearly crashing into Val and Jackson as they were descending the stairs. Shock registered for both Lex and Lyla as they realized who was carrying Christopher. The rogue alpha didn't give them any time to think; he pushed Christopher into Lex's arms, leaving behind dark red stains on his torn white tee shirt.

"Go, now." In the hallway behind them came the growls and howls of the other alphas. "Get him to the trauma unit in the nurse's office."

Lex and Val immediately turned with their fragile cargo and headed back out into the freezing rain, but Lyla stared at Jackson. "You have a lot of control right now."

He turned away from her to face the oncoming Weres, but not before he'd flashed his signature smirk. "You're not the only one who's phased before, Blackwood. Now get out of here."

Lyla left to the sound of the other werewolves crashing into Jackson, letting the door shut definitively behind her. As she ran, following the dim shapes of her sister and Lex, she remembered the quiet prayer that Mr. Wells had said at the Thanksgiving table and said one of her own. *God, please get us all out of this.*

Mr. Wells.

Thunder cracked overhead as the three of them reached Gibbous Hall, steps careful to avoid slipping on the puddles of water that were beginning to freeze over. Lyla glanced out toward the lawn and saw the shadowy figures of a large group of Weres, some fighting amongst themselves. She ignored them. They would keep for a little while longer.

Inside the building, they were met with the same red lights and the stench of phased wolves, fainter than it had been in the dormitories. Lyla grimaced as they reached the battered door of the nurse's office and were met by the aftermath of the battle between the group of Weres and the security betas. One of the betas was lying face down on the floor and the other slumped against the wall, spent gun across his lap. Lyla's foot collided with a bullet casing and it skittered away. She could smell the sharp pungent scent of silver in the air. It burned in her nose.

Val tried the doorknob, only to find that it was still bolted shut. She knocked against the door. "Marge, please open this door if you are in there!"

There was no answer. "Marge, it's Val and Lyla, please we need your help!" Val pounded a fist against the door, and then moved back several feet, motioning for Lyla and Lex to move back. She growled, summoning the reserves of her strength to attempt to break in.

"Val, wait." Lyla hear the soft scrape of the lock turning, and then the wary face of the school nurse appeared, shocked as she took in the sight of the three werewolf students carrying their friend. She glanced to the side and then quickly opened the door, doing little to hide her fear at the sight of the sharp claws that were wrapped carefully around Christopher's body. Lex laid him on the table, and Lyla saw the extent of the human boy's wounds for the first time. She turned to her sister and saw Val's eyes. She didn't need to say anything. Val already knew.

Marge locked the door behind them and rushed to Christopher's side, ripping back his torn shirt to expose the raw wound in his abdomen. Her hands froze on the fabric, and she shook her head.

"I don't know if there's anything I can do for him," she whispered. Her fingers moved to the side of his neck. "His heartbeat is barely there."

"But it is there," replied Val, gripping the sides of the table desperately. "Marge, you have to try."

"I'll do what I can to make him comfortable. I do have some morphine, but I'm not a surgeon, and even if I were, I couldn't do anything fast enough," replied Marge, pulling supplies out of a drawer. She hung an IV bag above the table on a silver hook and opened a sterilized package. Within the next few short minutes, she had a port in the boy's arm and hooked him up to the monitor.

"I can't believe he's still alive," murmured Lex. "Did Jackson..."

Val shook her head. "No. It was his alphas. I was too late. I didn't protect him."

Her sister turned to look at her, and Lyla felt the grief rolling like tidal waves through the bond. "You did everything you could."

"Please save him," Val whispered, sinking into a chair. Tears swam at the edges of her violet eyes. Lex moved back to stand by the door as Marge began laying out some rudimentary surgical supplies.

Lyla turned away, reaching down and fumbling with the zipper of her cargo pants pocket to remove her phone. Irritated, she shook it out onto the floor and pressed the button to see that there was no service. That didn't surprise her. She scrolled down to where she found Mr. Wells' number in the contacts and awkwardly typed four words into a text message.

MESSAGE NOT SENT
Will retry when connected to service.

...

"I'll try to repair as much of the damage as I can, but I could lose him at any moment, Val," Marge said gently. "Why don't you hold his hand?"

Trembling, Val wrapped her large claws around Christopher's hand, the paleness of his skin strange against the grayish hue of hers. Val leaned her head against the table, wishing there were something… she sucked in a harsh breath and reached out for Lyla's arm.

"I can save him."

Lyla's eyes widened as she understood. "No, Val, you can't."

"I have to do this."

Turning to the nurse, Val held out her arm. "Take my blood and give it to him."

Shocked, Marge stared at her. "Valentine Blackwood, you are asking for a death sentence. I will not have the death of two students on my conscience!"

Val glowered. "But you'll accept the death of one? Then you should have no problem with this. Do it, you know my blood is the most powerful thing you can give him, the only way he has a chance." She saw the nurse glance at the still form of the boy on the table. "Marge, please."

The monitor flatlined. The blood claim linking them shattered like a thousand needles plunging into Val's skin. With a cry, Val sank her teeth into her arm and held it over the gaping wound on Christopher's abdomen. "Marge!" she shouted.

Marge grabbed a large sterilized syringe from the tray and shoved the needle into Val's arm. Val growled at the harsh sting but held steady as Marge drew all the blood that the syringe would hold. "I don't have the right equipment," she muttered under her breath. Despite her shakiness, her hands were steady as she pushed the needle into the port in Christopher's arm, depressing the blood into his body. Val was already reaching across for another syringe on the tray, ripping the package open with her teeth. Another syringe filled. Another needle pushed into the port.

Val pulled her arm away from the wound, tears rolling down her cheeks. She looked down at her claws helplessly as Marge filled another syringe. *It's not enough. In the moment when it matters most, I can't save him. I've never saved any of them.*

CHAPTER THIRTY

BEEP.

Val gasped, staring at the monitor in disbelief. *There's no way it actually worked.*

BEEP.

Marge dropped the last syringe onto the tray, blinking down at the boy on the table. She quickly hooked up several other machines, punching in numbers and watching the screens. Val waited, still watching the tiny blip that appeared on the line of the heart monitor. It was faint, but it was steady.

"Thank God," whispered Lex. Val sank to her knees next to the bed, head swimming, the strain on her body finally showing. She drew in shaky breaths and felt her sister's gentle hand on her shoulder. Marge hurried around the room, pulling more packages out of the drawers and cupboards, and then disappearing into the small supply room behind the office.

"He's going to be okay, Val," said Lyla softly. Val reached up and grabbed her sister's hand, gripping it with as much intensity as she could muster. Their emotions flowed freely through the bond, each lending strength to the other.

Lyla spoke again. "I need to go, Val. The pack won't stay on the lawn forever, and the other students are in danger as long as we are not in control."

"Take Lex with you," replied Val. "I'll come as soon as I can."

With one last squeeze of her sister's hand, Lyla disappeared out of the door with Lex. Val was dimly aware of Marge's gaze on her. The nurse finished taking a blood pressure reading, and reached up to the cupboard, removing another white package. One that Val recognized.

"A suppressant?"

"He's a werewolf now, Val," replied Marge softly. "And although I expect him to be out cold for quite a while as his body heals, I'm not going to take any chances."

Val limply leaned back against the seat of the chair behind her. "Is it from the same crate as the others?"

Marge shook her head. "I'm not that dense, dear. This is one from November's crate, and I know that one works." She paused. "That was a brave thing you did. I don't know if he'll thank you for it, but it was a selfless thing to do."

"Do you need more blood?" asked Val, not knowing how to respond. Marge gave her a small smile and shook her head.

"No. We have more in the cooler." She must've seen the question that was forming on the young alpha's lips. "Not as strong as yours, but you've given him enough to bring him back. I can keep him alive now and stable until we can get him to a safe place for his first phase."

Val leaned her head back. She would face a jury for the crime she had just committed, and it would be unanimous. There were no exceptions—no special circumstances—allowed. Not even someone who was dying could be changed. She wondered briefly if they would even allow her to speak in her own defense. She imagined Dr. Carrington sitting on a chair above a courtroom, all of the other board members arranged in the seats of the jury, all pointing their thumbs down at her like some kind of gladiatorial sentence. She looked back at Christopher, watched as his chest rose and fell in a shallow rhythm. The wound in his abdomen was already beginning to heal, the torn flesh slowly knitting itself back together as the Trueblood alpha blood coursed through his veins.

It was worth it for you.

…

Lyla walked out into the frigid air. She was ready to face the pack outside, no matter what that might bring. She didn't know if she was strong enough to hold them all. There were so many. Suddenly, Lex' presence behind her felt comforting. Alphas squabbled, fighting amongst themselves, trying to separate the group into smaller packs. Betas chose their alphas and fought alongside them. The few stronger gammas that were in the group hung back and watched the others, restless and agitated but not willing to get in between the alphas.

The sounds of fighting faded slightly as the pack caught the scent of the Trueblood alpha striding toward them, head held high. Her eyes met each challenging gaze without fear as she walked through them into the middle of the pack. The rain cleared, and the air had frozen the water on the ground. The full moon shone defiantly through the murky haze in the sky. Steam rose from the bodies of the students around her.

This is it. Either they respect me as alpha, or they don't. Lex stood protectively at her side, waiting, glaring down the Weres standing closest to them, leaving no doubt whose side he was on. An alpha only a few feet away bared his fangs at her, not averting his gaze when Lyla looked him in the eye. He took a step forward, shoulders tense. Lex growled. Another alpha stepped forward to circle with the other. The rest hesitated, watching her. Lyla snarled at the two challengers as they inched forward, blood-red eyes locked on her.

…

Val stood up slowly. She knew that she had pushed herself to the limits, but she could feel Lyla through the bond and knew that her sister was having a hard time holding the pack. She took one last look at Christopher.

"I have to go. Don't let anyone in that door, Marge."

The nurse shook her head. "He's not going anywhere soon, and there are other students who may need my help."

Recognizing the determined glint in Marge's eyes, Val conceded. "In the basement of the girls' dormitory there is a bunker. We sent all the students we could down there, so they'd be safe. I know there are some that are wounded."

Marge was already packing a bag with supplies. Val reached for the doorknob, looking one last time at Christopher. As she exited the room, a faint buzz sounded underneath the chair.

SERVICE CONNECTED
MESSAGE SENT.

Val closed the door behind her and sprinted down the hallway as fast as her tired body would allow. Lyla needed her now. As she reached the doors, she heard a shuffle behind her and a click. Turning her body mid-stride, Val dropped her claws to intercept what she imagined to be another Were.

BANG.

The horrific, fiery burn of silver spread through her shoulder. She screamed, twisting as she caught sight of Principal Bleiz crouched in the doorway of his office with a gun, the barrel pointed directly at her. Val managed roll to the side as she hit the floor.

"Coward!" she shouted at him, gripping the wound with her opposite hand. If he fired on her again, there was a chance she could reach the door before the bullet reached her. "I'm helping them!"

She dove for the door, hitting it with her good shoulder and letting her momentum carry her out into the cold as the second bullet snicked into the metal inches from her head. She rolled onto the hard ground, staying still for a moment to catch her breath. She touched the hole in her shoulder and felt her head swim. The earth slowly steadied, leaving behind a sharp throbbing pain. *White fire.*

Clenching her teeth, Val stood up and took a shaky step toward the pack of werewolves on the lawn. Several of them had already turned, the scent of her blood reaching them.

The alphas stopped mid charge, their heads snapping back toward Gibbous Hall. The pack began to separate, and Lyla saw her sister walking toward her without sparing them as much as a glance. She walked with pride, but Lyla saw the bloodstain on Val's shoulder and the stiffness in her body as she moved. She felt Val's pain, sharp and stabbing. Her multiple wounds were quickly draining her strength.

Val stopped in front of her, then tipped her head back and let out a howl, deep and wild. Immediately, Lyla did the same, and their two voices sang together into the winter air. Lex joined them, and one voice at a time, the pack bowed to the authority of the two Truebloods.

A low rumbling began to rise beneath the wild sound, and Lyla turned toward the tall iron campus gates just in time to see a flash of headlights crash through. Trucks poured through the opening in the fence, rolling to a stop a safe distance away from the pack. Men in black military gear jumped from the back of the vehicles, guns raised and trained on the werewolves as they settled into formations.

Finally, they came. Lyla felt an apprehensive sense of relief as if the weight of the ordeal had been lifted from her shoulders. But then she realized that the bond was flooded with fear, and she glanced up to see Val growling, backing a step away. Lyla looked down to see red dots swarming like angry bees on her chest. The Weres behind her began to move back, angrily staring down the threat and ready to attack.

"Fire on the Truebloods!" someone shouted from the circle of guns. Lyla yelped and felt her body lurch backward as a bullet lodged itself in her left thigh, pain bursting through her leg. The pack leapt into action to protect their alphas, surrounding the Truebloods. Val went down to her knees as another silver bullet met its mark. Lyla felt Lex behind her, dragging her back behind the other Weres, but she struggled free.

"NO!" she shouted at the top of her lungs. "Do not attack!"

If she didn't stop them, they would all die. She heard Val screaming out a similar command, but their control over the pack had decreased in the fury of bloodlust and anger that gripped them all. She could feel her wolf slipping away with the exhaustion and pain that she could no longer hold at bay. She saw two groups of the armed team break off from the formation and charge into the pack, firing at any of the werewolves that attempted to attack them.

Howls and snarling mixed with shouting and gunfire. Pain exploded in Lyla's side. Her knees buckled, and she sank down to the grass. She was dimly aware of someone pulling Lex off of her. She heard his roar of fury, felt gloved hands grip her arms and drag her along the frozen ground. Her vision swam, and she thought that she caught sight of her sister for a brief second, surrounded by black uniforms and gleaming gun barrels.

Lyla was lifted off the ground and pushed into the back of one of the trucks, her shoulders scraping painfully over the grooved metal floor. Her body was going into shock. She felt the sharp sting of a needle piercing her neck, and then the cool rush of something spreading beneath her skin. There were steel-toed boots beside her. She heard the truck doors slam shut and the sounds of the mayhem outside disappeared. It was eerily quiet except for the low grumble of the engine as the truck rolled away from the campus. Lyla felt something cold and metal click around her wrists as her arms were pulled behind her back. The movement pulled against the wound in her side with inexplicable agony. The last of her strength fled as she slipped away from consciousness.

The forest was full of bird songs and the smell of fresh pine needles. Arka toddled after her big sister as quickly as her short legs would allow. Her simple dress swished against her knees and her hair flowed behind her, loose from its ribbon yet again. She was giggling so hard that it was difficult to run, and a wayward root sent her toppling onto her small hands.

Arka picked herself up, brushing off the dirt and dead pine needles on the front of her dress. Bright eyes scanned the trees as she started to pick up the chase once more, but soon realized that her sister was nowhere in sight. Her tiny footsteps shuffled to a stop and she frowned. For a moment, she paused to listen.

The birds went quiet, and Arka turned around again, sensing that she was not alone. Less than twenty feet from her in the trees was a werewolf. His violet eyes studied her as she stood, small and unafraid. She recognized the bracelet on his wrist, tied with little turquoise beads. This morning he had walked past her cabin, and she had waved to him from the porch with Sanzi. This morning he had been only a man with green eyes and teeth that sat in a straight line.

But there was nothing about him that scared her. She knew that someday she would change just like he did, and her hands would wear sharp claws. Her eyes would turn color and be a beautiful purple, just like Mama and Papa's. She liked purple better than red. Some of her friends had red eyes.

She lifted her hand and waved at him, tilting her head sideways and offering him a wide smile. When he smiled back, his lips pulled away to reveal his fangs, and Arka clapped with childish glee. His gaze moved to something beyond the little girl in the trees, and then he turned and loped away into the brush. Arka watched until he had disappeared. She heard a quiet step behind her and felt familiar hands reach beneath her arms and pull her up against a firm chest. A red beard tickled the side of her neck, and she dissolved into a fit of giggles. When he drew back, she tapped his arm insistently.

"Papa, did you see him?" she asked.

His eyes twinkled. "See who, little one?"

"The wolf."

Her father's voice dropped into a whisper. "Was it one of our wolves?" She beamed and nodded. His expression gave way to a cheery smile. "He was watching over you to make sure you were safe. What do we do to help each other?"

"Keep the pack safe," replied Arka dutifully. Her father tweaked her chin and then began walking back toward the little circle of houses. The little girl looked back into the trees where she had seen the werewolf, her little mind pondering new thoughts.

"Papa why are there people who aren't wolves?" she asked. The big man set her down carefully on a log and then took a seat beside her, his large frame dwarfing her tiny one. He squinted up at the sky.

"When we are born, each of us is given gifts. Those gifts make us what we are. Whether we have brown hair," he tugged at the strands hanging down her back, "Or red. Whether we are tall or short, whether we can heal or build, whether we have a soft voice or a loud one, these are all gifts that we are given. If we were all the same, we could not help each other. Being a wolf is one of those gifts, and it is important for us to learn how to use it well."

"Maybe it is so we can help the people who aren't wolves," remarked little Arka, kicking her feet against the bark of the log. Her father paused and looked down at her with a sad smile.

"I think you might be right." He reached his arm around her and hugged her to him. *"We should always share our gifts with the people who need them the most."*

Arka looked up at him with determination. "I will help them, Papa."

He chuckled. "I know you will, Arka. I know you will

CHAPTER THIRTY-ONE

Drip.

Drip.

Drip.

Was it blood or water? The sounds all blurred together, and Val could only hear them through the muffled humming in her ears. Someone far away was yelling her name, calling out for her.

She raised her hand, reaching out in the darkness for that voice. It was calm and soothing even though panic and anger laced through it. Somehow it broke through the violence of her mind's fevered thoughts. A broken howl echoed through her thoughts. **VAL!**

"I want that silver out… keep them alive… cell three… we need a confession…"

There are too many voices now. Where is the one that was calling my name?

Someone gripped her arm, and something cold was injected into her bicep. Val shuddered, back arching on whatever hard surface she was restrained to. Clarity rushed through her as adrenaline pumped into her veins, bringing with it the agonizing grip of pain. She thrashed and felt her world tilt. Nausea overwhelmed her, and she vomited.

They won't let me leave. I want to go home. Please let me go. White fire in my blood, it hurts so much.

"Stabilize her, damn it!" Dr. Carrington's voice was close, far too close. Val's eyes fluttered open, but the faces surrounding her were out of focus. The nausea crept up into her throat, clutching at her stomach. She could barely feel her limbs, ice cold and tingling with a thousand tiny needles.

And somewhere through the darkness… ***where are you?***

Val opened her eyes, blinking against the bright white, fluorescent lights. Her cheek was pressed into a concrete floor. She inhaled and coughed. The simple movement sent aching tremors through her body and she took a moment to focus on calming herself with slow, shallow breaths. Her wrists were encased in leather attached to a chain that hung from a metal bracket on the concrete block wall behind her. The ID bracelet was gone. The chain was long enough to give her minimal movement, but not more than a few feet from the wall. Her clothes were still hanging on her, torn and filthy. The bullet wounds in her shoulder and stomach were caked with blood.

Reaching shaky fingers down, Val pressed lightly against the wound in her stomach, taking deep breaths to steady herself when the pain made her head spin. She couldn't feel the silver bullet. Perhaps their captors had done her that small kindness at least.

There was evidence of an IV port in her forearm, and she knew she wasn't feeling the effect of her wounds nearly as much as she should. Her body wasn't healing like it normally did, as if her natural abilities had been dampened in some way. She saw one door leading out of the room, and an ancient security camera hanging from the ceiling above it. Then she noticed that she was not alone.

Lifting her head, she looked at her sister restrained against the wall next to her. They were far enough apart that Val thought she might be able to only just reach. She shifted as slowly as she could manage. Inch by inch, she shifted closer to Lyla, who was still slumped against the wall, the effort nearly rendering her unconscious again.

Val stretched out her fingers as far as they would reach. It wasn't far enough, and she dropped her hands to her lap in defeat. Watching her sister for any small sign of life, she realized she was holding her own breath. Then she saw the hair in front of Lyla's face flutter ever so slightly. Val exhaled in relief.

She leaned back against the wall, wincing, and holding her stomach. She wasn't sure what damage her internal organs had suffered, but she knew that with whatever had been injected into her body to slow her healing, she wouldn't last as long as she'd like to.

"This is it," she whispered to herself. Honestly, she was surprised she'd made it this far. That was mostly thanks to Lyla. After their parents died, Val had always expected to follow in their footsteps, especially after they were captured by the DAO and subjected to their programs. She briefly expected Cormoran to walk through the door with her clipboard, chiding them for their behavior. That would be a welcome sight compared to the bleak future Val envisioned for herself.

She coughed again and felt wetness on her lips. Running her fingers over her mouth, she saw flecks of blood staining her skin when she drew them away. She scoffed at it. *Two bullets. That's not even close to my silver limit.* A soft noise from Lyla drew Val's attention. The younger alpha moved stiffly, stopping with a grimace when her body protested.

"Hey," Val said softly.

Lyla's dark eyes slowly began to focus, first on the room and then on her sister's face. "What… are we…"

"I don't know where we are. No one else has been in here since I've been awake."

"Oh…" Lyla nodded, pressing her hand against her injured thigh, her pain-slowed brain attempting to reform the memories of what had happened. "They shot us. With silver."

The sharp retort of guns echoed through the campus. Val felt the impact in her stomach and her knees buckled. Somewhere in the distance someone called her name. A flash of red eyes and fury.

"Yeah. I don't think they like us very much." Val chuckled and coughed, quickly swiping the blood away from her lips before Lyla could see it.

Lyla looked toward the door. "I guess we'll just wait until someone comes in, and we'll explain what happened."

Val shrugged. "Maybe they'll let you out for good behavior." Her sister's gaze fixed on her, stern and searching.

"What do you mean? We'll just tell them—"

The door in the corner of the room groaned open, and a tall woman with stern features walked in. Dr. Quinn, holding her ever-present clipboard and pen. She stopped a safe distance away from the alphas, which nearly made Val laugh. As if they were in any shape to do her harm.

Val eyed her as she crouched down, balancing on her heels in front of the two sisters. She tapped the clipboard with the pen. "I must admit to being very disappointed in meeting you here like this," she said. "But you need to know that you have failed. Westbrook High and the other schools in our program have been secured. It will be much easier for both of you if you tell the truth and admit to your part in this."

Both sisters frowned in confusion. Val glanced at Lyla. Neither of them knew what to say, and Val tried to understand, her brain not cooperating in its pain-hazed state. "What?"

Dr. Quinn gave her a convincing smile. "I won't waste either of our time by playing games with you, Ms. Blackwood. You give me a signed confession admitting to your part in convincing the Trueblood students of our program to take control of the assimilation schools, and I will see to it that you and Lyla are made more comfortable."

"More comfortable…" was all Val could manage. She coughed.

Lyla stared at the woman in shock. "You think that we are responsible for this? Us? It was your worthless suppressants!"

"The same way it was our suppressants when your friend phased over Thanksgiving?" Dr. Quinn asked. "We have documented proof that Alexander was given a perfectly good dose. The only thing that changed in his routine was the two of you." When Lyla opened her mouth, Dr. Quinn held up a hand. "I understand that it is impossible for you to reject your nature. But we have plenty of evidence pointing to your involvement. Each school in our program was involved in this horrible tragedy, an act of violence led by Truebloods in every instance."

Val chuckled, and both Lyla and Dr. Quinn looked at her in surprise. She hid a cough behind her hand, the reinforced chains clinking next to her. "So that's it then. We're guilty until proven innocent."

"Will you sign the confession?"

Val shook her head. "No. Because you know we didn't do it."

Dr. Quinn sighed and stood up, tucking the clipboard under her arm. "Very well. The dose of silver in your systems is enough to stop your natural healing process, and you both need further medical attention. Should you choose to provide us with the truth of your involvement, we may be able to assist you. If not, we will have to take more definitive measures. I'll leave you to reflect."

She left, and Val and Lyla sat alone in the room. Val leaned her head back against the wall, the pieces of the puzzle falling into place. "So that's why they let us talk to the other Truebloods over break," she mused softly. "Why they let me pass the test when I failed. They wanted me in the school."

Lyla stared at her, and Val smiled sadly. "Don't look at me like that. I knew there was no way I passed."

"If I hadn't convinced them to let you come with me, maybe none of this would've happened," said Lyla, gripping the wound on her leg. A tiny trickle of blood seeped between her fingers.

"Lyla, I don't think it would have mattered," said Val. She coughed again and winced. The pain in her stomach was a steady, torturous pulse. "I need you to promise me something."

"What?"

Val fixed her gaze on the floor. "I want you to tell them that it was my idea. That you just followed everything I told you to do."

"You know I won't do that."

"You have to. At least one of us needs to make it out of this alive," said Val. Her eyes burned, but she swallowed back the tears. "I need you to live."

Lyla scowled at her. "Stop it. The other students will tell them the truth. There were witnesses that saw us helping."

"They saw us fighting. That's all the DAO will care about. This is a witch hunt, Lyla."

"We've survived this much already."

Val couldn't bear her sister's undying faith in their survival. She didn't want Lyla in her mind, so she pictured the barrier, shutting her side of the bond. Her thoughts were a tangled mess, and she needed to convince Lyla to follow her only plan.

"I changed a human. I'm only alive because they haven't had time to figure that out." The emphasis she was putting on her words strained her stomach wound, and she paused, taking breaths as deeply as she dared. "Don't try to play the hero. When they come for us, you need to tell them that you had nothing to do with it."

Lyla looked her over more closely, eyes lingering on the fresh blood seeping between the fingers Val had tightly pressed against her stomach. Val avoided her sister's gaze, focusing on the tiny specks of gray in the white tiles.

"We're valuable to them, Val," Lyla replied. For the first time, the faint note of desperation entered Lyla's voice. "We have to get out of here."

Val felt Lyla's fear, and how hard she was trying to hold it back. Her sister's mind trembled with the effort. Val realized that she felt almost peaceful. She hadn't expected to live through her days in the Domestication program. When her parents had been murdered, a part of Val had died, and it seemed like nothing would ever bring her back to life. Her only purpose had been her sister.

A boy lying on a cold white table, cheeks cloaked with the pale finality of death. Her blood mingled with his, bringing him back to a whole new life. And when he opened his eyes for the first time again, they would glow a beautiful crimson. **I will find you.** *Promise? I* **promise.**

Would he miss her as much as she missed him?

Val held the image in her hands, watching the boy. The boy with the notebooks and the quiet way of caring. The boy with gentle hands. Then she put it away, somewhere deep, and hidden. She would carry it with her into the dark, safe from the eyes of the world. **Val…**

When Val opened her eyes in the white room again, she saw Lyla staring at the far wall, anger radiating from her and trickling through the bond. "You can be as pessimistic as you want, but I'm going to get us out of here," Lyla gritted out between clenched teeth. "I will not give up, and you're not going to either."

"I won't let you throw your life away trying to save me," said Val. "It'll be my word against yours."

Lyla opened her mouth to retort, but the words died on her lips as the door to the room opened. A wheeled cart entered the room, followed by a lab technician wearing a surgical mask over his face. He didn't look at the two captives. Not a word was spoken as he stopped the cart beneath the glass window and locked the wheels. Then he turned and left the room.

Four large syringes sat on a metal tray with an assortment of other supplies. Val recognized the vials, and they brought a cold uneasiness to the room. The quiet was unsettling, stretching into long minutes as they waited for the technician to return. He didn't.

"Val?" The anger that had been so present in Lyla's voice moments before was gone. "What does it feel like?"

Val was a lot of things, but a liar wasn't one of them. "It hurts more than anything I've ever felt. It feels like fire in your blood," she admitted. "But it won't last long. Not with that much silver."

"I'm scared," Lyla whispered.

Val shifted forward again, moving as close to her sister as she could. She reached out with her uninjured arm as far as the restraints around her wrists would allow, biting her lip against the pain. Lyla did the same, and this time they were close enough that their fingers touched. Val gave her a little smile.

"If I could take it for both of us, I would," Val said quietly. "I've never been able to protect you the way I should have."

Lyla's lips trembled. "You have. More than you know. Worrying about you kept me from losing my mind through all of this. I always had someone else to think about."

Val chuckled. "I guess we'll just have to keep worrying about each other right up until the end."

"That won't be hard." Lyla squeezed the tips of her sister's fingers gently. "I'm not going anywhere without you, Sanzi."

"I love you."

"I love you too."

They stayed there, leaning against their restraints to feel the small comfort of the other's touch. Val finally dropped her arm and groaned at the stiff ache. Neither of them knew how long they'd been in that concrete room. The little red light on the security camera blinked hypnotically in the corner. Val slumped back against the wall, the remaining strength slowly ebbing from her body. Lyla watched her and made no effort to hide her worry. There was no sense of time in that little room, no way to know what hours ticked by in the outside world. Val sat with her arms around herself and shivered, her fever rising and bringing horrible chills with it. She wove in and out of focus, only brought out of her blurry haze whenever Lyla would quietly say something to her to bring her back.

Sometime later, she startled awake, thrown back into reality by the nightmares that plagued her deep within. The room was quiet, and she saw Lyla dozing with her head bowed on the opposite wall. Val looked down at the blood still trickling ever so slowly from her stomach wound. Stubbornly, she pressed her fingers in tighter, trying to keep her life inside just a little bit longer. Whatever was coming for them, she couldn't let Lyla face it alone. She looked up into the fluorescent lights, silently imagining that they were the sun.

*The scent of the forest was heavy and earthy, and it thrummed through her senses like its own kind of magic, calling to her. **Where are you?** She ran her claws along the rough bark of a tree, scraping gently enough not to leave a mark. The forest was home. It was the only place she truly felt safe. Here there were no labs, no vials full of silver, and no cages. She ran, seeing the forest's beauty, the morning* *dew drops sparkling like diamonds, hanging precariously from the fine lines of a spider's web. The autumn golds littered the ground like a palace carpet. **VAL.** The forest spoke her name gently, beckoning.*

"That was beautiful," whispered Lyla.

Val withdrew from the daydream, realizing that Lyla was sharing it with her through the bond. There was a sudden flickering, a buzz, and then the lights went out, leaving the two wounded werewolves in complete darkness. And this time there was no generator, no eerie red glow, to take the place of the lights. And in their soundproof concrete block room, there was only a resounding silence. Val's shallow breaths grew even fainter. She felt tears rolling down her cheeks, and she reached up a shaking hand to wipe them away, but there was nothing on her face. She realized that she was feeling them from Lyla. Angry at the restraints holding her back from her sister, Val immediately reached out to the bond, hesitantly brushing against Lyla's side.

Let me in. Val stood on the mental bridge between them, arms outstretched. She knew what her sister needed in that moment, but she waited for Lyla to choose, to open the doors herself. Whatever thin barrier was there slowly disappeared. Val stepped through that smoky silver space. She heard the voice call from inside her once again. ***Where are you?***

She became aware of Lyla's thoughts melding and twisting around her own as they sat silent in the utter darkness. There was little distinction between the feelings of one and the feelings of the other. The bond was completely open. Val closed her eyes and reached out in the chaos for her sister, drawing close to the girl curled up on the white floor. Her body felt lighter than a feather as she knelt down and gathered her sister into her arms in the only way she could. Every pain and every fear flowed between them and was met by strength. Their wolves howled from the deep, wild things refusing to admit defeat.

CHAPTER THIRTY-TWO

The quiet wrapped around them like a blanket, and eventually the lack of light became familiar. Lyla drifted in and out of restless sleep, her exhaustion winning over her need to be vigilant. They had no sense of time, no way of knowing how long the concrete room held them, no way of knowing what was happening outside the four walls. She became aware of Val's presence in her mind slowly fading, retreating back over the bridge between them.

Roused from sleep, Lyla sat staring at the space where she knew her sister had slumped against the floor. She reached out again for the fifth time in the past few minutes, searching for the faint pulse of life she could still feel from Val. She could hear her sister shivering in pain against the concrete, her body trembling out its last reserves. Lyla fumbled with her own restraints, still holding onto that shred of hope that she might be able to break free. She contorted her hands until they ached, trying to pull them through the hard leather and steel. Her wounded arm felt cold and numb and was nearly useless in her attempts.

Val, just hold on a little longer. I'll get us out. I'll get us out.

The room was slowly becoming a tomb. Lyla couldn't stop her mind from sorting through every moment since they'd been thrown onto the metal floor of the truck. Every little detail was dragged forward and examined.

They wouldn't leave us to die here. We're valuable to them. We're Truebloods. They need us for the experiments. They're just waiting to see what we do… if we can get ourselves out. The whole rampage was a test. The confession. They wanted to see what we would do. It was all fake, the blood and the bodies, all of it.

Lyla refused to acknowledge any other possibility. If she could free herself from the restraints, the door would open and Cormoran would come in, tell them that she was so proud of them. This was all another experiment. It would all be over soon. She heard Val whimper softly. It would all be over soon.

"Val?"

There was no answer. Even through the bond, Lyla was met only with the dim confusion of delirium. The bridge between them was growing too long for her to reach across. Lyla struggled to breathe, her chest growing tight. She growled and strained at the cuffs on her wrists. Her wolf raged, and she could feel her mind slipping further into the wild. She bared her fangs at the darkness, a snarl breaking free.

A sound.

Her keen senses picked up on the faint sound somewhere outside their prison, something that hadn't been there before. Her violet-flecked eyes darted around, making out the dim shapes of the wall corners and the faint glint of the silver door handle. The sounds grew louder. *Voices.* Lyla stiffened. She was ready to make her stand.

The room was flooded with light from an outer hallway as the door crashed open, thudding against the wall. Several men in full SWAT gear rushed in, the lights above their gun barrels piercing the room. Lyla growled and lifted herself to her feet with a strength that her body should never have had left. She lunged against the restraints, getting as close to the inert body of her sister as she could, her snarling fangs daring the first contender to step closer.

"Stand down! We found them!"

Lyla's growling continued, ignoring the man who had lifted his hand to the others and lowered his weapon. One of the others came forward, pulling the black helmet off of his head. He gestured the others to step back.

"Lyla Blackwood?"

This is a trick. We're the lab rats. Lyla crouched over her sister and snapped at him, but his voice was gentle as he held out his palm to her. "I'm Commander Shawn Branley. Peter Wells sent us to find you. We're going to get you out of here, okay?"

Wells… Mr. Wells… get us out of here. Something human in Lyla managed to respond to the words. She closed her mouth, her fangs disappearing once again behind her lips. She sank down to the floor, and choked out a cry, wrapping her good arm around herself. One of the other officers lifted a walkie-talkie to his mouth and spoke into it. The crackling sound was far too loud in the room that had been deathly quiet only moments before.

"We found them. I need stretchers down here stat. Medical team on standby."

Officer Branley stepped closer to Lyla, kneeling down to her level as he reached for her restraints, key in hand. "Lyla, I'm going to need you to help me, all right? We're going to get you and your sister out of here safe and sound, but I'll need you to stay calm. Can you do that for me?"

Lyla nodded numbly. "Val…"

"Don't you worry, we're going to get you both out of here, okay?"

The stretchers arrived and Lyla found herself released from the wall, lifted gently onto the canvas. When the straps were placed over her chest and arms, she struggled a little as fear gripped her. Commander Branley put a hand on her arm.

"Lyla, you're safe. This is just a precaution to make sure we get you to the ambulance all in one piece, all right?"

"Val…"

"She'll be right behind us," reassured the officer. Lyla strained to see as they carried her toward the door and saw a group of paramedics lift Val onto her own stretcher, her arms hanging limply over the sides. Out of the unknown building, upstairs, and into the bright light of the sun. Lyla closed her eyes, the light blinding her momentarily. Lifted into the ambulance, she felt an IV placed in her arm, but she was too far gone to care. She was dimly aware that one of the paramedics was talking to her. A cool, light feeling began to sweep through her and her breathing steadied. She closed her eyes.

…

The first thing that Lyla was aware of was the warmth of her own breath captured against her face beneath the oxygen mask.

The second was the three bright bouquets of flowers sitting on a table next to her. She blinked, eyes slowly roving over the four walls of the room. The window to her left was open, and the blue sky beyond was more beautiful than she remembered. Several machines beeped around her softly, and she looked down at the tubes connected to her arms, the electrodes attached to her chest and limbs. White gauzy bandages encased her shoulder, and she could feel more around her thigh beneath the blanket.

When she saw who was sitting in the chair next to her, she felt tears sting the back of her eyes. Jules had curled up in the puffy armchair, her hair falling over her face as she dozed. Lyla swallowed hard and blinked at the ceiling a few times. Her throat felt dry and sore. When she opened her mouth to say something, her voice was too hoarse. Frustrated, she reached up and carefully pulled the oxygen mask away. The pain in her arm had faded almost completely.

"Jules."

The omega stirred, wide brown eyes fluttering open groggily. "Mmmmhmmm." She looked up and saw Lyla watching her from the bed. Her eyes flew all the way open.

"You're awake," she whispered. She reached down to the remote attached to the side of Lyla's bed and pressed a button. "I'm so glad to see you, Lyla. You have no idea. We thought…" the thought trailed off into silence as a tear ran down the omega's cheek.

Lyla swallowed, irritated by her throat's lack of cooperation. "Val…"

Jules gave her a small smile. "She's in the intensive care unit right now. They weren't sure she was going to make it, but she's out of the worst of it now."

"I want to see her."

Jules reached out and took Lyla's hand, giving it a gentle squeeze. "They're not letting anyone in to see her yet. Lex and I have been taking turns sitting with you."

"Lex?"

"Yeah. He's here too."

I want to know… there are so many questions. "Where… what happened?" asked Lyla, not sure if she was ready to hear the answer.

Jules bit her lip. "I can't tell you everything, Mr. Wells wanted to talk to you as soon as you were well enough. There were men with guns that came and let us out of the bunker, but they pushed us all into the trucks and brought us here. We were all locked in the rooms until Mr. Wells took over."

"Where are we?"

"The D.A.O. center," replied Jules. "It's the only place equipped to handle everyone right now. There were… a lot of us."

Lyla frowned, sensing that there was more that Jules wasn't telling her. She leaned back into the pillows and reached out into the bond. She could feel Val's presence, but it was smooth like glass, the deep quiet of sleep the only response given to Lyla's questing touch. Just feeling her sister's presence stronger than it had been the last time gave Lyla more relief than the strength returning to her own mind and body.

"Hey, it's going to be okay," said Jules softly. "Do you want to talk to Mr. Wells?"

"Yeah."

Jules patted her hand and left. A nurse came in to check Lyla's vitals. Lyla watched a lazy white cloud meander across the blue outside the window while the blood pressure cuff slowly constricted around her upper arm. The moment that the nurse disappeared out the door, Lyla heard the soft step of men's dress shoes.

She tore her gaze away from the window to meet the eyes of Christopher's father as he sat down, placing his briefcase next to the chair. He gave her a smile and adjusted his glasses, folding his hands over his knees. Lyla took in the pressed white, collared dress shirt without a tie or jacket. She saw the same eyes that Christopher had, kind and gentle. He had no clipboard, no gun, and no lab coat. His plain gold wedding ring graced his left hand, recently polished.

Lyla took a deep breath. "Mr. Wells, I know how this all looks, but please believe me, Val and I didn't start the phases at the school. The suppressants didn't work, and—"

"I know you're not at fault, Lyla," he replied. "If anything, the two of you are the reason why things weren't much, much worse. We have witnesses to prove it."

"Oh." Lyla didn't know what else to say. She hadn't been prepared for him to agree with her so easily. He took out his phone.

"Why would you text me for help if you were responsible?" He shook his head. "No, I never suspected you of foul play. Lyla, I know that you have a lot of questions, and I'm going to do my best to answer them. But first let me explain where we're at right now. I've been placed in temporary control of the DAO's operations.

Things will be running very differently here going forward. We're working to bring justice to the current Board members. Several of them have escaped us for the moment, Dr. Carrington and Mr. August are still unaccounted for. We're going to need your help. If you're up for it, I'd like to hear your side of the story tomorrow. All of it."

Lyla sagged back against the pillows, her mind racing. "What happened?"

Mr. Wells nodded. "I've had questions about the D.A.O.'s practices for years, but never enough evidence for a formal investigation. But when I met you two, I knew that I needed to dig deeper. When I received your text message that night, I called in every resource I had available. We weren't able to reach the school before they'd taken the two of you."

"The other schools… Dr. Quinn said something about the same thing happening there?"

"Yes. It was a coordinated event across all of them. From the evidence we have, this has been planned for some time. We are still gathering information, but it seems that there was an intent to create a tragedy that would remove any doubt in the public's mind that Truebloods are dangerous and should be exterminated."

Lyla couldn't understand. "But why all the experiments? Why keep us locked up in cells for years if they were just going to kill us all anyway?"

"Dr. Carrington has been profiting off of his research here for years. And I believe he was waiting until he had the perfect catalyst," replied Mr. Wells.

"Me and Val."

"Exactly. We've searched the DAO center and Dr. Carrington's home, but he was prepared for us. We didn't find much. However, the witness of several suspects in question has provided us with more. We were able to retrieve Dr. Quinn and your handler, Ms. Cormoran. Your handler was not directly involved with the Trueblood scheme, and she has been very cooperative." Mr. Wells smiled and leaned forward on his knees. "The one thing they didn't expect is that we would actually find you. The bunker you were in was part of a safe house they hadn't used in years. But we did find you, and a gold mine of evidence exposing Dr. Carrington and the DAO center's involvement in activities targeting werewolves for decades."

Lyla desperately wanted to be surprised, but she wasn't. She saw something in Mr. Wells' expression that told her there was more to the story. "What did you find?"

"Lyla, this may be difficult for you, and it is important that we take this one step at a time."

"Please," Lyla closed her eyes. "I've waited long enough for answers. Whatever you found, I need to know."

"All right then." He reached down into his briefcase and pulled out an old folder with the words Carrington Labs across the front. Lyla silently cursed her shaking hands as she opened it. Her breath caught as photos of her parents and their cabin stared up at her. The papers in the folder gave all their personal details and history. She flipped through the pages until she reached the next set of photos. An image of her tiny body dancing through the woods, arms outstretched. A photo of Val sitting on the porch of their cabin with hands stained blue and full of berries. The next page held photos of their parents. Lyla felt sick. Her lips quivered as she ran a finger over her mother's cheek.

Mr. Wells spoke softly. "We found enough to believe that Carrington Labs was directly involved in, and perhaps even orchestrated, the attacks on what they considered to be 'rogue' packs during the Culling. We can't say for certain, but they had information on every member of the pack you and Val grew up in. It appears that Dr. Carrington has had an agenda since the beginning."

Lyla pushed the folder away, staring down at her hands. This long history of destruction and death was far more than even she had imagined the DAO capable of. "The schools… how many died?"

Mr. Wells hesitated. "The casualties at Westbrook were some of the lowest, Lyla. It would have been so much worse if you and Val hadn't done what you did to save them. Nearly all of the survivors are telling us the same story. The Truebloods were some of the first to intervene in every school."

Lyla swallowed. "How many?"

"At Westbrook, there were fifteen deaths. Twenty-seven seriously injured. The rest were minor injuries or unharmed. At the other schools… we still don't have the final numbers. At least four Truebloods were among the casualties."

"Mark and Dodger? The DAO blood bonded them over winter break. Are they all right?" asked Lyla. "Dodger's real name is William McLane."

Mr. Wells shook his head. "Mark saved the lives of quite a number of students at his school. He is recovering here from minor injuries, and the loss of a blood bond."

"Dodger?" Lyla whispered.

"The witnesses told us that he was separated from Mark during the incident and sacrificed himself trying to save a group of human students who were being attacked."

Lyla looked up at the ceiling. It had been so much easier when it was just her and Val against the world, and she didn't have to worry about anyone else. And the look of sympathy on Mr. Wells' face was almost too much for her to bear; she couldn't meet his gaze.

"We're doing everything we can to get to the bottom of this, Lyla," he reassured her. "And I know that nothing I can say will change what happened. But I do want you to know that your sister woke up a little while ago. You'll be able to see her later today."

"Is she going to be put on trial?"

Mr. Wells looked at her, surprised. "Trial?"

"You… you have to know what happened to Christopher. What she did." said Lyla. There was no way he didn't know. "Is he alive?"

He smiled. "Yes. He is alive and well, thanks to your sister. We are keeping him at home for the moment, I think Val needs some time to recover first. But there won't be a trial. Had he died, it would have been charged to the people responsible, not to Val. My superiors have dismissed all the charges that were submitted by the DAO."

Lyla stared down at the pictures of her parents. She hadn't been able to bring herself to close the folder. "How did you find us? You said the safe house was secret."

"It was. Ms. Cormoran was helpful to us in that regard. She was able to help us find files in the DAO archives that gave information to narrow down locations. But in the end, it was Christopher who was able to narrow it down."

"Christopher?" Lyla asked, surprised. "How?"

"He saw details about where you were taken." Mr. Wells folded his hands. "Just glimpses, but it was enough for us to pinpoint our search."

"He saw…" Lyla stopped. "They have a blood bond."

"We believe so, yes." Mr. Wells paused. "The nurse we spoke to was clear that there was a fairly substantial transfer of blood." His face was drawn, as if it pained him to think about what must have happened in that small office. "While Val is recovering, we have been using preventative measures to keep their bond quiet. We didn't want to cause any further distress."

There was too much. Even though she had wanted to know everything Mr. Wells had just told her, Lyla felt drained. She couldn't even begin to process everything. And she knew that she would only have more questions as the days went on. "Thank you."

"It has been my pleasure to be of assistance," he said. "Is there anything else I can do for you right now?"

"I just want to be alone for a little while," replied Lyla. Mr. Wells nodded and rose from his seat, leaving the room without another word. Lyla's shoulders slumped, letting go of the effort to keep herself upright during the conversation. She gripped the sides of the folder, leaning over the faces of her parents. And for the first time in years, she began to let herself feel. All the anger, the pain, and the sorrow crashed through her, and through the agony, there was a soft sense of freedom. It was a new feeling, one of being unable to breathe for so long that she'd forgotten how. And for the first time since those carefree days at the cabin, she came up for air.

CHAPTER THIRTY-THREE

Val picked up a handful of freshly fallen snow, letting it stick to her fingers and then fall to the ground in clumps after meeting the heat of her skin. Next to her, Lyla watched the other students who were getting out in the fresh air. Some wore bandages, others walked slowly along with them. For the most part, Val and Lyla had kept to themselves, only mingling with the others during mealtimes once Val was well enough to leave her room. She had been awake for five days now, and although the nurses kept reminding her to take all the time she needed to heal, she couldn't help feeling restless. Even under new management, the DAO center was still not a place that she wanted to be.

The bandages around Val's stomach and shoulder were the only sign of her wounds and were deceptively minimal for how close she had come to succumbing to the injuries. Her blood's healing power had returned in full force, and the physical reminders of the rampage were nearly gone, leaving behind only scars. Other wounds would heal much more slowly. The night terrors plagued them both, and most of their nights were spent trying to keep the monsters in the dark at bay.

Mr. Wells had offered to provide them with a counselor, but Val had refused for the time being. She wasn't ready to delve into the past just yet.

Val straightened, the slight twinge in her stomach irritating her. The silver that had been in her system had left her feeling sick for several days after waking up, but it was all beginning to fade. Since Val had woken up, Lyla hadn't left her side. They'd moved into a larger room together on the end of the building, which gave them a little bit of quiet. The center was full to capacity, and it was only within the last couple of days that some of the Were students who had sustained lesser injuries were released back to their families.

Val shuffled her feet a little through the little trails of snow that had fallen off the sides of the shovels earlier that day. She glanced sideways at her sister, who had paid less attention to their environment and more to Val the entire time they'd been outside.

"Stop that," she said. Lyla's left eyebrow arched. "Stop looking at me like I'm dying."

Lyla smoothly shifted her gaze out over the expanse of snow leading up to the tall chain-link fence. "You got pretty close."

"We're Truebloods," replied Val. "Even the DAO couldn't bring us down in the end."

Lyla paused on the sidewalk. "I have something to show you." Val waited with her as she dug something out of her pocket and held up a carefully folded piece of stationary. "Mr. Wells gave me this. It's a note from Cormoran."

"I don't want to hear anything from her."

Lyla shook her head. "They might not have found us without her, Val. She turned herself in when she heard what happened. If you don't want to read this, then we won't. I'll get rid of it, and we'll never talk about it again. But aren't you even a little curious?"

Eyeing the piece of paper, Val could see the faint outline of sophisticated floral stationary. She crossed her arms. More than anything else, she wanted to ignore it, leave it in the snow, and walk away. *Can I forgive her after everything?*

"All right, let's have it then." She turned away from Lyla, fixing her eyes on the blue sky as her sister unfolded the paper and began to read.

"To Lyla and Valentine,

I would not presume to gain your forgiveness by any words I could put down on this page. Whatever the circumstances were, I have failed you again and again by not speaking on your behalf when it mattered most. I have failed you by allowing my misguided belief in the organization's mission to cloud my judgment.

When you were entrusted to my care, I was given the task of protecting and guiding you, and in my conviction that my actions were for a greater good, I failed you. My current actions to shed light on the organization's unethical dealings do not excuse my past failures.

I am sorry, with all of my heart. Please know that if you ever find it in your hearts to forgive me, I will be most profoundly grateful. It is my fervent hope that others may protect and guide you to a better life than the one you have lived until now.

Sincerely yours,
Ms. Charlotte Cormoran."

As Lyla's voice trailed off, Val licked her lips. "She's got a lot of nerve."

Lyla watched her. "You don't think she meant it?"

"None of them have ever cared how much damage they did. Why start now? Maybe because there's a nice reward at the end of this if she tells them everything and pretends to care about our future!" Val paused, trying to steady her breathing. Lyla was not watching her anymore, and Val realized that she was being abnormally quiet. Shocked, Val forced her next words out. "You believe her."

"Yeah, I actually do."

Val's brain stuttered to a stop, the angry words dissolving on her tongue. "Why?"

Lyla considered. "Because for all the mistakes she made, I think she was misled into believing that she was really doing the right thing. I'm not saying she was right. But I think she meant what she said."

"You're going to forgive her?" Val asked, incredulous.

Lyla nodded. "I already did. I'm tired of being angry, and if I hold on to everything that has happened forever, then they win anyway. I'll never be more than what they made me."

Clenching her fists, Val held on to the anger with all her might. *I can't forgive her. I'm angry. I need to be angry. Because if I'm not angry, I'm...* the thoughts stopped abruptly.

Val ran her hands through her hair, pulling hard. She squeezed her eyes shut and tried to hold back the flood of memories and emotions that were threatening to crack the walls she had worked so hard to build. Inside her mind, she saw the scared face of a little girl with wide eyes staring back at her. The little girl huddled on a black floor with her arms around herself, her terror materializing around her like dark wraiths.

I'm not her.

I'm not her.

I'm not her.

I'm not…

Please just let me be angry.

Arms circled around Val's shoulders, and her head was pulled down against Lyla's shoulder. Her sister's presence in the bond was a soft whisper, but Val could hear her emotions echoed in Lyla's thoughts as well. Something deep within her stirred as she felt a comforting reassurance surrounding her from something far away.

Val, I'm here.

She fell into that gentle voice and into the promise of safety that it brought. She tightened her grip around Lyla, her tears soaking into her sister's light jacket. They stood like that until the tears had passed. Somewhere deep inside both of them, the first broken pieces were being sewn back together.

...

"So… it is a date."

Lyla groaned and rolled her eyes after glancing at herself in the bathroom mirror as discreetly as she could. At least her hair wasn't sticking out all over. She was ready to call off the whole thing if Val kept teasing her about it. She gave her sister the fiercest glare that she could muster, but Val just chuckled and leaned back against the wall with a smirk, glancing at Jules. Sitting on Lyla's bed in the DAO center room, the omega stifled a giggle with her hand.

"You two are way too pleased with yourselves," grumbled Lyla. She slid her shoes on absent-mindedly. There was a knock at the door. Lyla trudged over to it and turned the handle, revealing Lex on the other side. He was dressed stylishly in a heavy leather jacket and scarf. She ignored the fact that she had chosen to wear jeans and a nice jacket instead of her usual hoodie and sweatpants. It wasn't a date. Lex grinned and waved at the two girls sitting on the beds.

"Hey, Val. Jules."

"Hi, Lex. Have her back before ten o'clock," her sister said teasingly, calling the last sentence after them as Lyla quickly exited to the hallway, closing the door behind her.

"Sorry," she mumbled.

Lex laughed. "It's fine."

Lyla noticed the small basket in his left hand. "What's that?"

He turned and started walking down the hallway. "You'll have to come with me to find out," he replied with a smile. He took her to the door in the middle of the building that led to the roof. It was always locked, so Lyla was confused until she saw Lex pull a key out of his pocket. The door opened. When she raised her eyebrows at him, he just looked proud of himself and held his hand toward the stairwell. She walked past him and up the stairs, emerging out into the winter night. Her shoes crunched the layer of gravel on top of the roof. Above her, the deep night sky glittered with millions of tiny stars. It was crisp, cold, and so breathlessly clear. Lyla's mouth opened as she stared at the beautiful sight, lifted high above the ground. It was the perfect planetarium.

Lex approached her and set the basket down on the gravel, opening it to reveal a small box of crackers and a little plastic package of cheese. Lyla chuckled as she saw them. So much had happened since the time they'd sat on the school lawn, awkward and tense. She shook her head and took the cracker that Lex handed her. She sat down a couple feet away from him on a stone ledge.

After they'd worked through half the squares of cheese, Lex leaned back on his hands. "Do you like it? Not everyone has the kind of influence it takes to get the key to this place."

"Yes. It's much nicer up here." She took a deep breath. "It's almost like everything underneath us doesn't exist."

"How are you?"

The question surprised her. She looked at him and saw the concern in his face. If she was honest with herself, she didn't really know how to answer. Both she and Val had been coming to terms with everything, but all the new freedoms were still strange to them. She could choose to leave her room whenever she wanted. When Lex had asked her if she would be willing to hang out with him that night, he'd made it clear that there were no ulterior motives behind the request. But part of her was still curious, and she found that she looked forward to his company despite herself.

"I'll be okay. It's a lot to process, I guess."

He nodded. "The rampage by itself is a lot to process. I can't imagine everything else on top of that. It hasn't even been three weeks, but it feels like it's been so much longer. I don't even have words for it yet. I'm just grateful we're all still okay."

"Christopher might not describe it that way," said Lyla. "Mr. Wells said that he's doing well, but I can tell that the change has been hard on them."

"Has Val talked to him?"

Lyla shook her head. "Not yet." Val still didn't know about the blood bond, and Lyla knew that it would change a lot of things when she did. Lyla had seen fragments of the memories that haunted Val and what she had seen when she found Christopher in his room. "You know what still doesn't make sense to me? That Jackson decided to help her after all. He's obviously phased before. He had way too much control."

Lex hesitated, as if unsure what to say. "I've known him for a long time. He never wanted to go home during the summers. I don't know much, but I do know he doesn't have a good relationship with his dad. Jackson always stayed away from the omegas, even when we were in middle school. Had a real problem being friends with them."

Lyla could tell that there was more Lex wanted to say, so she waited patiently while he sorted out his thoughts. He drew his knees up and locked his hands around them. "When we first started at Westbrook as freshmen, he started a gang of kids that were as rough as him. I went along with them for a while, but then one time he cornered this omega student, and he said he wanted me to help him teach the kid a lesson. I couldn't do it, so I got the kid out of there and told Jackson to lay off. We never really talked again after that."

"Have you seen him?"

"Yeah, I saw him once a couple days ago. He got pretty banged up by the other alphas, but I think he's working through a lot more than that," replied Lex. He took another cracker. "What's next for you two?"

"We're not staying here. I'm sure they're going to make it a great place, but not for us. Mr. Wells gave us a few options. We'll probably leave in the next few days."

"That makes sense," said Lex. "I wouldn't want to stay here either. Do you mind if I tag along to help you guys get settled?"

Lyla was surprised. "Your parents won't mind?"

"I'm heading back to my mom's after you two leave, but I can just make a road trip out of it and detour for a few days. Besides, I don't know when I'll get to see you again."

The way he was looking at her made Lyla's stomach twist strangely. She looked back up at the stars and tried to make her tone as off-handed as possible. "You could always come and visit."

He smiled. "Yeah, I'd like that."

Lyla had grown used the idea of their little pack, and the familiarity of her friends was something she was realizing that she didn't want to give up. Besides, she knew that it was highly unlikely that Val would be eager to be apart from Christopher much longer. Lyla didn't know if Val had worked out all her feelings for him, but whatever it was, they needed to talk.

She wouldn't say anything to Lex yet, but Mr. Wells had already talked to them about returning to Westbrook next year. Another choice with the strange freedom to say yes or no. There had been no question about it for either of them. It was the first place away from the cabin that had felt even a little bit like a home. Well, there was one other place…

CHAPTER THIRTY-FOUR

Val fidgeted incessantly as the car drew closer and closer to their destination, desperately wishing that Jules was there to keep her mind off things. Lyla had given up trying to get her to calm down. Lex sat in the passenger seat in front of them next to Mr. Wells, who had elected to drive them himself. Hours earlier when they had driven away from the iron gates of the DAO center, Val hadn't known what to do with the exhilaration of turning her face away from the chain-link fence for the last time. As kind as everyone had been during the last three weeks, she was ready to leave and never look back.

Her fingernails dug into her palms. They were only days away from their next phase, but Mr. Wells had reassured them that there would be no suppressants, that they had been reserved a place where they could finally run free without fear.

She glanced out the rear windshield at the gravel road disappearing behind them and the tall walls of trees on either side. Her stomach was in knots. Lyla patted her knee and attempted to reach through the bond for what seemed like the hundredth time since they'd left. Val couldn't pay any attention. She could swear that she felt his presence growing stronger as they drove up the road toward the big house.

What will he say? What if...

The possibilities that presented themselves made Val feel sick. No matter how hard she tried, her brain was not about to slow down. It was like her own thoughts were getting a high from tormenting her. The car rolled up the driveway, and Val blinked as the wolf within her seemed to press forward, urging the rolling wheels to move faster. Something inside her was physically pulling, wrapping its fingers around her ribs, and dragging her through the grove of trees.

The car stopped a hundred feet from the house. Val watched the others get out and stretch their legs. She stayed inside, ignoring the pull. Whatever it was, she was starting to decide that it made her uncomfortable. Her car door opened, and Lyla reached in, poking her shoulder.

"Come on. You can't hide in here forever."

Val unclipped her seat belt and slid out of the car, her boots crunching on the layer of snow. Lex went around and unloaded their bags from the trunk. Mrs. Wells appeared from the front door just like she had before and offered welcoming smiles to the girls, but she didn't come to give them hugs this time. Val turned to pick up her duffel bag and hefted it over her shoulder.

The scent hit her first, and the duffel bag dropped back to the ground. She looked up and saw him walking out of the house, standing at the edge of the path with his hands in his pockets. He was the same golden-haired boy with glasses that had handed her homework papers, sat across from her in the library, and scribbled his observations in notebooks. The scent was still Christopher, and somehow it wasn't. It was different, richer, and stronger.

Val.

It was you. All this time, it was your voice.

Val froze still as a statue when she realized the voice in her head was his. All this time it had been his. Inside, she forced herself to breathe as she reached out toward the bond she'd always shared with Lyla, only to realize that it wasn't the only one she found. There was another thread linking her to the boy standing by the house, and it was something even stronger.

A blood bond. And with dreadful clarity, Val realized that he was holding it back. Carefully withholding his emotions and memories from her. She couldn't tear her eyes away from his. It was so obvious; she couldn't believe that it had never occurred to her. She struggled to grab hold of a coherent thought. His voice in her head was so clear.

Her gaze flew to Lyla, who was standing to the side with Lex. "You knew?"

Before Lyla could answer, the bond was flooded with warmth and a gentle brush against her mind. ***Let me show you. Please.*** Throwing her fears to the wind, Val took one step onto the mental bridge between them. There was no barrier, and he let her into his thoughts without hesitation.

If Lyla's mind was a forest, then Christopher's was a library, full of philosophy and curious pondering about life. Val paused, overwhelmed by the sheer magnitude of the memories and emotions that she was feeling. They were all new and foreign, and

Christopher wasn't in full control of sharing them yet. He sensed her discomfort and tried to lead her toward a specific memory. It was pieced together, fragmented, but powerful.

When she sat across the table from him in the library, eyes flashing with that wild glint as she tried to decide what to make of him, he felt a sudden thrill that she was talking to him. He saw the haunted look that she wore sometimes, staring off at something beyond what she could see. He saw the strength in her heart, and he loved her for it. And when he had finally told her that he loved her, he could see the pain in her. She wasn't ready.

But that night, everything changed. When the alphas broke through the wall between the two rooms, and he saw the predatory rage in their eyes, he knew that he wouldn't make it out alive. He knew that he was going to die, and fear shook him. But more than anything else, he wanted Val.

She felt the strain as he forced his mind to ignore the images of what happened next. He didn't want her to see them. Her heart ached.

He remembered floating in darkness. Waking up with a roar in a locked room as he discovered his body forever changed. His muscles and bones felt heavier. A sound exploded through his ears and he whipped his head to the side. The curtains were softly rustling against the window frame, but it was magnified somehow. He looked around the room again at all the sharp edges and textures. His glasses were lying forgotten on the side table. He put them on just for a sense of normalcy.

My mother looked at me the same as she always had, told me that they would help me however they could. But the first time she saw me with red eyes and fangs, she was afraid.

He could see a concrete room; feel pain radiating through his stomach to the rest of his broken body. But he knew that the pain wasn't his own. He could feel her shivering in the dark. He felt her fear, and then her calm acceptance of death.

Where are you? *He shouted into the space between them. Somehow, they were connected, a blood bond. But it was more than that. He felt every shuddering breath, his heart felt as if it were tethered to hers. He threw himself into frenzy, destroying his room in his family's house as he howled in anger. He had to reach her. Nothing else mattered.*

WHERE ARE YOU?

"Dad, please! Let me help you find her; I can feel her through the bond!"

"Christopher, we're doing everything we can—"

"IT'S NOT ENOUGH! SHE'S DYING!"

VAL.

Please tell me where you are.

The concrete walls were different from the DAO center. There was another location, a hidden place. He analyzed every little detail that he had seen, the style of the flooring and what era it might have been built, the camera in the corner that was at least two decades old. He tore through the records his father gave him.

He felt it when her mind slipped away into the edges of silence. He rocked on his knees in the middle of his room, tears falling onto his open palms as he felt the agony of helplessness. She was dying, and he would have to feel every moment of her disappearing from his grasp. Over and over, he replayed every memory he had of her.

"Christopher, we found them. They're alive."

"I want to see her." **I love her.**

"She's not stable yet; we need to give her time, son."

"…please." A whisper.

"She doesn't know that you have a bond. You have to wait for her to come to you. Let her decide for herself. She's going to be all right." His father's hand rested on his shoulder gently. "I know this is hard for you. Give her the time she needs."

"I can't lose her again."

I love you, Valentine Blackwood. I won't hide from you anymore, but I know you may not feel the same. I will never ask you to stay with me if it isn't what you want. Now you know the truth. All of it.

Val retreated back to her own mind with a gasp. All that time when she had felt the presence of his voice and hadn't known that it was him, the sound of it had made her feel safe in the midst of the chaos. Her feet moved of their own volition. He stood as still as a statue, letting her close the distance. She looked up at him and reached out to touch his hand with the tips of her fingers. His palm curled around hers gently. She felt the strength in his grip, and it surprised her. A gamma with the blood of a Trueblood alpha. His spirit was still the same, still as quiet and thoughtful as ever, but a powerful steadiness radiated from him now. *I feel safe with you.*

Tears welled up in her eyes. "I love you. Christopher Wells, I love you."

His eyes searched her face, and he hesitantly reached up to run a finger down the side of her cheek. He swallowed. "I think I'd like to kiss you now."

Val felt the blush all the way down to her toes, but she tilted her chin up. He leaned forward to meet her, and then his lips touched hers ever so softly, his hand cradling her head. It was a safe feeling, as if she had finally come home.

They pulled away from each other reluctantly, and Val smiled, their hands still locked together. She saw him watching her, his expression soft. "What?" she asked.

He squeezed her hand. "You don't know how many times I've dreamed of hearing you say that."

Lyla cleared her throat. Turning toward her sister, Val felt her face go even redder when she saw her sister's smirk. Lyla shook her head. "You guys really need to keep your thoughts to yourselves. We're going to need to work on that ASAP. I can hear Val loud and clear over here."

Val laughed awkwardly. "Sorry."

The younger alpha rolled her eyes. Suddenly, Lex turned to her and held out his hand. "Lyla, will you go for a walk with me?" Lyla glanced between him and her sister, and then silently placed her hand in Lex's. He gave her a huge smile and led her away toward one of the walking trails.

Val saw Mr. and Mrs. Wells disappear into the house. She knew that it was kind of them to offer her and Lyla a place to stay, but she couldn't help feeling guilty. They were still human, after all, and caring for three werewolves under their roof was a risk. She and Lyla weren't exactly normal even by Were standards.

Physically they were healing and strong but healing their minds would be a slow process.

I'll be here. Every step of the way.

She glanced up at Christopher, but she didn't know how to express the discomfort she felt. He cocked his head to the side, thoughtful.

"I'm not reading your thoughts," he said. "You are sending them to me. I can try to block you out if you want me to give you some privacy."

Val sighed and rubbed her forehead. "I've never had a bond with anyone besides Lyla, and this is… this is different. I don't know what to do with it." Her nightmares and flashbacks often bled through the bond link between her and Lyla. This was exactly why she'd been afraid to let Christopher close in the first place. She was a broken mess, and she didn't want to burden him with that.

She heard him huff next to her. "Val, please don't think like that." She could tell how hard he was trying to block her out, and how much he disliked it. He turned her so that she was facing him and waited until she met his gaze. "You are not alone anymore." He tugged at her hand. "Come on," he said gently, pulling her toward the house. "It's time to go home."

. . .

The old hunting cabin was deep in the woods, refurbished with minimal necessities. Phasing werewolves had little need for the luxuries of the human world. But it was perfect—far away from anything and anyone else, almost as if it were its own little corner of the world. The forest went on for miles in every direction. It was as close to Lyla's childhood home as she could imagine, and she was already in love. Mr. Wells had seen to it that the cabin was ready for them before they'd arrived. It was theirs as long as they needed it—the perfect place for them to phase and hunt.

Lyla wiped the sweat from her forehead with her arm and closed her eyes, standing in the middle of the trees and taking deep breaths of the earthy air. Lex thundered into the trees behind her, letting out a wild howl as he charged into the forest, eyes blazing red. Snow fell from the branches above him as he disappeared for a moment, only to reappear a few feet away from Lyla. He bared his fangs in a wide grin and waited, knowing that it would only be a short time before she was joining him.

Next to the cabin, Christopher was holding Val in his arms as she growled, her body shifting into the phase, violet eyes narrowed. Here there were no small white rooms and observation windows. They were free. Lyla tilted her head back and let her control slip. Strength flooded into her system, and the scents and sounds of the forest spurred her on. She crouched, eyes locking on Lex with a mischievous glint. He snarled playfully at her, and she attacked. Their claws locked and they crashed into the underbrush.

Lyla rolled to her feet and looked back to see Val coming toward them, still holding back. The bond link between them reverberated with the memories they carried from the last phase. Val walked forward and pressed her forehead to Lyla's. The bond hummed between them, unbound by suppressants.

Lyla pulled back. *Hunt with me.*

She saw Val's eyes shift at that, and the full strength of the violet shone through. *If you can keep up.* Without another word, Val bolted away, letting out a howl. The other three immediately followed suit, and they raced into the forest, their graceful footfalls nearly silent.

The forest welcomed them home, calling to the wild blood coursing through their veins. Overhead, the full moon shone through the early evening dusk, a bright silver coin covering the forest with its glow as the four werewolves wove in and out of the trees.

SEVERAL MONTHS LATER

Lyla took a deep breath, leaning back against a tree at the edge of the overlook. Beneath her, the edge of the cliff dropped away into a valley of treetops. It had been five months almost to the day since the rampage at the school. Five months since they'd woken up in the DAO's hidden safehouse, not knowing if they'd live out the day. Lyla closed her eyes, attempting to let her surroundings soothe away the thoughts that had been plaguing her for weeks.

She ran her fingers through her still-damp hair. Val was more content than she'd been since Lyla could remember. Christopher came to visit nearly every day. They had everything they could want, and as close to the life they'd had before as they could get. Lyla stepped forward to the edge of the overlook and peered over the edge. Sap. Pine. Dead leaves and the damp smell of the earth after the previous night's storm. Peace.

Lyla's eyes burned with tears of frustration, and her fingers curled into a fist. The photos in Carrington's folder haunted Lyla still, and everything Mr. Wells had told her about the DAO's dealings with the Weres had left an unpleasant edge beneath her skin, restless. There had to be more that she could do besides sit in her cabin hiding from the world. Away from danger.

"Lyla, Dr. Carrington and Mr. August are still unaccounted for. We're going to need your help."

She'd testified. She'd told them everything she could remember since the day they'd walked out to the carnage outside their parents' cabin. So had Val. They hadn't left out a single detail, and it had nearly gutted them both to relive it. And it still wasn't enough to catch the one man who was truly responsible.

"Lyla, if you ever feel so inclined, your skill set would be invaluable to us. If you want a spot on the team, it's yours. But it's up to you. I completely understand if you want to be left alone."

Lyla glanced to the side, knowing that Val was only a few feet away in the cabin. "I'll let you know."

The distracted memory of the last call she'd had with Mr. Wells could very well have leaked through the bond, and Lyla cursed her lack of control and spun on her heel. She took her time walking back to the cabin. She'd been left alone long enough.

When the cabin came into sight, a thin line of gray smoke rose gently toward the sky. Val was outside, chopping wood. She lifted the axe and swung, the blade making a sharp arc through the air before splitting the small log cleanly. Val tossed the pieces aside, not looking up.

"How was your walk?"

Lyla could sense Val's tension through the bond. She'd definitely seen something. Lyla straightened her shoulders.

"Good, it's a nice evening." She walked up to the cabin's porch and kicked off her boots. "You could go if you want. I'll watch whatever it is you're cooking in there."

Val swung the axe again, burying it in the large log and tightening the bandana keeping her long red hair out of her face. "Why don't you tell me what's going on? I thought we decided that keeping secrets wasn't how we were doing things now."

Lyla gripped the porch railing. They had waited so long for this. More than anything she wished that the words about to come out of her mouth could be anything else.

She sighed. "Val, I can't stay here."

ACKNOWLEDGMENTS

This book truly would never have reached publication without the support of some incredible people. Writing can be an isolating craft, but it takes a village to believe in the final product and make it the best version of itself.

My supportive and ever patient husband Ben, for believing in me through every step of this book. For getting excited with me and letting me lean on you when I was sure I was failing. I love you.

To my amazingly talented and creative other half, my best friend Sara. This book would not exist without your support, ideas, and artistry. From deep dives into Val and Lyla's psyche to the incredible cover you graced this story with, thank you for believing in me and in this book from day one.

To Gina. It's not easy being an editor for an author as free-spirited and scatter-brained as I am, but you have been nothing but the best. Thank you for seeing the diamonds in this story and helping me bring them to the surface.

To my amazing beta readers, Nickie, Kate, Beret, Kay, David, Christina, Grunke, Kate, Sadie, Joren, and Anada. Your support, critiques, and enthusiasm for my characters and their story has meant the world.

To Mom and Dad, who listened to chapters and chapters of my first messy written works and loved them anyway.

And finally, to my Lord and Savior Jesus Christ, who blessed me with the love of writing stories.

ABOUT THE AUTHOR

Tori Tecken has been a published author and motivational speaker since the age of 14. After obtaining a B.A. in English from Bethany Lutheran College in 2013, she is rekindling her passion for writing fantasy. Tori lives in southeast Minnesota with her husband, their three children, and their incredibly patient cat.

www.ingramcontent.com/pod-product-compliance
Lightning Source LLC
Chambersburg PA
CBHW051002180726
48291CB00006B/1937